MW01136243

Angelic Commission

Angelic Commission

by: Timothy Swiss

To All Who Cherish Truth,
And Who Love a Great Adventure

Angelic Commission
Copyright © 2019 by Author. All rights reserved.
Copyright Registration Number TXu 2-159-845
Issued under the seal of the Copyright Office in accordance with title 17, United
States Code, and made part of the Copyright Office records.

Introduction

Craig and Nancy were twins. They grew up in a typical American family and attended a neighborhood church. Their public school did not permit open prayer or other expressions of Christianity—such practices were in conflict with the Federally-established cult of Humanism. They both believed that there was a God, but the teaching and preaching they received left them with disturbing questions. They wanted answers, so they decided to consult Doctor Trustumbarger.

Eleazar Moosuka Trustumbarger was not a medical doctor, he was a librarian. No one knew why he was called *doctor*, and no one ever asked. Doctor Trustumbarger answered every question that anyone ever asked him, and his answers always seemed right. When Craig and Nancy asked him if everything that ever existed had a beginning, he explained that something had to exist without having a beginning or else nothing would exist; and he explained that something that exists without having a beginning can just as easily be an almighty God as a gaseous cloud of ether. This was the last question he answered for Craig and Nancy; because on the evening of their tenth birthday, he disappeared, and his library disappeared with him.

During the night preceding their seventeenth birthday, Craig and Nancy had an unusual experience—they both dreamed the same dream. They dreamed that Doctor Trustumbarger's library sat alongside a dirt road south of town, and they dreamed that a fox guided them to the library by moonlight. Deciding that the dream was a supernatural message, and knowing that they both had troubling questions, each of them wrote down questions for Doctor Trustumbarger on a sheet of paper. The day following their dream was a Saturday, and they asked permission to borrow the family car. That evening Craig drove the car while Nancy watched for a fox. A red fox appeared, and they followed the fox to Doctor Trustumbarger's library.

Doctor Trustumbarger smiled from behind a wooden desk when Craig and Nancy entered. His library was small, and the outside looked like an old cabin; but the walls within the library were crammed with books. Craig and Nancy each withdrew a list of questions. Nancy was less timid than Craig, and she was first to hand a list to Doctor Trustumbarger.

Nancy's list read as follows—*Can women be preachers? Can women teach men in Sunday school? Do wives have to take orders from their husbands? Can women wear jewelry? Why was Adam created first? What was Eve's curse? Did Eve's curse apply to all women? Are men and women the same spiritually? Is nudity a sin? Can saved people reject salvation and go to hell? Was Eve tempted by a snake? Was Satan really one of God's heavenly angels? Are Christians saints?*

Doctor Trustumbarger nodded his approval of Nancy's questions. This encouraged Craig, and he also relinquished a list of inquiries. Craig's list read as follows—*Is sex before marriage a sin? Is pornography a sin? Is masturbation a sin? Are Christians just sinners saved by grace? Is the Bible really true? Can people with different religions all go to heaven? What makes someone a Christian? Can Christians fight? Do Christians have to take orders from the government? Should it be against the law to pray out loud in school? What did Thomas Jefferson teach about the separation of Church and State?*

Again Doctor Trustumbarger nodded approval. Craig sighed in relief. The two lists were placed inside an odd wooden box, and then

Eleazar Moosuka Trustumbarger bowed his head and placed open palms on top of the box. Everything blurred, and it seemed that all of the books in the library flew from the walls and whirled together in a vortex above the box. Then Eleazar Moosuka Trustumbarger and the library disappeared. However, the odd wooden box remained, lying on the ground in a grassy field. When Craig and Nancy opened the box, they found a book inside. The book was entitled *Angelic Commission*.

Contents

* *

* * 3 * *

The Land of Who
46

* * 4 * *

The Golden Pathway
65

** 5 **

The Barren Land
91

** 6 **

Fiery Cauldron
160

* * 7 * *

Pursuit of Breath
251

* * 8 * *

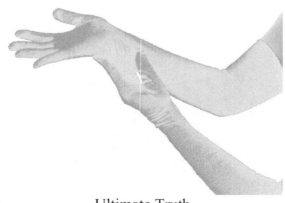

Ultimate Truth
274

Chapter 1

Andela

"April Fools' Day," muttered Andela. She stood outside the door to her second-floor apartment and steadied her hand to insert the key into the lock. "And I'd sure be a fool to even think of going back to work for Mr. Jergan again, that's for sure, the very nerve!" She stepped into her living room, turned around and closed the door with more force than usual, switched on the light, marched across the rug that covered the center of the floor, and collapsed into the solitary chair adjoining her sofa. Her breast was rising and falling. "I sure feel sorry for that man's wife," she berated, "and I bet she doesn't even know. What an abhorrent creep."

She quit jabbering and sat still. The sound of her own distraught breathing troubled her, and she felt odd about talking to herself aloud; but thinking out loud was something she tended to do in stressful situations, and this was a stressful situation.

"Bzzzz!"

"Oh no," Andela whispered.

"Bzzzz!"

She sat up and stared toward the door. Her fingers clutched the arms of the lounge chair. Mere minutes had passed since her boss made such indecent advance that she was forced to flee her workplace; and now, if he was at the door, she had no idea what he might try to do. "Who's there?"

"It's me, Jenny!"

Andela's grasp on the arms of the chair eased. She rose and strode across the room, and then she opened the door. Jenny, a married neighbor who lived in the apartment below, entered hurriedly. Her purse hung at her right side, suspended from a strap that looped over her left shoulder.

"Shut the door and lock it," Jenny spoke. She was not only Andela's friend and neighbor, she was also a coworker. Both women worked as secretaries under Mr. Jergan's supervision. Andela followed Jenny's instructions and closed the door and locked it.

"Pam just called me on my cell phone while I was driving home," Jenny continued, speaking while grabbing Andela by both wrists. "Mr. Jergan is on his way over here. She says he's higher than a kite over the way you treated him."

"I treated him!" retorted Andela, flinging her arms downward and breaking Jenny's grasp. "He's the one doing the treating! Do you know what he said to me?"

Jenny stood her ground, confronting Andela face to face. "But Dell, he never really does anything. He just carries on a little bit when his wife's out of town."

"A little bit! He wanted to take me out to eat, and then he wanted to have me come over for a while to visit, alone, just him and me at his house."

Jenny opened her mouth, but then paused and peered into Andela's eyes. She seemed a bit startled. "At his house?"

"Yes! And he said I might want to bring some comfortable clothes to wear after dinner," added Andela, expecting her words to shock Jenny.

Jenny shrugged and turned her eyes toward a corner of the room. "Well, Pam went over there once, before you were hired, and she says nothing happened. They just ate some popcorn and watched an old movie."

"Jenny," said Andela, waiting to continue speaking until her friend again faced her. "Pam is not like you and me. How do you know she's telling the truth?"

A pained expression appeared on Jenny's face. "Oh Dell, please, I don't want you to get fired. You're the only real friend I have at work. Can't you just do enough to appease the man? St. Louis is a big town, so no one's ever going to find out that you went over to his house and watched some TV."

Andela's eyes narrowed. "So, what would you do in my place, Jenny? Let's say you were the one Mr. Jergan invited to come over and bring a change of clothes—what would you do?"

"I wouldn't be in your place, Dell. I'm too fat."

Andela shrugged and shook her head. Jenny was somewhat overweight, but she was still attractive. "Not so, Jenny, the only reason you're not fair game for Mr. Jergan is because you're married and because you attend the same church that he does. And speaking of church, does he show up for services?"

"Show up? Sure he shows up—he's on the Board of Deacons."

Andela's eyes widened. "No…really? The Board of Deacons? What a hypocrite!"

Jenny fidgeted. "He behaves better at church."

Andela assumed a look of indignation.

Several seconds passed with Andela and Jenny peering into one another's eyes. Neither girl seemed to know what to say next. Jenny shook her head and wandered over to the sofa where she sat down. She seemed despondent. "Okay, I guess if I were in your place, I wouldn't go either. But you know how he is—he'll fire you if you don't do something."

"I don't think so," Andela replied matter-of-factly. She followed after Jenny and plopped back down in the chair next to the sofa, to Jenny's left. The chair and sofa sat at right angles, corner to corner, so it was easy for the two girls to face one another. There was a small coffee table situated in the angular space between the chair and sofa. "I'm quitting."

For several seconds Jenny sat in silence, but then she smiled and raised surprisingly playful eyes. When she spoke next, her voice gave no hint of despondency. "Thanks, Dell, you've done me a favor. I owe you a debt of gratitude. I needed someone to break the ice for me. So then, I guess we'll have to be looking for new jobs."

Andela stared at her friend. "We?" she posed.

Jenny grinned and nodded. "Yep, I'm quitting too."

"Really? I mean,…"

"Bzzzz!"

Both girls jolted upright in their seats. Jenny was the first to act. She sprang to the door and opened it just wide enough to stick her head outside.

"Is that you Mr. Jergan?"

A gruff and aggravated voice replied. "Yes it is. Is Andela in there?"

Andela again clutched the arms of her chair.

"Yes she is, Mr. Jergan, but can you wait for a couple of minutes? We've been anticipating your arrival."

There wasn't anything about Jenny's demeanor to suggest that she was drawing Mr. Jergan into a ruse. The words she spoke were true, but she fully expected Mr. Jergan to misinterpret them.

"I suppose so," Mr. Jergan returned. His voice still sounded disgruntled, but there was also a note of appeasement.

"Okay, I'll get back with you, but I'm going to shut the door for now."

"Shut the door? Why?"

"I'd rather not say, but let me ask you a question. How would you feel if you saw a woman plum naked?"

While Jenny conversed with Mr. Jergan, Andela lifted a wireless phone from a coffee table that sat between the chair and sofa. She was preparing to dial 911.

Mr. Jergan was tongue-tied. To Jenny's repulsion, he attempted to peek around the door. With a groan of disgust, she shoved the door closed and locked it. Then she strode back across the room. She sat on the arm of the sofa next to the coffee table, noting that Andela was holding the phone. It was easy to guess Andela's intention.

"No, not the police, Dell. I've got a better idea, one that will teach Mr. Jergan a lesson."

There was something about the tone in Jenny's voice that intrigued Andela. "You do? What?"

"Pastor Larken is home. I saw him going into his apartment when I drove up."

Andela knew that Pastor Larken lived next door to Jenny. He was the pastor where Jenny and Mr. Jergan attended church. She watched as Jenny took the phone from her hand and punched buttons. Jenny raised the phone to her ear, knelt to bury her face in the corner of the sofa, and covered her head with a couch pillow. Andela rose and leaned downward with her head near the pillow so that she could listen.

"Hello Pastor Larken, it's me, Jenny…yes…well, we're in a big hurry, but guess what's up here in Andela Tidmore's apartment, it's that book you've been wanting to borrow, the one by C.S. Lewis…yea, no kidding…sure, if you can get up here right now, pronto…great, I'll meet you at the front door of the apartment—apartment 217, bye."

There was a grin on Jenny's face as she rose from beneath the pillow.

"Jenny, I only one book by C.S. Lewis," whispered Andela. "It's *The Four Loves*."

Jenny raised an open hand. "No worry, the book's in my purse," she answered quietly. She slipped the purse strap from her shoulder and dropped her purse onto the sofa. Then she withdrew a paperback book—*Out of the Silent Planet*. She showed the book to Andela and flipped through several pages. "This is the first book in C.S. Lewis's *Space Trilogy*," she explained. "They're all three very good, but this one's my favorite, and I recommended it to Pastor Larken."

"Bzzz! Can you open the door now?" Mr. Jergan hailed from outside.

"It won't be long," returned Jenny.

Jenny held the book with one hand and stepped to the door where she began fumbling with the doorknob, making some clicking noises but taking care not to actually unlock the door. She placed her right ear against the door. Andela gazed for a couple of seconds, and then she stepped up beside Jenny and placed her left ear against the door. The two girls waited face to face, fueling one another's anticipation as they peered into one another's eyes.

"Why, Brother Jergan!" boomed the voice of Pastor Larken. He was blessed with an exceptional set of vocal cords and could easily preach to a congregation without the use of a microphone. "What a surprise to meet you here! What brings you to Andela Tidmore's apartment?"

A look of mutual glee erupted on both girls' faces.

"Pa…u…Pastor Larken," stammered Mr. Jergan. "Well…I…uh, well, here's the thing, I just came to give Andela her well-deserved reward for winning a contest…um…*Secretary of the Year!*"

"Secretary of the year?"

"Yes, that's right. It's a program I've developed to applaud fine performances by my employees."

Andela's brows rose in surprise. Jenny bit her lower lip to suppress a giggle.

"Really? How nice of you," responded Pastor Larken.

"Yes, well, with a business as demanding and productive as mine, it pays to compliment exceptional effort and dedication. But I'm in a rush, and no one seems to be answering the doorbell, so I think I'll stop by another time."

Mr. Jergan's abrupt footsteps evinced plans for escape, but his plans were thwarted—the door swung wide open. Jenny nodded to Pastor Larken and then stared toward Mr. Jergan.

"Mr. Jergan! What a surprise!" Mr. Jergan halted in his tracks and turned around. "I knew Pastor Larken was on his way over here to pick up a book that I'm loaning him, but what on earth brings you here?"

Andela held her breath as she peered through the open doorway. The expression on Mr. Jergan's face seemed that of a third-grade schoolboy caught pulling a girl's pigtails. He looked between Pastor Larken and Jenny, with only a glance back toward Andela. Andela wondered what words would manage to emerge from his chagrined lips, but then Pastor Larken intervened.

"It seems that Andela has achieved quite an honor," declared Pastor Larken, facing Jenny.

"Oh really," responded Jenny. She rendered herself a virtual personification of innocence. "What?"

Pastor Larken was no fool. He figured that something questionable was going on, and he surmised that Mr. Larken was the one receiving a well-deserved reward of sorts.

"Well you see," piped up Pastor Larken, speaking before Mr. Jergan could decide how to respond, "Andela has been chosen as *Secretary of the Year*." He turned his face toward Mr. Jergan. "I'm curious to hear what a profitable business establishment, such as yours, considers a just reward for its *Secretary of the Year*."

Mr. Jergan looked sheepish. "Five hundred dollars, Pastor Larken, and not a penny less," he proclaimed, reaching for his hip pocket. "I went to the bank and withdrew the money this morning, just for this occasion."

Andela's eyes widened. She worked for minimum wage, and a great deal less than five hundred dollars would have seemed a handsome bonus. Mr. Jergan shoved five one-hundred-dollar bills inside the door, and Andela withdrew them from his hand. Not a word passed between them.

"That's generous, Mr. Jergan. Your employees must be impressed with your incentive programs," commented Pastor Larken.

"Yes, well, nice to bump into you pastor. I've got to hurry along, so good night."

Mr. Jergan never looked back as he disappeared into the stairwell leading downward to the parking lot. No one spoke a word until the sound of his footsteps faded. It was plain to both Jenny and Andela that the smile on Pastor Larken's face disclosed awareness of their situation, but he made no comment.

Jenny raised the book by C.S. Lewis. "Here pastor, and thanks."

"Anytime," replied Pastor Larken. He accepted the book and nodded. "See you in church, Jenny, and congratulations, Miss Tidmore."

"Thank you," said Andela.

With nothing more than a gracious bow, Pastor Larken departed. Jenny closed the door. She spun around and leaned back against the closed door, staring at Andela and releasing theretofore restrained giggles.

Andela placed one hand on her hip and tried to look disapproving. "Jenny, that wasn't very nice," she choked, but she was trying so hard to hold back laughter that her efforts produced a ludicrous expression. Seeing Andela's face, Jenny erupted into laughter and sank to the floor while clutching her abdomen in bliss hysteria. Andela attempted no further restraint. She joined her friend in laughter, teetering across the room and collapsing onto the sofa.

One woman's glee fueled the mirth of the other. It was an emotional purge. The tragedy of losing their jobs shrank to inconsequential insignificance. Jenny regained adequate composure to rock forward onto her feet and stumble toward Andela. Andela's limbs were sprawled about the sofa. She had tossed the five one-hundred dollars bills onto the coffee table situated to her left.

"Well Andela, I thought that went rather well."

Andela sat up, permitting Jenny to sit to her right. There were a few seconds of thoughtful silence, and then Andela picked up the five one-hundred dollar bills and offered them to Jenny.

"Here, these are yours," said Andela, facing Jenny.

"No they're not," retorted Jenny. "He gave them to you, not me."

Andela's face grew firm.

"Okay, I'll take two and you take three. I'm not tearing one in half."

The two women sparred back and forth until Jenny finally took two of the bills, insisting that Andela would need the larger share of the money since she was now unemployed and had no husband. Once the money matter was resolved, Andela faced Jenny with a look of earnest. "What are you going to do?"

Jenny relaxed her posture and eased her shoulders and neck against the back of the sofa. "Well, as soon as I get good and pregnant, I'm going to stay home and have fun raising babies."

"You're pregnant!"

Jenny chuckled. "No, not yet. But hey, I'm on the journey to my destination, we're working on it."

Andela blushed and dismissed the subject. "So, will you be looking for another job?" she inquired.

"Nah," Jenny crooned, "no need to look. I've already had an offer, better pay too. I was just staying on with Mr. Jergan because I liked working with you."

Andela absorbed Jenny's words with appreciation, gazing upon the only close friend she had in St. Louis. She managed a smile. "Thanks, I liked working with you too."

"Hey, not so fast," said Jenny. "I'm sure I can get you hired with me. It's a toy distribution center. A girl like you—honest, hardworking, smart, good-looking—no problem. When do you want to start?"

"That's great, I mean, you've been a wonderful friend, Jenny."

Jenny sat upright. Her face wore an expression of perplexity. "Been? Been? What do mean by *been*?"

Andela eased backward, staring wistfully forward. She shook her head. "It's not like I thought it would be, living here in the big city. I think my chances are better in a smaller place, maybe even back home."

"Chances, chances for what?"

There was no response. Andela continued staring forward.

"Oh," declared Jenny, "so that's it. You're looking for a boy."

"No," rebuffed Andela, "not a boy. Boys and girls are what you have after you're married. I'm looking for a man, and it's not necessarily that I'm looking for a man, exactly, it's more like, well, I'm sort of hoping that a man might be looking for me, maybe, if the right man exists."

Jenny placed one hand on Andela's shoulder.

"There are lots of men in St. Louis, lots and lots. And believe it or not, there's plenty of time. There's no need to rush things."

"Plenty of time? You know what happened to me back home? I got up one Saturday and went out for a walk, and as I was strolling through a park, and I heard a little boy say to his friend—'*Look, there's the old maid that teaches the girls' Sunday school class.*'"

Jenny skewed her brows. "Dell, thirty-years-old does not warrant the description of *old maid*. Barbara Jones got married when she was thirty-five, and she has two kids of her own, and she and her husband adopted two others."

Andela paused and sighed. "Okay, I guess you're older than me."

"Yes, I am, but not much older."

An uncertain expression crept upon Andela's face. "And you were how old when you got married?"

Jenny shifted. "Maturity is not always measured by years."

"How old?"

"Okay, I was almost twenty-five."

"Ahah! Twenty-five! So then, that changes things. That means I've been an old maid for five years."

"That's ridiculous. You're not at all old by today's standards."

Rather than continuing the verbal dual, Andela again sighed; and this time it was a deep and ponderous sigh. Her facial expression grew somber. She turned her head and peered into Jenny's eyes. "I apologize. I know I'm not too old, and I'm not even sure if ever want to get married. But the fact is, Jenny, I'm downright bored—I've reached a point in my life that it's time for something to change, whether or not it means finding a man who I could consider marrying."

Jenny felt her heart sink into Andela's emerald-green eyes. She was speechless.

"As you know, Jenny, my parents are on the other side of the ocean, serving as missionaries. My older brother is in the Air Force, happily married, and my younger sister is in college, and she's engaged to be married. That leaves me—the single, grown-up working girl." Andela continued to hold Jenny's attention with her eyes. "And don't get me wrong, I'd stay single forever if I knew God wanted me to lead a solitary life."

"Dell!" intervened Jenny. "Being single does not mean you have to lead a life of isolation. Isn't your very favorite author Jane Austen?"

A quizzical expression crossed Andela's brow. "Sure, I love her books."

"Well then, did you know that she never got married?"

Andela appeared notably surprised. "Really? Never married? But how could that be? She wrote so much about romance and marriage."

"Yes, she did. And she no doubt experienced more depth of passion and romance in her imagination and heart than most women experience during a lifetime of marriage."

Andela stared at Jenny in silence.

"And she's not the only renowned female who never married," added Jenny. "It so happens that Susan Boyle, Greta Garbo, Susan B. Anthony, Joan of Arc, Queen Elizabeth the First, and Florence Nightingale never married."

The brows above Andela's eyes drew questioningly together. "Why do you know that?" she asked.

Jenny dropped her face for several seconds, and then raised sincere eyes. "You know that my mother's been single my entire life, don't you?"

"Yes, you've mentioned that to me before."

"Well, she told me a little about my father."

Andela nodded. "Go on."

"When they got married, he convinced her that she needed to go to work in order to help with the costs of living. She did, and she got a job that paid more money than his job, and then he quit working and started drinking alcohol. My mother worked hard to keep up with her job and then come home and take care of cooking, laundry, and house cleaning, all of which my father expected her to do. Meanwhile, he got meaner and meaner, abusing my mother verbally as well as physically, and refusing to get help for his drinking problem. And then it finally happened."

"What?"

"When she was five months pregnant with me, my mother got off early from work one day, and when got home there was loud music playing in the bedroom where she and my father slept. She found my father in bed with another woman."

Andela's shook her head. "That's terrible."

"Yes it is. And after my mother filed for divorce, my father disappeared. I've never met him, and my mother never received one penny of alimony or child support. She says there was only one good result that came from her horrible marriage and the nightmarish three years that she lived with my father, namely me. She also says that she was never even tempted to consider marriage again, and she advised me to live a happy life as a single woman unless I met a man who I was absolutely sure about."

Andela straightened. "So that's why you know so much about single women—you seriously considered staying single yourself."

"I sure did, and it took three years for Ralph to change my mind. I was a happy woman when I was single, and I sure didn't want to go through anything like my mother went through. But thank God, I have even more happiness now, living with Ralph, than I had before. It isn't always easy being married, but Ralph's a good husband, and he really loves me."

Several seconds of silence elapsed, with Andela and Jenny peering into one another's eyes.

Andela broke the silence. "You don't think I'll ever get married, do you?"

Jenny shrugged. "Don't get me wrong, Dell. I think there are all kinds of guys who'd marry you in a heartbeat. But you're one of the most joyful persons I've ever met, and one of the most caring and giving persons I've ever met, and I'd hate to think of what would happen if some insensitive bum got you to marry him."

"So you don't think I should get married?"

"I didn't say that, exactly. I'm just saying that I think you should be very, very careful. I believe you have everything that it takes to live a full and successful and happy life as a single woman, and I think it would take a very special man to complement a woman with as lovely and sensitive a heart as yours."

Andela patted Jenny's hand and smiled. "Thank you. You're more than a dear friend, you're a sister."

"Quite so," returned Jenny. "So then, you'll stay in St. Louis for a while? Right?"

Andela broke her gaze with Jenny. "Thank you, but no." Then, before speaking again, she again raised her eyes and met Jenny's eyes. "You're the one reason I'll hate leaving St. Louis, but I'm leaving. St. Louis is a great city, it really is, it's just not for me. I'm not a city mouse, I'm a country mouse, and I'm heading back to the country."

The two women sat for some time in silence, neither one of them feeling that the conversation was at a good stopping point. Jenny raised her hand and put it all the way around Andela's shoulders, pulling her close and administering an affectionate hug. "I'll miss you, and we'll still keep in tough, right?"

Andela freed herself and threw both hands around Jenny's neck. She laid her forehead on Jenny's shoulder. "I'll miss you too, and of course we'll keep in touch."

Soon both women were shedding tears. After laughing only minutes before, they conveyed no semblance of emotional composure. A minute or two later, Andela rose and stepped into her bedroom where she retrieved a box of Kleenex. She withdrew three for herself and handed the box to Jenny. They sat and talked for a while longer, wiping away tears and reassuring one another that they would continue their friendship forever, no matter how far apart they happened to live.

"Well, I guess I'd better get down and start supper," Jenny finally remarked. "I hope you know how much I love you, Andela."

"I love you too, Jenny," replied Andela. "Thanks for everything."

After escorting Jenny to the door, Andela found herself sitting alone. There was much to think about, but she wanted to rest her mind. She leaned her head back on the top edge of the sofa and shut her eyes. By and by she began feeling bored—she was not good at doing nothing—so she rose from the sofa and began humming a tune as she stepped into the kitchen. It was time for supper. After finishing the tune she was humming, she switched on the kitchen radio and adjusted the dial to the most uplifting gospel station in St. Louis.

With her mind made up to leave, Andela decided that there was no reason to linger. She would pack up and leave the next day. The apartment was furnished by the landlord, so all of her possessions would fit inside her car. Then, on a whim, she decided to celebrate her last night in the big city with a special meal. There were two steaks in her refrigerator, and she grilled both of them.

A stimulating aroma flavored the atmosphere as steak, potatoes, and crescent rolls were cooked to perfection. Fresh vegetables were sliced, diced, and compiled in a tossed salad. Andela felt as if she were carrying on like a five-year-old serving paper cookies and mud pies to dolls and stuffed animals, especially since she was cooking plenty of food for two persons. She imagined what it would be like to actually be cooking for two, such as Jenny was probably doing.

Suddenly an uncanny feeling rose within Andela's breast and evicted present thoughts from her mind. She straightened and stood still. The feeling came from nowhere, or perhaps from everywhere. Up to this point the day and had been eventful and tiring, but nothing that had happened seemed surreal; that is, not until now.

It seemed to Andela that an indefinable breeze swept through the apartment, despite the fact that all the windows were closed. An odd sensation evolved within her solar plexus—a queasiness in the pit of her abdomen—something that mimicked the sort of feeling she experienced prior to her first dance recital at age seven. But the feeling she now experienced was more unsettling than what she experienced at age seven. She was no longer a child, she was an adult; and she experienced a mature level of apprehension.

"Who's there?"

No one answered. Andela couldn't decide if she were experiencing excitement or terror. She sensed a presence—not a threatening presence, but a potent presence. The thought entered her mind that she should set the table for two persons. Then the room was back to normal—the feeling, the presence, was gone.

"Okay Andela," she spoke aloud to herself as she turned and leaned backward against the kitchen counter. "You're okay, you're not dead, you're still here, and you've been under a lot of stress."

Then the music resumed. Andela jolted and stared at the radio—it was sitting as usual on top of the counter. She did not remember the music stopping, but it must have stopped. It wasn't storming outside, and the radio was new; so something must have happened at the broadcasting station.

"Yes, that's it, the broadcasting station," Andela mumbled. She continued leaning against the counter and looked around the kitchen. She saw nothing unusual. After several seconds she decided that the sound of her voice had served to normalize the surroundings.

Everything was like it had been a minute or two before, all pretty average, except that she would never forget the feeling that had overwhelmed her senses a half-minute earlier.

"Okay then, no one in the world knows you're doing this. It's your apartment, so you can set the table however you want to."

Despite the reassuring nature of her voice, Andela decided to stop talking out loud—it seemed weird. She could not help but wonder if someone was watching her. Without further speech, she began setting the table for two persons. She was embarrassed by the thought of Jenny finding out that she was placing two plates, two glasses, and two sets of silverware on the small dining table in her kitchen. But nonetheless, she would not dare ignore the message that was impressed upon her mind— namely the impression that she should set the table for two. After the utensils and food were all arranged, she sat down in one of the four wooden chairs that surrounded around the square table. Rather than beginning her meal, she again glanced about the room.

The room was ordinary, a typical kitchen in a standard apartment. The radio continued producing music. Andela took a breath and looked down at the table. A moment later, she arose from her chair and stepped to the cabinet where she withdrew her only table ornament—a large, white, intricately fashioned wax candle. This would be the first time she lit it.

After lighting the candle, Andela ran water over the head of the match. Then she threw the match into a trash bag beneath the sink and returned to the table. Though she rarely spoke out loud to herself unless notably stressed, she often prayed out loud. She considered asking God to preserve her sanity; but if something supernatural were going on, he might be the one behind it. How would God feel if she asked him to clear her mind of hallucinations when it wasn't hallucinations at all—it was him? She decided to not mention her sanity. She closed her eyes.

"Dear Father God, thank you for this meal. Thank you for life, and especially for eternal life. There is joy in knowing you, and I ask for your perfect will in my life, whether that perfect will means that I remain a single woman, or whether that perfect will means that I will someday get married. I pray this in Jesus' name, amen."

Andela raised her head and looked about the room yet again. The room still seemed normal, and she felt normal, but there was something else too—she felt impressed by how special and wonderful her *normal* life really was. There was much to be thankful for, and much to look forward to, no matter what plans God might have for her. It struck her mind that life is both good and wonderful because God is both good and wonderful. With such pleasant thoughts, and with the comforting normalcy of her surroundings, she managed to ignore the extra place setting and the burning candle, both of which were reminders of recent sensations that were anything but normal. She cut a juicy slice of steak and began raising it toward her mouth.

The slice of steak never touched Andela's lips—it froze in place an inch from her mouth. The music had ceased, right in the middle of a phrase. Andela stared at the radio. The odd sensation that she had experienced earlier returned to the pit of her abdomen.

"Bzzzz! Kerslpank!"

The metal fork clanked against the porcelain plate a half-second after the doorbell rang. Andela could feel her heart throbbing. She grasped the edge of the wooden table with both hands to steady herself. She felt dizzy. Her knees seemed as though they might buckle at any time as she rose from the chair and made her way to the front door. "Maybe it's Pastor Larken," she uttered in a soft whisper, but she did not really think it was going to be Pastor Larken. As she reached the door, she regretted hanging an outside wreath that blocked the door's viewing lens.

"Whu...ah," croaked Andela, trying to gain sufficient composure to speak. "Huh...who's there?"

"A messenger."

The voice was crystal clear and calm—a stark contrast to the tone of Andela's inquiry.

"Ah...a messenger?"

"Yes."

It dawned upon Andela that she could peek out through a window to her left, the only window in her living room. She darted to the window. The adrenaline that pumped through her bloodstream no longer immobilized her; instead, she moved with agile swiftness. In less than five seconds from the time the visitor last spoke, she eased one section of a Venetian blind upward and peered out. Their eyes met—he was staring straight at her.

The overhead light in the outside corridor set the visitor's hair ablaze, and there were golden strands wrapped around his forehead. There was no way, however, that the overhead light could account for the resplendence of his gleaming eyes—it seemed that they could see straight through her, or perhaps peer deep inside of her. Andela surmised that the visitor's eyesight was not impeded by the door or walls; he saw her movement as plainly as if the entire apartment were lucent glass. He wore a white robe and golden sandals. *I'm not crazy after all*, Andela thought to herself. She deduced that what happened in the kitchen was supernatural, and that all the weird feelings she had been experiencing were leading up to this, namely an encounter with a messenger from God—a heavenly angel.

Andela was Christian. She often spoke with God. There were times she sensed the presence of God's Spirit as surely as she sensed anything; but up to this point, she had never experienced anything that she considered a supernatural phenomenon. Strangely, now that a supernatural phenomenon was transpiring, the whole event seemed quite natural.

Andela continued holding up the blind, staring into the angel's eyes. "Won't you please come in?" she spoke. Her voice was now stable.

The angel nodded. "Thank you," he said, and Andela was able to hear his voice as plainly as if he were standing inside the room beside her.

It did not surprise Andela when the angel passed into the room without opening the door. He stood in formal silence, apparently waiting for her to speak.

"Won't you join me for supper?" asked Andela. She was glad that she had responded to the impression that she should set the table for two persons, but then a quizzical look passed over her face—she wasn't sure if angels ate.

The angel smiled as if he were reading Angela's mind. "I will most gladly join you for supper. I smell something delectable."

With few additional words, they were soon seated at the kitchen table. The angel looked out of place, but he appeared at ease. It struck Andela's mind that the angel's drinking glass was empty. The various foods she had prepared were all on the table and ready to dish out, but she hadn't bothered to fill the glass at the second table setting.

"Oh, what would you like to drink?" asked Andela.

"Whatever you're having."

"Well, I'm just drinking water."

"Water is fine."

Andela rose as gracefully as she could and withdrew her nicest pitcher from an overhead cabinet. She filled the pitcher with cool tap water and returned to the table. After pouring water into the angel's drinking glass, she set the pitcher on the table and returned to her chair, sitting across the table from the angel.

"Shall we ask grace?" she inquired.

"You already have grace, my dear," the angel stated. He looked at Andela and smiled.

"Yes, well, I mean, should we thank God for our food?"

"Your previous prayer was both sincere and adequate."

Andela looked back at the angel. She wasn't sure what to say or do next.

"Nonetheless, I think another prayer would be acceptable," said the angel. "May I have the honor?"

The angel's manner and speech were congenial. Andela was able to relax. "Yes, please do."

Rather than shutting his eyes, or turning his face upward, the angel continued gazing straight ahead; but he seemed to lose focus with his eyes. His facial features depicted earnest concentration. "Father Creator, good and eternal God, thank you for granting everlasting begottenness to your beloved daughter who sits before me, and thank you for this mortal substance that nourishes her temporary temple. Blessed is the sovereign name of Jesus."

Andela smiled. Without further ado, the angel began eating. Andela followed suit. She assumed that angels eat for pleasure, not really needing to eat at all; but she decided not to ask about that—she figured that more important questions would come to her mind, and she did not want to bother the angel with trite inquiries. For a while nothing was spoken. It was interesting to watch the angel eat; he not only ate the skin on the potato, but also the bone in the steak, and he did not have any difficulty chewing the bone.

"Delightful meal, my dear hostess," the angel appraised after washing down the last bit of potato skin. "I predict that you will induce culinary celebration via a fortunate man's gastronomic perceptions."

Despite his odd choice of words, the angel's praise sparked Andela's interest. His words insinuated that he expected her to get married. "Thank you," she said. "I feel most honored by your presence."

The angel shrugged. "My presence is my privilege, my dear. Missions such as this one have a special appeal to me."

Andela's shoulders tensed with curiosity. "Missions?" she prodded. She knew that visits from angels, at least those recorded in Scripture, were associated with momentous events.

The angel peered into Andela's eyes. "Are you finished eating?"

Andela did not even look down at her plate. "Yes."

The angel smiled and rose from his chair, lifting his plate and utensils.

"Oh, um, I can get those," interjected Andela. It hardly seemed appropriate for an angel to be washing dishes.

"No, stay seated. I'll be right with you."

The angel placed his dish and utensils into the sink, and then collected Andela's. He rinsed the dishes and utensils and arranged them inside the dishwasher; gathered the platters of leftover food and placed them inside the refrigerator; and then blew out the candle and set it on the counter beside the sink. Andela felt abashed, but she did not interfere. When finished, the angel returned to his chair and leaned forward. He rested his elbows on the table and folded his hands. He gazed into Andela's eyes. She knew that she was about to learn the purpose of his visit. She could scarcely breathe.

"There are two among us, a son and daughter of God, who recently joined us. They were married during their lives upon the earth, and served as missionaries of a sort, though not paid by any religious organization. Furthermore, though it may seem foreign to human notions about missionaries, they lived in a settlement near this one. But no matter, it is not the nature of their missionary work that I am here to discuss. We want to provide care for two children left behind, and we hope that all parties selected for that purpose will choose to participate in the care of those children."

"Children?" inquired Andela. She was fond of children and good at taking care of them.

"Yes, two young children, a boy and a girl. They have been left to the care of one who is dead."

Andela's brow furrowed. She stared in silence.

"The dead one, it is determined, has the potential to fulfill your desires and dreams for a man-mate. Furthermore, you fulfill the dead man's fancies regarding a partner of the female gender. Thus, if you find the children adoptable, two matters may be resolved through a single mission, and I am especially fond of missions serving double purposes."

"Man-mate," Andela reiterated. "You want me to marry a dead man?"

The angel's face flashed an expression of dismay, but then he resumed his former composure. "Certainly not. The man must first choose to become a member of the kingdom of the living."

Andela was not fond of horror films, and the angel's words brought grim thoughts of ghosts and zombies. "You mean you want me to marry a man who comes back from the dead?"

A broad smile formed across the angel's face. "The proposed man-mate has never experienced the decease of his earthly temple, and he is quite alive in the biological sense, but this is hardly worth deeming the man *alive*—not in comparison to the begottenness that human beings are intended."

Andela settled back in her chair, dropping her shoulders in relief. "Oh, so he's physically alive, but he's not a Christian."

The angel sat and peered at Andela for several seconds. When he finally spoke, Andela had the impression that he was trying to simplify his response. "Given that the term *Christian* is defined as *Christ like*, and given that Christ is wondrously and eternally alive, then yes, I agree—he is not Christian, at least not yet. But I suppose you could still consider him to be alive in a limited sort of capacity, since he is, as you put it, *physically alive*."

"So, what am I supposed to do?"

The angel appeared startled by Andela's inquiry. After he regained his composure, however, his facial expression indicated approval. He addressed her with a gleam of admiration in his eyes. "Your receptivity is most welcome and inspiring. Now then, only one variable appears likely to threaten the success of my mission."

"One variable? You mean me? My freewill choice?" inquired Andela.

The angel peered upon Andela's face. "I fully acknowledge that you possess free will, and I also acknowledge that the mission is highly dependent upon your freewill choices. But you are not really viewed as a variable, but rather, as a constant."

"A constant?" responded Andela. "What do you mean?"

"Well, to use a colloquialism of this native region, we are banking on you."

"Oh, thanks," said Andela, producing a weak smile. She was flattered by the angel's praise of her stability, but she felt a little embarrassed. "Well then, please go on—you were saying that there is one variable that threatens *your mission.*"

The angel resumed. "Yes, the dead man's freewill choice, namely *to be* or *not to be*, is the variable. If he accepts *begottenness*, he will suffice. If not, well, that would not be good."

Andela continued facing the angel. The angel's proposition seemed to be a sophisticated blind date—a date with the challenge of wooing an unsaved man to Christianity. The entire proposition seemed daunting, and yet it seemed altogether intriguing and stimulating, a stark contrast to her present, rather boring routine.

"I think I understand, and yes, I'd like to accept your invitation—I'd like to participate in this mission."

The angel again appeared startled. "My dear, that is splendid," he praised. "But I cannot accept your offer until I explain a couple of details."

Something in the tone of the angel's voice made Andela nervous. "Details?"

"Yes. First of all, the dead man is affable, but stubborn. Through the persuasion of certain prayers on his behalf, and also in consideration of the children, it is granted that he may accompany you on a potentially insightful journey—a fantastic and wonderful journey—a journey such as neither he nor you have ever sought to imagine. The journey will be fraught with hope, but will also be dangerous."

"A journey? Where to? And what kind of danger?"

The angel addressed Andela's last question. "For you, little danger, merely loss of your earthly temple."

Andela interpreted the angel's language only too well. She stared at him with mixed emotions. "So then, you're saying that I could be killed on this journey, right?"

The angel gestured casually with one hand. "I like to think of it as a graduation—your next temple will be much superior to your temporal one."

Andela swallowed. "Okay, understood. So then, would there be the same danger for the man?"

"For the dead one, there is a greater risk. He will not be permitted to die physically during this journey, since he will be drawn into the journey without willful knowledge of his circumstances. In fact, he will most likely think the journey is a nighttime dream. But if things do not go well, he could return from the journey and realize that he failed to prevent your physical demise."

"So, how would that be a greater risk than my physical death?"

"The answer is quite simple—the dead man could blame his own failure on the Creator, not realizing the importance and impact of his own free will. Such misplaced blame could decrease any probability that the dead man will choose *to be*."

Andela pondered the angel's words. She experienced a sinking feeling that drifted downward from her breast to her stomach. All the excitement she felt moments earlier now seemed a taunting memory. "You mean that, if I fail on this mission, then the man you're talking about could end up going to hell?"

The angel responded with a solemn nod.

"Well then, I, um, I just don't think I could take such a risk," said Andela, casting her face downward in disappointment, almost in tears.

"Splendid!" proclaimed the Angel. Andela looked back up as the angel continued speaking, "You would set aside the opportunity to possibly fulfill your present dream of a man-mate, simply to better the chances of eternal life for an individual you have never met."

Andela sighed. "Yes."

"Then you are ready for the assignment."

Andela's forehead creased. "But, I thought...,"

The angel raised his right palm and stopped Andela's speech. "I know, my dear, I know," he stated, lowering his hand back to the tabletop. "The fact is, though, that the dead man's likelihood of choosing eternal life will be much increased if you proceed with the mission. In short, the eternal risk to the dead man is much greater if you do not participate in the mission than if you do participate."

Andela faced the angel for several seconds, and then a relieved and excited expression bloomed upon her face. "Are you certain?"

The angel peered deeply into Andela's eyes, more deeply than anyone had ever looked into her eyes before. "Yes, I am certain."

"Okay then, I'll go."

The angel scooted his chair backward and stood upright. His demeanor was wrought with dignity, like a herald announcing the arrival of royalty, and Andela felt certain that he was somehow paying her a compliment. "The journey will begin as soon as the dead man kisses you, provided the kiss is one of true and earnest affection. God be with you." He paused and reached to a pocket hidden within his robe. He withdrew a petite white scroll that was tied with a band of golden thread. Very formally, he placed the scroll down on the tabletop and faced Andela. "The dead man's address is written upon this parchment. He has decided to secure the services of a nanny to help care for the orphaned children, and you will be that nanny. You are hereby instructed to arrive at his house no earlier than tomorrow afternoon at five o'clock, and no later than tomorrow at midnight. You are not to contact him prior to arrival."

Andela stood also and stepped near the angel. She raised a finger of inquiry. "Okay, thank you, but…"

The angel vanished.

Chapter 2

Vacuum

"There's something I'm missing, something downright important," muttered Bill. Sweat dampened his long-sleeved flannel shirt as he continued working into the night; there was always plenty to do around a dairy farm. "This is just plain weird," he added, realizing that he couldn't remember ever carrying on an audible conversation with himself. He was feeling unsettled by recent changes in his household, and speaking out loud seemed to vent inner frustration. "It's a good thing no one can hear me, they'd think I was crazy."

Bill remained quiet long enough to contemplate how embarrassed he would be to find out that someone was listening to him; but then he assured himself that no one could possibly hear him, other than perhaps a squirrel, or a lizard, or a bullfrog on the bank of the pond some distance behind him. He dismissed his feelings of self-consciousness and decided that a dairy farmer, working all by himself at night, ought to be able to talk out loud if he wanted to.

"Just what am I supposed to do to make me feel like my life really matters, not just for the kids, but for me?" he remarked in a voice of inquiry, standing straight up and gripping the handle of his hammer. He paused from his task and gazed upward through churning oak leaves. Beads of starlight pierced through opening and closing gaps in the foliage like alien fireflies. The flickering light was mesmerizing; it held his uplifted eyes and drew his thoughts beyond his own feelings. Then a most mysterious sensation poured through his chest; it seemed that someone was listening.

Bill was frightened. He had the impression that he was not alone, and that something or someone was aware of his presence—something or someone capable of cognitive interaction. For several seconds he continued gazing upward, almost expecting a voice to speak from the stars; but then he jerked his face downward and shrugged off the sensation. He shook his head and snickered to himself, returning to his hammering and again speaking out loud. "What the blazes was that?"

The feeling returned, this time stronger. Bill felt his heart throbbing. Again he looked upward. "Can anyone hear me?"

"Whooo, whooo, whooo..."

The nearby screech owl nearly frightened Bill out of his own skin. He dropped his hammer and clutched the wooden gatepost he was repairing. One of his more contrary dairy cows, a large Holstein named Bertha, had butted the post halfway over when a wandering cocker spaniel paid his farm a visit earlier that evening.

"Just a hoot owl," murmured Bill, reaching back down to retrieve his hammer.

"Whooo, whooo..."

"Who?" returned Bill. "Why you, not me. I'm...I'm...or am I?"

Bill's mind succumbed to an unnerving sense of outer vastness that accentuated his sense of inner irrelevance. Did he exist, or did he not? Fathomless space stretched beyond the highest branches of the oak, but his thoughts stretched far beyond the nighttime sky. His soul awakened to hunger—an inner yearning to fill a longing void. The more he pondered his own being, the more he doubted it. He felt an urgent need to secure or become something. He began to...

"Ah!!! Fire ants!"

Bill's thoughts were interrupted by sharp pains. His cumbersome boots clanked down the well-beaten path from the fence gate to the front door of his house. He ignored the repeated stings of attacking ants long enough to ease open the door, not wanting to strike a small child; and then he flung himself onto the floor beyond the threshold to the doorway and began hollering. He yanked the boots and socks from his feet and slapped at his ankles, making unrestrained vocal sounds that had little resemblance to the English language. "Ah! Eeeyaa! Yiohyiaheee!"

"Unky, Unky!" a small girl cried out. From an upstairs bedroom burst Robin, Bill's robust, three-year-old niece. Close behind trailed Ricky, her five-year-old brother.

"Unky! Unky!" Robin continued screaming as she scampered down polished oak steps with one hand raised to slide her palm along a handrail. She ran across the spacious den; a room bedecked with sofas, armchairs, a television, and a pool table; and then she slid to her uncle's side, wrapping both arms around his neck like a baby possum clinging to its mother's back. Ricky, who was not as hysterical over the commotion, stopped five feet from the scene and watched with attentive eyes. Robin was plump, cute, and strong. Her curly brunette locks tickled Bill's throat as she clasped his neck. Ricky, in contrast to his sister, was slim, blonde, and blue-eyed—much like his uncle in appearance, except that Bill had dark hair.

"Bill Stroggins, if you don't beat any man I ever laid eyes on for carry'in on over nothin!"

Bill watched a slender figure kneel over his ankles. Graceful hands sought out the two or three ants that were still alive and crushed them.

"Fire ants," Miss Andela noted with disdain, "such despicable little varmints. I wish someone would have had enough sense to leave the critters in Argentina, or wherever they came from."

Bill smiled as Andela stood and faced him with a hand on one hip. Robin quieted to a series of pitiful whines; there were teary streams coursing down both her cheeks. Ricky responded to Bill's smile and smiled in like manner, moving his eyes back and forth between Bill and Andela. He was barely old enough for kindergarten, but he was old enough to realize that there was something special about the way his uncle and nanny looked at each other.

"Poor baby girl," cooed Andela. She stepped closer, leaned forward, and raised Robin in her arms. "Did Unky's big battle with the little ants scare our baby girl?" She rocked side to side with Robin's face drawn next to hers. "Yes, Aunt Dell was scared too, nearly swallowed her tooth brush."

Andela's eyes snapped at Bill. He was propped up on both hands with his legs and bare feet sprawled across the floor. One of his boots sat upright just inside the open door, and the other lay flat on the outside doormat. Andela's eyes only made Bill's smile broader.

Both of the children knew that Andela Tidmore, called Dell, was not a blood relative; but they called her *Aunt Dell* just the same. "Did fire ants really come from Argentina?" questioned Ricky.

Andela carried Robin as she retrieved Bill's boot from the doormat and closed the door. "Well, I think it was somewhere in South America, I'm not sure, but anyway, I know they're not from Kansas. Wherever they come from, though, they sure seem to have an appetite for men from Missouri, especially men with big feet."

Bill smiled and wiggled his toes as both Ricky and Robin stared toward his feet.

"Now," resumed Andela, "please help your wounded Unky into an easy chair while your sister and I look for something appropriate to treat his bites." She looked back at Bill. "I guess we'll find some lotion if there's no pepper sauce or rubbing alcohol."

Andela turned and strode toward an open doorway at the opposite side of the den. Bill watched her pass from sight. He shook his head in wonder. She had captured the children's hearts the day they met her; and after four months of serving as a live-in nanny, she was charming his heart as well. He could not categorize her—she was different than anyone he had ever met before—and he knew one thing for sure, namely that she impressed him more favorably than he had thought possible for a member of the human race. And what was more, he wondered if he were falling in love with her.

"Come on, Unky," coaxed Ricky, "Aunt Dell said for you to sit in a chair." Ricky used both hands to grasp his uncle by the wrist, and Bill rolled forward with a grunt, pretending that Ricky pulled him up. Bill had always adored Ricky and Robin, and he adopted them within days of their parents' funeral. It surprised him to learn how much he enjoyed serving as an adopted guardian; but then, this was especially true after hiring Andela.

Bill plopped down in the chair and permitted Ricky to inspect the boots, socks, dead ants, and wounds. "You have seven little red bumps on this ankle, and nine little red bumps on this ankle," noted Ricky.

"Very good," appraised Andela, reentering the room. Robin was now smiling as she rode in one of Andela's arms. "Don't you think Ricky is doing well with numbers, Unky Bill?" she mused as she tossed him a bottle of calamine lotion.

"I guess so," conceded Bill, "but I sure hope we can get him something else to count when he starts advanced math."

"Ah, a good point, Ricky wouldn't want to count that many ant bites, that would get boring—nothing but hair and little red dots," teased Andela. "But you know, there are bound to be other things to count. Ricky, have you ever seen what river leeches look like?"

Ricky's eyebrows rose high as he stared at Andela's face.

"Only kidding punkin," said Andela, patting Ricky on the head after seeing his fretful expression. "Now come on, I think Unky's going to be fine, and we have a big day planned for tomorrow, so back up to bed we go."

Andela ushered Ricky toward the stairs as she carried Robin. Robin shifted in Andela's arms and waved back to her uncle.

"Night, night, Unky."

Bill grinned from his chair. "Good night, sugarplum."

Good night, Unky Bill," Ricky interjected.

"Good night, space pilot," Bill responded. He was careful to keep up with Ricky's imagined vocations. Ricky was pleased by Bill's response, and he would spend hours dreaming of navigating a space craft through asteroid fields.

Andela and the children stepped beyond sight. Bill watched them disappear, and then he began reminiscing over the recent changes in his household. He reflected upon his first two months with the children, before Andela's arrival. Ricky and Robin were both wonderful, but watching two children while rounding up dairy cows was tedious. He had to keep an eye on both of them while managing a grade A dairy operation. The milk in his stainless steel vat was tested from time to time during unannounced visits from the health department, so its purity had to be maintained; and more importantly, he did not want anyone getting sick from contaminated milk due to mental errors on his part.

Bill leaned forward to finish applying lotion to his wounds and then sighed as he sat back up and settled himself in the recliner. Why did he work so hard to keep up a small-scale dairy farm? The inheritance he received after his parents were killed overseas was sufficient to support a household, so why did he continue to chase cows and shovel manure? But then, as strange as it might seem to some people, he liked dairy farming.

Bill's chest rose with contentment as he contemplated all the hard work it had required for him to establish himself in the dairy community. No doubt his life was different than what his parents envisioned for him; they had hoped he would become a renowned attorney. Thankfully, though, both his father and mother were proud of his hard work and success as a dairy farmer, and that was a memory he cherished. And at any rate, what would he do all day if he weren't busy on the farm? He loved music, but his skills on the piano and guitar were not polished enough for him to perform as a professional.

He settled farther back in his lounge chair and shifted his thoughts to the preceding four months, namely the span of time that he had spent in company with Andela. His decision to obtain a nanny came the day that Robin escaped his notice long enough to walk beneath Old Pat's belly. Old Pat was a sedate jersey, and she merely flicked her tail when Robin's hair tickled her drooped abdomen. But what would have happened if Robin had stepped beneath a temperamental Holstein? He shuddered to think what might have happened if Robin had stepped beneath Bertha rather than Old Pat.

"Well, all tucked in like June bugs in a bale of hay," Andela announced in a soft cheerful voice as she stepped from wooden steps to the carpeted floor of the den.

Bill gazed upon the most mysterious entity that ever entered his life. On the morning of April 2nd, he contacted newspapers to place ads for a live-in nanny. At eleven-thirty p.m., still on April 2nd, the doorbell rang—just after he sat down on the edge of his bed to remove damp wool socks. He remembered the night well. Great branches of lightning streaked through monstrous clouds, and clapping thunder echoed between the ground and sky. When the doorbell rang, he surmised that Stan Bradsbury was at the door. Stan lived across the road from Bill's dairy farm, and Stan supported a wife and four children by raising beef cattle. Bill figured the storm spooked some of Stan's cattle and that Stan needed help with rounding up strays; but it wasn't Stan Bradsbury who rang the doorbell, it was Andela Tidmore.

Andela strode across the rust-colored carpet and stood before her employer. *She still seems as enchanting as ever*, thought Bill. He recalled flipping on the porch light and opening the front door, expecting to see Stan's hefty figure. Instead, there appeared the graceful silhouette of a woman, and then he came face to face with Andela. She held no umbrella, but grasped two suitcases, one in each hand. Her golden hair was drenched into ropy strands that toppled over her shoulders. Glistening raindrops crept along her gilded locks. All else faded, though, when he met her eyes.

Bill would never forget the penetrating aura that possessed him the first time he looked into Andela's eyes. The enchanting hazel dashed upon emerald green that comprised the color of Andela's irises was merely framework to something far more potent and indefinable. He sensed something when he looked into her eyes, something very different and wonderful. Several times since then, when a quiet moment permitted a mutual gaze, Bill experienced the sensation again, still the same, difficult to accept as reality and yet somehow more real than anything he had ever known. And now, there she was again, her eyes appearing just the same, and the feeling they evoked within him being every whit as compelling as the first time their eyes met.

"Penny for your thoughts," posed Andela. She shifted her weight to one hip and smiled as she tilted her head toward her right shoulder.

Bill chuckled and peered downward toward his bare feet. "Whatever gave you the idea I was putting out the effort to think?"

"After cohabitating with you for four whole months, Mister Stroggins, it's plenty easy to spot when you're havin' a deep ponder about somethin'," said Andela. She often spoke with a profoundly country accent when bantering with Bill, though she was also capable of proper English.

"Whoa ho!" remarked Bill, loudly enough to cause Andela's eyes to widen and to bring a finger to her lips, reminding Bill to keep his voice down on account of sleeping children. "A *deep ponder*, huh," he said more quietly. "Well, I'd say that's one of the most backwoods expressions I've ever heard in all my born days, *deep ponder*. I guess I've never hiked far enough back in the sticks as to hear that expression before, *deep ponder*."

As Bill hoped, and as he awkwardly counted upon in order to avoid engaging in more serious conversation, Andela adopted the change of subject.

"Sticks!"

Bill grinned and took his turn at bringing one finger to his lips. Andela dropped her voice, but she did not hesitate to continue speaking.

"Sticks my foot, Mister Bill. I've yanked more sticks outa yer socks and jeans than a girl might expect ta find in a beaver dam. Why, I'd never been so *stickified* in all my born days as the first time I tackled your mucked up laundry."

Bill loved good-natured kidding, and Andela was capable of matching him; but as he lifted a chuckling gaze into her downcast eyes, he sobered. Andela possessed a marvelous sense of humor, but at times she struck Bill as out-and-out serious; and as he lifted his face toward hers, he was seized by a staid and earnest inquisition—an inquisition that seemed generated from the depths of her soul, far beyond the cajoling twinkle cast upon the outer surface of her eyes. His features grew stolid. For several seconds they regarded one another in silence. It was Andela who regained sufficient composure to speak.

"Well, maybe I was exaggerating a little. I guess I should just be glad that your toilets flush—my aunt Ruby had an outhouse."

There was such a contradiction between the triteness of Andela's words and the earnest expression besetting her features that Bill didn't know whether to grant a smile or to give a solemn nod. But then her seeming innocence and vulnerability plucked a delightful chord in his heart. Before he could think twice, he rolled back in his chair and laughed aloud; not really laughing at Andela, but rather laughing because it was such a pleasure to sit in company with someone so genuine and charming. It was unusual that someone could free Bill's heart to laugh so merrily. In fact, this sort of laughter had rarely risen from his breast before Andela came, laughter that sprang from a sense of something Bill knew too little of, perhaps joy. He was abashed, therefore, when Andela turned without saying a word and walked toward the dining room en route to the kitchen.

"Temperamental female," muttered Bill, though his foremost feeling was that of *clumsy male*. He was aware that he admired Andela. Maybe he even loved her. But he was uncertain of the latter; in fact, he was not sure that he even knew what it meant to really love a woman. Sometimes he almost convinced himself that he should share his personal feelings with Andela; but then, on the other hand, she was hired to take care of children, not to be annoyed by a lonesome bachelor.

"Ka-plash!"

Bill straightened and grabbed both arms of the chair. A crashing sound from the kitchen was more startling than loud, striking his ears during the midst of reverie. He sat paralyzed for a second, and then he rose and dashed toward the kitchen. He stopped in the archway between the den and the kitchen, staring downward.

Bill's heart quickened. Andela was slumped in the floor like a lily beat against the ground during a summer storm; and beyond her was a small pile of broken, glazed glass. Her blue satin robe flowed outward on the floor, and her golden locks hung like sheltering veils about her downcast face.

"Andela," Bill spoke, stepping forward and then kneeling to the floor.

Andela raised her face. It was streaked with tears. She locked Bill's eyes with a pleading stare. It was the most earnest stare Bill had ever beheld. "I broke your great-grandmother's glass guinea goblet," she said. "I'm so sorry."

Bill was speechless. He gazed in silence as a new tear trickled down Andela's cheek and splashed almost imperceptibly onto the tile floor. He leaned forward and wandered into her eyes. The communing of their eyes seemed a daring passage, but it was a passage that Bill found to be marvelous beyond anything he had ever imagined.

"I...," began Bill, wanting to speak soothing words; but he could find no words to embody the communication transpiring via their mutual gaze. There was much within the world of Andela's eyes that Bill could not comprehend, much that was remindful of the sensations he had experienced while gazing upward into the endless sky through churning oak leaves before he was attacked by fire ants, but there was also a look that would be difficult for any man to misinterpret.

Finally Andela smiled. It was an appreciative and consoling smile. Then she dropped her face back downward.

With courageous resolution, Bill reached out and took hold of Andela's body, lifting her in his arms. Her head came to rest on his shoulder. He carried her back into the den and placed her on a sofa. Then he sat beside her, longing to again look into her eyes. Her face was cast downward.

"Dell, I don't care anything about that old glass chicken, not compared to..."

"I know," interrupted Andela, grasping Bill's arm without yet looking up. "It's not that, it's, well…"

There was a long pause. Bill sensed intensity in Andela's touch and demeanor. She raised her face and met his eyes with a look so compelling that his heart rose and pounded against the inner wall of his chest. He found it unbelievable that anyone so beautiful and adorable could be looking at him that way.

"Listen, Dell," Bill stammered. He searched his mind for something comprehensible to say. "I've been working you too hard. I didn't mean to take a vacation from chores around the house when I hired you."

"No," retorted Andela. "I enjoy what I do here, and I appreciate the way you help with the children, and the way you sometimes pitch in with chores, but listen Bill…"

Andela stopped speaking and lifted her free hand to clutch Bill's other arm. She pulled him closer. Bill felt her warm breath.

"It's not my work I want to discuss. It's us, Bill, me and you."

"I, uh," choked Bill, finding his vocal cords difficult to operate. "I admire you, Andela, more than I could ever say. But…"

"But what Bill?"

"Well, I don't know. I don't feel like I'm on the same level of existence that you are. It's like I'm some insensible chunk of limestone just sitting out in the middle of the pasture, just sitting there and hankering to be like a gorgeous butterfly flittering and dancing in the sunshine."

Andela pulled Bill still closer. "Are you saying I'm that butterfly?"

Bill nodded. "Yes Dell, you are. You're something I'm not, I can sense it, I only wish…"

"Wish what Bill?"

Andela's passionate presence drew Bill's lips toward hers like bare iron to a magnet; but before their lips met she released his left shoulder and placed one finger between their mouths. She did not back away; and the impending consummation of a first kiss was tantalizing to both of them.

"I," she spoke, hesitating as she found herself panting. "I can't do this until I tell you something."

"Okay," said Bill.

"Do you remember the night I came here, four months ago?"

"Like it was yesterday," replied Bill. He could feel his breast pounding like a kettledrum.

"Well, hasn't it ever struck you funny that I showed up the same day that you called the newspaper to place an ad for a nanny?"

"That was quick," Bill acknowledged absentmindedly. Given his present situation, he had difficulty generating much interest in the newspaper.

"No, now listen. What I'm telling you is that the newspaper was not even printed until the next day."

Andela's statement managed to elicit an inquisitive wrinkle in Bill's brow. "So someone from the newspaper told you about my call, well, I'm thankful for that."

"Bill, no human being told me anything about you. It was an angel. Our meeting one another was the result of a heavenly commission."

Although Andela's words did not necessarily seem logical, Bill found himself embracing them without reserve. If she felt that heaven had placed the two of them together, then that had to be a good sign in regard to the way she felt about him.

"That's wonderful, Dell."

Andela's finger slid downward and Bill could almost feel her lips touching his; but then she raised her finger one last time.

"Bill," she said, catching her breath and whispering through quivering lips. "The angel said that a kiss of true and earnest affection will send both of us on a fantastic and wonderful journey, and the journey may be very dangerous, and I'd love to go on that journey more than anything, but…"

"Let's go," said Bill.

Andela was never certain whether she removed her finger, or if Bill clasped her hand and drew her finger downward; but soon her entire body melted within Bill's arms.

Bill felt Andela's lips meet his own. He was infused with ethereal ecstasy. The sensations he experienced were far beyond anything he expected from a kiss. His head began spinning, pleasurably dazed, and his body felt weightless.

Chapter 3

The Land of Who

B ill recalled the feelings he experienced during his first ride on a roller coaster, but his recollection of these feelings seemed dwarfed by the sensations he experienced while kissing Andela. A gasp lodged above his diaphragm; his heart raced and throbbed; and it seemed that his senses peaked and cleared. As their lips parted and he gazed upon Andela's face, the remainder of the universe melted into oblivion. Her eyes entreated him, and her golden hair danced about her head and shoulders. He was certain that he had never beheld anything so invitingly wonderful.

Within seconds of meeting Bill's lips with her own, Andela realized that she was losing contact with the material world. Only the firm and compassionate grasp of Bill's hands and arms remained perceptible. She knew that it was happening—whatever the angel had been talking about—it was happening. The room vanished. A glorious and frightening thrill pierced her breast. She was nowhere she had ever been, and perhaps she was nowhere at all. After their lips parted, she released Bill's arms and clasped his hands; and then reality dawned anew. But it was a very different reality, a marvelous and enthralling reality.

Bill broke his gaze and looked around, above, and below him. An astonished, quizzical expression beset his face. He was the first to speak.

"So then, I'm asleep, all this is a dream, ah shucks. I should have known it was too good to be true."

Andela surveyed her surroundings. Delighted amazement ensued as she beheld breathtaking sights and scenery. She and Bill sat on the ground, situated together on the peak of a quaint knoll. Soft green grass carpeted the knoll, bedecked by myriads of violet flowers with velvety petals. Nearby rolling hills were multicolored due to striking variations of floral adornment on shrubs and trees. Looking to her left, Andela noted that the landscape sloped downward to a winding river. Even from where she sat, it was obvious that the river was crystal clear—it appeared as a colossal, serpentine prism pierced by dancing rays of light. Downstream the river entered a forest of hemlocks and ferns. The forest was teeming with chirping birds, many of them swooping in and out of lofty branches.

"Oh Bill, isn't it beautiful?"

Bill stared at Andela. She was looking first in one direction, and then in another direction. He wondered if all dreams were like this dream while the dreams were taking place, seemingly real. He wondered if the Andela in this dream would be just like the real Andela.

"Isn't what beautiful?"

Andela turned her head to face Bill, but then she raised her eyes toward golden-purple mountains that rose beyond a span of foothills. She noted that the river appeared to originate from the mountains. She looked back at Bill. "Why, everything! Everything around us! The trees, the flowers, the hills, the birds…everything!"

Bill's eyes darted from side to side, and then he stared at Andela with a puzzled expression.

"And those mountains," Andela added, pointing back behind Bill. "And that river down there," she concluded, pointing to her left.

Bill turned his head from side to side, and then looked above and below him. A perplexed expression remained cast upon his brow. Finally his expression eased as he turned his face back toward Andela and shook his head.

"This has got to be the strangest dream I've ever had. Here I am floating on light that's solid enough to support my body weight, with nothing visible in any direction except for you, and you're trying to tell me how spectacular the countryside appears." He shrugged as he finished speaking, looking at Andela with interest, and wondering what she might say next. "But I'll tell you what," he commented before she managed any response, "I can't believe how real you look. It's just like you look in real life. And what's more, it's the strangest thing, I can feel you…I mean, I can sense that you're here, just like when you're in the same room with me when we're awake, you know, when it's real."

Andela peered at Bill. An expression of bewilderment settled upon her face. The angel that visited her apartment in St. Louis had stated that Bill might think he was dreaming, but she couldn't remember the angel saying anything about Bill not being able to see things. Her eyes addressed Bill in questioning silence while Bill gazed at her. Neither of them seemed to know what to do next, or what to say next.

"He does not see your land, daughter of God," a voice sounded from behind Andela. She was startled and leaped to Bill's side, clasping her arms around his shoulders while looking back toward the speaker. Standing right there, only a few feet from them, was an angel. He wore a white robe that draped downward to the straps of golden sandals. A golden belt was fastened about his waist, and the color of his hair matched that of his belt and sandals. "The dead cannot see the lands of the living," he resumed speaking, "they can only detect the beckoning light. The only thing that this dead man sees, apart from light, is you."

Rather than verbally responding, Andela leaned to one side where she could look into Bill's face. He still appeared bewildered, but there was also a pleased aspect to his countenance.

"He does not see me, nor does he hear me," spoke the angel. "He thinks that you have chosen to place yourself at his side, and he does not appear to object. You must guide him to his destination."

Andela faced the angel. "How? What destination? Where?"

"How what?" interjected Bill.

Andela again faced Bill. "I'm, ah, I'm talking to someone you can't see or hear."

Bill grinned. It seemed that the Andela in his dream was just as unpredictable as the real one. "Oh, someone I can't see or hear, huh. Okay then, go ahead."

Andela hesitated. She continued facing Bill, wondering if she should explain what was going on.

"I would surmise that the dead man thinks himself to be dreaming," said the angel.

Andela turned her face back to the angel and nodded. "Yes, and his name is Bill," she said. It gave her an intestinal cringe to hear Bill referred to as *the dead man*.

"So, what's your friend's name?" asked Bill. "That is, the name of whoever you're talking to that I can't see or hear?" Bill felt free to assert himself as he pleased, given that he was dreaming—he figured that a man should surely be in charge of his own dream.

"Tell him my name is *messenger*," instructed the angel, "and tell him that the message I bring is for him to follow you. Lead him upward through the hills until you reach the source of the river in the mountains. There are many wonderful things for you to see and experience in this land of yours, but do not be delayed here. Your mission is to reach his land, and to persuade him to invite Life into his land, so you must first journey to his land."

"Okay, but..."

Before Andela could formulate a concrete question within her mind, the angel disappeared. It struck her as rude for angels to vanish while she was attempting to ask questions, but then she figured that angels might have other tasks to carry out.

"Well, are you going to tell me your friend's name?" inquired Bill.

Andela became conscious of the fact that she was sitting close to Bill, and that he thought he was dreaming. She knew him to be respectful and considerate, but she figured that anyone might act differently in a dream. The frankness and tone of his speech suggested less shyness than he demonstrated when they were alone in Missouri.

"Um, his name? Sure," replied Andela, rising and standing before Bill. "He said his name is *messenger*, and he said that he wants me to take you somewhere. Would you like to go with me?"

Andela reached out a hand of invitation.

Bill peered at Andela. Her velvet robe enveloped her body like blue adorns the sky. Both of them were barefooted. He felt blood pulsing through his arteries—a much more genuine sensation than seemed feasible for a dream; and he could feel soft wind coursing over the surface of his skin. For several seconds he just sat and stared.

"Let's go," Bill finally consented, rising and extending a hand.

Andela clasped Bill's hand. She experienced an inner elation as his hand touched hers. She smiled with timid excitement, and then turned her face toward the purple mountains. She began leading Bill toward the river, intending to follow it upstream to its source. The surrounding scenery was breathtaking. Fruit trees grew from place to place, and each tree bore fruit that appeared ripe and delicious. As they drew nearer to the river, they came upon a grassy strip of ground that followed beside the river and coursed upstream toward the mountains. Andela turned and led them along this strip of ground. They both enjoyed walking while holding hands; it was their first time to do so.

A period of silence ensued. The silence made Andela uneasy, but she was nervous about starting a conversation. She hoped for more guidance when they reached the source of the river. Bill figured that several hours in a dream might be a few minutes of real time, or even a few seconds. And even if hours were passing, he was content walking side by side with Andela and holding her hand. He found himself hoping that he would dream a long, long time.

As they hiked onward, Bill ascertained that the thick substance upon which they walked inclined generally upward. He found himself getting a little winded. This surprised him since he figured that nothing that transpires during a dream should be tiring. Andela found herself staring at remarkable stones that jutted upward through the thick grass. The stones looked like giant gems, and they were more stunning than any rocks she remembered seeing in Missouri.

"Ouch!" exclaimed Bill.

Andela released Bill's hand and jumped in surprise. Bill reached down and rubbed the end of his right big toe. Andela had been walking to his left.

"What's wrong?" asked Andela.

"Something hit my toe."

Andela searched along the ground. She spotted a green stone that rose above the grass. She knelt and parted the grass from around it. It glistened when light pierced its sides, gleaming like a huge emerald.

"You felt this?" inquired Andela, looking up at Bill's face. "You can feel things here?"

Bill dropped to his knees beside Andela and stretched out his right index finger. Andela appeared to be rubbing her hands over the surface of something. He placed his finger between her hands.

"Feels like a lump of smooth glass," noted Bill.

"Yes, so, you can feel!"

Bill chuckled at Andela's exuberance. "Well, I guess that's progress, huh. I can't see, but I can feel."

Andela smiled uncertainly. "I guess so. I'll have to be careful where I lead you."

"Oh, okay. So, can you tell me where we're going?" asked Bill.

"To your land," answered Andela.

"My land?" retorted Bill. And before Andela could respond, he added, "Okay, that's fine, let's go." It struck Bill's mind that he shouldn't ask too many questions since doing so it might change the course of his dream, and he was enjoying the way his dream was unfolding.

An approving nod seemed the appropriate response, so Andela nodded toward Bill and rose to her feet. "Maybe you'd better walk right behind me so I can make sure we avoid stubbing your toes."

"Sure."

On they traveled. Bill found himself trying to decide if it were more enjoyable walking beside Andela and holding her hand, or more enjoyable following behind her where he had a full view of her figure. He noted the coordination of her lithe limbs, the perfect shape of her petite feet and toes, the bounce of her sunlit locks upon her back and shoulders, as well as other aspects of her feminine figure. He began comparing this *trek through dreamland* to long walks around the perimeter of his farm; and although there were trees, birds, streams, and woodland creatures that entertained and fascinated him back in Missouri, watching Andela stroll gracefully before him enthralled him more.

"Oh how marvelous! Look at the river!" exclaimed Andela, but then she covered her mouth with one hand and glanced back toward Bill, remembering his visual handicap.

Bill just smiled. He was aware that the Andela in his dream claimed to see things he could not see and to hear things that he could not hear; but that hardly mattered to him so long as he could see and hear Andela.

Andela dropped her hand from her mouth and turned back around. The river coursed some distance to their left, and something eye-catching had drawn her attention. The pathway they were traversing had risen far enough above the level of the river's surface for her to see the riverbed, and spectacular colors made her wonder if the bed of the river was a virtual flower garden. She peered ahead at the face of a mountain. The river issued from a deep gorge that was bordered by sheer cliffs. A thunderous sound rising from the gorge made Andela certain that a gigantic waterfall was cradled in the distance, somewhere in the majestic folds of the mountain's mantle.

Then Andela turned back toward the river. The mountain was close, and she figured a brief excursion wouldn't hurt anything. "I'll be right back," she said; and then she stepped down a grassy slope to the water's edge. Glittering white sand met the border of the grassy bank. The edge of the river looked as if it were aligned by the swipe of an artist's paintbrush. Beneath the water, the sandy bank sloped downward to the bottom of the river.

Gorgeous aquatic plants with millions of colorful flowers blanketed the floor of the river. Dancing upon the sandy white sides of the riverbed were crisscrossing rainbows—spectral bands of light clothed in red, yellow, purple, green, and all the hues between. In addition, there were fish more dazzling than the saltwater species Andela remembered admiring at a public aquarium in St. Louis. She knelt to her hands and knees at the edge of the bank and stared downward like a child peering into a goldfish bowl for the first time.

"Splash!"

"Bill, no!"

Andela jolted to her feet as drops of water splashed against her face. It was Bill; he had fallen into the river.

Andela recalled the angel's words—*There are many wonderful things for you to see and experience in this land of yours, but do not be delayed here.* She had allowed herself get distracted rather than following the angel's instruction. Bill's mishap was her fault. Would this change things? Would Bill disappear and find himself back at home? Would she disappear with him?

Andela stared at Bill. He did not vanished. He looked toward her and made stroking motions with his arms and legs. Apparently the journey would continue; and since Bill was an excellent swimmer, she figured that he would soon be emerging from the river. She gazed up toward her assigned destination, namely the mountain. What should she say to Bill after he climbed the river bank and stood dripping wet beside her? What would be the best way to persuade him to continue the journey?

These thoughts occupied Andela's awareness for some time, and then it struck her mind that there were no sounds of splashing. She looked back into the river. Bill was still visible, but he was drifting deeper and farther away. Her eyebrows skewed. Despite obvious efforts to swim, Bill was sinking. She bent downward with the intent of diving in after him, but then a voice to her right startled and delayed her.

"Oh my, dead weight, I think he'll sink. Only the living can swim in that river," spoke an excited, girlish voice.

Andela looked toward a bouncy little girl wearing a one-piece outfit that looked tie-dyed silk. The outfit was white with patterns of flowering shrubs. The girl also wore a long, black, beaded necklace.

The little girl turned her face to address Andela. It was a cheerful, elvish face bordered by brunette locks of hair. "You'd better go after him. The water won't go past his lips—it's that death-life barrier—he'd have to willfully take it in, and I don't think that he will do that right now."

Andela looked back and forth between the little girl, who was prancing from one foot to the other and babbling advice; and Bill, who was sinking. His limbs were thrusting in swimming motions that should have propelled him through the water, but his efforts were to no avail.

"Well, shall we just let the man drown? I'm too little, you know, but I'll try if you want me to try. It's all up to you, you know, so what are you going to do?"

Andela glanced once more at the little newcomer, and then looked back toward Bill. There was no more hesitation. She drew a deep breath and dove through the surface of the water.

By this time Bill was in a panic. He was surprised when he walked past Andela and felt his leading foot give way. His body lunged forward and splashed into water. He surmised that he had fallen into the river that Andela mentioned; and since he could swim, this did not frighten him. But then things got weird.

As he attempted stroking upward toward Andela, his body continued sinking downward. It felt as though his feet and legs had gained the atomic mass of iron. He could not swim vigorously enough to thrust himself toward the river's surface. Looking above, he could see the wavy silhouette of Andela standing on what he presumed to be the invisible bank of an invisible river, and he also spotted a shorter figure standing beside her.

Oh well, from dream to nightmare, time to wake up, thought Bill, and he closed his eyes, waiting for something to happen. Several seconds later, however, the thought struck his mind that he was having a heart attack in his bed. Why else would he feel pain in his chest and perceive sensations of asphyxiation? On the other hand, maybe the house was on fire and he was inhaling poisonous gas! What about the children! He had to wake up! He tried to open his eyes—his real eyes—but everything was blacking out, and then someone was fighting him!

As she dove into the river, Andela noted that the water felt different from any liquid that had ever touched her skin. Warmth enveloped her body like molten sunshine. She neither seemed to rise nor sink, and she could swim as easily in one direction as another. Like Bill, she was an accomplished swimmer. She had no difficulty holding her breath long enough to reach Bill, though swimming downward to his body took longer than she expected—the water was deeper than it appeared from the surface.

Andela had served for two summers as a lifeguard, so she knew how to approach Bill from behind and clasp an arm under his chin. His body felt limp; so she figured he was unconscious, which would proffer an easy rescue. But then, as Andela began swimming upward, Bill went ballistic. He thrashed like a shark reeled to the side of a boat on a harpoon. Arms and leg shot in all directions, and his left elbow caught Andela in the stomach, knocking all the air from her lungs. She knew she had to surface, and she twisted around to swim away; but Bill's right hand caught her flowing hair. For a few moments she struggled. Her head was drawn backward and a strong arm wrapped around her waist.

Struggling was useless. Bill clung like a man grasping the trunk of a tree during a tornado. Andela's muscles weakened. Her vision was dimming and there seemed no chance of escaping Bill's grip. She hoped the process of drowning would not be too painful, but she was much more concerned about Bill. And what about the children? Who would take care of the children?

Andela sensed unconsciousness settling upon her. Her chest relaxed. Rather than causing a spasm in her throat, inhaled water began filling her lungs. She did not fear death, but the thought of Bill finding her lifeless body in his arms when he returned to his home in Missouri was awful. *God, please help me*! she pled from her soul. Blackness thickened before her eyes.

Then vitality thrust throughout Andela's body. It was like being awakened from sleep by a douse of ice water; but at the same time, she felt wonderful. At first she thought that she was awakening in heaven, but then she realized that she could feel Bill's body, and there was a school of blue and golden fish swimming a few feet before her. Her mind had revived; in fact, she could not recall ever experiencing such exuberant awareness. She was breathing the water, and it felt marvelous, even joyful! "Wow, this water is rejuvenating!" she exclaimed, discovering that she could speak beneath the river's surface.

Andela freed herself from Bill's limbs and then spun around to face him. Her smile faded. Bill looked dead, or at least unconscious, and there was no indication that he was attempting to breathe.

It was not difficult for Andela to stroke through the water while pulling Bill along with her. She surfaced and dragged him onto shore, positioning him on his back. Then she collapsed to the ground at his right side and placed her left ear to his chest. She detected a heartbeat, but she felt no movement of the chest wall—he was not breathing.

"He's still alive, quick, breathe for him! Lips to lips revitalization!"

The little girl would have made Andela laugh if the situation were not so serious. Andela turned Bill's head to one side and pressed downward on his chest. No water came from his lungs, and she suddenly realized that no water came from her lungs either. She passed from breathing river water to breathing air without any notable transition.

Andela then turned Bill's face upward and tilted his head backward, using her left thumb and forefinger to pinch his nose. She began mouth-to-mouth resuscitation, praying to God from her heart while providing Bill with air from her lungs. She knew that the angel in her apartment told her that Bill could not die on this journey, but he seemed to be dying, and what would happen if he seemed to die, even if he didn't really die? Why hadn't she asked that question when she was discussing this journey with the angel?

"Bill, please," Andela besought between breaths. "Please come back to me, please…"

From deep within a warm red fog of corporal awareness, Bill rose into consciousness. At first he perceived faint light, a mild tingling in his lips, and warm air passing into his chest. Then the tingling spread across his shoulders, down his spine, and to the tips of his toes. He remembered that he was dreaming, and he remembered his dream deteriorating into a nightmare; but now he experienced increasing pleasure. Before even opening his eyes, he realized that Andela's lips were pressing against his own lips, and that her breath served as his own breath. He wasn't exactly sure how he knew it was Andela—perhaps he had learned to perceive her presence by some means other than the five physical senses; but nonetheless, he knew it was her, and he also knew that he was experiencing bliss beyond anything he had ever imagined.

"He's breathing!" blurted the little spectator, dropping to her knees and clapping her hands.

Andela rose to her hands and knees, panting from her efforts. She observed Bill's eyes open. Her body almost collapsed in relief. For several seconds he held her in his gaze; then to her surprise, he turned his head toward the child beside them.

"You can see now!" exclaimed Andela, rocking back to a sitting posture.

Bill smiled, looking from face to face between Andela and the jovial child. He sat up and fixed his eyes upon Andela. "For a while there I was hoping that I would wake up, but now, whoa doggies! Now I'm glad I didn't."

"What do you mean?" the little girl inquired. "You look awake to me."

Andela realized that Bill's *whoa doggies* was in reference to his resuscitation, namely to the experience of their lips touching for the second time, and she blushed.

Bill turned his attention toward the little girl. It seemed to Andela that he was surprised to hear the girl speak.

"Who are you?" asked Bill.

"I'm Pat," announced the girl, tapping her right fist against her breast. "Who are you?"

Bill grinned, musing to himself that this little girl was a creative addition to his dream. He determined to remember this dream after he awoke, though he wasn't certain how to guarantee any such recollection.

"Hey, I told you my name, now it's only fair that you tell me yours," persisted Pat.

"Of course," returned Bill, chuckling as he spoke. The little girl reminded him of a perturbed kitten. "My name is Bill."

As Bill and Pat conversed, Andela found her attention drawn by the flowing movements of blue-green grasses carpeting the riverbank. Full-figured, long-leafed willows sat along the river's edge, decreasing in number as the riverbed rose toward its source in the mountain. There were tall lean waterfalls bedecking both sides of the gorge in the distance, appearing like strands of molten silver; and she was able to espy a great roaring waterfall farther up the gorge.

"Bill, Bill, now that's a rather nice name. Don't you think so Andela?"

Andela was startled at hearing her name. She focused her eyes upon the little girl. "How do you know my name?"

Pat looked flabbergasted. "How do I know your name? Why, you're kidding! You've got to be kidding! How could I not know your name? Why, everyone in this land knows your name, except maybe for someone from the outside, like this Bill here. But Bill seems nice, doesn't he?"

Andela sat spellbound. She stared at the little girl in silence.

Bill was next to speak. He regarded himself as the initiator of all events taking place in his dream, so he felt slighted by the little girl's reference to him as an *outsider*.

"How could you not know Andela's name?" he reiterated, rising to a semi-reclined position. "What do you mean by that?"

"Why, this is the land of who she is!" proclaimed Pat, springing to both feet as she spoke. "Everybody knows that. Well, time for me to go."

Without giving a chance for anyone to ask another question, Pat spun around on one foot and darted toward the wooded hills behind them. "Kawoooo!" she called, sounding like an exotic bird. Her lighthearted cry permeated the atmosphere, echoing from distant hillsides and mountains. The birdlike cry and receding echoes delighted Bill; he considered them reflections of his innate inventiveness—after all, this entire affair was manufactured through his own knowledge and imagination, or so he thought.

Meanwhile, Andela pondered Pat's words. *So, this is the land of who I am*, she thought. *It must be some sort of physical manifestation of my inner being.*

"Kawoo! Kawoo! Kawoo!" resounded hawk-like calls; but Bill did not hear these calls. A large bird resembling a crow appeared from over the crest of the nearest hill, being visible to Andela, but not visible to Bill. The bird swooped downward before a backdrop of green conifers. It flew more like a swan than a crow, with great wings that tapered to points at the tips of huge feathers. After diving toward Pat in the manner of a falcon intending to seize a mouse, it opened and batted its wings to stop its descent, and then it dropped to the ground and folded its wings against its body.

Pat sprang forward and grabbed hold of the bird's neck. She swung upward and plopped onto its back, stretching her legs around its neck and removing her long, black necklace. She looped the necklace over the bird's head, and the bird took hold of the necklace in its beak. Then Pat grasped the necklace in both hands and whistled.

Great wings spread and flapped. The bird rose with its little passenger and flew back over the crest of the nearest hill, disappearing from sight. Andela leaned toward Bill, intending to ask him if that were not the most wonderful bird he had ever seen. When she glanced at his face, however, she halted her speech. He had a strained, contorted expression that gave every indication that he was about to burst out laughing; and then he did just that. His mouth opened widely and he flopped backward to the spongy ground, laughing so heartily that his chest and stomach undulated like a teeter-totter.

Andela was perplexed. "What are you laughing about?"

Bill paused and cocked his head forward to address Andela, but then he plopped his head back to the earth and resumed laughter, raising one hand and pointing in the direction where Pat disappeared.

"The little girl riding the bird?" inquired Andela. "Is that what you're laughing about?"

Bill heaved several times, permitting gradual diminution of his laughter. Then he rolled onto his left side and propped himself up on one elbow, facing Andela. "Bird? What bird?"

Andela blinked. "What bird? Why, the bird that the little girl sat on—the bird that flew away with her on its back."

Bill stared at Andela with scrutiny. Besides an endless expanse of light, all that he had seen since his dream began, other than Andela, was a comical little girl who called herself Pat; and Pat had just floated away in a most ludicrous manner.

"Hum, okay, whatever you say, Dell. But I didn't see any bird."

Andela felt her emotions sink. She thought some sort of breakthrough had occurred and that Bill could see; but apparently she was wrong. She could not restrain a reactive frown. "But, you spoke to Pat. You saw her, didn't you?"

Bill found Andela's question exasperating. He was enjoying his dream. Apart from one brief episode where he almost drowned, the dream was creative and entertaining. Andela was seldom annoying in real life, so why should he permit her to be annoying in a dream that he was fabricating within his own mind? After all, wasn't he the one who was determining Andela's words and actions?

"Listen, Dell, why don't we make an agreement—you see whatever you see, and I'll see whatever I see, and let's both have a good time, okay? Now, all I've seen since this dream started is you and that little girl, no bird."

Despite Bill's annoyance with Andela's pestering question, the look that mounted her face made him regret his words. Her lower lip puckered and the look in her eyes left little doubt that she might cry. He quickly came to the conclusion that people cannot totally control their own dreams, and he searched his mind for the right words to erase his last statement. He wanted to say something that would get his dream back on a pleasurable course. When he drew a breath to speak, however, he was preempted.

"He only sees you, and those of us who represent you," pronounced a masculine voice.

Bill and Andela were seated close to one another and were engaged eye to eye. Neither one of them heard anyone approaching. Bill jolted, lunging to Andela's side with his left hand fastened to her right shoulder. Andela peered back and to her right, and then she found herself looking almost straight upward into a face that hovered above her.

"He like ta' scared me to death," gasped Bill, releasing his hold on Andela as both he and Andela pivoted around on the grass to face the newcomer.

Standing over them with both hands on his hips was a tall, muscular man dressed in a green tunic with matching trousers. He wore brown leather slippers that matched a broad leather belt. The belt was fastened in front by a golden buckle engraved with a flying eagle. On the man's head sat a pointed felt cap the color of his belt buckle, and the cap was bedecked with a long, plush, green feather. Curly locks of hair sprang freely from beneath his cap, locks the color of ripened wheat. He wore a smile that seemed winsome to Andela, and his golden-brown eyes danced with exuberance.

"I do not scare persons to death," the visitor stated, making it obvious that he overheard Bill's comment. "Quite to the contrary, I am much more likely to stir someone to life."

"Do what?" responded Bill.

"Who are you?" interjected Andela.

The intruder withdrew a perusing stare from Bill and smiled toward Andela, bowing and then straightening to his full height. "Allow me the privilege of two introductions," he spoke with a cordial air. "First, the spontaneous little girl you just encountered is Miss Patience. She calls herself Pat because it's quicker."

Bill chuckled. "Miss Patience, huh, well, she sure seemed in a hurry for someone named Patience."

"Yes," conceded the visitor, eyeing Bill. "Patience is a little unpredictable in this land. It is hoped that she will mature over time."

The man's eyes turned upon Andela as he completed his statement. Then he addressed both her and Bill, looking back and forth between them. "I have a name that is well known in this land. My name is Hope."

"Hope," Andela echoed in a whisper. She surmised that the land through which she and Bill were traveling was a virtual reality of her inner being. Her inner qualities were manifested as living personalities. Pat's behavior suggested that she had a lack of patience, something she already suspected; and she was relieved to learn that she apparently excelled in another desirable quality, namely hope. She also fancied that the gorgeous scenery and marvelous wildlife somehow reflected her artistic qualities and her zest for life. Bill could not see or hear the surroundings, but he could see and hear the persons characterizing her personal traits, such as Pat and Hope.

"Patience, Hope," recapped Bill, looking irritated. "What's going on here? Is this dream becoming some sort of Old English morality play?"

"Play! Who's playing, man? This is much more important than any play!" proclaimed Hope.

Bill grew flustered. "Look, Mr. Green Pants," he said, standing to his feet, "you're probably the product of some half-digested pickle, and I'm having far too good a dream to let some vinegar-soaked cucumber step up as master of ceremonies."

Andela grew apprehensive and rose to her feet beside Bill. She wanted to say something that would keep Bill and Hope from becoming adversaries, but she wasn't sure how to begin.

Hope placed both hands on his hips. "So, a giant pickle, am I? Well, man, let me present you with some simple facts. First..."

"Wait! Hope! Wait!" interjected a girl's voice. Pat appeared from nowhere. She stood beside the canopy of a nearby willow and peered at Hope. "Not too much, not too fast, you must have patience!"

Hope, who dwarfed Pat in size, bit his lower lip and eyed Bill.

"You do great work, Hope," continued Pat, "but it's not time yet. Rebelon is strong in this man's land. We must work together as a team in order to help change the forces within his land, and I may play an important role."

Pat's words were curious to Bill and Andela, but Hope seemed to understand. His eyes rose toward the peak of the mountain facing them.

"Yes, of course, you are right," said Hope. He turned his face toward Pat. "But you could show up a little sooner, and maybe hang around a little longer."

Bill felt a twinge of disappointment as Hope permitted Pat to curtail the argument. On the one hand he felt like punching Hope in the nose; but on the other hand, he sensed a desire to get better acquainted.

"Yea, I guess you're right," returned Pat, looking sheepishly toward her bare feet. "I haven't learned when to stay put and assert myself." She folded both hands behind her back and jostled one toe in the turf.

"Ah, but here you are!" attested Hope. "Do not worry, my dear. Each day you grow in wisdom and strength. Some day you may acquire enduring and graceful beauty, like Madam Patience of the Northern Pool."

Pat's face beamed; she looked up at Hope and smiled. "Thank you," she chirped, and then she spun around and ran back across the riverbank toward a grove of fruit trees. Before vanishing into the grove, however, she stopped and whirled back around, cupping both hands to her mouth. "I'll be around," she hollered. Then she darted away and disappeared amongst the trees.

As Bill and Andela observed Pat's departure, Hope turned and sprang into the river. Andela heard the splash as Hope's body met the surface of the water. She turned to see what was happening. Bill heard no splash, but his attention was drawn by Andela's movement. He looked in the same direction as Andela and spotted Hope. It was apparent to Bill that Hope was swimming; though to Bill, Hope appeared to be swimming through white light.

"Hope! Wait!" hailed Andela.

Hope stopped swimming and bobbed to the surface, turning his head to face Andela as he treaded water.

Andela spoke again, "I've got some questions!"

"I'm sure you do," acknowledged Hope, "but Miss Patience has spoken wisely. I recommend that you heed her words. I'll be keeping an eye on you."

"But, what about Madam Patience of the Northern Pool? Who is she? And what is the Northern Pool?"

"Madam Patience is divine patience. There is much for you to learn, but I have spoken enough for now, my lady."

"Well, at least tell me about Rebelon."

A gust of chilling air cut through the atmosphere. Andela noticed Bill clutch his chest. An uneasy feeling settled upon her shoulders. The grasses and trees seemed to shudder. She looked toward Hope and saw that his face was raised toward the sky.

"Justice!" cried Hope.

Andela's uneasiness lifted as quickly as it had settled upon her. The surrounding environment calmed.

Bill looked startled. "Whoa," he said, "what a relief. I felt like I was having a heart attack, and that's the second time in this dream that I've felt like that."

Andela smiled weakly at Bill, and then looked toward Hope. "What happened?"

Hope's expression was stern. "Well, let it suffice to say that you should avoid inquiring about that name again, at least while you have him with you," he said, nodding toward Bill.

"What name, Rebelon?" inquired Bill. "Who is Rebelon?"

Andela gasped and looked about her, but nothing happened. Apparently, at least in her land, Bill's words did not elicit the same results as her words.

Hope ignored Bill's question and spoke to Andela. "Journey to the tallest peak in the mountain. You must climb that peak, a peak situated at the edge of your land. His land lies parallel to yours, and you may reach his land through the realm of the Northern Pool. That is your destination. You will reach his land by way of the Land of the Northern Pool."

"My land?" inquired Bill.

Hope looked at Bill, but then returned his eyes to Andela before speaking. "I won't be far away. Goodbye."

"Wait, what about my..." Bill began, but Hope twisted around and ducked beneath the water, swimming away so swiftly that both Bill and Andela stared in wonder. It seemed to Andela that he swam more like an otter or dolphin than a man. Soon he passed beyond Andela's view, and Bill saw him fade away into endless light.

Bill turned and faced Andela. "So, do you know what he was talking about?"

Andela turned her face toward Bill, searching her mind for the proper response. "Who?" she asked with feigned absentmindedness. She was not certain about how she should answer. She knew that Bill thought they were in one of his dreams, so she decided to try and take advantage of his mistaken assumption. She decided to act clueless, figuring that a ploy of ignorance might give her some time to think. And besides, they might meet up with someone who knew how to answer Bill's questions better than she did, and she had plenty of questions of her own, so how could she possibly begin to answer Bill's questions?

A look of perplexity mounted Bill's brow. He raised one hand and pointed toward the location where Hope had last spoken. "Him, Mister Pickle—the product of some sour morsel of food I ate for supper."

Andela stepped close to Bill and placed one hand on his shoulder. She smiled and peered into his eyes, leaning forward so that their faces were mere inches apart. "Oh yes, I think I remember now. Well, whatever he was talking about, we get to travel some more together, you and me."

Bill felt his spine tingle. His dream seemed to be changing again, and he liked the change. For several seconds no one spoke, and then Andela took a step back and reached out an inviting hand.

"Coming with me?"

The appeal of Andela's eyes was irresistible. Bill wondered what he would do if she ever looked at him that way in real life. Any questions he had about Hope or Rebelon dissipated from his mind. As he accepted her hand, he surmised that he was somehow gaining more control of the mood and progression of his dream.

"Okay, follow me," Andela instructed. She released Bill's hand and turned toward the mountains.

Chapter 4

The Golden Pathway

Time was difficult to measure during the trek up the nearest mountain. Whether an hour passed, or many hours, Andela could not tell. She never grew hungry or thirsty, and the upward climbing did not seem strenuous. There was no visible ball of fire in the blue sky, but pervasive light flooded forest, mountain, and plain. There were wooded regions where pastel twilight cradled flowers and ferns, and these regions were often juxtaposed to brilliantly illuminated glens and copses. All in all, the light in the land was constant and enduring, giving no hint to the passing of time.

Over and over again, Andela had to bite her lip to keep from commenting on breathtaking sights. There were quaint waterfalls that sprang to freedom from recesses above the trail and then dropped into crystal basins like curtains of iridescent diamonds. Stunning rock formations rose like multicolored stone gardens; and cavernous entrances opened through sheer stone walls, divulging glistening gullets studded with gems. Since Bill could see none of these sights, Andela resisted the temptation to venture off the main trail.

The trail was easy to traverse, as if it were shaped by a colossal forest sculptor and worn smooth by flocks of mountain sheep. By and by, Andela and Bill made small talk as they coursed along the way. Subjects such as food, animals, hobbies, movies, books, cooking, and farming provided the menu for dialogue. Andela liked to think that she and Bill were getting to know one another better as they conversed back and forth. It was the type of thing two persons should do; that is, two persons who might someday join in matrimony.

Bill was enjoying the trek. Watching Andela walk before him was intriguing, and he liked conversing with her. He began wondering if he were somehow interacting with the real Andela—perhaps she was also dreaming, and perhaps they were somehow communing with one another. He came to realize that he sensed Andela's presence through some capacity other than his eyes and ears, and the sensation was marvelous. And in addition to that, he could tell that she sensed him too, even when her back was turned to him. They were not holding hands, and yet they were touching each other; and though the touch was not physical, it was very real and very wonderful. He began speculating upon whether or not a man can fall in love with a woman during a dream.

Meanwhile, Andela felt growing fondness for Bill, and she knew that their journey was no dream, she knew it was real. The bond of affection that developed at the farm in Missouri was persisting and intensifying. The importance of her mission now became more than a matter of eternal life and death for Bill, though that was certainly the weightier matter; it also became the realization that she wanted Bill to be her husband—her living husband.

Bill was telling a wild story from his teenage years as they ascended the final slope of the mountain's tallest peak, a story about attempting to put a saddle on a cow and train her to cooperate as a surrogate horse. They were both laughing when Andela entered a white cloud that rested on top of the peak. The cloud hovered in place; it did not appear to move or change form. As she entered the cloud, Andela noted that it seemed to be composed of condensed light rather than mist or vapor. She felt her way along the ground, unable to see anything other than white light; but when she glanced back at Bill, she could see him clearly. It was obvious that he could see her too; he smiled winsomely when she looked back in his direction. There was no indication that Bill perceived any change in the environment when they entered the cloud of light.

Then Andela emerged from the cloud. Her senses awakened to sights and sounds that were imperceptible a short distance behind. The mountain terrain looked much the same as it did before entering the cloud, but Andela took little notice of terrain—her attention was drawn to an immensely tall, sheer, golden cliff that rose some fifty yards before her. Ascending straight upward like a wall of polished glass, the cliff appeared to soar higher than any cliff or tree Andela had ever seen. Pouring over one portion of the cliff was a waterfall that plummeted downward and crashed into a churning pool of water; and this pool served as the source of a river that flowed into the white cloud behind her. Given the short distance to the great cliff, and its tremendous height, it was impossible to see what lay beyond the upper edge of the cliff.

Andela peered to her right and left. She noted that the landscape was bordered on either side by clouds of light, much like the cloud behind her. These walls of light blocked her from seeing anything past them. Remarkably, the well-beaten trail that Andela had followed into the cloud continued as a golden pathway. Andela walked forward on the golden pathway, captivated by the sight of the golden cliff. The smooth surface of the cliff seemed like sunlit water on a windless sea. Her steps quickened. Bill followed.

"It looks like a huge wall of pure gold," she commented as she slowed and gazed upward, opening the palm of her right hand and reaching outward to touch the immaculate surface. It felt cool and smooth.

Bill began feeling agitated by Andela's comments. Besides Andela, he saw only light. He tilted his face upward to follow her gaze, but he did not stop walking as he stepped around her. He felt the surface beneath his feet change from a solid, smooth substance to soft and spongy ground.

"Bam!"

Andela turned just in time to witness Bill's chin rebound from the side of the cliff. His fingers clawed at the flawless surface before him, but found nothing that he could grasp. He felt himself lose balance. As he toppled backward, the thought entered his mind that he would awaken in the soft mattress of his bed.

"Thud."

The soft ground beside the golden pathway mitigated Bill's fall, especially since Andela managed to get one hand behind his neck to slow his descent. The weight of Bill's body tugged her right arm and caused her to topple down on top of him. For a few seconds they lay there, staring into one another's eyes. Bill surmised that he was not yet awakening, and the feel of Andela's warm body upon his own body was enough to make him shun any prospect of his dream coming to an end.

Then a new thought struck Bill—if he might awaken at any moment, then what should he do right now? Perhaps this was the last episode of his dream, and he might never have such a dream again. He was awed by the virtual sensations in his breast and limbs; in fact, the sensations he experienced seemed at least as real as sensations he would expect when awake. Andela's eyes were poised above him, and he stared into them, wondering how such marvels could be generated by a man's dream.

Both hearts began racing as Bill's right hand brushed through Andela's hair and coaxed her lips toward his own. Their eyes never parted until their lips touched; and then Bill and Andela kissed. When their lips parted, their eyes engaged once more. There were no words either could conjure to express the communing of their eyes.

Andela spoke first. "Bill, I've got to tell you something."

"What?" asked Bill. He was savoring every moment, and he resolved that he would have to find the courage to reveal his feelings to the real Andela when he awoke.

"I know you think you're only having a dream, but…"

"There you are!" blasted a sweet yet vigorous voice.

Andela and Bill were both befuddled. Andela rolled from atop Bill's body and sat up on the ground, pulling the edge of her gown over her knees and downward toward her ankles. Bill also sat up, and then he spotted the little girl who called herself Pat. She was still wearing the same outfit.

Pat turned and looked back toward the white cloud from which Bill and Andela had emerged. "Hope! They're up here!"

Bill rose to his feet at the mention of Hope's name. Andela followed suit and stood beside him. Seconds later Hope broke into view. Like Pat, he wore the same outfit as before.

"Well," boomed Hope as he stepped along the golden pathway. "I see you've run into a bit of an obstacle. That wall must be two-hundred feet high, and you need to get above it."

Bill stared at Hope.

"Yes," remarked Andela. "It's very high and very smooth. I couldn't imagine being able to climb it."

Bill turned his face toward Andela. He deduced that Andela wanted to get over an invisible wall. "Why do we want to climb it?" he inquired.

Hope answered first. "Why do you think, man? To get to your land, of course! Your eyes will be able to see the ground and trees in your land."

"My land?" queried Bill, looking back toward Hope. He remembered Hope mentioning *his land* previously. "Just what is my land?"

"I'm sure you can handle this Hope. I've got to go," announced Pat. "Bye, bye."

Hope smiled and shook his head as Pat bounded down the pathway and disappeared. "Darling lass, but she can't stay put more than a second," he mumbled. Then he turned to address Bill. "Well, let's just say it's a land where you're in charge, a place where you're the official governor."

It seemed to Bill that a man should be in charge of his own dream regardless of being in any particular land; but then, this dream had already proven difficult to manage. "Okay," he responded, "so we're trying to reach my land, and we have to get over a huge wall that's invisible to me, though apparently it's a wall that everyone else can see. Does that sum things up?"

"A fair summary," Hope replied flatly.

Bill frowned.

"How are we going to get over the wall?" inserted Andela, facing Hope. She still found herself trying to keep Bill and Hope from squabbling.

Hope gazed upward, and Bill followed suit; but all that Bill could see was white light.

"Time to call for some help," announced Hope.

"Hopefully someone with plenty of rope and some experience repelling," said Bill, "unless you're good friends with the Jolly Green Giant."

Hope shrugged one shoulder toward Bill, and then stepped forward to address Andela. "I doubt that our helper will bring any rope, and he may not appear very impressive to your visitor," he stated, glancing toward Bill as he pronounced the word *visitor*. "But I assure you that he will be more than capable of giving us the assistance we require."

Andela grew curious. Apart from an angel, the only persons she had met since the journey began were persons representing features of her own nature. Now Hope spoke of someone with great capabilities. Did she possess some special trait or feature that was notably outstanding? Was there an attribute in her personality that would manifest itself as a hero?

"Okay, who is this superman?" Bill posed with a note of sarcasm.

Hope flashed feisty eyes toward Bill. He straightened his collar and addressed Andela with an air of formality. "It is my pleasure, madam, to request that you call a very close friend of mine. He will respond when you call his name."

Bill, though flustered, found himself tucking his shirt beneath his belt. The atmosphere thickened with a sense of celebrity.

"Who should I call?" inquired Andela.

"Faith."

"Faith," Andela echoed, smiling introspectively.

Bill looked on without saying a word. He wasn't sure about faith, or faiths, but he figured there might be something behind them; and he figured that whatever made Andela seem so alive and wonderful might have something to do with faith. Perhaps, if he kept his mouth shut, he would learn something new about her. It seemed curious that he could discover anything new in a dream since he assumed that everything in his dream come from his own mind; but on the other hand, maybe there were things he knew in his subconscious mind or unconscious mind that could be transferred to his conscious mind while he was dreaming. Or, as he had contemplated before, maybe the real Andela was also dreaming, and maybe they were engaged in some sort of psychic communication.

"Do I just call his name?" asked Andela.

"Yes," replied Hope.

Andela looked around. "Where from?"

Hope pointed back down the golden pathway toward the white cloud. "From beyond the cloud."

Andela nodded and smiled in anticipation. She turned her face back toward the cloud. There were numerous occasions during her lifetime when she was praised by friends and relatives for her faith; they all seemed to agree that she had a great deal of faith. What sort of champion might appear from the boundary of the cloud, she could only imagine. She raised her right hand to her mouth. "Faith!"

A rustling of wind was followed by expectant silence. All eyes were turned in the direction of Andela's land. No one spoke. Long seconds passed. No one moved a muscle.

"At your service, my lady," spoke a permeating voice that seemed to come from all directions at once.

Andela and Bill both turned their heads from side to side, searching for the speaker. Hope stepped forward and bowed from his waist. He extended his right hand all the way to the ground and permitted Faith to climb atop his index finger and then step to the middle of his palm. He then rose to his full height and held Faith before Bill and Andela.

Before anyone could speak again, Bill burst into laughter. He laughed for several seconds with both hands propped on his knees, and then he rose back to an upright posture and chuckled as he looked between Hope and Andela. Andela knew why Bill was laughing, and she felt abashed by the revelation of Faith's stature—he wasn't big enough to wrap both arms around an apple core. She looked at Bill and produced a weak smile. Her cheeks were tainted. Then she broke eye contact with Bill and stepped close to Hope. She rose to her tiptoes so that her lips came close to Hope's ear.

"Are you sure he's the right one?" she whispered. "I mean, he's so tiny."

Hope cast a disapproving look toward Bill. Bill's face still wore the caricature of laughter. Then he brought the index finger of his free hand to his lips and turned his head so that he could whisper back to Andela. He dropped his free hand to his side. "Shhh, do not say such things, you might shrink him. Just imagine how many mustard seeds he could contain at his present size."

Andela thought for a moment, and then took heart. She was familiar with the passage in the Bible about faith the size of a mustard seed, and she recalled that such faith granted the potential to move a mountain. She ruminated over this Scripture as she leaned forward to inspect her miniature guest. Hope raised his hand so that Faith was positioned mere inches from Andela's eyes.

"What's all the whispering about?" questioned Faith. His voice was now subdued to the level of volume that one would expect from a miniature man.

Andela managed a cordial smile, peering into Faith's keen little eyes. He stood about two inches high, and was neatly dressed in white satin slacks and a matching, long-sleeved shirt. He wore a silver cape. His belt, slippers, and bushy head of hair were as golden as the sheer cliff that towered above them. His little eyes were bright and blue.

"Oh, nothing important," replied Andela.

"How true," acknowledged Faith, making it clear that he overheard every word whispered between Andela and Hope. Then he turned his head and pointed one finger toward Bill. "Who's that?"

Bill watched with a sustained look of amusement, straining his ears to try and hear what the pint-sized Lilliputian was saying.

"That's my dear friend Bill," replied Andela, carefully choosing her words in hopes of initiating a good relationship between Bill and Faith.

"Well, there is certainly Hope," stated Faith, staring hard at Bill. Then he turned his eyes back toward Andela. "Now then, why is it you have summoned me?"

"Well, we need to get over that wall," disclosed Andela, pointing to the golden barrier.

Bill could hear Andela speaking, but could not make out the words spoken by Faith. He stepped a couple of paces closer and leaned forward so that he could hear how the puny newcomer might respond. He was impressed by Faith's blue eyes.

"By what means would you prefer to transcend this obstacle?" Faith asked.

Bill could hear Faith speaking now, and chuckled. "I think a spiral staircase would be suitable," he mused. As far as he was concerned, his dream was drifting toward whimsical fantasy.

"Does that suit you, my lady," responded Faith.

"Well, sure," Andela stuttered. She knew that Bill was not taking anything seriously that was spoken by Faith.

"Very well, put me down, Hope."

Without saying a word, Hope placed Faith onto the ground.

"All right, when I say three, everyone lie flat on the ground, face down, and you won't get hurt," Faith spoke loudly enough for everyone to hear. He then faced Andela. "When I'm finished, you may lead your friend up the stairs. Hope and I will always be with you, even if you do not see us as you do now. We bid you farewell."

Andela glanced at Hope, who had already kneeled to his knees, and then she began squatting downward herself. "Okay," she said.

Bill smirked as he stood and crossed his arms over his chest. He had to suppress laughter when he saw Andela and Hope positioning themselves flat on their stomachs.

"One, two..."

"Bill, get down!" warned Andela, lifting her face and espying Bill.

"Three!"

Andela fretfully followed Hope's example and buried her face in the soft grass.

"Ka—Whoooom!"

Bill stared downward and watched the tiny man wave his arms. At first Bill grinned, but then his face sobered. There was a brief moment of stillness followed by a terrific blast of wind. Bill's body was lifted and hurled, carried aloft as if he were a leaf blown from the branch of a tree. For a few seconds he was airborne, spinning head over heels, and then he dropped into something thick and bristly, though fortunately soft. The first thing to enter his mind as he grappled within the bristly milieu was that he had plopped into a gigantic pile of furry caterpillars. He had no phobia of normal caterpillars, but invisible caterpillars were a different prospect, and he knew that some species of caterpillars could inflict nasty stings.

"Ahhh! Get them off me! Ahhh!" he hollered. And no matter which way he rolled or twisted, he remained engulfed in the fuzzy maze.

Andela felt the gust of wind whip past the back of her body. A couple of seconds later she raised her head. She seemed to be alone, no one was in sight. Then her attention was drawn to a large shrub about twenty yards behind her. The shrub was dense, and it shook wildly. Andela figured right away that Bill was caught in the shrub, and then his frantic cries for help made his presence obvious.

Andela rose and dashed over the mountain turf. As she drew nearer, the bush grew quiet and still. Peering at her through fuzzy limbs and twigs were Bill's imploring eyes. He was staring without batting an eyelash. It struck Andela that he saw her more easily than she saw him; apparently he saw through the shrub as if it were not there. For several long seconds they stared at one another. Then it struck Andela that Bill was waiting for her to disclose the details of his predicament.

As Andela continued gazing into Bill's eyes, it occurred to her that he seemed cute staring at her that way, comparable to a pleading puppy. Looking behind her, she determined that they were indeed alone; there were no other persons in sight. There was, however, something that caught her eyes as she glanced backward. There was an opening in the base of the cliff, an opening that wasn't there before; and discernible above that opening were smaller openings that were evenly spaced along a straight line upward. It was Faith's spiral staircase.

"Mmmm…," Bill managed to mumble without much lip movement.

Andela looked back toward Bill. Waves of trepidation contorted his face as he tried to communicate without moving. His wide eyes were glued to her face. As Andela studied his expression, she mused over his likeable sense of humor. She knew that the more time she spent with him, the more she learned to exercise her own sense of humor. It was obvious that Bill thought he was caught by something other than a bush. An idea popped into her head, one that made her smile.

"Is something wrong Bill?"

It was all Andela could do to keep from laughing at the astonished look that beset Bill's features. "These worms!" he eked, still trying to speak without moving his face. "I can't get them off me!"

Andela moved her eyes all around Bill.

"You know Bill, if you don't move a muscle, I don't think anything will eat you."

It surprised Andela to see Bill's eyes grow even wider. Apart from the expansion of his eyelids, he lay still. She stared into his eyes and walked toward him, wading through the ticklish tips of furry limbs. As she grew closer and closer, Bill's lugubrious facial expression grew desperate.

"No! Get back or they'll devour you too!" hollered Bill, relinquishing his body to whatever fate might assail him in order to protect Andela.

Andela took a step back. Bill tensed his muscles, thinking this would make it more difficult for little worms to chomp down. Then Andela smiled and remarked, "Bill, you really care about me, don't you?"

Bill remained stiff, staring toward Andela. After several seconds he deduced that he was no longer in danger, not with Andela staring at him with such a peaceful expression. His body eased as she leaned forward and grasped his cheeks. She gave him a smack on the lips.

"Bill, this is a bush. You're just caught in a bush."

Andela's words were confusing. But as he thought about it, Bill concluded that he was never in any danger at all since he was merely dreaming. Furthermore, he decided that he was taking his dream too seriously. Of course a pile of carnivorous worms could change into a bush when the worms and bush were merely parts of a dream, even if the worms and bush were both invisible. Why, anything might happen in a dream.

As Bill contemplated his circumstances, he decided that he needed to take more initiative—he needed to assume more control. He threw his right hand behind Andela's head and drew her lips back to his lips. He then delivered a full-fledged kiss; and although it was wonderful, it was rather unsettling that the sensations pulsing through his body felt so real. He was perplexed as he released Andela and looked into her eyes—nothing about the kiss seemed less than flesh and blood reality. Dream or no dream, he could feel himself blushing.

Andela reached out a hand and helped Bill dislodge himself from the shrub.

"Coming with me?" she posed.

"Sure," replied Bill. Given the way he felt after kissing Andela, he decided to postpone the idea of taking more control of his dream. After all, things were progressing nicely. He followed behind Andela until she stopped and gazed upward, and then he stopped behind her.

"It's a spiral staircase," said Andela, "just like you suggested. It enters the cliff and then circles up, and it appears that there are windows in the cliff to allow light to enter the stairwell."

Bill remembered his offhand request for a spiral staircase. He experienced a strange sensation of power. "You don't say?"

"Yes, it's marvelous! Follow me, and be careful not to stub your toes on the steps."

Bill felt out the steps with his bare feet and made his way upward behind Andela. He noted that the faint sounds of their footsteps echoed about them, sounding indeed as if they were transcending a great vault. Now and then he brushed against the smooth sides of the stairwell. The light, which was all that he could see besides Andela, seemed somewhat dimmer now than before he started climbing, though there were occasional rectangles of brightness that Andela claimed were windows. Bill noted that they passed one of the bright rectangles with each full loop as they spiraled upward. And as they continued upward, a compelling idea began formulating within his mind.

As Bill observed Andela climbing before him, he began contemplating what he wanted to happen in his dream. Despite the fact that he was dreaming, the *Andela* he saw before him seemed exactly like the real Andela. She even surprised him with actions and comments that seemed unlike anything that would come from his own mind. Perhaps, then, he could find out some things about the real Andela by questioning this *Andela*, perhaps asking questions that he was reluctant to ask in real life. As they continued upward, the thought of asking such questions grew stronger and stronger, becoming peculiarly compelling.

At last Andela emerged from the golden stairwell. Far to the right, and far to the left, were two more great clouds of light, both ascending upward like pillars supporting the sky. Directly before her lay a gorgeous garden of terraced shrubs and beautiful flowers. The landscape surrounding the garden was beset with verdant glades encompassed by cypress-like trees. Within the glades were pools of clear blue water; and the uneven ground between the glades was adorned by rivulets, petite waterfalls, and gushing waterspouts that danced upon the landscape like liquid ballerinas. Although the grasses in the garden did not appear mowed or cut, and although the shrubs did not appear trimmed, everything in the environment seemed perfectly matched and proportioned, with the exception of a large body of water in the distance to her left.

Andela peered back at Bill. The exit from the stairwell was a safe distance from the edge of the cliff, so she was not fearful of his falling. He responded with a disarming smile, and he focused solely upon her without granting any attention to his surroundings. This made it evident to Andela that Bill was still not able to see the environment surrounding them. She turned and again faced forward.

Perhaps a half-mile ahead of them rose another golden cliff, and this one was even taller than the cliff they had just transcended. Across the top edge of the cliff lay a colossal cloud of light. This cloud stretched to the right and left until it joined great cloud walls on either side. A large waterfall poured over the edge of the cliff and plunged into a pool of water that fed a river coursing to their left. The golden pathway continued straight ahead toward the cliff.

"There's another golden cliff in the distance, and the pathway leads that way. Will you still come with me?" asked Andela, pausing and turning to face Bill.

"Sure, why not?" responded Bill, and then he experienced an eccentric sensation of supremacy—a feeling that he was gaining due control over his dream—an impression that he had every right to be totally in charge. He figured that he was on the verge of awakening, reaching that stage of dreaming that permits more conscious management of events. Then a vexing thought struck his mind—if he were about to wake up, he might not have much time to test his hypothesis, namely the hypothesis that he might learn things about the *real Andela* from this *dream Andela*. He quickened his pace, drawing closer to the woman before him.

"Say, Andela," he called, sounding much more confident than he felt. The thought of personal conversation with the fascinating female who stopped and turned to face him seemed to cause his stomach to curl upward and crawl into his esophagus.

As the woman in his dream stood facing him, Bill got the unmistakable impression that he should take as much care interacting with this *dream Andela* as he would with the *real Andela*, but he determined to ignore this impression since he deemed it illogical. He stopped about two feet from Andela.

"I, um, I just wanted to, ah...," Bill stuttered.

"You wanted to what, Bill?" coaxed Andela.

Again Bill reminded himself that he was dreaming. "I just wanted to talk with you for a while, you know, ask you some questions."

Andela felt simultaneously nervous and delighted. "Sure Bill," she replied. She noticed that her voice quaked. Before speaking again, she drew a deep breath and attempted to steady her nerves. "Why don't we sit down?"

Andela seated herself on a soft bank of grass to the right of the pathway. Bill stepped forward and sat closely beside her, more closely than he would have situated himself in real life. Soon afterward, dream or no dream, he felt his heart quicken and his skin tingle. For a few moments he forgot all about his plan of interrogation—his mind was too filled with wonder over the sensations spawned by his proximity to Andela.

"Okay, what would you like to ask me?" Andela politely prodded.

Bill remembered his plan, and the sense of urgency returned—he had to find out what he could before he woke up. If he could extract data from the mind of this *dream Andela*, it might help him figure out how to approach the real Andela. He faced her, but discovered that such an approach wouldn't work; facing Andela made him lose track of what he was planning, or perhaps it made him think that what he was doing was somehow erroneous or insignificant; so he looked downward instead. "To begin with, why did you really come to the farm?"

Andela was stunned. Although she knew this was more than just a dream, it still seemed like a dream, and up to this point she felt free to act like it was a dream. But the question Bill posed now, so personal and crucial, was a question he had never before asked her.

"I, well, Bill, do you still think you're dreaming?" she questioned.

Bill found himself annoyed by the fact that this *dream Andela* seemed to be evading him. Of course he was dreaming, and shouldn't he be able to govern his own dream and ask a few simple questions? And furthermore, shouldn't he be able to get some straight answers? Feelings began swelling up within his breast that transformed the *dream Andela* into an adversary.

"Now listen, Andela, quit stalling. Just answer my question, and answer it now."

The stern tone of Bill's voice and his dismissal of her inquiry left Andela heart-stricken. Bill had always seemed to appreciate her sensitivity, and this behavior seemed unlike him. She stared toward his averted face. She was waiting for him to look back at her.

"Well," persisted Bill, perturbed by the thought that he might awaken prior to obtaining the information he desired. He chose not to face Andela, because facing the *Andela of his dream* affected him the same way as facing the *real Andela*. He meant to get an answer to his question, and the lack of response was making him mad.

Andela struggled to hold her composure, but the harder she struggled the more she hurt inside. She tried to gather her thoughts, but she was uncertain of how to respond.

"Okay, I'm waiting, you can talk now," Bill scolded.

That was more than Andela could endure. "Oh Bill, what's wrong with you?" she asked in a pleading tone of voice. Then she dropped her face into her hands and tried to hold back a sob.

Bill figured he might awaken at any second, and this was not the way he wanted his dream to end. "Knock it off!" he ordered gruffly. He rose in disgruntlement, and his thigh bumped Andela's shoulder and she toppled to her side.

The insides of Andela's breast seemed to shatter. The fall was gentle enough, but Bill's words tortured her heart. Within seconds, salty moisture coated her eyes and wet tears began streaking down her cheeks. She sobbed uncontrollably.

Bill watched with sustained agitation. He was too frustrated to speak, feeling that his dream was decaying into a total waste.

"Okay Bill, what do you want from me?" Andela finally spoke. She rose to a sitting position and leaned back on one hand. She swept hair from her face and looked up.

Bill opened his mouth to deliver another scoffing remark, but then his eyes met Andela's eyes. He struggled to assure himself that he was gazing upon the figment of a nighttime dream, but somehow his heart could not grant him that certainty. Those eyes were so much like Andela's eyes—genuine, powerful and appealing. And what was more, they appeared deeply hurt.

Andela sensed a change in Bill's attitude. Hope swelled within her heart. Bill knelt in reverence beside her. He reached out and placed his right arm around her shoulders.

"Andela," he spoke.

"Yes Bill."

Bill searched his mind for the right words. To simply say *I'm sorry* after seeing the look on Andela's face seemed insufficient. It no longer mattered to him whether he was dreaming or not. He drew comfort from the fact that Andela seemed to be reading his mind, or perhaps his heart, or perhaps something deeper—something beyond both heart and mind. She stared into his eyes and smiled.

Then Bill's eyebrows furrowed and his eyes changed. The thought that he had been tricked seized his mind. He decided that this *dream Andela* was manipulating his thoughts. "No!" he spoke crossly.

A look of confusion and fear seized Andela's countenance; and then, with no warning, she felt Bill's body ripped away from her. Something or someone snatched him from her side like a bear swapping a salmon from a stream. The violent force of his abduction lugged her forward and dropped her onto her stomach, knocking the air from her lungs. Her eyes rose from the ground and espied two brilliant red boots. They stood upon the golden pathway with toes pointed toward her.

Above the boots were coal-black trousers. Andela rose to a sitting position and peered up at a scene that struck terror through her breast. A tall stranger clutched Bill in his arms. One forearm pinned Bill's chest while the other pressed into Bill's throat. Bill was barely moving.

The stranger wore a long-sleeved red shirt that matched his boots. His face was handsome but sadistic. Sharply cut features defined a Roman nose and hollowed cheeks. He had black hair and dark eyes, and he displayed a haughty jeer. His demeanor seemed that of a heartless demon.

Andela was shocked. Desperate questions flooded her mind, but she took no time to contemplate answers. "Stop!" she screamed, rising and lunging at the stranger like a cornered bobcat. She grabbed at the arm that wrapped around Bill's neck.

"Let go! This is my land!"

A fierce knee rose and caught Andela in the center of her stomach, raising her feet from the ground and thrusting her backward onto the grassy turf. She rocked forward to her knees and gasped for air, disregarding intense pain. She was determined to attack again as soon as she was able.

The stranger stared downward with malignant pleasure. Cold-blooded eyes dared Andela to approach again. She realized there was little hope in attacking without a weapon.

"Who are you?" she groaned.

"My name is my own business, but you can rightly call me Justice. I deserve the name *Justice* because I'm giving this coward the justice he deserves for failing to take control of a worthless wench like you."

"You're killing him!" Andela accused, having regained her breath. She disregarded the stranger's insults.

"No!" roared the stranger, raising his face and laughing. Then he peered back down at Andela. "You're as foolish as you are feeble. He cannot die here because he did not come of his own free will. You tricked him into coming here. I'm freeing him—a little while longer and he will awaken back where he belongs. And he will awaken a wiser man, wiser for having discovered that the woman who scammed him into an absurd quest is a conniving con artist."

Andela felt a degree of relief as the stranger reminded her that Bill could not be murdered, but then she remembered the angel telling her that the journey might pose a risk to Bill that was worse than the risk of physical death—it was the risk that he would be hardened against truth, and that he would remain a *dead man* forever. She deduced from the stranger's words that if Bill died, or seemingly died, then both she and Bill would return to Missouri, but her prospects of bringing him to Life might be crippled.

"You want me to call you Justice," Andela criticized. She rose to her feet and faced the stranger. "Okay then, the *just* thing to do when you're in someone else's land is to obey the master of that land. This is my land, and I demand that you release Bill!"

"You demand!" chided the stranger. He seemed elated by the opportunity to argue. "Well then, perhaps I must do as you say, if you are truly a master. Who are you, master?"

Andela opened her mouth to speak, but then she stopped short—she realized the error of her words. She continued facing the stranger, wondering if she were facing Satan.

"My mistake, I am not the master of any land. But I am the governor of this land, and that makes me the one who chooses the master, and I have chosen…"

"I know who you have chosen, young fool!" roared the stranger. Andela collapsed to her knees. The stranger again raised his face and laughed, and the laughter reverberated against the golden cliff and dissipated into the clouds of light. Then he dropped his face downward and eyed Andela with relentless hatred. No trace of humor remained upon his countenance. Andela felt an icy shudder run up her spine.

"This is not your land, pretty one."

Andela lowered her gaze. Bill hung motionless in the stranger's grasp. She felt helpless. Her heart seemed to sag downward into the pit of her stomach, yet she began rising to her feet; she had to try again, she had to fight.

"Nor is it your land, Rebelon!" asserted a strong, feminine voice. It was a voice that stirred the environment like the roar of a lioness. Andela almost collapsed from shock, but she remained standing. There beside her, just to her left, stood a beautiful, majestic woman. The woman wore a scarlet silk gown that flowed downward to her ankles. A purple belt fit snugly around her waist. Her skin was smooth and fair; and her long, thick hair was richly dark. Her eyes were also dark, yet brilliant, like burning stars in the depths of a nighttime sea.

Andela had no idea who this woman might be, but her presence encouraged Andela's heart. The woman boldly faced the stranger holding Bill, the man she called *Rebelon*. "You have spoken a lie in the Land of the Northern Pool, for you could never *rightly* be called *Justice*. Lying is not welcome here—the real Justice will deal with you."

As the woman finished speaking, Andela turned her eyes back toward the cruel stranger. She gathered from the woman's words that she was no longer in her own land, but rather in the *Land of the Northern Pool*. She also gathered that Bill's attacker was not *Justice*, but rather *Rebelon*. There was an alteration in Rebelon's facial expression. The look of hatred was now blended with one of terror. Then she sensed a powerful presence.

"No!!!" issued a horrid shriek from Rebelon's throat, and then Rebelon disappeared. Bill's body plopped to the ground, and the sensation of a powerful presence melted away.

Andela looked around. There was no one in sight other than the woman who stood beside her; and Bill, whose body lay crumpled on the ground. She rushed to Bill and knelt down beside him, and then she turned him onto his back and attempted to ascertain whether or not he was breathing. She was about to conclude that he was not breathing, and that she needed to initiate mouth-to-mouth resuscitation for a second time, when he took a deep breath. He was still unconscious, but he was breathing.

"He will be fine, at least physically," spoke the woman. She walked to a position just behind Andela. "He will have to decide the other."

"He's okay?" inquired Andela, still staring at Bill's face. "He looked dead when I first turned him over."

"No, Rebelon is not permitted to work such feats in this land. He has seldom been invited here, so he is ignorant of the laws. Your friend is now sleeping."

Andela raised her face to address the woman. The woman responded by smiling and seating herself on the golden pathway beside Andela.

"So then, Bill's sleeping?"

"Yes."

"When will he wake up?"

The woman paused and gazed into Andela's eyes. "After I've answered some of the questions that burden your mind, then I will disappear, and he will awaken."

Andela gazed back into the woman's eyes. "Who are you?" she asked.

"I am Madam Mercy of the Northern Pool, wife of Justice."

"Mercy," breathed Andela, moving her lips without speaking loud enough to be heard. She looked back at Bill's face. His skin had regained healthful coloration. This woman certainly brought mercy. Then something Madam Mercy said wrought an inquisitive wrinkle across her forehead. She faced her. "Thank you Madam Mercy, thank you so much, but, you're married to Justice? How is that? I mean, aren't you opposites? And is he invisible?"

Madam Mercy responded with a merry little laugh. "He is not always invisible," she replied. "And I know what you ask in regard to our marriage. The answer is not so complicated, really. True mercy must be *just* mercy. If this were not so, do you think a loving Father would commission his Son to pay the price of his own blood on a cruel cross in order to purchase mercy? Indeed, it is divine justice that begets true mercy."

Andela remained held within Madam Mercy's eyes. She knew what Madam Mercy referred to, but she had never before heard anyone present the crucifixion of Christ in that manner. "You mean that Jesus had to die on the cross? It was a requirement?"

Madam Mercy's face grew somber. "No, my dear, it was not a requirement. God could have lived forever without the company of those who have been redeemed by the blood of Christ. He did not have to send his Son, but in his divine love, he chose to do so."

Andela contemplated Madam Mercy's words. "So then, for us to live, or I mean, for me to live, Jesus had to sacrifice his blood on the cross."

"Yes. In order to purchase your eternal life, Jesus was required to pay a price both perfect enough and great enough to satisfy God's holy justice. You see Andela, God the Father did not create himself. In fact, he was never created at all. Before all time, and before anything else, he *is*. His nature and essence were never predetermined, they have always been, and they never change."

"So, God is just."

"Yes, he is just, and his mercy must be just. Only he himself was capable of providing the divine sacrifice that met the measure of his innate, divine justice." Madam Mercy paused, delving more deeply into Andela's eyes. "He is also love, and he is the standard and definition of goodness. His love and goodness are the heart of eternal joy."

Andela leaned farther toward Mercy. "That explains, well, why there's no other way into heaven."

"Yes, that is why."

Andela leaned back. She gazed downward in thought. She understood what Madam Mercy was saying, and she knew, in her heart, that Madam Mercy's words were true. In her mind, however, the exclusive avenue through which sinners could escape eternal death and gain eternal life was difficult for her to grasp.

"I know the Bible teaches that God is holy and just," Andela spoke without looking up, "but a lot of people think that, well, since he is a God of love, that he accepts people into heaven from other religions besides Christianity, especially people who try to live decent lives."

Madam Mercy drew a ponderous breath. "Like I said, Andela, God did not create himself. There is no doubt that he wants every human being conceived upon the earth to receive eternal life in heaven, but his own nature requires individuals to meet the standard of his holiness in order to obtain such life."

Andela looked back up. "But is it possible for anyone who reaches an age of moral accountability to do that?"

"Of course," responded Madam Mercy. "The blood of Jesus Christ has the power to save any individual who repents from sin and chooses the lordship of Christ, and such salvation meets the standard of God's holiness. It is the sacrificial death and shed blood of Jesus Christ that enables individuals to obtain eternal life."

"Yes, I understand," said Andela, "and I know you're right. It's just that, well, a lot of people wish God were different than you're saying. They wish he were more lenient."

"Too true," acknowledged Madam Mercy, not acting a bit surprised by the progression of Andela's questioning. "There are many who would recreate God, but whatever notion could be more vain or foolish? God did not even create himself, albeit that the Son was begotten of the Father, so how do mere human beings think that they can take it upon themselves to recreate God?"

Andela focused upon Madam Mercy's eyes. The measureless significance of the words Madam Mercy spoke began unfolding within her heart and mind. "Oh my," Andela softly exclaimed. "I never thought, I mean, I never realized…"

"Indeed," affirmed Madam Mercy, sensing Andela's mental and spiritual cognizance. "If not for the holiness of God—that very aspect of his nature that made it necessary for the eternal Christ to come to the earth within a temple of mortal flesh and pay a blood sacrifice for human sins, and that very aspect of his nature that means many souls will be damned to hell because they reject the sacrifice and lordship of Jesus Christ—then the words hope, faith, love, and life would be void and meaningless. No Andela, it would not be a good thing if God were more tolerant of sin. In fact, it would be reasonable for every human being upon the face of planet earth to begin each wakeful day by proclaiming, *my soul rejoices, for God is holy*."

Andela continued facing Madam Mercy, feeding from Madam Mercy's eyes. She felt that she was seeing God more clearly than she had ever seen him before. She knew she was Christian, and that Jesus Christ was her Lord and Savior, and that she would go to heaven if she died; but she was beginning to realize that there was a whole lot more to learn about God than she had ever known before, and she was discovering that the holy God of the universe was more wonderful than she had ever imagined.

"So then," spoke Andela, "what about the people who say that a good and loving God could never send anyone to hell? What about the people who say that America's multiple religions are a good thing—a *melting pot* that blends us all together?"

These questions wrought a look of exasperation upon Madam Mercy's features. She replied with a firm voice. "What greater folly could a human being achieve than setting oneself up as God's judge? God is not merely good, he is the only reason that good exists. Without God, there would be no good and evil—in fact, there wouldn't be anything. There is no authority or basis for goodness in the mere existence of humanity, and besides that, humanity could not even exist without God."

Andela faintly nodded, but there was still a look of inquiry in her eyes.

Madam Mercy continued, "If a man or woman desires more mercy than that ordained by God, then such mercy is evil. If a man or woman desires more justice than that ordained by God, then such justice is evil. God's nature delineates goodness. God is good—not because he is the way that any man or woman wants him to be, but because he is the origin and basis of goodness. Persons who would redefine goodness, and use that definition to determine what God should or should not do, are exercising a damnably fallacious philosophy. The goodness of God is the joy of eternity, but to deny his goodness is suicidal megalomania.

"And the very idea that a *melting pot of religions* is a good thing is satanic propaganda. Perhaps a melting pot of culture, art, and music could be a good thing, adding variety to those fields of human activity. But a melting pot of religions generates an amalgam of fodder fit to fuel the flames of hell. How could anyone who claims to be Christian condone a melting pot of religions? Jesus Christ made it clear that he is the only avenue to salvation, and this is made very clear in the Bible, such as in John 14:6. Any other proposed avenue to heaven apart from Jesus Christ leads to everlasting death. Is it a good thing for most people to go to hell? Of course not! So to say that a melting pot of religions is a good thing is equivalent to calling our Lord Jesus Christ a liar, and it condones the eternal destruction of human souls."

"Whoa," uttered Andela. "I guess that means that several denominations that call themselves *Christian* are teaching dangerous stuff." Andela paused in thought before speaking again. "So then, what's the best denomination? I mean, what denomination teaches the best doctrine? Is it the Baptists? Or Roman Catholics? Or Episcopalians? Or Methodists? Or Presbyterians? Or what?"

Madam Mercy reached into a pocket in the scarlet gown draped over her figure. She withdrew a petite scroll; untied and removed a sheer, blue ribbon that bound the scroll; and handed the scroll to Andela.

Andela accepted the scroll and unwound it. Her eyes fell upon the following title and paragraph:

* * * * * * * * * * * * * * * * * * *

God's Church

God's Church resolutely affirms our sole and total creed to be the Holy Bible, consisting of sixty-six books as canonized by our assembly in the fourth century A.D. through the grace and provision of God.

Absolutely no additions or deletions may be regarded as creedal or binding to the Church. Furthermore, let it be known, as Christ's words confirm, that the originally scribed Scriptures constituting the Holy Bible were and are absolute truth without error.

* * * * * * * * * * * * * * * * * *

"God's Church," said Andela, handing the scroll back to Madam Mercy. "Okay, so where do I find one of those churches."

"Wherever two or three children of God are gathered together to worship him, there you will find God's Church."

"But, which denomination is best?"

"It is best that there be no denominations."

Madam Mercy looked upon Andela with patience, awaiting Andela's next comment or next inquiry. Andela felt as though there were a thousand questions regarding a thousand topics that churned within her mind; but after glancing toward Bill, she knew what she wanted to ask next.

"So, this is the Land of the Northern Pool, right?"

"Yes."

"Exactly what is that?"

Madam Mercy looked out across the plush landscape. "It is the invitation for all lands to be living. There is no land that does not touch the border of this land, not unless the time of choosing is over."

"The time of choosing?"

Madam Mercy's eyes focused back on Andela. After looking for some time upon Andela's face, Madam Mercy's eyes revealed her awareness that Andela already knew the answer to her question. Still, Madam Mercy was gracious enough to respond. "It is the time in the lives of earthly human beings that is measured from the beginning of spiritual accountability to the point of physical death."

This response appeased Andela, but she was ready with another question. "Okay, so Rebelon was not permitted to kill Bill in this land, namely the Land of the Northern Pool. And besides that, I understand that killing him would just send him back home to the farm in Missouri since he did not come on this trip knowingly and voluntarily, right?"

Madam Mercy nodded.

"Okay, but there's another question I want to ask. So then, I know we are supposed to go to Bill's land." Andela paused and faced Madam Mercy with a look of deep concern. "Can Rebelon kill Bill in Bill's land? I mean, like he almost did just now? And exactly who is Rebelon? Is he some sort of rebel?"

Madam Mercy seemed more challenged by these questions than by any of Andela's preceding questions. She gazed thoughtfully toward the distant waterfall that plummeted downward from the cloud of light at the upper edge of the golden cliff. After several seconds she turned her face back toward Andela. "Well, let me answer your questions in two parts. First, Bill is the governor of Bill's land. He is granted the freedom to choose. Rebelon could not kill him there unless Bill chose to permit such an atrocity. In fact, Rebelon could not even attack him there, not unless Bill willfully invited such an attack."

Andela's lips parted to retort such a suggestion, but Madam Mercy raised a hand to stay Andela's words. "Bill does not seem the type that would permit any such thing on the part of Rebelon, and that is to his credit. But now let me continue answering your questions."

Andela was calmed by Madam Mercy's positive comment about Bill. She reclined into a listening posture, leaning back on straightened arms with her palms on the golden pathway beneath her.

Madam Mercy resumed, "Rebelon is the personification of rebellion. He is wholly evil, and therefore, he is not the personification of all rebellion, for not all rebellion is evil. In fact, rebellion against evil is more refreshing to me than words could ever manifest, and such rebellion is only too rare in your present world. But more specifically, Rebelon is the embodiment of rebellion against true love and against life. It would only be if Bill were drawn to extremes of rebellion against love and life that Rebelon could gain the power to slay Bill in his own land—unless, perhaps, Bill were insane—but Bill is sane."

Andela nodded. "So then, my mission is to persuade Bill to choose love and life rather than choosing rebellion against God."

Madam Mercy smiled, and her countenance conveyed approval of Andela's words. She sat for several seconds while gazing into Andela's eyes, and then she arose. Suddenly thousands of tiny flowers bloomed across the grassy turf, glimmering and sparkling like myriads of multicolored fireflies. Madam Mercy turned her face upward and spoke toward the sky, "I am Mercy of the Northern Pool, faithfully married to Justice of the Northern Pool." Her voice was deep yet feminine, resonating throughout the atmosphere and arousing wonder within Andela's heart. Waterspouts that bedecked the landscape shot upward with liquid fingers. Madam Mercy raised one arm and directed Andela's attention toward a cloudy bank, the bank of light that was to Andela's right when Andela first entered the Land of the Northern Pool. She turned her face back toward Andela. "His land lies next to yours…"

"Oooh, aaah," groaned Bill. Memory of the crushing pain he experienced only minutes before began returning to his mind.

Andela glimpsed downward toward Bill, and then looked back upward. Madam Mercy had vanished. The waterspouts receded to their former heights.

Bill sat up and palpated his chest. At first he was puzzled to discover that his chest was not sore, but then he reminded himself that he was only dreaming. He was glad that Andela remained beside him. "Lands to Betsy! I just had another one of those nasty nightmares in the middle of this dream," he declared, addressing Andela.

"Really, what kind of nightmare?" asked Andela.

"A grizzly bear grabbed me, and he nearly crushed every rib in my body."

Andela smiled and peered at Bill. "Well," she spoke at last, "I think you look better than the average man would look after taking on a grizzly bear with his bare hands."

At first Bill looked perplexed. But as he sat and contemplated Andela's remark, a pleased expression replaced his visage of perplexity. He stared into Andela's eyes, recalling that he was attempting to get information out of this *dream Andela* before he woke up. Somehow, though, the idea of extracting information no longer seemed to matter. If he could simply enjoy the rest of his dream without getting crushed, drowned, or eaten; then he would be content. "Yep, I guess I could be worse off after wrestling a grizzly," he commented with a shrug.

Andela rose and reached a hand toward Bill. "I think we were on our way to your land. It's that way," she said, nodding in the direction that Madam Mercy directed.

"My land?" responded Bill, accepting Andela's hand and rising. "Oh yea, I remember. Sure, let's go."

Chapter 5

The Barren Land

As they entered the cloudy bank where Madam Mercy directed Andela to lead Bill, Andela found that she could see nothing but light, just like when she entered the cloud bank at the northern tip of her land. She chose to enter this cloud where the ground was grassy and level; and the surface of the ground remained consistent after entering the cloud. Passing through the cloud banks made her appreciate the fact that Bill had walked without seeing the ground beneath his feet during the entire journey. And then as she exited the other side of the cloud, she noted that the landscape was very much like the previous landscape; so she deduced that this was a continuation of the Land of the Northern Pool. For Bill, however, exiting the cloud presented a great change.

Andela felt Bill clutch her arm. "Look, Andela! Over there!"

Andela looked in the direction Bill pointed, namely in the opposite direction from the great golden cliff that continued along the northern border of the Land of the Northern Pool. There was something different about this section of land—there was no cloud of light forming a wall at the southern border. The land simply ended at the edge of a cliff; and far in the distance, below and beyond the cliff, stretched another landscape—a very different landscape. Andela figured that the land below was Bill's land. She also figured that Bill was now able to see.

Then Andela noted another difference about this section of land. There was no river pouring into the land that lay below the cliff to the south of them. There was a waterfall plummeting downward from the cliff to their north, but this water was totally contained within a great lake in the distance before them. Looking more closely, she realized that the southern tip of the lake was bolstered by a colossal stone wall—an enormous dam. The dam prevented water from flowing into Bill's land.

"You can see?" Andela inquired, pulling her eyes from the landscape and facing Bill.

"Yep," replied Bill, facing south.

"That must be your land down there."

"I reckon so."

Bill released Andela's arm and strode forward.

It was not far to the southern border of the Land of the Northern Pool. Andela was excited over Bill's ability to see. She observed his behavior with hopes of pressing forward in her quest to woo his soul. But then her eyes widened with alarm—Bill was not slowing as he neared the edge of the cliff! She deduced that he was seeing his land, but that he was not seeing the Land of the Northern Pool, and that meant that he was not seeing the ground beneath his feet.

"Bill stop!" screamed Andela, launching forward and stretching out a hand.

Bill slowed and turned his face back toward Andela, but he did not stop walking. He would have stopped, in another step or two; but instead, he felt his right foot drop downward. He was in the process of turning around to face Andela when his foot plunged into thin air, and then he toppled sideways over the edge of the cliff.

"Aaaaaaaaaah!" a masculine squeal erupted. The sound of Bill's cry faded as his body plummeted downward. Andela was frozen in dread, but only for a moment. She regained the use of her limbs and continued forward to the spot where Bill disappeared, and then she dropped to her hands and knees in the lush grass. She crawled to the edge of the cliff and lay flat on her stomach, with knees and toes pressed into the ground; and then she inched forward until her head protruded beyond the cliff's upper edge.

The face of the cliff was smooth and golden, just like the cliff at the northern border of her land. A bleak landscape was visible below. There were huge tree trunks rising from place to place with small, broken limbs that held very few leaves. Rocky hills formed skeletal dunes that stretched on and on in the far distance; and eastward, below the great stone wall at the southern tip of the lake to Andela's left, ran a deep gorge. Andela noted the environment only briefly—her eyes fixed themselves straight downward.

Perhaps a hundred yards from the tip of Andela's nose, lying motionless on the cracked ground, was Bill. Andela felt a pang of remorse grip the pit of her stomach. Why hadn't she been more alert? Why hadn't she been smart enough to predict that Bill would only be able to see his own land? Her lips began quivering, and a soft moan thrust itself upward through her throat. But then Bill moved. He rose to his feet and looked around.

"Bill! Bill!" called Andela. Her heart quickened.

Bill did not respond. He peered in all directions, including upward; but he did not seem to see Andela.

"Bill! It's me! I'm up here! Bill!"

Bill gave no indication that he heard. He stepped forward and reached a hand outward toward the face of the golden cliff, and then he bolted backward as if surprised to have touched something. Then Andela felt a hand touch her shoulder.

"Easy," spoke Madam Mercy as Andela flipped over on her back. Madam Mercy offered a helping hand.

Andela released a gasp of air and rose to a sitting position, reaching upward and grasping Madam Mercy's extended hand. "It's Bill! He…"

"I know," interrupted Madam Mercy. "He is not injured. It is not permitted for an accident in the Land of the Northern Pool to result in injury or death in another land."

"He's okay then?" Andela inquired, releasing Madam Mercy's hand after rising to her feet.

Madam Mercy paused.

Andela did not like the look of contemplation that beset Madam Mercy's countenance. "He's not okay?"

Madam Mercy faced Andela in silence. After several seconds, she turned and stepped a few feet back from the edge of the cliff. Then she turned back around and sat down on the plush grass, motioning for Andela to move a safer distance from the edge of the cliff and sit beside her. Andela was eager to pursue Bill, but the look in Madam Mercy's eyes restrained her. She stepped forward and sat down beside Madam Mercy. She then addressed Madam Mercy with inquiring eyes.

"There is great danger, and you must act to dissuade devastation."

Andela's eyes widened. This was not what she wanted to hear. "What? What kind of danger?"

"I know how the Enemy will first choose to strike—he will employ one of his most fruitful weapons of wreckage."

"The Enemy? Who's the Enemy? And what kind of weapon?"

Madam Mercy settled into the lawn. Her face grew intent as she faced Andela. "When I say *the Enemy*, I am referring to the *father of all lies* and to his minions. The weapon he will wield first is that of a temptress."

Andela felt her heart skip. "A temptress?"

"Yes. I'm sure they'll send Decevon. There's no more apt seductress in any land."

"But, I mean…" stammered Andela. The threat of a seductress caused a throbbing in her abdomen. Her speech faltered and her mind whirled with disturbing contemplations. "I don't think Bill would, but wait, he thinks he's dreaming! What if this temptress, Decevon, makes Bill think they're married?"

Madam Mercy shrugged. "Within the boundaries of marriage, dreams of marriage, thoughts of marriage, and hopes of marriage, the gift of sex blooms in beauty and holiness. The bed is undefiled at all ages and all stages of development, so long as the mind, heart, and conscious imagination keep the gift of sex within the divinely ordained boundary of monogamous, bisexual marriage. I would add, though, that unmarried men and women should keep imaginary partners imaginary—they should not entertain fantasies of being married and having sex with someone who really exists."

"But Bill isn't dreaming," blurted Andela. "This is real, right? I mean, if he has sex with this temptress because she makes him think they're married, then he will really be having sex, right?"

Madam Mercy leaned forward and grasped Andela's shoulder, staring into Andela's eyes. "Do not worry, she won't do that. Decevon will make no attempt to make Bill think that she is Bill's wife." Then Madam Mercy released Andela's shoulder and settled back to her former posture. "Our adversaries have nothing to gain by persuading Bill to engage in sex within morally permissible boundaries. If Bill thinks he is having sex with his wife, then what moral wrong is there? Is there anything wrong with a man having sex with his wife?"

Andela felt desperate. "But, but this is no dream. He would be having sex with a woman who is not his wife."

Madam Mercy nodded. "I understand, and I understand that such a thing would torment you. But it won't happen—it won't happen because the Enemy wants more than to torment you, he wants to destroy Bill. Therefore, he will try and get Bill to commit a moral wrong."

Andela's face blanched. "You mean Decevon will try to seduce him, even without trying to make him think that they're married?"

"Oh yes child, you can count on it."

"No," Andela stated. She drew a deep breath and the color returned to her cheeks. "I don't think Bill would do such a thing."

Madam Mercy proffered another shrug. "Well, he does have remarkable character for a dead man. There may be a chance that you're right."

"A chance?" retorted Andela.

"We are in the midst of battle. Decevon is not a weapon to be underestimated. She may use the fact that Bill thinks he is dreaming to attempt diminishing his defenses against fornication."

"But, would that still be a moral evil? Even if Bill thought he was dreaming?"

"Yes. The willful meditations of the heart should be kept within the boundaries of God's statutes, how else could a man commit adultery within his heart? If Bill chooses to daydream of having sex, or if he has any conscious control over a nighttime dream of having sex, then his sexual partner should be his wife. And as I stated before, if an unmarried man dreams of having sex with his future wife, then that wife should be imaginary, not an actual person."

An introspective look crept across Andela's face. She peered into Madam Mercy's eyes. There was inquisitive wrinkle across her brow, but she seemed hesitant to speak. Madam Mercy perceived that there was something Andela wanted to ask, and she waited in patient silence. Finally Andela's lips parted. "I guess girls can dream too, can't they?"

"Of course," returned Madam Mercy.

"So, if a boy or girl, or a man or woman, is dreaming about having sex with a marriage partner, well…"

"Well what?" coaxed Madam Mercy.

Resolution rose within Andela's expression. Madam Mercy was knowledgeable, and there was something Andela wanted to know, even if she found the subject to be embarrassing. "I was in a church revival service several years ago," she began, "and there was an evangelist who preached that masturbation is a sin."

Madam Mercy frowned. "Really?"

"Yes. He said that God slew O'nan in the Book of Genesis because O'nan committed masturbation."

The frown on Madam Mercy's face transformed to a look of anger.

Andela felt vulnerable. Madam Mercy seemed so insightful; surely Madam Mercy would know why Andela was bringing up the subject. It seemed to Andela as if she were openly admitting that she masturbated. A knot of apprehension formed in her stomach. She had tried to give up masturbating, but it seemed impossible to refrain from easing the sexual tension that mounted within her body from time to time. She looked upon Madam Mercy's face and waited for a response.

"Matthew chapter eighteen, verse six, makes it clear that it would be better for a man to have a millstone tied around his neck and be thrown into the sea than for him to offend a young child of God," Madam Mercy spoke in a firm voice. "I believe this verse applies to offenses that might drive a child away from God's family."

Andela stared in perplexity. "What are you saying?"

"I am saying that an evangelist who teaches that masturbation is a sin may end up with blood on his hands. His false teaching may spurn souls down the roadway to hell, souls who otherwise may have chosen the pathway to heaven. And such an evangelist places himself in jeopardy of judgment. Revelation chapter twenty-two, verse eighteen, teaches that plagues may befall a man who adds to the Word of God. In other words, it can be a serious offense against God to claim that the Bible teaches that a particular act is a sin when the Bible teaches no such thing."

"So then, masturbation is not a sin?"

Madam Mercy still seemed affronted. "What do you suppose might happen if an evangelist taught that urination is a sin and that anyone who urinated should repent and stop the horrible practice of urinating?"

Andela was taken aback. "Um, well, no one would believe him. Everyone has to urinate. It's just natural."

"Perhaps so," returned Madam Mercy. "But what if some persons did not need to urinate? What if some persons had ureters that emptied into their intestines so that urine passed out with bowel movements? Would that mean that other persons with urinary systems such as yours would no longer need to urinate?"

"Of course not," Andela replied.

"Well then, there may be persons with no physiological need to masturbate, but masturbation is a normal and natural physiological process for many, and it is a cruel lie to teach that such a process is sin."

"But what about the Bible? Isn't the story about O'nan in the Bible?"

"Of course it is," returned Madam Mercy, "but O'nan's sin was not masturbation. He sinned because he disobeyed his father's instruction to place seed within the body of Tamar. In ancient Old Testament times, it was a custom for a man whose brother died to take his brother's widow as a wife, and for her firstborn child to be deemed the child of the brother who died, as is made clear in Deuteronomy chapter twenty-five, verses five and six. O'nan's father, Judah, instructed O'nan to take Tamar as a wife and bear a child. Tamar had been the wife of Er, but Er was slain.

"O'nan disobeyed his father's instruction to get Tamar pregnant, and he did so by spilling his seed outside her body. Disobeying a parent was considered a serious offense by Old Testament standards, as is revealed in Deuteronomy chapter twenty-one, verses eighteen through twenty-one. This disobedience was O'nan's sin. Judah clearly understood that God slew O'nan because he refused to get Tamar pregnant, as is shown in Genesis chapter thirty-eight, verse eleven. In this verse, Judah asks Tamar to remain in his house until his younger son, Shelah, grows old enough to take her as a wife, so that Shelah will not also be slain. Thus, O'nan was slain because of disobedience, namely because he deprived Tamar of a child—not because he masturbated. In fact, it is not even clear that he masturbated at all—he may have simply withdrawn from intercourse just as he was about to eject seed."

"Oh, wow, so the Bible never says that masturbation is a sin?"

"Of course not," stated Madam Mercy. "But note that there are two categories of uncleanness disclosed in Scripture. There is moral uncleanness, which is sin, and there is social uncleanness, which is a matter of physical sanitation. Moral uncleanness is presented in such verses as Matthew chapter twenty-three, verse twenty-seven, and First Thessalonians, chapter two, verse three. In these verses it is apparent that *uncleanness* refers to matters of the mind, heart, and spirit. Social uncleanness is addressed in such verses as Leviticus chapter fifteen, verse nineteen, and Leviticus chapter fifteen, verse sixteen. The social uncleanness in verse nineteen applies to women during menstruation, and the social uncleanness in verse sixteen applies to men who spill semen on themselves when they ejaculate apart from having sex with a wife. It is also social uncleanness when men spill semen on both themselves and their wives during sexual intercourse, as is disclosed in Leviticus chapter fifteen, verse eighteen.

"Masturbation, then, is a part of sexual development and maturation, as is menstruation. Both menstruation and masturbation are normal physiological processes, as are urination and the passage of stool. It is tormenting oppression for religious leaders to teach that any of these processes are sin, though it is proper for each to be done in a healthy and appropriate manner. Remember, though, that the meditations of one's heart should always be acceptable to God, so when one daydreams of having sex, it should be done in a manner in keeping with the boundaries and instructions God has given for sexual conduct."

Andela stared upon Madam Mercy's face. The subject of masturbation was one that had beleaguered her for years, and it was dumbfounding to hear the subject explained so simply. It then struck her mind that she had a couple of other sexual questions.

"Okay, thank you for that explanation," said Andela. "So then, what about petting and oral sex during dates?"

Andela felt a little flushed after posing additional sexual questions, but her desire to learn more about sex superseded her shyness.

"For the sake of time, I'll proffer conclusions first, and then support my assertions," responded Madam Mercy. "One may argue that affectionate kisses are acceptable while dating, and one may make such an argument in light of the instruction found in First Peter chapter five, verse fourteen—*Greet ye one another with a kiss of charity*. One should exercise serious discretion when it comes to kissing, of course, since serious diseases such as herpes and mononucleosis can be transmitted through kissing. Also realize that romantic kissing should be considered an intimate act, and should not be taken lightly, but I do not believe that kissing is prohibited outside of holy marriage. I believe one should refrain, however, from manually stimulating sexual parts of another person's body while dating. Furthermore, I believe one should refrain from orally stimulating sexual parts of another person's body while dating, and from assuming positions of sexual intercourse. Such activities as erotic petting and oral sex should only take place between a husband and wife.

"Before proffering Scriptures that shed light on the subject of proper sexual conduct, let me point out that what is written in First Corinthians chapter seven, verse one—*It is good for a man not to touch a woman*—does not refer so much to petting as it does to a man remaining single and leading a life of celibacy. Christ even goes so far as to comment upon the permissibility of a man making himself a eunuch for the kingdom of heaven's sake, as is found in Matthew chapter nineteen, verse twelve. One may construe from such permissibility that the instruction given to Adam and Eve to multiply, as found in Genesis chapter one, verse twenty-eight, does not apply to later generations inhabiting a populated earth. Thus, birth control is not a sin, but rather, having a child with no intention of providing for that child is a sin, as pointed out in First Timothy chapter five, verse eight."

"Oh," said Andela. She had heard arguments both for and against birth control, and she had already come to conclusions consistent with what Madam Mercy stated.

"Bible verses supporting what I have told you regarding sexual conduct during dating are verses such as Second Timothy chapter two, verse twenty-two, Proverbs chapter five, verses one through twenty-three, Ecclesiastes chapter eleven, verses nine and ten, and Ezekiel chapter twenty-three, verses three and twenty-one. The Bible teaches that having sexual intercourse outside the bond of marriage is sin, and it is reasonable to conclude that manually or orally stimulating the sexual parts of another person's body outside the bond of marriage is also sin."

Andela faced Madam Mercy for several seconds, grateful for answers to arduous sexual questions. Then her mind shifted—she felt an urgency to find Bill. "I'd better go," she said, leaning on a straightened arm in order to rise.

"Wait," Madam Mercy stated, retaining Andela by again placing a hand on her shoulder. She waited until Andela was settled back down and their eyes again met before withdrawing her hand. "Remember this—true love is stronger than misguided lust."

"Okay," returned Andela, nodding in affirmation. She was anxious to rise and get going.

"One more thing," added Madam Mercy, "you can't go down there the way Bill did. If you jump over the edge of the cliff it will be no accident, and you will be killed. There is a stairwell on this side of the lake. The stairwell was formed at the same time that Faith wrought the stairwell leading upward from your land. The opening into the stairwell is near the edge of the cliff. Now go!"

Andela felt abashed about almost departing without even knowing how to descend to Bill's land, but she felt more concern than embarrassment. She nodded her understanding, and then, with a look of determination set upon her face, she rose and turned toward the lake. She took two strides, but then she froze in place. A second later she turned back around to face Madam Mercy. "But, what if I fail? Is there still hope for Bill?"

Madam Mercy rose to her feet and looked upon Andela with so grave an expression that Andela's heart seemed to chill. "There is still hope, my child. Any living man, woman, or child dwelling within a human body during the period of spiritual accountability, who will repent from sin and receive the true Master's lordship, will receive eternal life."

Andela appreciated Madam Mercy's words, but she also sensed that there was something more—something that Madam Mercy was holding back.

"What else can you tell me?" asked Andela.

Madam Mercy took one step forward and then stood facing Andela. "There are many creatures on your planet that have been given the nature to be monogamous, and they generally conduct themselves according to that nature. Bald eagles among the fowl, angelfish among other aquatic species, beavers and red foxes among the four-footed mammals, and white-handed gibbons among the primates—and I'm referring to those primates that are not spiritual beings."

"Spiritual beings?"

Madam Mercy looked surprised by Andela's question. "Human beings are the only primates presently living upon the earth, in the biological sense, who are begotten spiritually. They are destined to one of two eternities—eternal life, begotten of God, or eternal death, begotten of the Evil One. The other primates, such as apes, monkeys, and chimpanzees, are merely animals."

Andela realized that she had asked a rather simple question. She blushed and nodded for Madam Mercy to continue.

"Even though there is only one God, he is plural in person, and he communes with himself. Thus, he was able to say—*Let us make man in our image*—as recorded in Genesis chapter one, verse twenty-six. Man, on the other hand, is single in person. Although human beings can reason within themselves, and can even talk to themselves, each human being is only one being, and is only one person."

Madam Mercy paused and waited for Andela to indicate whether or not she was following her explanation.

"Okay," responded Andela, wondering just how this information was going to reflect upon Bill's danger. "I understand, please go on."

"Very well, when the first man was created, he was given charge over a portion of God's creation, and he was meant to enjoy the beauty and wonder of his surroundings. This first man was never meant to die, and he was given the ability to love and honor God, thus glorifying God. One way this man was meant to love and honor God was through obedience. There were many marvelous and attractive entities surrounding the man, including many good things to eat, and including many enjoyable things to do, but he was commanded to avoid one thing that appeared attractive within his environment, namely the fruit of one tree. And by avoiding this particular fruit, he evidenced his allegiance to his Creator. This first man obeyed God, and things went well, but there was a problem with this man, namely, it was determined that he was alone—too alone.

"So God made Eve," interjected Andela, thinking she would speed things along.

This time Madam Mercy did not appear surprised by Andela's interjection. "Not yet," she stated. "At this point in creation, the first man was one-hundred percent *man* spiritually, but on the physical level, he was not yet what you think of as a *man*. And notably, when God first decided that Adam was too alone, he did not immediately create Eve. He tried something else first."

Andela was perplexed. "What? What do you mean?"

"The terms *man* and *him* and *his* and *he* and *son* can be generic in the Bible. They may refer to an adult human male, or to an adult human female, or to a human that by whatever circumstance is neither male nor female. They may also refer to a boy, or to a girl, or to a baby, or to an unborn infant still in his mother's womb. In regard to Adam when he was first created, the term *man* refers to a human being who was only partially a member of the animal kingdom."

Andela's wrinkled brow divulged confusion. She had heard the story of creation over and over again, but she had never heard such a statement. Despite her great respect for Madam Mercy and respect for the words that Madam Mercy spoke, her forehead became creased in doubt. "What do you mean?"

Madam Mercy paused for several seconds, cognizant of the impact her words might have upon Andela's mind. "Let me ask you a question, Andela—do you think the Creator would have given sexual abilities to the first man without giving him a sexual partner? It is forbidden for mankind to have sex with any creature other than one of his own kind, and even then he may only have sex with a human of the opposite sex, and only in a marriage relationship. Furthermore, the Bible teaches that the marriage relationship ordained by God is monogamous, taking place between one woman and one man. Only under influence of the fallen nature did man delve into polygamy, and I think it is notable that the first recorded polygamist was also a killer, namely Lamech. So, does it not make perfect sense that the first man, living without the existence of any other human being, was not yet a sexual creature?"

The creased expression faded from Andela's forehead, but a look of compelling curiosity ensued. Madam Mercy's words were reasonable;

but still, the information was different that anything she had ever heard about the creation of Adam and Eve. "Okay," she granted, "that would seem logical. I don't suppose Adam was supposed to have sex with anyone, or anything, since there were no other humans. But God knew he would be making Eve later, didn't he?"

"We do not know all that is in the mind of God," responded Madam Mercy. "But let me ask you another question—if God knew he was going to create Eve, then why didn't he?"

Again Andela's brow wrinkled. "What do you mean? He did create Eve, right?"

"Of course, my dear. He has not given the power to create life to others, not really, and certainly not spiritual life. But what I'm saying is that the first human lived for quite some time before another human was created."

"He did?"

"Of course. The first man was alone from the time that he was created until God determined that the man was too alone, and no one knows how long that was. And then, when God determined that the *single being* and *single person*, namely Adam, should not be alone, he did not initially seek to remedy the situation by creating Eve. He tried something else first—he made other creatures as candidates for solving Adam's aloneness."

Andela presented inquiring eyes. "Really, well, why isn't that written in Genesis? I mean, if that's really true, then why don't we read it in the creation story?"

Madam Mercy smiled. "Ah, but it is written in Genesis, my dear. I have no doubt that you have read it many times."

Andela was startled. "I've read it? Read what?"

"When the Creator first determined that man should not live alone, he did not respond by creating another human."

"He didn't?"

"No. He first created beasts, cattle, and fowl that Adam named."

"Beasts, cattle, and fowl?"

"There were apparently no fish created at this point, but what kind of coequal companion would a fish be?" Madam Mercy remarked with a chuckle. But then a worried look mounted her face, like the look that might appear on a schoolboy's face if he thought he had just given the wrong answer to a question. "Please do not misunderstand me," she spoke with a note of apology. "I imagine that God could certainly create a fish that could serve as a coequal companion if he determined to do so, but there is no mention in the Bible that God created such a fish."

Andela smiled at Madam Mercy's discomfiture regarding the subject of fish, but then the preponderance of Madam Mercy's words began impressing her mind. "So, you're saying that God created some animals between the time that he created Adam and the time that he created Eve? And you're saying that this is recorded in the Book of Genesis?"

"Yes, and the Bible says that God brought these animals to Adam so that Adam could decide what to call them, and that Adam's decision determined the *name* thereof. In this instance, the Biblical term for *name* means *an appellation, as a mark or memorial of individuality*. It is the same Hebrew word for *name* as that used when Adam later called his wife's *name* Eve."

"Hold on," spoke up Andela, raising and then lowering both palms. She stared at Madam Mercy for several seconds, unconvinced by Madam Mercy's words. But then, as she thought about it, she recalled a passage in the second chapter of Genesis that described the creation of animals after the creation of Adam, and these animals were indeed created prior to the creation of Eve.

"Oh my," said Andela. Her eyes widened and she peered at Madam Mercy's face. She could hardly believe that she had read about the creation of these animals so often without realizing what was written. She remembered one of her Sunday school teachers remarking that the Bible is so full of information that a person can learn new things after reading the same passage a hundred times. "So, those animals created after Adam, they had names?"

"Yes. And it's important to note that the verse in the Bible that tells about the creation of these special animals, namely Genesis chapter two, verse nineteen, comes right after God's proclamation that he would *make* Adam a *help meet*. God did not proclaim that he would bring animals to Adam that had already been created, and that he would let Adam name those animals, rather, he plainly stated that he would *make* a *help meet*. It is inappropriate to interpret verse nineteen as saying that God had already made these animals. The King James Version of the Bible is correct by saying that God *formed* the animals, and the New American Standard Bible is also correct, but the New International

Version of the Bible is incorrect by saying that God *had formed* the animals."

"So, you're saying that Genesis chapter two, verses eighteen and nineteen, teaches us that God created animals between the creations of Adam and Eve?"

"Yes, and there are several other factors to support what I am saying," explicated Madam Mercy. "At the end of Genesis chapter two, verse eighteen, Adam was considered to be alone, even though there were many animals created before Adam. It would be illogical to think that Adam had no interaction with the animals created prior to him, especially when there were no other human beings. So it appears that the presence of these animals, namely the animals created before Adam was created, was not sufficient to keep God from proclaiming that it was not good for Adam to be alone. Then, at the end of Genesis chapter two, verse twenty, it no longer appears that Adam was considered to be alone, but rather, the problem was that there was no *help meet* found for Adam. In other words, the animals created between the creations of Adam and Eve sufficed for Adam to no longer be alone, but none of these animals sufficed as a *help meet*."

Andela stared at Madam Mercy in thought. "How's that? I mean, if Adam was considered to be alone when there were animals created before him, then how could he no longer be alone because animals were created after him?"

"That's the point!" proclaimed Madam Mercy. "Adam was considered to be alone in the presence of all the animals created before him because those animals were not spiritual beings, they were mere animals."

A look of awe emerged upon Andela's face. "Spiritual beings?"

"Yes," avowed Madam Mercy. "Even if the Hebrew verb for *formed* in Genesis chapter two, verse nineteen, can mean either *formed* or *had formed* if interpreted by itself, it's obvious that the Hebrew verb should be interpreted as *formed* when taken in context. It would be ridiculous to think that God would consider a non-spiritual animal as a candidate for being a *coequal companion* with Adam, for the Hebrew words translated as *help meet* indicate a companion of equal status. To be of equal status with Adam, an animal would have to be created in the *likeness of God*, or in other words, the animal would have to be a spiritual creature, not merely a physical creature. I am not saying that the animals created between the creation of Adam and the creation of Eve were created in the image of God, as was Adam, but I am saying that these animals were made in the *likeness of God*, and could therefore be rightfully considered of coequal existence with Adam."

"Wow, spiritual animals," said Andela. "So, did the animals created between Adam and Eve know their own names? I mean, could they talk? I know that animals have their languages, sort of, but I mean, could they talk like we're talking?"

"Of course they could talk," returned Madam Mercy. "What kind of *coequal companion* would an animal be if that animal could not talk? Did Eve give any indication of surprise when the dragon, Satan, spoke to her?"

Andela paused and stared at Madam Mercy.

"Did you say dragon?"

Madam Mercy smiled at the startled look on Andela's face. "I believe that Satan had legs before he was cursed and made to crawl around on his belly, so I think he was what you would call a dragon, though I'm not certain that he had wings."

"Really?"

"Yes. The Hebrew word *serpent* is derived from the hissing sound that snakes make, and I believe Satan spoke with a hissing sound before he was cursed. And notably, the words *serpent* and *dragon* appear to be used interchangeably in the Bible. The Hebrew word for *serpent* found in Exodus chapter seven, verses nine and ten, is the same Hebrew word that is translated as *dragon* in most of the Old Testament. And a different Hebrew word is translated as *serpent* in Exodus chapter seven, verse fifteen, but it refers to the same serpent that is mentioned in verses nine and ten where the Hebrew word that is also translated as *dragon* is used. And this different Hebrew word is the same word that is translated as *serpent* in Genesis chapter three, verse one, referring to Satan. And in addition to this, Satan is referred to as both a dragon and a serpent in Revelation chapter twelve, verse nine. So when Satan was first created, I believe that he was what you would call a dragon, and I also think that both the Hebrew and Greek words that are translated as *serpent* can rightly be applied to Satan."

A nervous sensation evolved within Andela's stomach. One of her favorite figurines was a pink dragon. "So then, are dragons evil? I mean, I've collected some souvenir dragons, and I especially like a pink one."

Madam Mercy's serious mien lightened. "Who do you think created the body of the first dragon? Satan is evil, beyond any question, but note that the design of his body was altered after he became the father of all lies. The King James Version of Psalms chapter one-hundred and forty eight, verse seven, begins with the words—*Praise the Lord from the earth ye dragons*—and a well outside of Jerusalem was referred to as the *dragon well* in Nehemiah chapter two, verse thirteen. Also note that in Isaiah chapter forty-three, verse twenty, the Lord proclaimed that the beasts of the field shall honor him, the dragons and the owls. The Hebrew word translated as *dragons* in Isaiah chapter forty-three, verse twenty, is the same Hebrew word translated as *dragon* in Isaiah chapter twenty-seven, verse one, where we read that the Lord shall slay the dragon that is in the sea. So in summary, Andela, I think it is quite acceptable for you to keep your pink dragon. And furthermore, I do not think that the bodily forms of any of the creatures that God created should be considered evil."

Andela gazed into the fathomless orbs comprising Madam Mercy's eyes, pondering Madam Mercy's words. "Okay then, back to what we were talking about—these animals, namely the ones created after Adam was created, were they definitely spiritual beings?"

"Of course!" reaffirmed Madam Mercy. "Do you think that the dragon that spoke to Eve was just a dumb beast? It was Satan himself! The Bible never says that the serpent was possessed by Satan. Rather, the serpent was, in fact, Satan."

"Really?"

Madam Mercy gazed thoughtfully into Andela's eyes. "You know what, there's too much tradition taught by religious leaders, rather than what's in the Bible. Satan was obviously one of the beasts of the field that were created between the creations of Adam and Eve. Genesis chapter three, verse one, states that the serpent was more subtle than any beast of the field which the Lord God had made. In verse fourteen of that same chapter, the serpent was cursed above every beast of the field. His body was changed so that he had to crawl around on his belly. And note that God's judgment against the serpent affected the serpent's seed, showing that the serpent had a physical presence on the earth and that he bore offspring."

Andela's face paled. "Offspring," she reiterated. "Do you mean there are snakes crawling around that are descendants of Satan?"

Madam dropped her face downward and drew a pensive breath. "The animals now born upon your planet are of the earth only. Apart from human beings, there are no longer spiritual animals inhabiting the earth as natural, physical inhabitants of the planet. The Spirit of God oversees all of his creation, but the earthly animals that you have seen during your lifetime upon the earth are not innately spiritual beings—that is, of course, other than for the earthly animals such as yourself, namely human beings."

"So then, the animals created between Adam and Eve were spiritual beings. Well then, were all of those animals killed? Why aren't there any of them now?"

Madam Mercy turned her face back toward Andela; and as their eyes met and engaged in somber silence, Madam Mercy presented such a grievous expression that Andela's stomach tightened. At last Madam Mercy spoke. "You can read Genesis chapter six, verse seven," she said in the most solemn voice Andela had ever heard. "And note that only one individual was said to have found grace in the eyes of the Lord in Genesis chapter six, verse eight, and that one individual was a human being, namely Noah." She took a deep breath and again turned her face away. "The nonhuman animals taken aboard the ark were not spiritual beings. And I would add this, none of the animals taken aboard the ark were genetically capable of bearing offspring with humans through the deplorable act of bestiality."

Andela was a little puzzled by Madam Mercy's lack of emotional composure, but then it occurred to her that Madam Mercy was the embodiment of mercy. Perhaps Madam Mercy mourned the fact that these animals, namely the animals created after Adam, rejected her—they rejected mercy. And Madam Mercy's comment about bestiality sparked further contemplations within Andela's mind. Perhaps some of these spiritual animals were the *sons of God* that saw the *daughters of men* and took some of those daughters as wives before the great flood in Genesis. Andela recalled that these *sons of God* took wives *of all which they chose* from the daughters of men, and it struck her mind that a couple of major religious leaders, namely Joseph Smith and Muhammad, men who initiated antichrist cults—cults that deny that Christ is a Person of the One God—took many wives for themselves. Perhaps these polygamous men were possessed of evil spirits that once inhabited animal bodies, and perhaps these evil spirits still coveted the daughters of men through the flesh of the men they possessed. Perhaps some of the *giants* and *mighty men* and *men of renown*; referred to in Genesis chapter six, verse four; were physical hybrids resulting from the interbreeding of nonhuman spiritual creatures with human beings. Perhaps all human beings surviving after the flood are, at least to some extent, physical hybrids.

Andela further recalled that Genesis chapter six is the chapter in the Bible that discloses God's plan to pass judgment against the evils of the earth with a great flood. Noah found grace in the eyes of the Lord, but apparently human beings were the only spiritual beings whose physical lives were preserved upon the earth. Afterward, the *sons of God* presented themselves before the Lord, among them Satan, in the first and second chapters of Job. Perhaps these *sons of God* were disembodied spirits; and perhaps they had opportunities after the flood to turn from evil and receive mercy, but rejected such opportunities to the point of final judgment, or perhaps their judgment was already final when the flood occurred and they were disembodied through death by drowning. Either way, if these disembodied spirits became the evil gods and demons of the earth—demons and gods who are antagonistic to God's plan for mankind; and who are elevated to godhood by the freewill choices of men; and who are damned to everlasting death through rejection of God's will and authority; and who hatefully compete for the souls of mankind—then no wonder Madam Mercy found it emotionally stressful to speak of them.

These thoughts brought a question to Andela's mind that puzzled her. "I appreciate your answering my questions," she said. "But, the Bible says that, prior to the flood, the *sons of God* took the *daughters of men* as wives. In fact, it says they took all the women as wives that they so chose. This was obviously something that God considered wicked. So then, why are creatures that behaved so wickedly referred to as *sons of God*?"

Madam Mercy kept her face turned away. "Have you read the genealogy of Christ in Luke chapter three?"

"I think so," replied Andela.

"That genealogy goes all the way back to Adam, and according to that genealogy, whose son was Adam?"

Andela had never given much consideration to genealogies. She was stumped. "I think, well, I don't know."

"He was the *son of God*. And do you know why he was referred to as the *son of God*?"

Andela thought for a moment. "Well, God made him, he didn't have a mother and father, so I guess you could say he was the *son of God* because God made him."

"Quite so. And the animals created between Adam and Eve—how does the Bible say they came to be?"

"Well, um, doesn't it say that God made them?"

"Yes. Genesis chapter two, verse nineteen, reveals that God *formed* these animals, and the Hebrew word for *formed* is the same Hebrew word that is used when the Bible states that God *formed* man in Genesis chapter two, verse seven, namely the word *yatsar*. This word, meaning *to mold into a form* or *to squeeze into a shape*, is comparable to the Hebrew word translated as *made* in Genesis chapter two, verse twenty-two, namely the word *banah*. The word *banah* means *to build*, and it is used in reference to when God made a woman. Notably, the words *yatsar* and *banah* are never used in the creation story in reference to any creatures other than Adam, Eve, and the animals created between the creations of Adam and Eve."

"Really?"

"Yes. And since the first man—a spiritual being in an animal body that was formed by God—is referred to as a *son of God*, then it makes sense that other spiritual beings in animal bodies that were formed by God would also be referred to as *sons of God*. And it also makes sense that, since Adam was begotten with free will, then candidates for finding a coequal companion for Adam would also be created with free will. I believe this *free will* is very special, permitting creatures to bless God with the choice of loving him. I believe such *free will* contrasts with the *will* of heavenly angels—I believe the *will* of heavenly angels is wholly and irrevocably subject to the sovereignty of God, and that you will never find a heavenly angel disobeying God. Mankind is given the choice of accepting or rejecting God's sovereignty through the exercise of his free will, thus enabling a man to bless God by choosing to love God, but a man's rejection of God's sovereignty results in that man's damnation, showing that God has ultimate sovereignty. If mankind were not given the ability to reject God's sovereignty, then no man would ever commit an evil act.

"And what's more, God did not create *free will* for the purpose of any creature ever performing an evil act. He created *free will* in order to be willfully loved. God is not half-light and half-darkness, he is wholly light without any trace of darkness. God was so terribly grieved when the gift of *free will* was widely misused upon the earth, that he once repented of even creating mankind, as stated in Genesis chapter six, verses six and seven. And note that the Hebrew word for *repent* in these verses is the same Hebrew word used the vast majority of times when the word *repent* appears in the Old Testament. And also note that God did not need to repent for any wrongdoing on his own part, for it was not wrong for God to desire a relationship with creatures who could willfully love him. Numbers chapter twenty-three, verse nineteen, reveals that God does not lie, and he does not commit sin for which he must repent, as do the sons of men. God's repentance resulted from the misuse of free will by spiritual animals, including mankind, all of whom existed because God had made man on the earth. God's repentance did not result from any personal wrongdoing on God's part, it resulted from personal wrongdoing on the part of creatures to whom God bestowed the gift of *free will*."

Madam Mercy's explanation was easy for Andela to follow. "Thank you. So then, what happened in the Garden of Eden after God made spiritual animals with free will?"

Madam Mercy looked back toward Andela. Her face softened. She appeared thankful to be moving on to another subject. "Well, none of the spiritual animals proved adequate—not one of them sufficed as a *help meet* for Adam. Adam was still too alone."

Andela continued facing Madam Mercy as she lowered herself back to the ground and motioned for Madam Mercy to again sit down beside her. She knew that the creation of Eve would come next, and she wanted to hear everything Madam Mercy had to say about the creation of the first woman. After all, she was a woman, and she was keenly interested in anything she could learn about womankind.

Madam Mercy acquiesced, situating herself on the ground beside Andela. She looked upon Andela's eager face and smiled as her lips parted to speak, "Then it happened, the Creator decided to extend his image and likeness into an entire species. Adam, the man who was *too alone*, would come to experience the emotional essence of the animal kingdom, mating and bearing young, raising a family, having friends of the same species, and though he would still be totally spiritual, he would also become totally physical, like the first created animals, except that he was never supposed to die. Thus, the first human being was given divinely administered anesthesia, and when he awoke, there were two human beings—two sexual human beings. Both were the same spiritually, begotten of their Father Creator, but physically they were different, as were other members of the animal kingdom, having differing genders."

Andela nodded her understanding, but she was ready with a question. "So, why was the first human being made into the male?"

Madam Mercy's expression sobered; she appeared to take Andela's question seriously—so seriously, in fact, that Andela began fearing that she would receive some sort of reprimand for asking the question.

"A fair question, and an acceptable one," stated Madam Mercy.

"Thank you," returned Andela.

Then Madam Mercy's expression lightened and she gestured with a shrug. "I don't know really, and I don't know that it would matter much. The first human had to be one or the other—the spirit of a human is not something that can be split up into separate persons. Each new human is a unique, begotten creation, so the first human had to be made either male or female. This did not mean that one sex was superior to the other. I've given it some thought, though, and I have a theory as to why the Creator may have made the first human male, and the second female."

"Really, why?"

"Well, remember that it was the *too alone* condition of the first human that prompted the creation of the second human. In a sense, the Creator may have considered the first human responsible for the fact that the second human needed to be created. In the animal kingdom, it is sometimes the male that has greater responsibility for protecting a family, and the Creator may have determined that this greater responsibility should fall upon the first human, namely the human that was accountable for necessitating the creation of the second human. Furthermore, in the case of human beings, I think the Creator has generally put more responsibility on the male when it comes to provision. Thus, it would seem appropriate, at least to me, that the primary responsibilities of protection and provision should, to the greater extent, fall upon the shoulders of the human being that was not satisfied with solitary existence as a human."

Angelic Commission

Madam Mercy's explanation was not difficult for Andela to follow. "Okay, that makes sense, but I'll tell you what, I wish everything you just said was written in Genesis. It seems to me like some things are left as mysteries."

A mischievous glint sprang within Madam Mercy's eyes. She turned her face askance in feigned contemplation. "Maybe we could proffer some other explanation for Adam being the male."

"Oh?"

"Maybe the *too alone* human was not considered worthy of having the best looks, so the second human was made female, and the first was stuck with being male."

Andela smiled weakly. She appreciated Madam Mercy's compassion and encouragement, but the subject of the sexes was a serious matter to her—a deeply emotional matter—and she found it difficult to dismiss the subject tritely. She dropped her face. "Okay, I guess so."

"No!" Madam Mercy spoke with passion, sensing Andela's despondency and looking upon Andela's downcast face. "Listen to me Andela—when your heart is compelled by the Spirit of the Creator to find answers, especially when the explanations of men seem contrary to the Spirit's leading, then do not accept fables and doctrines of mortal men rather than the truth of your Creator, and do not accept the offhand jest of an uncertain tutor. Many teachings regarding women have come from the Enemy, teachings comprising erroneous lies meant to torment the souls of women and men alike. Such teachings are meant to turn women and men against each other, and they are meant to destroy marriages and families. The Evil One has attacked females, as well as males, ever since he first approached Eve in the Garden of Eden—do not forget that."

Andela's face rose. She engaged Madam Mercy eye to eye. "I've always been taught to submit, and accept the truth," she spoke with a tone of dejection.

Madam Mercy did not break eye contact. Compassion emanated from her soul. "Accept the truth, yes, always. But the *truth* preached by men is not always the truth of God. Submit, yes, whenever it is true and right to submit. But remember, there is only one God, and no one else has the right to assume his role. The Enemy does not accept truth, and he rebelled so vehemently against godly submission that he ushered into existence the reality of spiritual death, and his actions served to spark the fires of hell. There is no end to what the Enemy will do to create *false truths*, or what he will do to destroy any relationship that has been ordained by the Creator."

Andela was aware that many of the *truths* she had been taught regarding women did not seem right. "So…," she began, coaxing Madam Mercy to continue.

"So you should always submit to truth, but never to falsehood, and you should seek wisdom and knowledge so that you can know the difference. There is one true God, and you should never replace him with any lesser god, whether that god be male or female, human or material, physical or spiritual, friend or foe, alien or family, peasant or king, secular or clergy—it matters not! There is only one true God, and it is his truth that guides mankind into the joys of life eternal, whether that life follows physical bliss or physical woe during the brief span of mortal existence."

Andela wanted to hear more. "Okay, so, can I ask another question?"

Madam Mercy hesitated. She was aware of the importance of Andela's mission, and she did not want to delay Andela's departure much longer; but she knew that truth bestowed through spoken words could impart spiritual guidance, and that such guidance could help equip a young female for battle. And beyond all doubt, she knew that Andela would be venturing into battle when she entered Bill's land. "What is your question?"

"Well, since Eve ate the forbidden fruit first, does that mean that husbands now rule over their wives? Is there a curse on wives now?"

Madam Mercy took some time deliberating, but she never turned her face from Andela.

"There were several judgments that occurred after mankind chose to disobey God," explained Madam Mercy. "For one thing, mankind was ejected from the Garden of Eden, removed from access to the Tree of Life, and doomed to physical death. This judgment applies to all human beings born upon the earth from that time forward. In a sense, mankind became totally animal, totally like the animals created before Adam. But unlike the other animals that now inhabit the earth, mankind remains totally spiritual, and men are inescapably destined to one of two fates—eternal life, or eternal death."

Andela nodded. She was anxious to hear about husbands and wives. Her eyes made it clear that she was ready for her tutor to continue.

"Another judgment was cast upon the Dragon, also referred to as the Serpent. His body was transformed to that of a snake. Furthermore, God decreed that there would be negative relationships between the Serpent's descendants and the descendants of Eve—something that would make it more difficult, one would think, for Satan's descendants to influence Eve's descendants in the manner that Satan influenced Eve. Thus, the judgment cast against the Serpent involved generations to follow."

Again Andela nodded.

"Now I want to point out something important about the judgment against Adam," said Madam Mercy. "All men die, but not all men have to work and sweat in order to eat bread. Some men are born into wealthy families and never have to work at all. The ground was cursed, and that affects mankind in general, but the judgment against Adam, namely that he would eat bread by the sweat of his face, was placed against Adam himself—Adam personally. No one else is named in this specific judgment. And notably, Adam's descendants are not named. Unlike judgments made against mankind in general, such as the eviction from the Garden of Eden, the judgment that Adam would eat bread by the sweat of his face was a judgment against Adam in particular. It is still true that, as a result of Adam's sin, many men have to work in order to obtain bread, but such is not true for all men."

Andela did not nod; she was too busy thinking. She was searching her mind for the exact words applied to the judgment against Eve in the third chapter of Genesis. Was it a judgment against women in general, or a judgment against Eve in particular? She couldn't quite remember— this was not a passage of Scripture she memorized verbatim, and she could not recall how it was written.

Madam Mercy continued. "God pronounced judgments against the woman. They were pronounced against *the woman*, singular, not against women in general, and not against the woman's descendants. It is consistent with the entire Word of God that individuals sometimes reap consequences for their own misdeeds, and this applied to Eve. And the first two judgments pronounced against Eve were that she would get pregnant often and bear children in sorrow, judgments that obviously do not apply to all women—some women never get pregnant at all, no matter how hard they try.

"And then there was the other judgment against Eve, namely that Adam would *rule over* her. Notably, *rule over* in this passage uses the same two Hebrew words later used to point out that Cain, the firstborn, would *rule over* Abel, the second born, though this was contingent upon Cain's life pleasing God. We know, of course, that Cain's life did not please God, and that he ended up murdering Abel rather than *ruling over* him. But at any rate, *rule over* in both of these instances means having a higher position of social influence. Thus, Eve lost social influence as a consequence of her sin, and remember that her sin was not only that of yielding to the Dragon's temptation, but also that of persuading Adam to do likewise."

Andela faced Madam Mercy for several seconds. She sensed a burdensome frustration dissipating from her mind as she contemplated Madam Mercy's explanation—the explanation that Eve's judgment was not cast against all women. Madam Mercy's answer was simple enough; in fact, it was so simple that Andela wondered how she missed seeing it herself. She had often heard the passages regarding the judgments that came after Adam and Eve sinned, but she never really grasped the particulars of how those judgments were written, not until Madam Mercy pointed them out.

"So," said Andela, "the judgments against Eve in Genesis were against Eve herself, they don't mean that wives have to do whatever their husbands say, right?"

Madam Mercy's expression gravened. Dark eyes held Andela in staid regard. "The Creator has given each human being the freedom to choose who will ultimately rule his or her heart, and it should never be another human, or self, or anything besides the Creator. Even Eve, with the particular judgments that were cast against her, should never have disobeyed God in order to follow directions from Adam. It is true that one of the judgments against her reduced her influence with Adam—Adam was given more authority than Eve in their ongoing mortal relationship—but even then, Eve's *god* was meant to remain God. Adam was not to take God's place in Eve's life."

Andela peered at Madam Mercy.

Madam Mercy continued. "Any woman permitting her husband to have ultimate rule over her heart is guilty of idolatry, a dire sin, and any husband who turns his back on God in order to please or serve his wife is also guilty of idolatry. A wife may serve her husband in submission to the Creator, and her husband may serve her likewise, but neither should be ultimately ruled by the other—no human being should ever become a god to another human being."

"Okay, so, what does the Bible mean when it says that Eve was created to be Adam's *help meet*?" posed Andela. "That was before Adam and Eve sinned, so it couldn't have anything to do with the judgment against Eve. Are all wives just supposed to be *help meets*?"

"Just *help meets*?" returned Madam Mercy. "Don't you remember my explanation as to why a non-spiritual animal could not be a *help meet* to Adam? I think you have the wrong idea of what the Bible means by *help meet*."

"I do?"

"To begin with, the Bible never states that Eve was Adam's *help meet*, it just infers it. When God decided that Adam needed a *help meet*, he first made animals that Adam named, not Eve. Nonetheless, I would agree that the inference that Eve was Adam's acceptable *help meet* is strong enough to conclude that Eve was, in fact, Adam's *help meet*. But what do you think the term *help meet* means?"

Andela's mind was musing over spiritual animals being created as candidates for Adam's *help meet*, but she managed to focus on Madam Mercy's question. "Well, isn't that like a plumber's assistant or something—someone who just helps someone else who is in charge of a job?"

"Not hardly," replied Madam Mercy, speaking in a remonstrative tone. "The Hebrew word for *help* in Genesis chapter two, verse eighteen, is the word *ezer*. The Hebrew word *ezer* is also translated as the word *help* that is found in Psalms chapter thirty-three, verse twenty, where David says—*Our soul waiteth for the Lord: He is our 'help' and our shield.* And the root word for *ezer* in the ancient Hebrew language, namely *azar*, is translated as *helper* in Psalms chapter fifty-four, verse four, when David declares—*Behold, God is mine 'helper.'* The word *ezer* means *help* or *aid*, and it derives from the word *azar*, which means *surround*, *protect*, *aid*, *help*, and *succor*. When one looks at the use of the word *ezer* in the Old Testament, it appears appropriate to conclude that the *helper* is generally above or more capable than the one receiving help."

"Whoa," exclaimed Andela. "That sure turns the tables. So then, was Eve was created above Adam? Does that mean…"

"Hold on," interjected Madam Mercy. "You've forgotten the word *meet*—Eve was Adam's *help meet*, not just his *help*."

"Oh, so what does that mean?"

"It means that Eve was created equal to Adam, not above him. The word *meet* comes from the Hebrew word *kenegdo*, meaning *face-to-face like of him*, or more loosely translated, *like companion*. The prefix *ke* means *like*, the suffix *o* means *of him*, and the word *neged* comes from *nagad*, meaning *face-to-face*. So in short, I believe it would be appropriate to say that Adam and Eve were coequal helpers, helping one another."

Andela's mind drifted back to what Madam Mercy said about the animals that Adam named. "Well, in that case, were the animals that Adam named—the animals created after Adam—coequal with Adam?"

"I think there was that potential, at least for one of them."

"One of them?"

"During the period of creation demarcated by Genesis chapter two, verses nineteen and twenty, I believe these animals, namely spiritual beings created between the creations of Adam and Eve, were created with the intent of coming up with a *help meet* for Adam. However, the end of verse twenty states that none of these animals sufficed as a *help meet* for Adam, and at that point, or perhaps sometime after the creation of Eve, I believe that God gave dominion over all of these animals to mankind. Such dominion is made evident in Genesis chapter one, verse twenty-eight, and this turn of events may have played a role in the Dragon's evil rebellion and his hateful temptation of Eve." Madam Mercy dropped her face. "I have no relationship with demons, they hate me, they hate all that is good."

Andela felt a cold shiver climb her spine. She decided to redirect the conversation. "So Adam and Eve were created as coequals, okay, but what about now?"

Madam Mercy recovered her bearing and raised questioning eyes. She said nothing.

"What about all that stuff written in the New Testament about wives submitting to their husbands?" Andela blurted.

As before, Madam Mercy appeared grateful to be moving to a subject other than that of the spiritual animals that were created after

Adam. "English is one of my favorite languages," she responded, "it's so colorful and versatile. But the New Testament was not written in English."

Andela skewed her brows. "So, are you saying the Bible doesn't mean what it says in English?"

Madam Mercy raised an open palm and flipped her hand outward, seeming to wave Andela's statement aside. "I did not say that. The King James English version of the New Testament is quite useful for those who will take it in context and seek the Spirit's guidance, as are several other Greek to English translations of the New Testament."

"Okay, I'm willing to learn," returned Andela, feeling frustrated as old questions surfaced in her mind—questions that had bothered her for years. "So what does the Bible mean when it says for wives to submit to their husbands?"

Madam Mercy sensed Andela's frustration and impatience, but on this particular point she would not be rushed. She settled more deeply into the grassy surface of the ground beneath them and addressed Andela with a look of longsuffering contemplation. Only after Andela relaxed furrowed brows did she resume speaking.

"One term for *submit* in the Greek means to *place under*," Madam Mercy explained, speaking in a didactic manner. "This word can be translated into English as either *submit* or *obey*, and it is always the New Testament term used in regard to wives submitting to or obeying their husbands, with the one exception of a particular reference to Sarah and Abraham, but I'll come back to that. Thus, each wife should place herself under her husband's protection and provision, though I realize that many women must help provide for their families and help protect their families, especially when husbands are disabled, or when husbands must work far away from home."

Andela resisted the temptation to ask questions that might be jumping ahead. She did not want to miss anything that Madam Mercy had to say about husbands and wives.

Madam Mercy continued, "In the book of First Peter, all Christians are instructed to be *subject* one to another, and this is the same Greek term, the term meaning to *place under*, that is used when instructing wives to *submit* to their husbands. It would be ridiculous to interpret this instruction to mean that Christians can give each other orders, bossing each other around. This instruction means that Christians should care about one another, support one another, and respect one another, and it also means that they should be willing to accept protection and provision from one another. Likewise, it would be ridiculous to interpret this same Greek word to mean that a wife has to take orders from her husband and do whatever he tells her to do, the word simply does not have that meaning."

"So," interjected Andela, "all Christians are instructed to *submit* to each other, and the Greek New Testament uses the same word for *submission* that is used when wives are instructed to *submit* to their husbands, is that right?"

"Yes."

"So, does that mean that Christian husbands are supposed to submit to Christian wives? I mean, since both of them are Christian, and since all Christians are supposed to submit to each other, then wouldn't that mean that husbands are supposed to submit to wives as well as wives being supposed to submit to husbands?"

Madam Mercy looked somewhat startled by Andela's question. "Well, yes, when husbands are commanded to love their wives, it would be absurd to interpret this to mean that wives do not need to love their husbands—Christians are all supposed to love one another. And when wives are commanded to submit to their husbands, it would be absurd to interpret this to mean that husbands do not need to submit to their wives—Christians are all supposed to submit to one another. But still, the specific instruction given for wives to submit to their husbands implies special responsibilities, especially for the husbands."

"Special responsibilities?"

"Yes. Remember that human beings are one-hundred percent spiritual beings, and also one-hundred percent animal beings. There is no difference between men and women spiritually. Verses twenty-six through twenty-eight of Galatians chapter three point out that humans become children of God through Christ Jesus, referring to spiritual life, and those verses go on to point out that, in regard to spiritual life, there is no differentiation between men of differing nationalities, no differentiation regarding social status, and no differentiation pertaining to gender. On the other hand, there are differences between men and women on the animal level. It is common for responsibilities to vary between sexes in the animal kingdom, and while living temporal lives on earth, human beings are members of the earth's animal kingdom as well as being spiritual creatures."

"Well then, are wives to submit more than husbands?"

Madam Mercy could not help smiling. "If what you mean by *submit* is to accept protection and support, then generally this is true, yes."

"But surely this doesn't mean that a husband can sit back and give orders to a wife, and she has to do whatever he says, does it?" inquired Andela, posing her question with a note of exasperation.

Madam Mercy laughed. "No it does not. But if a husband is all he should be, a woman might be able to accept some requests now and then, which brings us back to the subject of Sarah and Abraham."

"Oh yea, you said that they were some sort of exception?"

"Yes," said Madam Mercy. "There is another word in the Greek that is sometimes translated as *obey* in English, and this Greek word means *to listen attentively to*. This word appears in Scripture in regard to children obeying their parents, and in regard to servants obeying their masters, and in regard to the wind and the sea obeying the Lord—it indicates that what is said should be listened to, and should generally be done."

"Generally be done?"

"Yes, generally—not always."

"What do you mean?"

Madam Mercy shrugged one shoulder. "Well, remember that Peter and other apostles disobeyed the reigning High Priest and Council when they were asked to do something they considered ungodly, or against the will of God. Remember how they replied—*we ought to obey God rather than men*."

"Okay, so if a husband asks his wife to do something against the will of God, then she doesn't have to do it, right?"

Madam Mercy shook her head. "Of course not, but that applies to everyone—no one ever has to disobey God under any circumstances. But remember, the Greek word for *listen attentively to* is never used in directing wives to obey their husbands, it's only used as an example of what may occur in a relationship such as that between Sarah and Abraham."

"How's that?"

"In the book of First Peter, chapter three, verse one, wives are directed to be in *subjection* to their own husbands. And as is always the case with such instruction, the term *subjection* comes from the Greek term meaning to *place under*."

Madam Mercy paused, and Andela nodded her comprehension. Then Madam Mercy continued, "In verse five of the same chapter, a particular reason is presented as to why women should be in subjection to their husbands, namely because in the *old time* the *holy women* were in subjection to their husbands. And again, the term *subjection* comes from the Greek word meaning to *place under*. Note that this verse is not instructing wives to submit to their husbands, such as already occurred in verse one—rather, it is pointing out a specific reason why wives should submit to their husbands."

"Okay," said Andela, indicating her continued comprehension.

"Then finally," resumed Madam Mercy, "in verse six, a remarkable example of the *old time* women is given—*Even as Sarah obeyed Abraham, calling him lord*. It is important to note that this example is not a commandment to women, rather, it is a unique example of a relationship between a wife and husband that existed among the *old time* women. This one unique example, regarding Sarah obeying Abraham, is the only time in the entire New Testament that the Greek term for *listen attentively to* is used in reference to a wife responding to her husband."

"So, are you saying that Sarah actually took orders from her husband?"

"Well, let's just say that Abraham won sufficient respect from Sarah that she was willing to generally follow his advice and instruction, yes. But here's my point—this passage about Sarah and Abraham is not a commandment to wives, rather, it is an example of something that is okay, and even desirable. It is not difficult to believe that a woman could accept and follow directions from a godly husband such as Abraham— a husband who is supportive and provides his wife with servants, a husband who has such a relationship with God that both he and his wife are visited by angels, and a husband whose relationship with God results in the miracle of his wife having a baby that she greatly desires when she is too old to get pregnant. Sarah respected her husband and was able to follow his leadership, and was even able to respond to his verbal requests—there's nothing wrong with that. But again, this is an example, not a command. Wives are not commanded to *listen attentively to* in regard to their husbands, and they are not commanded to call their husbands *lord*, such as Sarah did Abraham—though when a man arises upon the earth worthy of such respect, then it appears that such is permissible."

Andela nodded. "Okay, so the Greek term that means *listen attentively to* generally suggests following orders, but not without regard to right and wrong, and not without regard to the will of God. But this term is never used when wives are instructed to obey or submit to their husbands, it's always that other term—to *place under*."

"Correct, and do not think that the absence of the instruction for wives to *listen attentively to* their husbands is some sort of oversight or mistake. When one considers how many times the instruction to *submit* or *obey* appears in the New Testament in regard to husbands and wives, the fact that the Greek term for *listen attentively to* never appears in regard to wives being instructed to submit to or obey their husbands is a significant factor. And besides that, Christ taught against the idea of human beings trying to *lord over* other human beings, as can be found in verses such as Matthew chapter twenty, verses twenty-five through twenty-eight, and Luke chapter twenty-two, verses twenty-five through twenty-six."

"That's a relief," stated Andela. "It's rather frightening to think that getting married means a woman has to do whatever a man says, especially when it's a man that she's supposed to live with for the rest of her life."

"Quite so, but I believe there are good reasons why the Bible stresses that husbands should love their wives, and that wives should submit to their husbands. When God made Adam and Eve, he made them part of the animal world, male and female, and he put special psychological and emotional needs within their physiological makeups. Surely a woman wants honor and respect from her husband, but I believe she has a special desire for love, to know that her husband cares about her, is true to her sexually, and is concerned about meeting her physical and emotional needs, as well as being willing to protect her with his life. And surely a man wants love from his wife, but I believe he has a special desire for honor and respect, to know that his wife supports his efforts to meet her needs, and that she is true to him sexually, and that she looks to him above all others, apart from God, for sustenance."

"Oh, I agree," acknowledged Andela. "But still, it's a relief to know that wives aren't meant to take orders from their husbands like privates taking orders from sergeants in the military."

"No doubt," rejoined Madam Mercy. "I think it's undeniable that the common misunderstanding of the term *obey* in the English version of the Bible has placed a great deal of undue stress upon the shoulders of newlywed husbands."

Andela began to nod her heartfelt agreement, but then she stopped and stared upon Madam Mercy's face. "Husbands? You mean wives, don't you? I mean, you meant to say that the misunderstanding of the term *obey* has placed a great deal of stress upon the shoulders of newlywed wives, right?"

Madam Mercy faced Andela in silence. She found herself amused by Andela's befuddled countenance. At last she responded. "It is far easier for human beings to perceive stress and frustration from their own perspectives than from the perspectives of others, and there is no doubt that misunderstandings of the term *obey* can be a real frustration and aggravation to wives. But consider this—what if wives were taught that they would be miserable failures before God unless they could somehow coerce their husbands into taking orders from them? There are too many challenges and irritations within the fallen society of mankind without adding a false sense of failure in the home and marriage due to incorrect doctrinal teachings regarding the word *obey*. Husbands should not be made to experience tormenting feelings of failure if they cannot somehow force or convince their wives to take orders from them, the Bible simply does not mean this when it refers to wives obeying their husbands. What the Bible does mean is that wives should acknowledge their husbands' responsibilities, and that they should give deference to their husbands above all others apart from God in regard to accepting support and protection. Both husbands and wives are free to say yes or no when requested to do something by their partners, but in good and loving relationships, one would expect more yeses than noes."

"Wow," said Andela, "I never thought of it that way before. I guess it really could put a lot of stress on a man to think that he was a failure unless he could make his wife take orders from him. So then, understanding what the Bible teaches about submission in marriage could be a great relief to both wives and husbands—thanks for pointing that out."

"You are most welcome."

Andela rested her mind for a few moments, relishing the truths she had learned and facing Madam Mercy with an expression of heartfelt appreciation. She realized that some of her most important questions were getting answered, and she felt better, but not all better. She continued facing Madam Mercy as she reengaged her mind in thought, grappling to find appropriate words to manifest the feelings churning within her breast. Such feelings often prodded her to learn more about something, or perhaps to pose a challenging question about some religious doctrine that many of her friends took for granted. During hours and hours of studying and pondering the Word of God, both in groups and on her own, she had developed a sense of inner guidance, something she attributed to the Holy Spirit.

"I will cherish the knowledge you've given me," said Andela, "but..."

"But what?" Madam Mercy asked.

"But, why not Sarah? Abraham was great leader, and I know that Sarah was a great woman, but God chose Sarah and Abraham mainly because of Abraham, right? Why can't women be great leaders?"

Madam Mercy eyed Andela with a piercing expression. "Have you read only part of the Bible?"

Andela sensed that she was being reprimanded, but she felt more curious than chastised. "Why no, I've read it all, the whole thing. But what do you mean?"

Madam Mercy tossed her head and turned her eyes toward the golden cliff to the north, as if drawing inspiration from the realm beyond the great wall. Her mannerism reminded Andela of a majestic mare shaking its mane above an open plain. Then she peered back at Andela. "It is true enough that the animal roles of human beings lend themselves toward males assuming roles of social leadership more often than females, but human beings are totally spiritual as well as totally animal, and they are supposed to be ruled more by the spirit than by the flesh. In other words, the spirit is to have preeminence."

Andela leaned forward, drawn by the tone and elements of Madam Mercy's words. "And?"

Madam Mercy folded her hands upon her lap with her legs draped beneath the folds of her scarlet gown. "In matters with strong ties to the animal kingdom, there are distinctions between *male* and *female* that do not exist in the spiritual realm," she began, locking eyes with Andela. "Due to animal distinctions, sex and marriage are only to be shared between male and female, and many physical tasks and activities are better suited to one sex or the other, giving more variety and depth to the physical experience of human beings on earth, and this is good."

"It's good," echoed Andela, sensing something wonderful and inspiring about her femininity, but also sensing that there was something else, something apart from, or perhaps beyond, animal gender.

"On the other hand," continued Madam Mercy, "in matters set further apart from the animal kingdom, there is less distinction between *male* and *female*, and oftentimes no distinction at all. For example, when it comes to membership in the family of our Creator, there is no male or female distinction—each individual is a member just the same, regardless of gender. Therefore, women are eligible for service in the spiritual realm, and note this Andela, women are also eligible for service in the physical realm, as is evidenced by the fact that among the judges that the Creator raised up to judge over Israel was a woman, namely Deborah. There is no indication that God considered Deborah less appropriate for her position than a man, or that she was less honored."

"Really?" returned Andela. She had heard Deborah mentioned in Sunday school class, but never in the manner that Madam Mercy presented her.

"Yes, really. And consider the prophets named in Holy Scripture. Surely one of the greatest honors bestowed upon a Biblical prophet was that of personally witnessing the coming of the Messiah and proclaiming his presence to the people of Jerusalem. Did you know that this honor was bestowed upon a female prophet?"

"A female prophet? You mean there was a female prophet?"

Madam Mercy smiled. "You've never heard of Anna the prophetess?"

Andela blinked in surprise. "Oh, oh yea, I have, I just never, um…"

"You never realized that she was an official, bona fide prophet?"

"I guess not."

After playfully shrugging one shoulder, Madam Mercy spoke again. "And in regard to the early Church leaders, can you name a female deacon? One who was a leader or ruler of many, including Paul?"

"What?" retorted Andela. "A female deacon? A ruler? A ruler over Paul?"

Madam Mercy gazed upon Andela's awestruck features for several seconds, and then lifted her head and laughed merrily. "You should learn Greek, my child."

"Greek?"

"Please do not misunderstand what I am about to say," requested Madam Mercy, looking back toward Andela. "The translators were quite good—some of your English versions of the Bible are surprisingly accurate, but there are some little things that annoy me sometimes, like the Greek word translated as *servant* in reference to the woman named Phebe, who…"

"Oh yea!" interjected Andela, interrupting Madam Mercy in mid-sentence. "I remember her. Are you saying Phebe was a deacon? Or, I mean, a deaconess? That is, if there is such a thing."

"Certainly there is such a thing," affirmed Madam Mercy. "And as I was beginning to explain, the word translated from Greek to English as *servant* in reference to Phebe is the same word translated as *deacons* in its plural form in First Timothy, so I'd feel much better about it if the word *deaconess* were used in reference to Phebe rather than the word *servant*."

"Wow, I never knew that," said Andela.

"Furthermore, the imperative statement made in First Timothy that deacons should be the *husbands of one wife*, a phrase that may be translated from the Greek as *one woman adult males*, does not mean that a single man cannot be a deacon, but rather, it means that a male deacon is not permitted to be married to more than one woman. In other words, if a man is a husband, then he needs to be the husband of only one wife in order to be a deacon. And this statement obviously does not mean that a woman cannot be a deacon, because Phebe was a deaconess. Furthermore, the statement that a bishop must be *blameless, the husband of one wife*, means that a male bishop is not to be a polygamist. A literal, Greek to English translation of the first portion of First Timothy chapter three, verse two, would read as follows—*Fall short now the overseer unblamable be, one woman adult male. A good* translation into English, then, would read as follows—*Now the bishop should not be guilty of falling short in the following, being a man who limits himself to one wife.* Thus, if a bishop is a man, he should not be a polygamist. So then, this instruction to men is not saying that a woman cannot be a bishop, since a woman is not guilty of *being a man who is a polygamist.* It may be assumed, however, that a female bishop should not have more than one husband."

"Wow, really? No one's ever told me, I mean, thanks for explaining that," Andela stuttered. Her mind was trying to digest so much information that she found it difficult to speak.

"And would you like to hear more on the subject of women in the Bible," asked Madam Mercy.

"Oh, sure," said Andela.

Madam Mercy appeared pleased. "Okay then, when it was translated that Phebe had been a *succorer* of many, including Paul, the translators came up with an English word that only appears once in the entire King James Version of the Bible, namely *succorer.* This English word *succorer* is translated from a Greek word referring to a leader or ruler. In fact, the actual Greek word translated as *succorer* is a feminine derivative of the Greek word translated as *rule* in the passage that states—*Let the elders that 'rule' well be counted worthy of double honor.* And furthermore, the same Greek word that is translated as *succorer* could be translated as *patroness* or *protectress* or *a woman set over others*, and it is the feminine form of a Greek word that can be translated as *leader* or *champion.* So, I think it is logical that a good Biblical translation should point out that Phebe was a deaconess, and that she was a noteworthy ruler."

"Oh, wow, a female deacon. That's so, well, refreshing."

"Um hum," said Madam Mercy, nodding as she looked at Andela. "Don't forget, though, that one of the most crucial physical tasks assigned to any male or female upon the earth is that of raising children, and this is a task that may be shared by those men and women who are not fortunate enough to bear their own children."

"Oh yes, I agree with that," said Andela. "But it's kind of nice to know that women can do things like Deborah and Phebe."

"Of course, and don't forget the honor bestowed upon Mary, the physical mother of our Lord and Savior. Do you realize that the Messiah came to this earth through the bloodline of a woman?"

"What?" inquired Andela. "What do you mean?"

"In Matthew chapter one, verse sixteen, we read that Jacob begat Joseph, the husband of Mary, and this is correct—a man named Jacob was the physical father of Joseph."

Madam Mercy paused, letting this point settle in Andela's mind.

"Okay," said Andela.

Madam Mercy resumed, "In Luke chapter three, verse twenty-three, we read that Joseph was *of Heli*, or at least that is what we read in the Greek. In the English translation, the words *the son* were added by the translators, so we read that Joseph was *the son of Heli*, but in fact, Joseph was not the physical son of Heli, he was Heli's son-in-law."

"His son-in-law?"

"Yes, Heli was the father of Mary, and the long lineage of Jesus given in Luke chapter three, going all the way back to Adam, was the lineage of his mother, Mary."

Andela gazed at Madam Mercy in wonder. "I've never heard that before."

"No? Have you never noticed that the names in the lineage given in Matthew differ from those given in Luke until you get back to David the son of Jesse?"

Andela looked puzzled. "I guess, um, I guess I've never paid that much attention to all those names."

"Joseph was a descendant of Solomon the son of David, and Mary was a descendant of Nathan the son of David. The Bible verses found in Numbers chapter twenty-seven, verse eight, along with Numbers chapter thirty-six, verses six through eight, make it clear that Mary was able to transfer the rights of her lineage to Jesus, given the fact that Mary had no brothers, and given the fact that she married within her own tribe. Both Mary and Joseph were members of the tribe of Judah, and they were both of the house and lineage of David. Thus, the prophetic bloodline of the Messiah came through a woman. And if you think about it, the physical bloodline of the Messiah had to come through a woman, because Jesus was born of a virgin."

Andela was awed. "Oh my, I never knew that. I mean, I knew that Jesus was born of a virgin, I just never knew about the bloodline."

"And don't forget about the woman who, along with her husband, was a religious teacher. Priscilla and her husband Aquila held church in their own house, and there is no indication that Priscilla only taught women—she apparently even taught the eloquent evangelist Apollos, as did her husband."

Andela's eyes danced with excitement. She began realizing that many of the customs and teachings regarding women that had troubled her heart for so many years were doctrinally incorrect, and she sensed power in Madam Mercy's words—power to release her mind from ignorance and power to free her heart to rejoice in the truth of God. But then she remembered a couple of other matters that puzzled and disturbed her. "Great, that answers a lot of questions," she said, focusing upon Madam Mercy in a manner that evidenced a new concern. "But what does the Bible mean when it says that the husband is the head of the wife? And what about women covering their heads?"

"You leave no stone unturned," commented Madam Mercy, presenting a fond smile in response to Andela's questions. "I'll answer your second question first. There are a couple of times in the Book of First Corinthians that Paul expresses his personal opinion, meaning that he is permitted to express his own personal view rather than giving a commandment of God. To me this is enlightening, for it shows that we are permitted to have personal opinions in many matters—we do not all have to agree about everything. There are crucial *spiritual truths*, of course, and I'm not saying that we shouldn't agree about those, but there are also many less important matters, and I think it's nice that we are permitted to have different opinions when it comes to less important matters, don't you agree?"

"Sure," responded Andela, anxious to hear what Madam Mercy was leading up to.

Madam Mercy continued, "In First Corinthians chapter seven, beginning with verse six, Paul says—*But I speak this by permission, and not of commandment*—and he goes on to state his own personal opinion that it is good for the unmarried and widows to remain single. Now don't misunderstand Paul, he makes it clear in First Corinthians chapter nine, verse five, that it would have been totally acceptable for him travel with a wife, as did other apostles. It is simply his personal view that remaining single is a better choice. And certainly those men and women who live their lives as single adults may find encouragement and comfort in noting Paul's opinion."

"Yes, I agree," said Andela.

"Then," resumed Madam Mercy, "in First Corinthians chapter eleven, verses three through fifteen, Paul expresses another personal opinion that is not a commandment from God, namely that women should wear long hair when they pray or preach in a church service, and that men should wear short hair."

"Preach!" interjected Andela. "You mean, Paul says that a woman can preach in church?"

"Certainly," responded Madam Mercy. "The second verse in the first chapter of First Corinthians begins with the words, *Unto the church of God which is at Corinth*, and it is most appropriate to conclude that Paul's instructions in the eleventh chapter of First Corinthians are in regard to church gatherings. Furthermore, the Greek word translated as *prophesieth* in verse five of First Corinthians, chapter eleven, notably a word referring to women, can also be translated as *preaching* or *speaking God's message*—it comes from the same Greek root word as the Greek word translated as *prophesieth* in First Corinthians chapter fourteen, verse four, where Paul compares speaking in an unknown tongue to speaking words that can be understood and thereby edify the church."

"Wow, no one ever told me that," stated Andela.

"Well, there is much to learn from Scripture," said Madam Mercy. "But now then, back to Paul's teaching about hair when it comes to praying or preaching in a church service."

"Sure, go on," consented Andela.

"Paul contends that nature teaches us that long hair is a glory to a woman and a shame to a man. He feels so strongly about the hair issue that he issues a personal command for the Corinthians take his advice, as revealed in First Corinthians chapter eleven, verse one. Long hair is presented as a covering that every woman, in Paul's opinion, should wear on her head when praying or preaching in church, and he also contends that every man who prays or preaches in church should have short hair. But a key verse that must be observed in this passage of Scripture is the concluding verse, namely First Corinthians chapter eleven, verse sixteen—*But if any man seem to be contentious, we have no such custom, neither the churches of God.* In other words, it is Paul's opinion that you should remain single, and that you should keep long hair if you want to pray or preach in a church service, but it would be no breach of God's commandments for you to shorten your hair and preach in church, and also get married, even though it would be contrary to Paul's advice. It is very notable, at least in my opinion, that Paul makes it clear that the Corinthians are not necessarily in the wrong because they fail to follow his personal command regarding hair—he would prefer that they conduct themselves in accordance with his command, but he recognizes that he is not God, and that men and women are not guilty of sin against God because they do not go along with his personal views when those views are not commandments from God."

Again Andela nodded, and this time she also shrugged. "I like the long hair," she stated. She made no mention of marriage—she figured that Madam Mercy knew that she was on a mission to bring a man to spiritual redemption and then to hopefully accompany him to the marriage alter.

"Your other question I've already answered, at least in part," resumed Madam Mercy. "When I explained that the Greek word used in the Bible for *obey*, regarding wives obeying their husbands, means to *place under*, well, that is why the husband may be referred to as the *head*. The head of a river is the source of water that supplies the river with water, and a husband is to be a source of emotional fulfillment for his wife, and he should seek to nourish her inner sense of self-worth. When he is able, the husband should also be a source of physical provision and protection. Understand that a wife should also seek to protect her husband, but a husband is generally given greater responsibility when it comes to protection, so long as health and other circumstances permit. Also, in keeping with what I taught you regarding obedience, the term *head* does not mean *boss*—it does not mean that a husband is like the foreman at a work site. Rather, it means that he is someone who seeks to support, protect, and nourish his wife, even like Christ serves the Church."

"So, does this make the husband the spiritual head of the family?"

Madam Mercy winced, steadying herself with one hand on the soft ground. She peered at Andela with a surprised look of concern—the question was apparently one that she did not expect. She raised an open palm and drew a deep breath, and then lowered her hand as she began speaking. "Remember, my dear, that the human race is both spiritual and animal. And remember that sometimes, in Scripture, comparisons are made between spiritual and physical relationships. There are certain roles in the human family that exist because of the animal component of mankind. It is within the physical realm that the husband is the head of the family, not the spiritual realm."

Andela stared in bewilderment. This was not what she remembered learning in Sunday school. "So, who is the spiritual head of the family?"

Again Madam Mercy looked surprised by Andela's question, but she managed to maintain her composure. "Christ, my dear, Jesus Christ is the spiritual head of all believers, male or female, married or single, child or adult—there is no other spiritual head. Remember Galatians chapter three, verse twenty-eight—*There is neither Jew nor Greek, there is neither bond nor free, there is neither male nor female: for ye are all one in Christ Jesus*. If there is neither male nor female in Christ, then obviously there is neither single nor married in Christ. And remember Romans chapter twelve, verse five—*So we, being many, are one body in Christ, and every one members one of another*. Thus, all Christians make up one body, and Christ is the head of that body.

"And furthermore, a good Greek to English translation of Paul's remark in First Corinthians chapter eleven, verse eleven, would be as follows—*Nevertheless, neither is man distinct from the woman, neither the woman distinct from the man, in the Lord*. And also remember Colossians chapter one, verse eighteen—*And he is the head of the body, the church*. So then, Christ is the spiritual head of every member of the body, women and children included, and no member of the body of Christ is meant to have two spiritual heads."

"Wait," interjected Andela, sensing an epiphany within her heart and mind. "You mean a woman has no spiritual head other than God? I mean, Christ? But then, Christ is God, right?"

Madam Mercy smiled in affirmation. "There are many members in the body of Christ, and those members have many different gifts, talents, and callings, but there is only one head to God's family, namely he himself, in the Person of Jesus Christ." Then a serious and admonishing expression beset Madam Mercy's features. "No man, woman, or child should ever enter idolatry by granting spiritual headship to any person or being other than God himself. A husband, wife, father, mother, or child may provide spiritual leadership within a family as guided by the Holy Spirit, but Christ should always be recognized as the spiritual Head."

Andela opened her mouth to respond, hoping to encourage Madam Mercy to tell her more, but Madam Mercy raised both hands and politely shook her head.

"There is more for you to learn about marriage, wives, and women in the Bible, but you must pursue this at a later time. We need to get back to the subject that started all of this discussion so that you can go after Bill," stated Madam Mercy.

"Oh yes, Bill," said Andela, rising to her feet. "I'd better be going."

"Sex!" hailed Madam Mercy before Andela could take a single step. "I need to finish with the subject of sex."

Andela halted, turned, and sat back down; staring toward Madam Mercy with curiosity and concern. She waited for Madam Mercy to speak.

"I'll be brief. Before the first disobedience against God, the *original sin,* mankind possessed the physical nature to be monogamous, and to be true to one's spouse. There are several animals with almost equivalent nature, though sometimes these animals sexually cheat from time to time, something that man was never meant to do. Anyway, the original physical nature given to mankind was far different than the fallen nature, and by *fallen nature*, I mean the nature that mankind acquired through disobedience to God. And furthermore, man was not originally subject to his physical nature, rather, the spiritual component ruled over the physical, even though there was little or no conflict between the spiritual and physical natures."

Andela spoke up. "Tell me more about the original nature of man, I mean, especially in regard to sex."

"Well, if you look at Scripture, neither the male nor the female had to wear clothing. There was no propensity to engage sexually with any creature other than with one's mate, and there was no friction or adversity between the spirit and the flesh. The human anatomy could be admired in unveiled beauty by either sex without temptation to betray one's sexual partner, and this would have remained true as Adam and Eve bore children and their children bore children, if not for the greater betrayal—the betrayal of True Love."

"What do you mean?"

"The Creator is Love, and he desires love. He has stated quite plainly—*If you love me, you will keep my commandments*. One way for the first begotten humans to love him was to keep a commandment, namely a simple commandment to abstain from eating the fruit of one particular tree."

"Then there was really a tree, I mean, a real tree?"

"There were many trees," stated Madam Mercy, "many trees and plenty of good fruit. There was only one tree that bore fruit that Adam and Eve were commanded to refrain from eating. And note that the Bible never says that the tree of the knowledge of good and evil was a seed-bearing tree, rather, it was a solitary tree that bore forbidden fruit."

Andela nodded and raised one finger. This was a subject she had pondered extensively, and she had questions about the tree of the knowledge of good and evil. "Well, if obeying God is one way to love him, then will there be another tree in heaven? I mean, another tree with fruit that should not be eaten?"

"There is no mention of such a tree in the last chapter of Revelation, only the Tree of Life is mentioned. I believe the presence of those who have chosen to obey God during their lives upon the earth will bestow honor and love to the Creator forever, even in the absence of evil temptations."

"Good," declared Andela, "and hopefully there won't be any more uprisings among the angels, either."

Madam Mercy turned her eyes upon Andela and stared for several seconds before responding. "What do you mean by angels?"

Andela began feeling uneasy. There was something about the look in Madam Mercy's eyes that made her feel tentative. "You know, Lucifer and the angels—the angels that rebelled against God and were kicked out of heaven."

Madam Mercy shook her head. "Do you not remember our discussion about the dragon? Let me ask you this—do you believe that Eve ate an apple in the Garden of Eden? More specifically, do you believe that the forbidden fruit was an apple?"

"Oh no," returned Andela, sensing inner relief at having knowledge of the matter. "The fact that the fruit in the garden is often referred to as an *apple* is just a tradition that sprang up over the years, I think in the Middle Ages?"

Madam Mercy nodded. "That is correct. And likewise, it is traditional hearsay to teach that there were heavenly angels that rebelled against God."

"Wha, what?" stuttered Andela. "But what about all those verses about Lucifer? And what about the angels that fell from heaven?"

Again Madam Mercy shook her head; but then she faced Andela with an expression of patient endurance. "The word *Lucifer* only appears once in the entire Bible, namely in Isaiah chapter fourteen, verse twelve. Verse four of that chapter establishes the fact that verses four through twenty-three comprise a proverb against the King of Babylon. Verse sixteen plainly states that Lucifer is a man, and this is made very obvious since verse twenty-two reveals that this man's son and nephew were to be affected by God's judgment against him. Thus, the term *Lucifer*, which can also be translated as *Day Star*, refers to a man, namely the King of Babylon."

"Really?"

"Yes, and what's more, verses one through nineteen of Ezekiel chapter twenty-eight also refer to a man, namely the prince of Tyrus. The words about him being a cherub and being in Eden are figurative descriptions, just as the next chapter describes Pharaoh as being a great dragon, and just as chapter thirty-one describes the Assyrian as a cedar in Lebanon made fair by the multitude of his branches so that all the trees of Eden that were in the garden of God envied him. Thus, these two sections of Scripture, one from Isaiah and one from Ezekiel, both refer to men, not to heavenly angels."

"Whoa, no one ever told me that before."

"And in regard to the fallen angels," continued Madam Mercy, "let me point out that the Biblical term *angel* comes from a Greek word meaning *messenger*. This particular Greek word can refer to a human being as well as to a heavenly angel."

"Human being?"

"Yes. The same Greek word that is translated as *messengers* in Luke chapter seven, verse twenty-four, and again in James chapter two, verse twenty-five, is also translated as *angels* in Second Peter chapter two, verses four and eleven, and in Jude verse six. It is clear that the *angels* referred to in Second Peter chapter two and in Jude verse six are human beings for a couple of reasons. First, they are reserved in hell until judgment, whereas Satan and his *angels* roam the earth and seek to work evil against mankind. And second, the more commendable *angels* in Second Peter, chapter two, are described as *greater in power and might* than the false teachers mentioned in verse one of the same chapter, and it would be unnecessary to point out that *heavenly angels* are greater in power and might than mortal men. Thus, these verses in Second Peter chapter two compare greater messengers, who do not bring *reviling accusations against dignitaries*, to false prophets, who *speak evil of the things they do not understand.*"

"Oh, wow, I've never heard that before either," said Andela. "But then, isn't there something about angels falling from heaven in the Book of Revelation?"

Madam Mercy responded, "Revelation chapter one, verse twenty, states that the seven stars are the angels of the seven churches, and the following chapters in Revelation make it obvious that the *angels* of the seven churches are the *pastors* of those churches."

"Right, I remember learning about that," acknowledged Andela.

"Well then, doesn't it make sense that the *stars* that were cast to the earth by the dragon's tail in Revelation chapter twelve, verse four, were fallen religious leaders? And if you'll notice, the war in *heaven* between Michael and his angels, and the dragon and his angels, occurred after the birth, crucifixion, and resurrection of Christ, as is made clear in verses five, ten, eleven, twelve, thirteen, and seventeen of Revelation chapter twelve. And remember that the word *heaven* can refer to different things in the Bible, such as the upper atmosphere of the earth, or the visible elements of outer space, or the abode of God. Perhaps the *sons of God* who are mentioned in the first two chapters of Job were able to ascend into the upper regions of the earth's atmosphere, or even beyond, and were able to present themselves before the Lord, but perhaps they were cast down to the lower regions the earth after the victorious resurrection of Jesus Christ. And note that the description of Satan's purpose in appearing before God in Job chapter two, verse one, is exactly the same as that described for the *sons of God*—namely to present themselves before the Lord. This identical purpose, along with the fact that these *sons of God* and Satan were in company with one another, lends evidence that these *sons of God* are Satan's demons—or Satan's angels—whichever one may wish to call them."

Andela thought back to the previous time that Madam Mercy mentioned the *sons of God*, back when they were discussing the great flood. She stared at Madam Mercy in wonder. "So," she finally managed to utter, "Satan and his angels were never angels in heaven? I mean, they were never angels like Michael and Gabriel."

"I should say not."

Andela drew a deep breath. "Good, I'm glad. So I guess heaven, namely where Christians go after they die, is a secure place."

"Yes."

"Oh good," declared Andela. She rested her mind for a few moments and stared upon Madam Mercy.

Madam Mercy surveyed Andela's eyes. "Now, let's get back to what we were discussing. I believe we were discussing the forbidden fruit in the Garden of Eden."

"Oh yeah, well, did anyone else, or anything else, eat the fruit of that tree? I mean, was the fruit okay for someone else to eat?"

Madam Mercy looked upon Andela with startled admiration. "You are a deep thinker, but time is an issue at present. Permit me to point out that Adam and Eve were informed that to eat the forbidden fruit would result in death."

"So, was the fruit poisonous to their biochemical systems? Did it alter brain function or cellular function?"

"They were altered, yes, though I cannot tell you how much of that alteration, if any, came directly from the fruit. Their disobedience comprised spiritual betrayal against the Creator. Thus, Adam and Eve chose another god, namely the Evil One. The Creator is just, and he respected the choice that was made—the Evil One became an alternate god, though a god of death rather than life. True to his holy and just nature, the Creator had to send a Person of himself, his Son, to shed perfect and precious blood in order to bring mankind back into the position of begottenness with God—back to eternal life."

"I think I understand why Christ had to shed his blood for the forgiveness of sins," acknowledged Andela. "But, can you tell me more about the physical change that occurred after Adam and Eve ate the forbidden fruit?"

"Well, the Creator would not permit mankind to go on living forever in the fallen state of betrayal, so Adam and Eve were driven from the Tree of Life."

"So, that tree was real too?"

Madam Mercy appeared taken aback by Andela's question. "Mankind was made part of the animal world, but it was not intended that human beings should age and die like the creatures that were merely animals, that is, not until after Adam and Eve sinned."

"Okay, so there was fruit that somehow sustained physiological equilibrium in a manner that mature adults did not deteriorate? Right?"

"Something like that, I guess," replied Madam Mercy, smiling at Andela's choice of words.

"Okay, but what about sex? What happened as far as sex is concerned?"

Madam Mercy turned her eyes momentarily away, and then addressed Andela with a look of distress. "The natural instinct for human beings to conduct themselves according to the Creator's will was terribly perverted, so perverted that it became an inner battle for those desiring to obey the Creator to overcome the natural cravings of their own flesh. The first hint of such perversion was the realization that sexual acts could be committed with other beings—Adam and Eve felt compelled to cover their nakedness, even in the presence of the Creator."

"Really!" remarked Andela. "Why? I mean, why would they need to cover their nakedness in the presence of God? He created them, right?"

Madam Mercy paused thoughtfully, and then peered questioningly into Andela's eyes. "Have you read much Greek mythology?"

"Some. We had to read it in school."

"Then you must recall that the Greek writers depicted quite a bit of sexual intercourse between the mythological gods and human beings."

Andela appeared shocked. "Oh yea, I know, but that was just mythology."

"It was mythology created by the minds and imaginations of human beings, and once Adam and Eve fell under the curse of sin, their thoughts and imaginations became subject to evil influence."

"So, what are you saying?" Andela asked in a tentative tone of voice.

"I'm saying that after Adam and Eve disobeyed God, they experienced immoral sexual temptation, sexual shame, and sexual fear, and they did not even want to stand before their own Creator without having their nakedness covered."

Andela could guess what Madam Mercy was hinting at—maybe Adam was afraid that God would want to have sex with Eve. And maybe Eve feared the same thing. And even if there was no fear of God committing some sort of sexual act, maybe such thoughts caused Adam and Eve frustration and shame. Andela recalled the Bible stating that

Adam and Eve hid from God because they were ashamed of their nakedness.

Then Andela posed another question, "Did being naked become a sin? I mean, after Adam and Eve ate the fruit, did it become a sin to be naked?"

"The Bible doesn't say that it bothered God for Adam and Eve to be naked," responded Madam Mercy. "The shame was in their own hearts and minds. Do you remember how God responded to their behavior?"

"How?"

"He wanted to know who told them that they were naked."

"So then, are saying that it's not a sin to be naked?" inquired Andela. "I mean, I once attended a Sunday school class where a married couple thought it would be fine for mature Christians to all go naked. They claimed that the blood of Christ regenerates us back to the position and condition we had before the fall of Adam."

"I am familiar with that argument," said Madam Mercy. "And although I would not agree that the flesh is regenerated to the condition that existed before the fall of Adam and Eve, I would agree that true Christians are ruled by the Spirit rather than the flesh, so let me first say that the argument is, to some extent, probably correct."

"What?" gasped Andela, not expecting such a response from Madam Mercy.

"Hear me out," said Madam Mercy, laughing at Andela's reaction. "Terms such as *uncover the nakedness* or *see the nakedness* or *look upon the nakedness* which are found in the Old Testament in verses such as Leviticus chapter eighteen, verses six through nineteen, Leviticus chapter twenty, verse seventeen, Ezekiel chapter sixteen, verse thirty-six, Habakkuk chapter two, verse fifteen, and Genesis chapter nine, verse twenty-two, do not mean to merely see someone naked, but rather to have sexual intercourse with that person. That is why Noah cursed Canaan, the son of Ham—it was because Ham had sex with Noah's wife and she gave birth to Canaan, and that is also why Canaan is mentioned along with Shem, Ham, and Japheth in Genesis chapter nine, verse eighteen, since Noah's wife gave birth to Canaan. It is having sex with someone outside of marriage that the Old Testament defines as sin, not merely seeing someone naked. If all the world were populated by mature Christians, and if there were no fornication, no adultery, no homosexuality, no infidelity, and no lusting to commit sexual sin, then

I would have to agree that there would be no need for clothing—people could go naked, appreciate the natural beauty of their bodies, and live holy lives."

Though Andela was still a little dazed, she felt somewhat relieved by Madam Mercy's explanation. Certainly the world was not free of sexual sin, so it seemed reasonable that Madam Mercy was not condoning social nakedness. "But the world's not that way," she stated.

"No, it is not," agreed Madam Mercy. "And in consideration of the deplorable state of sexual conduct upon the earth, I must take sides with the arguments for wearing clothing."

Andela sighed in relief. She had been rather disconcerted by thoughts of Madam Mercy favoring nudist colonies. Then, as she reflected upon Madam Mercy's words, her eyebrows drew upward in an expression of inquisition. "The arguments for wearing clothing? What arguments?"

Madam Mercy appeared more than willing to respond. "First of all, God clothed Adam and Eve. He never said it was a sin for them to be naked, but he clothed them nonetheless. In my opinion, the clothing was given to Adam and Eve as an outward symbol of an inward intent—the intent to have sex only with one another. Even though Adam and Eve were both aware that sexual acts could be committed with other creatures, they apparently determined not to commit such acts, and thankfully, there is nothing in the Bible to indicate that either Adam or Eve ever committed fornication or bestiality."

Andela nodded, hoping Madam Mercy would present arguments for wearing clothing that were more compelling than simply the fact that God covered Adam and Eve with animal skins.

"Secondly, remember what Paul taught about eating meat that had previously been offered to idols?"

"Yes, he said that it was not a sin for him to eat such meat, but he said that he would not do so if it might cause someone else to sin."

"Precisely," returned Madam Mercy. "And this is an appropriate illustration for my second point. Eating meat offered to idols in the time of Paul was associated with fornication, namely having sex with temple prostitutes. Paul knew that he could eat meat previously offered to idols without it tempting him to patronize a temple prostitute, but he did not want to eat such meat if it meant that one of his weaker Christian brothers might be drawn back into idol worship and fornication. Likewise, there may be mature Christians who could live free of sexual sin in a world of nudity, but there are many individuals who are weak when it comes to sexual temptation. In fact, ungodly sexual lust may be the most prevalent weakness in your society. So, in a world where large numbers of men and women fall prey to temptations to engage in sex outside of marriage, I think that persons should care enough about the spiritual welfare of others to wear clothing, given that nudity is generally more conducive to sexual temptation than wearing clothing, even though some persons would try to argue that point."

"I agree with you," said Andela, feeling rather peculiar about the need for such complex arguments to defend the appropriateness of clothing. She had always taken it for granted that people shouldn't walk around naked.

"You remember how Paul said that all things were *lawful* for him, but not all things were *expedient*," inquired Madam Mercy.

"Yes."

"Well, Paul did not mean that murder and adultery were lawful for him. What he meant was that when he considered all of the many things that he could do without breaking God's laws, not all of those things were wise or beneficial. And although this particular passage of Scripture likely reflects upon Paul's objection to Christians taking other Christians to court before pagan judges, other passages of Scripture indicate that eating meat previously offered to idols was something that he decided to avoid. Now remember, Paul was very capable of eating meat previously offered to idols without sinning or being tempted to sin. However, he lived in the midst of persons who were tempted by idolatrous gods and prostitution-laden religions, so for the sakes of those persons, he chose not to eat meat previously offered to idols."

"Okay," said Andela. "So what you're saying is that, just like Paul decided not to eat meat that had previously been offered to idols, even though he could have done so without sinning, it stands to reason that those persons in our present society who are mature Christians should wear clothing for the sake of the spiritual well-being of others in society, even if those Christians are capable of going naked without sinning."

"Yes, I believe you have summed up my second point very well," Madam Mercy stated with finality. But then she resumed speaking. "And as for your *internet*, a marvelous tool that can be used for good or evil..."

"I know," Andela butted in, "there's all kinds of trash on the internet."

"Indeed," conferred Madam Mercy, "it offers a veritable smorgasbord of hellish whoredom devised to purloin pocketbooks, assassinate souls, massacre marriages, and raze families." After a few silent moments to reflect upon the prodigious reality of her declaration, Madam Mercy continued. "But it's not the trash on the internet that I wish to discuss."

"Oh, so what do you want to discuss?" Andela inquired sheepishly, realizing that she had butted in before Madam Mercy finished her sentence.

"Nude art need not be pornographic, and certainly mature Christians should be able to admire the beauty of God's creation without yielding to temptations to lust sexually, including the beauty of the human body. So, considering that there may be some rare sites on your internet that attempt to present wholesome, non-pornographic nude art, how should mature Christians feel about such sites and such art?"

Andela stared at her tutor in perplexity. "Um, well, I, I don't know."

"An honest answer," praised Madam Mercy, sensitive to the fact that Andela seemed a little embarrassed about the subject. "This question is not a simple one. It is more complicated than one might think."

"How's that?" rejoined Andela.

"There are two aspects to bear in mind," disclosed Madam Mercy. "First, the aspect we have already considered, namely the example of eating meat previously offered to idols. If a mature Christian views purportedly wholesome nude art, but doing so places another person in jeopardy of yielding to temptations of sexual sin, then I would say that such a practice is not wise or beneficial. And furthermore, even if Paul could have eaten meat offered to idols in secret, what if a weaker brother asked him if he ate meat offered to idols? Don't you think Paul's best service to weaker brothers was to avoid eating such meat altogether?"

"Right," agreed Andela. She felt that she had a good grasp of Paul's lesson about eating meat that was previously offered to idols, and she was curious to find out what Madam Mercy would present as the second *aspect to bear in mind* when it came to nude art.

"Secondly," continued Madam Mercy, "what about the emotional and psychological well-being of marriage partners? One of the most basic, sensitive, God-given needs in the emotional core of a woman's heart is the sexual devotion and faithfulness of her husband. How many wives, living in a society such as yours, could comfortably accept the assertion that their husbands are viewing nude women simply to admire the beauty of the women's bodies? Certainly, in a chaste society, men should be able to view nude art without lusting or sinning, and perhaps there are spiritually mature married couples that could mutually enjoy nude art without sinful lust or concern over possible sexual betrayal, but can you imagine the distress a woman might have, living in a society plagued with sexual sin, if her husband habitually views nude art? What is the greater loss—a man deprived of viewing a limited portion of God's creation, or a woman robbed of sexual and emotional peace and joy?"

Andela faced her tutor thoughtfully. "I would hope that the wife's well-being would be more important to the husband than simply depriving himself of a little pleasure, even if it's not sinful pleasure."

"Exactly," concurred Madam Mercy. "After Adam and Eve sinned, human existence became a battle of love verses lust, with lust sometimes masquerading as love, and only very powerful and devoted love for the Creator, such as that demonstrated by Enoch, ever came close to boosting human behavior to what was originally intended. Only by regeneration through the blood sacrifice of the Messiah and the empowering of the Holy Spirit is mankind enabled to overcome the warped nature that compels him to sin. Sin merits eternal death, and only the blood sacrifice of Jesus Christ can bring life to the *walking dead*—namely those persons who are ruled by the flesh rather than by the spirit."

Andela could not help but think of Bill when Madam Mercy used the term *walking dead*, and this brought her mind back to Bill's predicament. She decided to wrap up her conversation with Madam Mercy. "So, the instinct to do what the Creator intended, when it comes to sex, was lost," she summarized.

"Oh no," rebuffed Madam Mercy. "The law of God is written within the hearts of men. But, after the betrayal, men became aware of other choices. Men became aware that carnal, sexual pleasure can be obtained outside of the boundaries established by the Creator. And even without any prodding from the Enemy and his agents, human beings are often tempted to sin sexually, meaning that they are tempted to indulge in sexual activity with some person or creature apart from a marriage partner of the same species as guided through God's Word."

"You can say that again," remarked Andela. "But Bill, I think he's different than most men. I mean…"

"Yes," interjected Madam Mercy, "that is true enough. But he is vulnerable to temptations from the Evil One, and the Enemy will fight for Bill's soul. Bill is not as strong as Enoch. As Scripture points out in Romans chapter three, verse twenty-three, along with Romans chapter six, verse twenty-three, and along with Hebrews chapter six, verse one, all human beings on earth who reach ages of moral responsibility commit sin, and they obtain life in only one manner—by repenting from sin and choosing redemption through the blood of the Redeemer."

"I know, but, what I'm saying about Bill is that…"

Suddenly Andela was cut short. The sentence she began to speak dissipated from her mind. Madam Mercy had raised an open palm and snapped her face toward the land below. Then, dropping her hand to her side, she looked back at Andela with alarmed eyes.

"What is it?" asked Andela, feeling her heart quicken.

"She has come. You must go."

"She? Who?"

"Decevon."

A chill pierced Andela's breast. "The seductress?"

"Yes."

"But, what should I do?"

"Remember that true love is greater than carnal lust. Call him from a heart of true love, and Decevon may appear as the demon who she is."

"Call him? But…"

"To his land! Now!"

* * * * * * * * * * * * * * * * * *

After toppling over the edge of the cliff, Bill expected to awaken in his own bed, clasping his blankets with a frightful feeling in the pit of his stomach. Instead, he felt his body decelerate as if his fall were cushioned by an invisible air mattress; and then he settled on hard, dry earth. For a few moments he lay still, assuring himself that his eyes beheld the ground. Then he arose and peered back upward from where he had just fallen. He saw only a blue sky. And strangely, looking forward into the distance before him, he saw nothing but light. It appeared as though the ground on which he stood simply ended, reminding him of rumors about what people believed in the days of Christopher Columbus, namely that the world was flat and ceased to exist at its edges.

Remembering past experiences in his odd dream, Bill approached the nothingness before him with caution. He raised one hand as he moved forward; and even though he half expected to find something solid, he was still startled when his hand met a hard, smooth surface. He tested the surface as far upward as he could reach, and then tested the surface for several feet to either side. There was no break in the flawless, invisible wall before him. Then he turned around and shifted his attention to the visible land that continued on and on in the opposite direction. The land stretched farther than he could see. He also noted that the landscape extended indefinitely to his right and left.

Looking to his left, Bill perused a span of cracked clay soil. The ground dipped to the edge of a gorge; and the gorge's steep walls dropped so far downward that Bill could not see the bed of the gorge. Beyond the gorge was a narrow plain—a flat stretch of packed sand extending to a jagged line of hills; and beyond the hills rose austere mountains.

"Magnificent," Bill muttered to himself as he gazed toward the mountains, realizing that this was his land. He experienced an indefinable sense of pride. After a deep breath, he mentally compared the vast landscape that stretched on and on before him to the *nothingness* of Andela's land. He realized that Andela claimed that her land was beautiful, but what good was beauty that was invisible?

Bill turned his face and focused on the sights straight ahead of him. Colored sand dunes squatted on bone-dry ground like desert tepees. Bizarre trees dotted the landscape; and there were occasional thickets that seemed the crusty remains of forsaken gardens. Most trees were small, but a few had monstrous trunks more than thirty feet in diameter. Branches jutted outward from the tops of the larger trees like the jointed legs of colossal spiders standing on their heads. Leaves were sparse and oddly colored—some green, some yellow or orange, and some purplish or brown.

Despite the desolate aspect of the landscape, Bill perceived his surroundings as being grand and glorious. He thought of Andela, and of how impressed she would be by the spectacle of his land. So where was Andela?

"Andela!" Bill called out in different directions, but there was no response. As he looked this way and that, Bill became even more intrigued with the environment, especially as he espied moving creatures. An animal about the size of a rabbit, dark black and appearing like a lanky-legged mouse, scampered up the side of a tree to his right and disappeared through a hole in the trunk. Then, high in the distance above the tree, there appeared three large birds that turned and swerved upon extended wings like miniature aircraft.

Bill backed against the smooth, invisible wall and slid downward to a sitting position. He decided to wait for a while and see if Andela showed up. He observed the environment and wondered what other astonishing creatures might appear. He watched the dwarfed branches of the trees sway sporadically as they were stroked by varying breezes. By and by a large orange lizard shaped like an iguana dashed from behind a tree and streaked toward the open gorge to his left; and just then a large raptor appeared, plummeting from the sky like a guided missile. The orange lizard dove over the edge of the gorge and disappeared; but the raptor, oily black with red wings, emitted a loud screech and swooped into the gorge, rising a few seconds later with the lizard in its talons. The winged carnivore flew over the far edge of the gorge and faded into the rough terrain to Bill's left, dropping behind the crest of one of the taller hills beyond the narrow plain.

"Whoa, that was spectacular," Bill remarked aloud, impressed by the vastness and complexity of his land. The farm he owned in Missouri covered almost two hundred acres, but this territory was far greater. Then he shook his head and chuckled to himself for gloating over something that was merely the fabrication of a dream.

"There is much that is spectacular in your land, Master Bill," crooned a female voice.

Bill was shocked by the near presence of another person, a person whom he did not see or hear coming. He rose to his feet and was further shocked when his eyes beheld the woman who was approaching from his right. She walked casually toward him, carrying a pair of western boots in one hand. Her body was tanned and voluptuous, clothed in a makeshift bikini of animal hides. She did not stop walking until she stood so close that he could feel her breath when she spoke.

"Welcome, Master," she spoke with a fawning smile. Her eyes were dark, and her flowing hair was chocolate brown. "Your office quarters and some refreshments are prepared for you. I've brought your socks and boots. Put them on, and follow me."

The woman's breath was seductive. She dropped the socks and boots to the ground, and then brushed against Bill's body as she walked past him, heading toward the gorge to his left. Bill hesitated, looking about the landscape for any sign of Andela.

"Coming?" inquired Decevon, stopping and looking back over her shoulder.

Bill felt uneasy about his sensual guide, but she seemed polite.

"Where did you say we're going?" he asked.

"One of your outpost offices, Master. You know, your little place in the gorge. So, are you coming?"

"I guess so," consented Bill. He dropped to the ground and began pulling on his socks and boots. They were identical to his socks and boots back home.

Decevon turned and strolled on ahead. Bill finished pulling on his boots and then rose and followed after her. He had no problem catching up. She walked to the edge of the gorge and then led Bill down a crude rope ladder with wooden rungs. When she reached the cracked surface of the riverbed, she headed southward—opposite the direction of the Land of the Northern Pool. She appeared perfectly comfortable walking barefoot on the rough ground. Bill followed.

The sandstone walls of the gorge were marked with curious swirls of amber and auburn; they seemed the petrified eddies of an ochre sea. Here and there caves opened into the sides of the gorge, and some were large enough to enter. Decevon ignored the caves, leading Bill onward. The riverbed zigzagged. Bill was never able to see more than seventy yards ahead. The ground crackled like eggshells, and Bill wondered if his land were experiencing a drought.

The absence of conversation and the nonchalant demeanor of Bill's guide magnified the provocative manner of her physical carriage. Her appearance was no less sensual than if she were naked. Once Bill thought he heard a scream, and later he thought that he heard eerie cries that echoed through the canyon; but his guide gave no indication of alarm. After passing several cave openings and then walking about fifty feet, they arrived at a wooden door. The door was situated to their left, and was carved from cedar or some other reddish wood. It was bedecked with meticulous carvings of forest trees and wildlife. There were no windows in the wall of the gorge; but there was a small, oval window in the door.

The door's window was about four feet above the ground. Decevon stopped and leaned forward to peer through the tinted glass of the window, cupping both hands about her face. After about ten seconds she straightened and faced Bill. She smiled as she noted a blush in Bill's cheeks.

"You like my outfit?" she asked, clasping her hands behind her back.

The first thought that ran through Bill's mind was, *what outfit?* There was little substance to his guide's attire. "Sure, it's fine," he stated. The scanty garment gave the impression of a cave woman's underwear.

Decevon reached beneath the strand of hide stretching across her right breast and withdrew a translucent strip of material the color of pure gold.

"I meant to surprise you with a new garment," declared Decevon. She lifted one end of the golden strip held it before Bill's eyes. It dangled downward toward her waist. The material was like tinted cellophane. "I needed twice this much fabric to make my outfit, though, and those nasty Cherinedes hid the thread I needed. When they found out that I was collecting their hair to sew myself clothing—hair left lying around in the woods after they cut it off—they started burying it, simply burying it out of pure spite."

"Hair?" stammered Bill, trying to make sense out of his escort's statements. "You make clothes out of hair?"

"Yes," affirmed Decevon. "I weave material from Cherinede hair. Cherinedes are little nomadic creatures that roam about the plains and woods. They're not so becoming as most of your loyal subjects, but they grow the most beautiful hair."

"They do?"

"Yes, and they hate wearing long hair, so they trim it on a regular basis, letting it fall where it will, or at least they used to let it fall, until they noticed that I was walking about the woods collecting it, several strands at a time, so that I could weave a garment suitable for such a find lord as yourself. And when they found out why I was collecting their hair, they got jealous of me, though I've never done anything to make them jealous, and they started burying their hair trimmings so that I couldn't have any. It's terrible!"

Decevon clasped her arms to her sides as she finished speaking.

Bill thought it sounded inconsiderate to bury hair trimmings in order to keep someone else from making clothing, though it also entered his mind that someone ought to be able to decide what to do with his or her own hair. These thoughts were crowded to the back of his mind, however, by thoughts of how the woman posing before him would appear if concealed by nothing more than translucent bands of golden fabric.

"All you have to do, being lord of this land, is to decree that the Cherinedes give all requested hair to my valet, and then I can finish my garments," Decevon explained.

"Squaah!!" interrupted a high-pitched squawk from the upper edge of the canyon wall.

Bill and Decevon both looked up and espied a large bird flapping its wings madly and streaking toward the west. It disappeared beyond the western edge of the canyon wall.

"What was that?" asked Bill.

Decevon stared for a few seconds, and then dropped her eyes back toward Bill. "A bloodblatt, very dangerous. I suggest that you make a decree for that bird to drop dead."

"Decree that it drop dead?"

Decevon pointed back toward the west, continuing to face Bill. "Those things sneak up on people during their sleep, and a single scratch from one their claws paralyzes their prey, and then the whole flock of them have a midnight snack." She dropped her arm back to her side. "You're lord of the land, so you can do away with that nasty bird."

"Whoa! They eat people alive!" responded Bill. "In that case, I command that all bloodblatts drop dead."

A confounded expression appeared upon Decevon's face. "No, I didn't say…," she started; but then she shrugged and smiled. "Never mind, I think you were about to decree that the Cherinedes give all requested hair to my valet. My valet's name is Rebelon."

"Your valet?" responded Bill. He remembered Rebelon's name being mentioned back in Andela's land.

"Yes, Master, he's my servant, just like I'm your servant," lied Decevon. "Just say the following words—*I decree that the Cherinedes give all requested hair to Rebelon*. That's all you have to do. After that, I'll be able to finish my outfit." Decevon held the band of gold about her waist. "Please, Master, I'm just doing it for you."

Bill felt uneasy; not only because a nearly naked woman was pleading for his assistance, but also because of something else—he had the heartfelt suspicion that his escort was asking him to serve as an accomplice in thievery. Decevon sensed Bill's reticence. She did not give him time to gather his thoughts.

"It's your land, Master, and everyone here exists for only one reason—to do your bidding. Won't you please help me? These old clothes are so scratchy! Please?"

Bill shrugged. After all, like she said, it was his land, so why shouldn't he be able to decide what happened to some spare hair? "Okay," he conceded. "So then, what was it you wanted me to say?"

"It's simple, Master, just say—*I decree that the Cherinedes give all requested hair to Rebelon.*"

"Okay, I decree that the...the what?"

Decevon squelched any outward sign of annoyance. Her smile was a portrait of amiable patience. "Cherinedes."

"Cherinedes, okay, I decree that the Cherinedes give all requested hair to Rebelon."

Decevon exhaled and stuffed the golden strip of material back beneath her upper garment. "Well, everything's ready inside," she stated gaily, turning and pulling on the door handle. The door swung open to the outside. She motioned for Bill to enter first.

Bill stepped inside a dim room. It was about the size of his den in Missouri. The inner walls were comprised of engraved hardwood panels. Engravings on the panels featured forest scenes and animated wildlife, with human figures interposed from place to place. Most of the figures were female.

Indirect lighting illuminated each wooden panel like an exhibit in a museum. Adjacent to the largest panel, to Bill's left, sat a small wooden table with sculptured legs; and atop the table were hors d'oeuvres in marble bowls. Two chairs were positioned at opposing sides of the table, and on the tabletop before the chairs were golden goblets filled with purple fluid. A sense of pride infused Bill's breast; he granted himself credit for whatever existed within *his land*.

Against the wall to Bill's right rested a rustic desk with papers scattered about the desktop. The appearance of the desk gave him the impression that whoever sat at the desk held a position of great importance, and he knew that the desk belonged to him. Straight before him, at the far end of the room, sat a four-poster bed. Carvings of slender nymphs composed the bedposts. Covering the bed were flowing linens topped by an embroidered comforter with a woven portrait of two reclining snow leopards; and above the bed hung a painting encompassed by a golden frame.

Featured within the golden frame above the bed; in bold detail against a blue, pastel background; were two images—Bill's escort and himself. He was receiving a back massage as he lay on his stomach with his hands folded beneath his head. His escort straddled his thighs. He wore a pair of jeans, and his escort wore small strips of ermine. Bill was gazing at the picture as Decevon closed the door to the chamber. She slid a bolt into place to secure the door.

"Let's have a drink, master, my throat is parched," coaxed Decevon as she crossed to one of the chairs at the table. She took the closer chair, motioning for Bill to sit in the chair that faced the bed. Bill accepted the invitation and seated himself. The aroma of steaming cinnamon rolls and mint chocolates made his mouth water. He lifted an elegant chalice to his lips and sipped the most delicious grape juice he ever tasted.

Although the purple drink was cool to his lips, warmth permeated Bill's abdomen. Perhaps it was not grape juice that he drank; perhaps it was wine, strong wine. He held the chalice in his hand and peered across the table at his escort. She produced a genial smile.

"It's the finest wine in your kingdom, master," she remarked. "Rebelon insists upon nothing but the best for your private quarters."

Bill observed his escort's face transform into a playful image of alarm. She pushed back her chair, rose, and stepped to the side of the bed. "Oh no, I almost forgot, master. I'm sure you'll want your customary massage before dining." Decevon faced Bill matter-of-factly. Then she turned and crawled onto the bed, positioning herself on her hands and knees and smiling toward Bill in a manner that signaled an invitation—an invitation for much more than a mere massage. "I'll let you rub me first, as usual."

Decevon was careful not to say that she wanted Bill to engage in sex; and there were no pictures on the walls depicting sexual intercourse.

The entire affair was orchestrated with utmost caution and subtlety. Rebelon, the mastermind behind Decevon's scheme, had warned her that Bill would not be easy to seduce. He explained that an anglerfish draws its prey toward gaping jaws with a fleshly lure, and that Bill was the prey, and that she was the lure.

Bill was aware that the sensations he experienced in this *dream* seemed very real. He paused in confusion, staring at the young woman before him. She lowered her elbows to the mattress and rested her head on folded hands, never breaking eye contact. Her alluring smile burned into Bill's heart and mind.

Bill shrugged and chided himself for taking his dream too seriously. It was like he told the rude and presuming character who called himself *Hope* back in Andela's land—the entire affair, the whole dream and everything in it, was probably the result of some half-digested pickle. A good back rub might be all he needed to quit dreaming and pass into a deeper stage of sleep.

Bill rose from his chair. A fleeting expression of malign confidence crossed Decevon's face as Bill looked down toward the top button to his flannel shirt, drawing both hands upward to the button. But when he looked back up, she was smiling as before. He stepped to the center of the room as he reached for the next button.

"Bill, no!!!" pierced a bloodcurdling scream.

Bill froze. The scream was silenced. Somehow, though, the essence of the scream continued, permeating the silence, persisting within the chamber, penetrating Bill's heart and awakening the conscience of his soul.

Then memory of the scream dissolved. Bill's eyes were captured by a sight that struck terror through his breast. The bed before him changed into a black-velvet casket; and black velvet shrouds dipped downward and spilled into a smoldering pit of rotting carcasses and moldy bones. Worms, maggots, flies, and slimy, wart-covered, pale-green toads hopped, swarmed, and wriggled through decaying, putrid, human skulls and flesh. And back on top of the casket, his attractive escort changed— her eyes became greenish-black caverns with the haunting impression of meaningless death; and her entreating smile transmuted into the fangs of a bloodsucking vampire. Her voluptuous body wilted into a wiry skeleton with parched flesh stretched between bones. For one mesmerizing second, Bill perceived the spiritual visage of sexual debauchery.

Decevon felt a power pass through the chamber—a power she despised. She cast hateful eyes toward the door through which she and Bill had entered. Then she regained her composure. She gazed upon Bill as if nothing had happened, and then she arched her back and eased into the most provocative posture that she could proffer. Her face displayed moral abandonment and the promise of sensual pleasure.

"I'm ready Bill," posed Decevon.

Bill stared upon his seductress with astonishment. She was gorgeous—he had never seen any fleshly image more attractive. The horrid revelation had vanished, but it had vanished only from his eyes, not from his heart, and not from his mind. His fingers were frozen at the second button to his shirt.

Decevon perceived a threat to her plans. "I can't wait to feel those firm hands of yours," she beckoned.

Bill continued staring upon his seductress without moving or speaking. Her body was beautiful, but now her beauty seemed the glossy sheen of a venomous spider. He turned and dashed to the door, fidgeting with the bolt until it banged to an unlocked position. He opened the door and sprang outside. After looking up and down the gorge, he dashed off to his left, coursing farther down the gorge. There was a leftward bend about sixty feet away in that direction, and he headed straight for the bend so that he could turn out of sight, just in case the woman, or whatever she was, pursued him.

Bill dashed around the bend in the gorge, but then his heart sank. The gorge swerved back to the right and then continued on and on in a straight line. This meant that anyone pursuing him could spot him in the distance. The sides of the gorge appeared to decrease in height in the distance, but they still looked steep; so Bill figured there was little chance that he could climb out before being seen. Then he sighted what appeared to be the opening of a cave some distance ahead and to his left. He ran on ahead until he came to the opening, paused to peek in, and then he ducked inside.

The opening was not really a cave; it was just a small hollow in the side of the gorge. Nonetheless, it was deep enough for Bill to crawl inside and hide. He sat down at the end of the hollow and leaned back against cool sandstone. He was breathing hard, but his breathing slowed to normal after a couple of minutes. He faced the opening of the hollow in thought, trying to decide what he would say if the woman appeared at the mouth of the hollow. Minutes passed, but nothing happened. There was no indication of pursuit.

Still sitting at the back of the hollow, Bill began thinking about his dream. It seemed odd that one dream could contain so many events. Perhaps he had dreamed other dreams just as eventful without remembering them. It occurred to him that if he could only go to sleep, he would awaken back at the farm. He closed his eyes and tried to erase all thoughts from his mind—his dream was not fun anymore—it was time to wake up.

Bill opened his eyes. He had been sleeping. He recalled all that had happened during his dream, and apparently he was still dreaming—he was still sitting at the back of the hollow. He had the eerie impression that he had been dreaming while he slept, though he could not remember what he dreamt. It gave him an odd sensation to contemplate sleeping and dreaming during a dream. Why didn't he really wake up?

Then he perceived faint, clopping sounds; the sounds of a horse galloping across hard, dry ground. The sounds grew louder and louder, rousing him to full consciousness. He faced the opening to the hollow.

A horse and rider appeared in the middle of the gorge, a jet black mare ridden by a cowgirl. The cowgirl wore a lustrous red hat with a wide brim, and the brim was trimmed in white lace with cottony white balls dangling side by side below the edge of the hat's perimeter. Her long-sleeved, red and white blouse was richly embroidered; and her jeans matched her blouse. She wore a wide, pearly-white belt; and her white boots looked freshly polished. Bill had no problem recognizing Cowgirl Jane, a fictitious heroin from a storybook his mother read to him during his childhood.

Decevon pulled back on the horse's reigns, causing the horse to rear upward on its hind legs and kick its front hooves in the air. Then the horse dropped both front hooves to the ground with a thud. Decevon's assignment had been changed. Rather than sexual seduction, she was now on a mission to perform psychosocial manipulation. She and Rebelon were determined to utilize whatever means necessary to deter the governor of their land, namely Bill, from withdrawing allegiance to the land's real master—the Father of Lies.

Spurs on the backs of Decevon's boots jangled as she vaulted from a western-styled saddle and landed to the left of the horse. The horse stood in place, prancing from one foot to the other. Then Decevon strode doughtily toward Bill.

This is more like a typical dream, Bill mused to himself as Cowgirl Jane approached. She knelt down at the face of the hollow and peered at him.

"She perta'neer gotcha, didn't she?" commented Decevon, speaking with the western drawl and confident tone that Bill expected from Cowgirl Jane.

Bill realized that Cowgirl Jane was referring to the woman from whom he fled. For a moment, as he looked into Cowgirl Jane's chocolate-brown eyes, he felt uneasy, almost alarmed, but then he dismissed the feeling and nodded. He recalled that Cowgirl Jane had brown eyes, so he figured that it was just a coincidence that Cowgirl Jane's eyes looked identical to the eyes of the woman in the chamber.

"I reckon," returned Bill. He was not inclined to disagree with Cowgirl Jane.

"Well, she'll be straight afta ya, or she might be sendin' somethin' even worser afta ya. You'd best hop right up here behind me. Midnight'll get us outa' here pronto."

Bill knew he would rather escape by waking up in his own bed than by riding off on a horse, but he couldn't seem to succeed in awakening, so he crawled from the hollow and followed Cowgirl Jane to the black mare. The great horse looked similar to pictures he remembered admiring in his childhood storybook. Cowgirl Jane mounted the saddle with ease. Bill was a little surprised as the horse shifted and he nearly failed in his first attempt to mount, but Cowgirl Jane grabbed hold of his shirt and steadied him as he settled on the mare's loins behind the saddle.

"Hold ta the straps back thar," instructed Decevon, but Bill was already wrapping leather straps around both of his hands, straps that dangled from the rear of the saddle. "Gettiup Midnight!"

Bill felt leather biting into the palms of his hands as Midnight took off, but the pain eased as the powerful mare settled into a smooth gallop and coasted over the floor of the gorge. "Yee hah!" whooped Decevon. She detested the cowgirl character she portrayed, but she could endure almost anything in order to serve the Father of Lies, for her seductive heart fed from his hatred.

Bill was impressed by Midnight's smooth stride and swiftness. He had ridden many horses while growing up in rural Missouri, but few of them could gallop like the black mare beneath him. Within three minutes they were far down the gorge. The sandstone walls to either side diminished in height and became less steep. All at once Cowgirl Jane wheeled Midnight's reigns to the right. Midnight turned and plodded up the bank of the gorge, barely slowing as her pounding hooves thrust them upward. Again Bill felt the leather thongs biting into his hands, and the biting pain continued until Midnight leveled off on the sandy turf above.

As they emerged onto the plain, Bill noted a change in the landscape. Trees were fewer and farther apart, and they were smaller—though they passed one gigantic tree with an enormous trunk. The sand below Midnight's hooves was packed firm, and the desert floor was the same color as the sides of the gorge. Tall cacti rose from place to place, featuring varieties Bill had never seen—some truncated and green with rounded limbs curving upward in symmetrical patterns, and others with spiraling vines laced together in thorny domes of bright purple, yellow, and red. The landscape stretched onward as far as he could see, though he could not see very far due to haze.

"I juss luv deserts," Decevon remarked. "Look's lika storm abrewin', so I'd best getcha ta yer cabin."

Bill felt Midnight bolt faster ahead as Cowgirl Jane prodded the mare's flanks with silver spurs. "Yee hah!" Cowgirl Jane hollered. Midnight galloped for several minutes. The dust and sand thickened in whirling winds. Bill had to squint to keep sand from stinging his eyes.

A small, solitary structure appeared ahead. It was a single-level ranch house with a sandstone chimney. The walls were also sandstone. As they drew nearer, a wooden door appeared in the middle of the wall facing them—the north wall. A single square window was situated west of the door.

A hitching post jutted upward from the ground a few feet west of the window. Decevon drew the horse to a halt at the hitching post, slid from the saddle to the ground, and stepped back to the door. She turned and faced Bill. "Come on down Bill. We'd better getcha in wherit's safe, 'cause the storm's gettin' worser."

Bill dismounted and walked toward the wooden door. Midnight stood in place before the hitching post. Cowgirl Jane swung the cabin door wide open—it opened to the outside like a barn door. She reached inside and flipped a switch that was mounted on the inner wall, turning on lights that dangled from an overhead chandelier.

"Get on inside thar," instructed Decevon. "Thar's grub in the frig', and yer bed's nice an' cozy. Thanks fer lettin' me barra yer bed now an' then. It's easier fer me ta drop ta sleep in that bed than anywhar, it's one swell bed. Well, I gotta get Midnight on back home afore that thar storm gets downright ornery, so adios!"

Decevon left Bill holding the handle to the open door while she strode back to her mount. She leapt into the western saddle and spurred Midnight's flanks as she turned the mare's head toward the western desert. Midnight launched into a gallop.

"Thanks!" hailed Bill.

"Yee hah!" returned Cowgirl Jane, never looking back. She and the black mare vanished within the thickening atmosphere. Several seconds later, sounds of Midnight's hooves beating against the desert floor faded beyond perception.

The dust and sand churned in meandering eddies. Bill turned and pulled the door closed as he entered the cabin. There was a simple metal latch that dropped into place to secure the door. Bill lowered the latch.

The interior of the cabin was clean and tidy. Bill stepped to the center of the main room, a large living room. A sandstone fireplace sat in the center of the eastern wall; a wagon-wheel chandelier hung from the ceiling above; a rectangular throw rug lay in the center of the floor; and two side-by-side lounge chairs were positioned at the northern edge of the rug. The lounge chairs faced a sofa that sat against the southern wall. The colors of the furniture and inner walls were all earthy—reds and browns that matched the fireplace. There was only one picture; it hung on the southern wall above the sofa. The picture was a large canvas painting depicting a calf roper at a rodeo. An excited crowd cheered from wooden bleachers beyond the calf roper, and a rodeo clown leaned against a gate post in the periphery. Bill felt at ease within the cabin.

After perusing the living room, Bill commenced a brief exploration. He discovered that the cabin had one bedroom containing one large bed, one bathroom, a living room with a fireplace, and a kitchen, and all of the rooms had electric lights that he flipped on as he snooped around.

He sat down at a small table in the kitchen and ate some leftovers that he found in the refrigerator. There was only one window in the entire cabin—a small, single-paned window west of the main door. Bill ate roast beef and green beans as he thought about the unusual dream he was experiencing. He wondered if he would remember any of his bizarre experiences after he awakened.

Then an idea popped into his mind—why not go to sleep in the *cozy bed* that Cowgirl Jane lauded so highly? The bed looked comfortable; and if he could fall asleep again, then maybe the next time he woke up, he would wake up in his own bed in Missouri.

He rose from the table and walked to the small bedroom. Much of the room was occupied by a ponderous featherbed encased beneath a great quilted blanket. Two plush pillows rested against a cedar headboard. Since the bedroom had no window, Bill was able to make the room dark by flipping off the bedroom light and nearly closing the bedroom door. He left a sliver of illumination showing from the main room.

After pulling off his boots, Bill sprawled back on the bed. The pillows were filled with down feathers. He felt sleepy.

Chapter 6

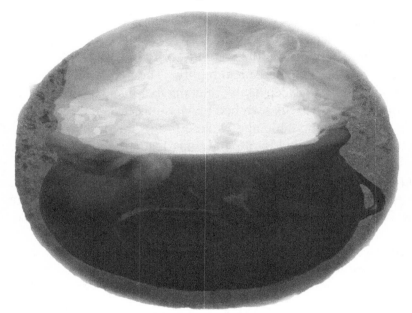

Fiery Cauldron

*C*all *him from a heart of true love, and Decevon may appear as the demon she is*, Andela repeated in her mind as she ran toward the stairwell leading down to Bill's land. Madam Mercy followed. As she drew nearer the lake, Andela was impressed by the clarity of the water, but she was too intent upon her mission to spend time admiring the lake's beauty. She had to get to Bill—she had to reach him before something awful happened.

Andela spotted the opening to the stairwell. Rather than entering, she veered to the right of the opening and dropped down on her stomach. She crawled forward and thrust her head over the edge of the cliff. She peered below.

A skewed look of concern emerged upon Andela's features. She held to the edge of the cliff with both hands, breathing hard after dashing across the grass. Below her, and some distance to her left, a basically naked female disappeared over the edge of a deep gorge, and Bill followed after her. Though Andela did not get a good look at the woman, it was apparent that the woman was physically attractive.

"It's Decevon, no doubt about it," stated Madam Mercy. She stood just to Andela's right.

Andela rolled to her back with alarm in her eyes, staring up toward Madam Mercy. "What do I do?"

"I cannot tell you what to do," Madam Mercy divulged. "You are here of your own free will, and both your earthly life and his eternal life are in jeopardy. You must do what you willfully choose to do."

Andela experienced a few moments of bewilderment, but then a look of strong-willed determination formed upon her face. She lunged toward the stairwell.

A smile lighted upon Madam Mercy's lips. She rushed to keep Andela in sight, following down the spiral stairwell. Andela sped down the steps as if she were pursued by a giant serpent rather than being trailed by a supportive comrade. She reached the end of the stairs and dropped to her hands and knees on a golden slab that ended in an opening to the outside world. After crawling forward and extending her head through the opening, she discovered that the stairwell ended about sixty feet above the parched ground of Bill's land. The sheer surface of the cliff continued straight downward.

"You'll need these," Madam Mercy spoke. Andela turned and rose to a sitting position, observing as Madam Mercy reached into a pocket on the side of her gown. Madam Mercy withdrew a pair of golden gloves, a sleek pair of golden slippers, and a long, thin, golden cord. "Put on the gloves and slippers and hold onto one end of the rope. I'll let you down."

Andela donned the gloves and slippers without taking time to speak; and then she accepted one end of the golden cord, wrapping it several times around her right hand and then grasping the cord above her right hand with her left hand. She lowered herself to her stomach and then slid backward, thrusting her legs out through the opening in the cliff. For one worrisome second, she thought of asking Madam Mercy if she were strong enough to hold up the weight of a grown woman; but then she decided that the question was not necessary—Madam Mercy possessed an aura of strength, and Andela figured that she could probably hold up the weight of a baby elephant.

"Once you are out, you will no longer be able to see me or hear me."

Andela paused and peered up into Madam Mercy's eyes. "You mean I'm on my own down there?"

Madam Mercy shook her head and smiled. "Oh no, my dear, a begotten child of the Creator is never on her or his own. I am present in Bill's land in the form of certain trees. Once you enter the land, your presence will make a difference—your presence will send a shudder through the hearts of our enemies and will add vibrancy to Hope and Truth. Now hurry!"

Andela held to the golden cord and resumed scooting backward until her body slid downward against the surface of the cliff. At first she was alarmed by how fast she descended, but her descent gradually slowed as she dropped lower. Looking up, she observed that the golden cord continued straight upward and then disappeared. She could no longer see where the cord entered the opening in the face of the cliff. The higher reaches of the cliff entered a white cloud of light. She did not remember seeing the cloud when looking downward from above. There was no visible sign of Madam Mercy.

"Flap, flap, flap, flap, splick!"

Andela's eyes widened with terror. A weird, batlike creature—black in color and about the size of a crow—crashed against the cliff and clasped the golden cord in long, orange, bony claws; and then it began gnawing at the golden cord. She glanced downward—she was still fifteen feet above the ground.

"No!" screamed Andela, looking back upward and shaking the cord in an attempt to dislodge the antagonistic creature. The little beast only shrieked in response, pecking and clawing at the golden cord.

"Whip, whip, whip, whip, whip, splat!"

Andela detected a whirling sound from somewhere below, and then a stone slammed into the creature above her. The stone ricocheted from the creature's crushed body. Blood splattered from the wall above and dropped downward along with the maimed creature, passing close behind Andela.

Andela clung to the golden cord and peered back behind her as she continued descending. Rolling hills and straggly trees stretched as far as she could see. Approaching from the base of the nearest tree—a huge tree with a hole in the center of its trunk—was a petite stranger wearing a loosely-fitting gray robe. The hood on the robe was pulled so far forward that Andela could not see the stranger's face. At his side he carried a sling—not a slingshot, but rather an old-fashioned sling such as David used to slay Goliath. He ran across the ground toward her.

"Creeech! Creech, eech, eeech!"

Shrieks echoed over the landscape, rebounding from the cliff and resounding between rolling hills. Shifting her gaze upward, Andela spotted a black cloud moving in her direction. Within seconds the cloud drew near enough for her to discern creatures just like the one that tried to sever the golden cord. The prospect of those creatures lighting all over her—biting, clawing, and ripping her flesh—petrified Andela in fright.

"Bend your legs and drop, now!"

Andela did not take the time to estimate her height above the ground. The hooded stranger had given an order, the stranger who had hurled the stone that slew her assailant. She held tightly with her left hand as she dislodged her right hand from the golden cord, and then she released. Her body plopped to the ground, and then she rose to her feet.

"Spites! I'll have to draw them away. They'll come after me once they know who I am." The stranger threw off the gray robe as he continued speaking. "You need to pursue Bill. Watch out for Resants— nasty, burly, yellow-eyed creatures covered with green fur like animated shag carpets. They are the embodiment of embittered resentment against the Creator, and they despise me, so they'll despise you. Move silently and swiftly down the canyon floor. If the Resants hear you, they'll come after you, and they're dangerous."

As the stranger's gray robe fell to the ground, Andela became captivated by his appearance. He was a vivacious little man with the figure of a woodland sprite. His hair, combed neatly to his shoulders, was as golden as the sheer cliff. He wore a tight-fitting, long-sleeved shirt with matching trousers. Both his shirt and trousers were ocean blue. His belt and slippers were the color of his hair; and from a golden sheath on his belt he withdrew a sword more stunning than any weapon Andela had ever seen—a sword that seemed a sharpened ray of lightning.

"Creeech! Acreech! Eeech!" cried the attacking spites.

"Catch me if you can, you weasel-mouthed flying scum bags!" hollered the elfish stranger, waving his glistening sword and running back toward trees to the south.

Andela watched for several seconds. The assailants swerved and flapped furiously in pursuit of the little man. He was swift, zigzagging first in one direction and then another; and from time he stopped and faced his adversaries, bisecting those that were closest upon him with quick swipes of his brilliant sword. She turned and dashed eastward. When she reached the edge of the gorge, she looked for any sign of Bill in the distance; but the gorge curved too much to see far, and she saw no sign of him. She cupped her hands to her mouth to call out, but then she remembered the little stranger's warning about creatures called Resants, and she restrained herself before anything more than a faint gurgle made its way from her throat. She stepped to the ladder.

After descending wooden rungs, Andela stood at the foot of the ladder and looked in all directions. There was no one in sight. She crept southward along the western wall of the gorge. The gorge was well lit, even though there was no visible sun in the blue sky. She paused whenever she came to a large opening or cave, listening for any sound from inside, but only perceiving silence that was reminiscent of placing one's ear to the opening of a seashell. About a mile down the gorge she came to the largest cave that she had yet encountered. It was in the eastern wall of the gorge, and it was about seven feet in diameter. She crossed to the eastern side the gorge and again paused to listen at the mouth of the cave. This time she heard something, the faint sounds of distant voices.

Stepping a few feet within the cave, Andela noted that the cracked clay soil changed to coarse sand. She walked with care, feeling her way along the stone wall as the cave grew darker. Then she spotted a dim light; and as she made her way toward the light, she again heard voices; and this time the voices were louder. None of the voices were familiar. She did not hear Bill speaking, and she did not hear any voice that sounded like the voice of a woman.

The light ahead of Andela came from a side tunnel adjoining the cave—a tunnel that coursed off to Andela's right. She crept to the edge of the tunnel, intending to peek around and see if she could spot Bill; but then she changed her mind. The speaking intensified. Andela pressed her body back against the wall of the cave and listened.

"Rebelon says the stranger is a serious threat," croaked a harsh, guttural voice that made Andela think of a buffalo. "He says we need to find her first, before they do, and before she finds Bill."

"She won't be a threat once we finish with her," cackled a similar voice.

Andela felt a quiver run up her spine. She knew they were talking about her.

"So then, where's Bill now?" questioned the second speaker.

"Decevon took him into her chamber."

"Ahha, perfect, she'll take care of him. Say, there's a wooden door with a window, so why don't we watch? It's only a short hike down the gulley."

"It's light out there, and you know I hate open light."

Andela heard the statement about *hating open light* only faintly, because she was moving back toward the gorge. Once outside, she turned to her left and began running, looking to both her right and left in search of a wooden door with a window. After rounding a curve, she paused at the mouth of large cave to her left—she thought she saw something moving within the shadowy interior—but then she resumed running. Shortly thereafter, she espied what she was looking for, a wooden door in the wall of the gorge to her left. She did not slow down until she reached the door. She was breathing heavily. She leaned forward to peer through an oval window that was framed in the center of the door.

Andela raised both hands to the sides of her face and pressed her nose and forehead against the window for a better view. What her eyes beheld as she gazed through the small tinted window caused a sickening gasp to rise from the pit of her stomach and lodge at the top of her chest. The woman in the room with Bill presented a horrible threat—the threat of sexual betrayal. If the woman had been holding a knife to Bill's throat, it would have aroused no greater alarm within the emotional seat of Andela's soul.

Even though she and Bill were not yet married, Andela hoped to someday marry Bill; and the feelings she experienced as she gazed into the room were the feelings of marital betrayal, and she had never imagined that the feelings associated with sexual betrayal by one's marriage partner were so excruciating. It seemed to Andela that the agony mounting within her breast would rupture her heart.

As Bill stepped to the center of the room before Decevon, Andela reached to open the door. Just as she discovered that the door was locked, she sensed something—something evil. She became aware of thumping footsteps. She looked to her left and espied a burly green monster bearing down upon her. The beast appeared to be seven feet tall. It continued lumbering toward her, unabashed by the fact that she faced it. Long, disheveled fur hung like Spanish moss from lanky limbs, chin, and torso.

Andela turned her face back toward the window and drew a deep breath.

"Bill, no!!!"

A musty paw closed over Andela's mouth, but the sound of her voice reverberated up and down the gorge and poured out over the edges of the stone walls that rose before and behind her. Andela sensed an eerie and pervasive awareness of her presence; it was as if Bill's land, up to this point, had only vaguely perceived her intrusion, but now she was known to all. Her body was lifted like a rag doll, and she felt the back of her head pressed into a furry chest. The beast continued muffling her mouth, and the broad pad of his paw made it difficult for her to draw a breath. She was carried back up the gorge, and then the huge beast ducked into the cave that Andela had passed before reaching the wooden door to Decevon's chamber.

As the grisly beast turned into the cave, Andela managed a sideward glimpse down the canyon. The wooden door swung open, but the beast lugged her into the cave before she could see who emerged. Andela struggled with all her strength, but the beast dropped his hand from her mouth and suffocating arms tightened about her chest, thrusting all the air from her lungs. She almost blacked out, and was only able to resume breathing after she ceased struggling and the arms enfolding her slackened. The thought of screaming came to Andela's mind, but she decided against it—the sound of her voice might not carry into the canyon, and the monster might crush her to death if she cried out for help. For several more seconds the brutal beast lumbered onward into thickening darkness, but then the darkness gave way to reddish, flickering light.

The reddish light revealed a tunnel with grayish walls that arched upward and formed a vaulted ceiling. The stone comprising the walls and ceiling looked like limestone rather than sandstone, contrasting with the red and yellow walls of the outer gorge. Flickering torches protruded from crude holes in the walls. There were occasional black fissures in the ceiling, and these fissures accommodated ventilation; but a sulfurous odor still hung in the air. The floor of the cave was packed sand.

Time passed slowly in the clutches of the lumbering beast. There were no sounds other than those of the beast's padded paws thudding against the floor of the cave and the sonorous hisses of the beast's labored breathing. Andela found herself thinking about Bill, and about the emotionally devastating scene within the secluded chamber. She presumed that the person coming out of the chamber was Bill, or at least she hoped so. Her heart ached as she wondered what happened. Where was Bill now?

Holding Andela with one arm, the beast opened a great iron door. Metal hinges creaked, and Andela was able to perceive other sounds, sounds of scuffling, clattering, and husky voices. Her abductor passed through the door, still holding her in one arm. They entered a great room, and then the room fell silent. The beast lowered her to a sandy floor, keeping a secure hold on her shoulders with great green paws. She faced outward.

Andela gazed with horrified wonder at the scene before her. A large, domed chamber was illuminated by scores of burning torches set within small recesses in gray stone walls. The sulfuric odor she had noticed in the passage behind her was less pungent here—the ceiling was high and streaked with crevices, and air seemed to move inward and upward from connecting fissures and passages so that smoke was lifted toward the overhead crevices. There were many creatures gathered, all similar to the one that abducted her. They were apelike with long green fur; and they varied in height from about three feet to seven feet.

A huge, round, rough-hewn stone table sat in the middle of the chamber; and to Andela's left rose an elevated shelf of stone that stretched from one side of the chamber to the other, forming a natural stage. On this stage sat three wooden thrones, with the center throne much larger than the ones to either side. There were also several wooden chairs positioned in a semicircle on the sandy floor. These chairs all faced the stone stage, and they were all situated between the stone table and the stage. At this point, all of the chairs were empty—none of the creatures were seated.

For several unnerving seconds nothing happened; the dreadful creatures stood and stared as if frozen in time. Then one of the larger ones, already situated near the stage, clambered up crudely carved steps and pompously situated himself in the center throne. He was followed by a somewhat shorter creature who sat to his right, and then by a third creature of even smaller stature who sat to his left. It became apparent to Andela that the creatures were enacting some sort of formal ceremony. Several of the other creatures began seating themselves in the wooden chairs.

There were fifteen chairs in addition to the three thrones, and each of the fifteen chairs was claimed by one of the creatures—each creature seating himself in a ceremonial manner. It was obvious that each occupant was assigned to his particular chair. About twenty creatures remained after the seating was completed, mostly the smaller ones; and these creatures seated themselves on the sandy floor between the chairs and the stage. One of the smallest creatures ambled to the door behind Andela and closed it, and then apparently locked it—she heard what sounded like a bolt slamming into place. The squat little beast then walked back and joined the others that were seated on the sand. Like the larger creatures that seated themselves in the chairs, the smaller creatures arranged themselves with the fronts of their bodies toward the stage. Curious, loathsome eyes turned and peered at Andela.

As the creatures assembled themselves, Andela made a more detailed perusal of her surroundings. She looked past the bizarre congregation and focused on the far side of the cavern; and as she did so, taut lines of concern drew across her forehead. The far wall receded as it dropped from the ceiling to the floor; and there were three large, black, metal cauldrons lined along the wall. The center cauldron was larger than the other two. Above the cauldrons were gaping holes, apparently ventilation shafts.

On the ground surrounding the cauldrons; barely visible over the far edge of the stone table; were mounds of white, meatless bones, including manlike skulls. The cauldrons were large enough to hold two or three humans; and above the center cauldron hung a net—an ominous-appearing hammock. The harrowing setup gave Andela the impression of a gruesome, makeshift barbecue. She strained her eyes to examine the net more closely, but then her eyes shifted as the silence was broken—the large creature who was seated in the center throne began speaking.

"My fellow Resants," he spoke somberly. His voice was low, resonant, and surprisingly refined. "Church will now begin. The priests may enter."

Andela was dumbfounded. Was this supposed to be a church service? Faint chanting commenced and then increased in volume, emanating from the dimly lit mouth of a large cave in the rear of the chamber, located to Andela's right. Andela could not interpret the words being sung, but she was quite certain that the creatures were singing in Latin; and the exquisite quality of the singing astonished her. Then her mind reflected upon the phrase first spoken by the leader; namely, *My fellow Resants*—she remembered her golden-haired rescuer, the petite swordsman who lured the weird batlike varmints away from her, warning her to watch out for Resants. These creatures certainly fit his description—thick, green fur hung like shag carpet from arms, legs, cheeks, and chins; rough, yellow nails hung like leathery leeches from blunt fingertips; and burning, yellow eyes peered like glowing lanterns from deep, dark, foreboding sockets.

The melodious chanting grew louder as the first priest emerged from the opening of the cave. If Andela had closed her eyes, she could have envisioned a line of Franciscan monks singing in a great medieval cathedral; but her eyes were far from closed, they were wide open. The lead priest was short, perhaps three feet tall; but the second priest was tall, at least six feet in height. Those that followed varied in height, with a total of twelve robed priests emerging from the rear cave. Each wore a muddy brown robe with a hood that hung about a lugubrious, melodramatic face. When a foot appeared from beneath the edge of a robe, it was covered with a brown slipper. The robes on the largest priests fit fairly well, while those on the smallest priests hung like drapes, concealing any trace of the creature within. The priests were all empty-handed with the exception of the seventh priest to enter; he was the largest of the priests, and he carried a huge book bound in leather.

As the last priest entered, several of the creatures that were seated on the sand and in the chairs about the stone table joined in singing. It became obvious that the priests were chosen based upon their ability to sing, because most of those joining them in song sounded like bloated bullfrogs or crooning warthogs. The priests continued marching ceremoniously, stepping in rhythmic unity until they were all situated before the stone stage, facing the large monster who was seated on the center throne. They continued singing until the green leader rose and waved his right arm; his hefty upper appendage looked like a lichen-laden branch swinging in a blustery breeze. Then the leader's arm dropped and all the singing stopped, followed by silence.

The towering leader turned his head and fixed his eyes upon Andela. She could feel the cold stares of all the occupants within the cavern, but the fearsome eyes of the grotesque leader overshadowed all else—eyes that were both captivating and dreadful. Then the leader shifted his eyes from Andela to the creature that held her beneath his paws. "I see, Org, that you have brought a visitor to our sacred gathering. Who is she?"

Andela felt a quiver pass through the furry hands that set upon her shoulders. "Lord Gelus, great and merciful, noble and wise, I beg your humble pardon—I do not know her name."

A threatening scowl became apparent upon the face of the Resant leader, who was addressed as Lord Gelus. "You do not know her name!" he roared, stomping a great foot against the stone beneath him. "I demand to know her name! Now!"

The hands upon Andela's shoulders began quaking. Despite the malfeasance her abductor had committed against her, Andela pitied him. "My name is Andela," she spoke aloud.

A gasp passed through the chamber. An ominous smile replaced the scowl upon Lord Gelus' face, and the trembling hands upon Andela's shoulders grew still. The intimidating leader's eyes shifted back to Andela's face. "So," he said, "you have voluntarily spoken in the midst of our church service." Then he was silent. He began looking up and down Andela's body as if she were a prize animal on display at a county fair. She did not like the way he looked at her.

Then Lord Gelus shook his head in a punitive manner. "Your attire is not very respectable. Is this the way you dress to attend church on Sundays?"

Andela felt affronted. Lord Gelus' demeaning words and degrading stare made her angry; but she was more frightened than angry. Her blue gown was modest and attractive, but it was not something she would wear to church; and it was certainly not something she preferred wearing when a horrid ogre's scandalous yellow eyes were fixed upon her body. "Oh, no, I usually wear a nice dress on Sunday mornings."

Lord Gelus tilted his head to one side and continued glaring with a look of interrogating contempt. He said nothing.

"Uh, and sometimes other things, my nicest shoes, and my nicest pearl necklace and earrings, and sometimes a hat and gloves," added Andela, realizing that she was including paraphernalia that she wore on Easter Sundays.

The hands upon Andela's shoulders eased their grip. She felt some relief as a look of appeasement appeared upon Lord Gelus' face. He raised one finger to his chin in a gesture of contemplation. "Perhaps you are not quite as degenerate as your choice of attire suggests. Hum, tell me, have you ever done anything to contribute to the success of the church?"

Andela was perplexed. She felt like she was on trial without knowing what crimes were charged against her. She glanced toward the mounds of bones scattered beneath the black cauldrons; and then she turned her face back toward Lord Gelus. "Yes, I've given tithes and offerings, I've helped in children's church, I've worked in the nursery, and I've taught Sunday school."

"Just little children, I assume," Lord Gelus interjected.

"Oh no," rebutted Andela, "I've taught adults too."

"Just women," returned Lord Gelus, waving a dismissing hand toward Andela and turning his face toward the audience of Resants.

"No, men too," said Andela; but the word *men* barely escaped her lips before she felt a queasy sensation pierce her abdomen. The word *too* faded in fearful uncertainty. She sensed something, something that made her mistrust Lord Gelus.

Lord Gelus turned his face back toward Andela. His yellow eyes had transformed into fiery, denunciating embers; yet when he spoke, his voice was mellow. "I see, well, perhaps, then, you are spiritually mature enough to realize that the church is a useful establishment?"

Andela nodded. "Yes sir," she affirmed, but she gained no sense of relief. Lord Gelus' face and voice conveyed appeasement, but his eyes were repulsive. Andela perceived that the flesh of Lord Gelus' eyes was inadequate to veil fiendish wickedness that seared outward from the depths of his soul.

"And you have concluded that church is a useful place to learn of such matters as Adam's transgression, and how sin may be atoned."

Andela opened her mouth to speak, but then faltered. As she stared into Lord Gelus' eyes, she determined that his questions were components of a treacherous plot. Again she glanced toward the black cauldrons, and then she turned her eyes back toward Lord Gelus. Rather than speaking, she proffered a fearful nod.

"I'll accept that as a *yes*," stated Lord Gelus. He turned his eyes away from Andela and sat back down on his throne. "Igmor, bring me the Holy Bible."

All twelve priests were standing before the stone stage, and the seventh in line still held the huge book that he had carried into the cavern when he entered. He clambered onto the stage and then he knelt before Lord Gelus. Using both hands, he raised the book to Lord Gelus.

Lord Gelus accepted the book; and then he waited until Igmor made his way back into position with the other priests. After bowing his head and lifting the book to his lips, Lord Gelus straightened and ritualistically opened the book in his lap. He turned several pages before stopping and resting his right palm on a selected passage of Scripture. He raised his face with a look of solemn virtue, and then he began directing his eyes back and forth across the group of creatures assembled in the cavern.

"The time has come, my fellow Resants, to grant our guest the courtesy of fair testing," he stated. "Pegus, you may assist Org in placing the woman, Andela, within the cords of divination above the cauldron of guilt."

Cruel faces peered back and forth between Andela and the netted hammock that hung above the center cauldron. She jolted with all the force her body could muster; but great, furry hands locked upon her shoulders like vice grips. Lord Gelus fixed venomous eyes upon her, and she became motionless, like a young deer with bright lights flashed into its wild eyes on a dark night, or like a field mouse caught in the merciless fangs of a viper. Pegus, one of the largest Resants in the assembly, rose from a chair and plodded across the sand to assist Org. Together they lifted Andela above their heads and carried her to the ominous hammock above the center cauldron.

Andela was helpless. Her heart throbbed with fright as Org and Pegus thrust her into the net and tightened it around her body until she was bound like a caterpillar in a cocoon, unable to move her arms or legs. One of the priests approached Org and handed him two strips of brown cloth. Org rolled up the smaller strip and climbed up onto the lip of the cauldron, holding the net to steady himself. He then attempted stuffing it into Andela's mouth. Andela resisted Org's attempts for several seconds, but then Pegus joined Org and grabbed hold of Andela's head while Org forced her mouth open and gagged her.

After gagging Andela, Org tied the second strip of cloth, a much longer strip, around her head. He pulled the second strip tight and forced it between her lips and teeth, and then he secured it in a knot behind her head, making it impossible for her to speak coherently. He and Pegus then climbed down from the cauldron and joined their fellow Resants. Andela was positioned so that she faced downwards. Her arms were bound against the sides of her body. Her feet, still clad with the golden slippers given to her by Madam Mercy, were aimed back toward the shadowy wall of the cavern. By raising her eyes, Andela was able to view the stone table and several Resants; but she had to force her face upward to see across the room.

It was futile for Andela to attempt moving her arms or legs; she could scarcely breathe. Her eyes darted involuntarily from place to place beneath her. She was puzzled to realize that there were no coals, logs, sticks, or ashes on the sand about the base of her cauldron, even though such debris was cluttered about the bases of the other two cauldrons. This lack of coals or ashes was puzzling in a sickening and ghastly way—there were plenty of bones about the base of her cauldron, so how did the pitiable creatures whose bones lay beneath her die?

Also puzzling was the appearance of the great cauldron itself. It was almost full; not of fluid or earth, but of a solid, black substance that looked like smooth, glistening basalt. The surface of the substance looked cool—a far cry from anything capable of boiling human flesh; but whenever Andela's eyes shifted back upon the mounds of bones stacked about the base of her cauldron, she could not help but dread that her captors were planning to make a meal of her. And as she thought about it, the stacks of meatless bones brought a verse of Scripture to her mind—*your adversary the devil, as a roaring lion, walketh about, seeking whom he may devour*. She knew that this particular Scripture warned against being devoured spiritually; and she knew that being devoured spiritually was something far worse than physical death; but nonetheless, her circumstances made it easy to interpret the passage of Scripture literally, and to view her captors as devils that intended to gnaw the meat from her bones.

"Let us show proper reverence for the reading of the Word," pronounced Lord Gelus.

Andela did not attempt to turn her face upward. She did not relish the thought of looking into Lord Gelus' yellow eyes.

"Natah-loo, symba-low, shemombelockambah-low…," the entire assembly of Resants began chanting. Their words no longer sounded Latin; they sounded like something intoned by a clan of delirious hyenas vying for strips of a bloody carcass. Andela raised her eyes. The Resants were rocking back and forth, seemingly entranced by the words and rhythm of the demonic music. A sense of inescapable doom passed through Andela's body—not only were these beasts heartless, they were also becoming mindless.

"First Timothy, chapter two, verse twelve," a clear, strong voice reverberated throughout the cavern. Andela quivered. Apparently the book that Lord Gelus read from was a genuine Bible. The chanting continued as he spoke; in fact, it grew louder. *"But I suffer not a woman to teach nor to usurp authority over the man, but to be in silence."*

Andela recognized the text. She had agonized through several Bible studies that addressed this passage of Scripture, and generally the person leading the study failed to give any clear explanation as to why the passage did not really mean what it seemed to be saying. There was a period of time when she actually maintained silence in church services when men were present; but when other women noticed what she was doing, she was badgered into abandoning such a practice. In fact, even most of the men considered her application of the words in the passage rather odd; though there was one outspoken male who maintained that she was behaving exactly as she should—he affirmed that all women should keep silent when there were men present in a church service. It was troubling. She was a sincere Christian woman, and she accepted the Bible as the True Word of God, so how could she ignore what these words seemed to be saying?

Andela's mind was grappling over the issue of women speaking in public church services when one of the larger priests stepped before her. He was so tall that his eyes were almost level with hers. She raised her face. Fiery, yellow eyes addressed her from within the draped hood of the priest's robe. "Be in silence," he spoke with a melancholy voice—smooth, sincere, and tormenting. "Be in silence, be in silence, and yet you spoke. You did this knowing, I am sure, that you are a woman, and knowing that church was in session, for Lord Gelus made that clear, yet you still chose to speak."

The hooded accuser cast his eyes downward, looking at the mound of bones and shaking his head from side to side. "Guilty, guilty, guilty," he crooned. "One who has admittedly attended church should know of a simple passage in the book of First Timothy, not that ignorance should be considered a proper excuse, but to willfully disregard the Holy Bible, oh my dear child, you are so inexcusably guilty."

Andela felt the priest's words wrenching her gut. She began to question her motives and sincerity in interpreting Scripture. Did peer pressure coerce her to accept falsely lenient doctrines? Was she wrongly driven by a desire to discover that women are not second-class citizens? Was she too proud? Did she search for answers with the wrong attitude? Was she vain? Was she rebellious?

Andela shuddered in mental anguish. Hadn't she always been willing to accept truth, if only she could know the truth? Couldn't she remember that something deep within her, or perhaps from far beyond her, had persuaded her that the passage in First Timothy must mean something other than what it appeared to mean? But then, was she right to respect such persuasion? Where did these feelings come from?

A ripple on the black surface below arrested Andela's thoughts. It was caused by a tear that dropped downward, her tear, but the surface no longer appeared solid; it was now liquid. What was happening?

"And that is not all, my dear," spoke a different voice, a scathing voice.

The first priest turned aside and stepped away, replaced by a somewhat shorter colleague. This second priest raised his yellow eyes to meet those of Andela; and then like the first priest, he turned his face downward and shook his head. "The Good Book says, *But I suffer not a woman to teach, nor to usurp authority over the man*, and yet you openly admit that you have committed the sin of teaching men!"

The priest had raised his voice in spurning accusation as he finished speaking. The chanting in the room rose to a pitch of frenzy, and some of the Resants rose and began pacing and stomping about the cavern, still rocking from side to side in rhythm with their merciless chanting. Andela grimaced; this was something else that bothered her, the matter of women teaching men. Madam Mercy had pointed out that Priscilla taught men, but was Madam Mercy mistaken? And as she began contemplating this issue, she perceived heat rising from the cauldron beneath her. Focusing downward, she was disturbed to note greenish bubbles rising and bursting at the surface of the thick, black brew—the mysterious concoction was boiling!

Lord Gelus spoke next, poring over the open book that lay in his lap. His voice was still fairly steady and dignified, but not so much as before; he was not immune to the emotional fervor waxing among his comrades. "First Timothy, chapter two, verses nine and ten, *In like manner also, that women adorn themselves in modest apparel, with shamefacedness and sobriety; not with braided hair, or gold, or pearls, or costly array; but, which becometh women professing godliness, with good works*."

A third priest, even shorter than the second, now appeared beneath Andela. Like the two priests before him, he raised his hooded face and peered at Andela with burning, yellow eyes; then he dropped his gaze downward and shook his head. He spoke more loudly than the previous priests—he had to speak more loudly in order to be heard over the rising din of the chanting throng behind him. "You have already admitted your guilt! Not with pearls, says the great and holy Book, yet you publicly proclaimed the sin of wearing pearls! Even to church! And doesn't the Fourth Commandment of the Ten Commandments instruct you to remember the Sabbath day and keep it holy, and yet you admit going to church on Sundays instead of Saturdays!"

Andela felt the net sag; apparently the cords suspending the net were sensitive to heat—the net stretched downward as the cords grew warmer. And now her mind, already in a state of torment, was further burdened with the thought that she disobeyed the Bible by wearing pearls and by not going to church on Saturdays. She desperately pondered the idea of crying out with her soul for God's forgiveness, yet she was not at all certain that wearing pearls was a sin, or was it? And didn't the early Christians meet together on the first day of the week rather than on the Sabbath?

"And your statement about Adam's transgression!" declared the third priest, still speaking loudly. "What transgression?! Does the Good Book not say, in First Timothy chapter two, verse fourteen, that *Adam was not deceived, but the woman being deceived was in the transgression*?! How dare you try and blame the wickedness of your fallen gender upon a man!?"

The net lowered yet farther toward the cauldron of torturous death. Tears were no longer detectable as they dropped into the bubbling brew.

Mist rising from the cauldron was rank and disgusting, but Andela hardly noticed the putrid odor—her senses were overwhelmed by her psychological turmoil and physical suffering—her skin was now glistening with sweat and painfully hot. She resisted screaming. She did not want to grant Lord Gelus the satisfaction of hearing her scream, but she feared that her bodily suffering would soon surmount her ability to resist screaming.

The third priest faded back into the throng of Resants, a mass of madly chanting beasts, swaggering, beating their chests, and pounding their palms on the stone table in tempo with the incessant chanting. It was easy to imagine the participants of such a barbarous orgy ripping the limbs from a boiled victim's body and gnawing flesh from bones.

Andela thought her physical life would soon be extinguished. The net dropped still lower and the heat and fumes grew unbearable—surely she would faint and die. She had not yet screamed. "Oh God," she moaned. The pitiable sounds she made would have been unintelligible to anyone listening. "God, please forgive me for anything I did not understand correctly. I would not want to disobey you in any way, whether knowingly or unknowingly. I have always desired to know Truth."

"Ignorance! Ignorance!" arose yet another voice from before the fuming cauldron, a voice that somehow managed to penetrate Andela's ears above the din of insane revelry.

Andela had not noticed another priest approach—apparently the heartless Resants did not consider the tortures delivered by the first three priests to be sufficiently nerve-racking. Her eyes gazed through fetid, steamy mist and focused upon the newcomer. She did not have to lift her eyes far, for this was the shortest priest of them all; the edges of his robe dragged far along the floor behind him. But then something happened that Andela did not expect—her eyes met his eyes, and a hope she could not have imagined ignited within her heart. Blue! His eyes were not yellow, and they were not burning with accusations, they were brilliant blue; and although she could not see his face very well, his two eyes showed from within his shadowy hood like lighthouse beacons piercing the darkness of a murderous storm.

"Ignorance of the kind that young children should have long ago left behind them," he spoke loudly enough for Andela to hear; but now that he had Andela's attention, he did not speak as loudly as before. Only the Resants passing nearest behind him could possibly be able to decipher any of his words, and few of them seemed apt to pay any heed to what he said—they were too consumed in pandemonium. Just in case they did chance to listen, though, the blue-eyed speaker made the tone of his words condemning and reprimanding. It was fortunate, though, that the Resants could not see his eyes.

"You are obviously ignorant of the Hebrew idiom, an idiom used throughout most of the New Testament in accordance with particular, God-given rules—rules that are supernatural and consistent. This idiom applies to over two hundred verses in the New Testament, and you can quell your ignorance in regard to this idiom by studying a book entitled *New Testament, Supernatural & Inerrant: Proof per Hebrew Idiom.* What false guilt you suffer! You are so ignorant!"

Though the words spoken by the petite stranger were harsh, his eyes were comforting and encouraging. Andela thought she recognized those eyes, but she did not tax her fatigued mind to try and bring the little priest's identity to memory; she simply fed from his eyes, drawing sustenance and hope from the courage and compassion that those uplifting eyes conveyed. And she determined that, if she survived her present ordeal, she would certainly search Amazon for the book the stranger mentioned.

Then the stranger spoke again, "The Hebrew idiom is identified in Biblical passages where *not this, but that* appears, or sometimes just *no, but*. It is an abbreviated way of saying, *not only this, but also that*. If I were of ancient Hebrew culture, and I said that I did *not eat apples, but oranges*; I would actually mean that I ate *not only apples, but also oranges*. Do you not feel ignorant?!"

Andela somehow found the strength to absorb the little priest's words. She did not know exactly why, but she felt that it was of utter importance for her to comprehend every word spoken. It was obvious that his comments about her ignorance were intended to pacify the savage mob behind him; he spoke much louder and turned his head slightly to the side when commenting about her ignorance, and much more intently and confidentially otherwise. He never turned his head far enough, however, to break the continual connection of their eyes.

"In Exodus chapter sixteen, verse eight, Moses told the children of Israel that their murmurings were not against him and Aaron, but against the Lord. However, in the same chapter, verse two, it plainly states that the whole congregation of the children of Israel murmured against Moses and Aaron. What Moses obviously meant by what he said was that the murmuring was not only against him and Aaron, but also against the Lord. The words *only* and *also* are not actually written down, but they are understood—this is the Hebrew idiom of which I speak. Is this not simple, ignorant one?!"

Andela nodded, holding her mutual gaze with the little priest. This was the first time she had ever heard about a Hebrew idiom, but what the little priest said made sense.

"In Genesis chapter thirty-two, verse twenty-eight, God says to Jacob, *Thy name shall be called no more Jacob, but Israel*. And yet in Genesis chapter forty-six, verse two, we read, *And God spake unto Israel in the visions of the night, and said, Jacob, Jacob*, so obviously this is an example of the Hebrew idiom—Jacob was no longer called *only* Jacob, but *also* Israel. And note that our Lord himself used the Hebrew idiom. In John chapter eleven, verse four, he said that Lazarus' sickness was not unto death, but for the glory of God. Then in John chapter eleven, verse fourteen, he plainly stated that Lazarus was dead. How could Lazarus be dead if his sickness was not unto death? What our Lord meant, then, was that Lazarus' sickness was not *only* unto death, but *also* for the glory of God. Again, the *only* and *also* are not written down, but they are understood due to the Hebrew idiom. Do you not comprehend such simplicities, oh ignorant one?!"

Andela nodded again; and although she was fully attentive to the little, blue-eyed priest, she also noticed that the searing heat from the cauldron below seemed less intense, or at least it was no longer increasing; and she also noticed that the net was no longer sinking downward.

"There are many other times the Hebrew idiom appears in Scripture. The phrase, *Labor not for the meat which perisheth, but for that meat which endureth unto everlasting life*, does not mean that we should not work in order to obtain food, oh ignorant one! It means that we should not *only* labor for physical gain, but *also* for spiritual gain. And when the Scripture says, *let us not love in word, neither in tongue; but in deed and in truth*, it certainly does not mean that we should never say, *I love you*, rather, it means that we should not *only* love in word, but *also* in deed and in truth. And when Peter told Ananias that he had not lied to men but to God, he obviously meant that Ananias had lied not *only* to men, but *also* to God, since Peter was a man. Is the ignorance of such things common?! And note this, when the Scripture says that women should adorn themselves *not with braided hair, or gold, or pearls, or costly array; but with good works*, it means that women should not *only* adorn themselves with fancy hairdos or jewels or expensive clothes, but *also* with good works, oh ignorant one! It means that inner beauty is more important than outer beauty, but it does not mean that the act of wearing pearls is a sin. Do you not comprehend your great ignorance?!"

Andela definitely felt the heat beneath her diminish. She could even detect the net rising. And it was not only outer pain that the petite priest's words quelled, but also the gnawing pain of doubt and confusion within her heart and soul. One of her favorite verses from the Psalms came to her mind, *As the hart panteth after the water brooks, so panteth my soul after thee, O God*. The words the little priest spoke were comforting, refreshing, and inspiring, even in the midst of her dire circumstances, and she realized that her heart had been thirsting for the information imparted by the little priest for a long time.

"And now, grant me your most sincere and effectual attention."

Andela laid all her thoughts to rest, concentrating so that she could mentally absorb whatever words would be spoken from the mysterious shaded realm of the sapphire eyes. She wondered what the face encompassing those eyes looked like, but it was difficult to see into the shadowy draped hood of the oversized robe—only the eyes were clearly visible.

"Considering that First Timothy chapter two, verse twelve, definitely contains the Hebrew idiom, a precise and accurate translation into modern English would read as follows, *...moreover it is not only permitted for a woman to teach, nor only to exercise authority over a man, but also to be quiet*. And it is notable that when the Hebrew idiom applies in Scripture, emphasis falls upon whatever follows the word *but*, whereas, those words that come before the word *but* and after the word *not* are considered to be of more obvious content, stating information that was more generally known when the Scripture was penned. Thus, when Paul wrote to Timothy in the second chapter of First Timothy, he treated the affirmation that women could teach men as a known fact. The intended emphasis in verse twelve was that women must follow the same order of conduct as men, and this was true even if those women recently departed from pagan, priestess-dictated religions of those times, such as the widespread, prevalent, adulterous cult of Isis where women ruled as sacred prostitutes. Oh the bane of ignorance!"

Though the scoffing charge of ignorance was intended to evade suspicions on the part of the Resants, Andela could not have agreed more—she had indeed been ignorant. But ignorance was apparently not too rare when it came to understanding Scripture, because no one had ever before taught her about the Hebrew idiom. The torturous agony that she experienced off and on for several years over this very segment of Scripture, namely First Timothy chapter two, verse twelve; was indeed a bane of ignorance, but it was ignorance shared by many. Now understanding the grammatical composition of this verse for the very first time, she sensed harmonies of Spirit and Scripture ringing within her heart like bells pealing victory and peace. Then again the little priest called her senses to attention.

"And that is not all, oh ignorant one! The Hebrew idiom is used again in verse fourteen of the same chapter, meaning that not *only* Adam was deceived, but *also* the woman, therefore, they were both in the transgression. And when one considers how the Hebrew idiom was constructed in this instance, the verse indicates that it was generally accepted that Adam was deceived. There was good reason, however, for emphasizing the fact that Eve was also deceived, for despite any ancient beliefs to the contrary, even the holy priestesses of Isis were guilty of sin, and even those priestesses needed redemption through the blood of Christ. And as verse fifteen points out, illustrating the depth of God's love and mercy, even a pagan priestess who is pregnant from religiously sanctioned whoredom, can repent of her sin, accept salvation through the blood of the Redeemer, and be a member of God's family. And her illegitimate child may be born and raised as a member of God's family."

Andela pondered the little priest's spoken words for several moments, and then she realized that one of the most confusing and troubling passages of Scripture that she had ever encountered was made rather simple to comprehend, namely First Timothy chapter two, verse fifteen.

"And regarding the Sabbath, remember that Christ never sinned, even though he broke the Sabbath as far as the Jews were concerned, declaring himself to be Lord of the Sabbath. Colossians chapter two, verses six through seventeen, make it clear that Jewish laws regarding eating, drinking, holydays, seasons, and the Sabbath no longer apply to the body of Christ. Christians, therefore, are free to meet on the first day of the week or whenever they choose. Every day is holy for Christians, whether at work, at rest, at worship, or at play."

The little priest paused, and Andela began realizing that he had effectually relieved her of all the guilty feelings she experienced from accusations made by Lord Gelus. She no longer felt any heat rising from beneath her. For the first time since locking eyes with the little priest, she broke her gaze and peered downward. She stared in wonder; the substance within the cauldron was no longer boiling. In fact, it was again a solid, glistening, black surface; and it appeared as cool as refrigerated Jell-O.

"Now listen," spoke the little priest, again capturing Andela's attention. "The end of a rope will fall through the ventilation shaft above you. When it does, you must secure it about your hands and arms, and then tug downward. You will be hoisted upward to the outer surface. I will most likely be detained, but they cannot kill me—I am immutable and invincible. Others above will help you. The air above is growing foul, they will have…"

"Silence!!!" roared the voice of Lord Gelus. At this point Lord Gelus stood on the sandy floor, positioned between the stone stage to his left and the stone table to his right. He had joined his emotionally drunken throng of followers while the second priest was verbally tormenting Andela.

The little priest stopped speaking and turned to face the throng of Resants. The riotous clamor within the chamber ceased, dissipating in reverberating echoes that coursed through passageways encircling the chamber. After the echoes faded away, all was quiet. Lord Gelus stood and peered into the little priest's shrouded hood. His hoary, green face became contorted with suspicion and hatred.

The little priest turned his face back toward Andela, and then he leaned forward and grabbed the lower edge of his robe. With one sweeping motion he removed the robe and slung it back toward the bewildered mob behind him. To Andela's surprise, there stood the little man who rescued her from the batlike creatures when she first entered Bill's land; he was still wearing the same blue and golden attire, and his sword was sheathed at his left side. "Catch yourself!" he exclaimed, still facing Andela. He used his right hand to withdraw his stunning sword, and an instant later he leaped high into the air and swung the sword in an arc, bisecting the net over much of Andela's body. He then dropped nimbly back to the floor, turning in midair to face the befuddled band of Resants.

Andela felt her body drop. Reaching upward and outward with both hands, she managed to grab portions of the severed net and steady herself as she lowered her feet to the solid, black surface below. It then took several seconds to disentangle her feet from the dangling net and kick it backward so that it hung behind and to the right of the cauldron. The little man's sword had sliced one of four ropes suspending the hammock. Glancing upward, she noted that the ventilation shaft opened directly above her; and it was more than large enough for the passage of her body. Then her attention was drawn to a familiar voice, the voice of Lord Gelus.

"So," Lord Gelus sneered, "it's you. I see that you've grown larger in this land."

"And my sword along with the rest of me," returned the little man, holding his sword outward. The golden blade was dazzling; it seemed to illuminate the entire chamber with golden rays. There was no hint of fear in the little man's voice.

"Perhaps so, but your brain must have atrophied while the rest of you grew larger."

Andela stood and listened, thankful that the little man had his sword. She removed the gag from around her head and withdrew the brown cloth from within her mouth; and then she tossed both of the detestable rags to the ground. Despite her activity, the eyes of Lord Gelus and the eyes of his followers all remained fixed upon the little man. Andela again looked upward into the opening above her, glimpsing a faint circle of light in the distance; but she did not look upward long—she did not want to draw attention to her avenue of escape.

The little man made no reply to Lord Gelus' insult. Andela wondered who was supposed to lower a rope downward from the outer surface. Lord Gelus seemed annoyed by the little man's silent composure. He signaled for some of the larger Resants to move toward the only two passageways into the cavern, one being the entranceway used by the priests, and the other being the doorway where Org entered holding Andela. Then Lord Gelus turned his face back toward the little man. Although he had not hesitated to insult the little man, it was apparent that he regarded him with fearful respect; and none of the Resants came near the raised blade of the golden sword.

"You had no right to interfere with the enactment of justice," spoke Lord Gelus. His voice was again mellow and refined. "By what inadmissible incantation have you thwarted the cauldron of guilt?"

"The black cauldron festers from false guilt as well as true guilt, as you well know, Lord Gelus," rebuffed the little man. "I dissolved false guilt."

Andela peered downward. So that was why her tormenting sense of guilt was followed by the sensation of scorching heat; the substance now supporting the weight of her body was transformed into a blistering brew by a sense of guilt, and it did not matter whether the guilt was based on truth or falsehood. She looked back up at the little man, the man whose teaching freed her from the tortures of false guilt.

"You lie!" bellowed Lord Gelus, raising his arms and taking a step forward. But then he halted—his eyes were fixed upon the golden sword. After a few tense seconds, he stared back down into the little man's face and lowered his arms to his sides. He then raised his left arm and pointed toward the vacated stone stage where the huge Bible lay open at the foot of the center throne. "I'm quite certain that you know what great Book lies before my seat of honor."

"I know that Book," replied the little man, avoiding any comment as to whether or not the large throne was a *seat of honor*.

"And you are bound by the words therein," Lord Gelus stated.

"I am bound by the words of Holy Scripture," the little man replied matter-of-factly.

"Um humm," croaked Lord Gelus without parting his lips. He flashed disdainful eyes about the room. "Igmor, bring me the Holy Book. And Org, bring that chair to the table."

Org grabbed the largest wooden chair and dragged it to the edge of the table. Lord Gelus stepped to the table and seated himself. The seventh priest arrived thereafter with the Bible, laying it down on the stone table and then backing away among the other Resants. The little man watched every move, never lowering the golden sword.

As she looked on, Andela sensed that her rescuer was pleased by the time-consuming proceedings. She figured that he wanted to keep the Resants at bay until the loose end of a rope dropped through the shaft above her. Her ears were on the alert for any sound suggesting a falling rope, but she could not help but listen to the conversation between the little man and Lord Gelus.

"Now," stated Lord Gelus, thumbing through the oversized Bible. "Ah yes, here it is, Romans chapter thirteen, beginning with verse one, *Let every soul be subject unto the higher powers. For there is no power but of God: the powers that be are ordained of God. Whosoever therefore resisteth the power, resisteth the ordinance of God: and they that resist shall receive to themselves damnation.*" He looked up at the little man, having pronounced the word *damnation* with staid emphasis. After a few suspenseful moments, he dropped his gaze back downward and continued reading. "*For rulers are not a terror to good works, but to the evil. Wilt thou then not be afraid of the power?*'"

Lord Gelus laid great, green paws on each open leaf of the Bible and peered upon the little man with a look of burning indignation. "I am the elected ruler here, officially placed in authority by the vote of the gathered assembly and given sole and complete power of governing over all that takes place within this cavern. Thus, you must subject yourself to me, or face damnation, and I decree by all authority of this realm that you must depart at once and leave the girl with us."

Andela felt her heart quicken. The hard surface beneath her feet seemed to soften. She had never understood the verses Lord Gelus quoted, but she had always assumed that those verses couldn't really mean what they seemed to say; and furthermore, she knew that she would disobey human rulers under certain circumstances. After all, should the Christians who were in Germany during World War II have subjected themselves to Adolf Hitler? And what about the Christians in Russia during the reign of Joseph Stalin? And the Romans—this passage of Scripture came from the Book of Romans, and surely God did not ordain a Roman Emperor as evil as Nero, did he? And what about the time that Peter and the other apostles disobeyed the high priest and the Jewish council, saying, *We ought to obey God rather than men?* On the other hand, could it be that she was guilty of disbelieving the Scriptures in Romans chapter thirteen just because they did not make sense to her? At any rate, she hoped the substance that she stood upon would not grow even softer.

The little man stood in silence. He neither moved nor spoke.

"Well?" Lord Gelus pressed. His voice was strained with impatience.

The surface beneath Andela's feet grew slippery and warm.

"Well what?" returned the man, speaking so calmly that his speech seemed more compatible with an afternoon tea party than the grim circumstances surrounding him. He then continued speaking before Lord Gelus had a chance to respond. "You are highly educated and intelligent, Lord Gelus, and I am fully aware that you know the term *higher powers* in Romans chapter thirteen, verse one, refers to the Creator and his divine angels, not to mortal rulers. The *he* in verse four of that chapter refers to an angel of God, whereas the *they* in verse six of that chapter refers to mortal rulers. When verse three says, *Wilt thou then not be afraid of the power?*, it is referring to situations where mortal rulers are upholding God's laws and principles, it does not apply when human rulers are ungodly. And speaking of mortal rulers, the first portion of verse three is written in the form of the Hebrew idiom, and it should be properly understood as follows, *For rulers are not only a terror to good works, but also to the evil.* You see, Lord Gelus, the Christians in Rome knew very well that rulers could be a terror to good works, but Paul wanted them to cooperate with mortal authorities when mortal laws and decrees were in keeping with God's laws and principles. On the other hand, Lord Gelus, when an individual in a position of mortal authority makes an evil decree, it is proper and right to challenge and resist that decree."

Though the little man never raised his voice, his words caused the yellow in Lord Gelus' eyes to ignite. Andela, meanwhile, felt the substance beneath her feet become cool and solid. She was very thankful for this—she did not relish the thought of sinking into the foul, fuming substance that had previously boiled beneath her. And in addition, she determined not to slip into feelings of guilt when Lord Gelus spoke; rather, she would wait and listen to what the little man had to say in response. After all, the little man's words were enlightening, and they held amazing power, including the power to maintain a solid surface beneath her feet.

"Lies!" Lord Gelus screeched, pounding his right fist against the surface of the open Bible. The group of Resants in the secluded chamber grew tense, as if expecting a vindictive order from their leader, an order to plunge into violence. But Lord Gelus gave no such order. Instead, he eyed his enemy thoughtfully, as if sizing up the little man both physically and intellectually. When he resumed speaking, his voice was again mellow and condescending.

"Surely you must realize that you are mistaken," said Lord Gelus, staring straight into the little man's eyes, "and I pity you for the unfortunate ignorance that someone has instilled into your misguided mind regarding the so-called *Hebrew idiom*. Do you think the passage in Matthew chapter six, verse thirteen, that states, *And lead us not into temptation, but deliver us from evil*, actually means, *And lead us not only into temptation, but also deliver us from evil?*"

The little man smiled and answered without hesitation. "You surely know better than that, Lord Gelus. In the Greek text of Matthew chapter six, verse thirteen, the Greek word for *and*, namely καὶ, comes directly before the Greek word for *not*, namely μὴ, and therefore, the Hebrew idiom does not apply. Aren't you familiar with Rule #5 in the list of rules that govern application of the Hebrew idiom, as plainly explained in the book entitled New Testament Supernatural & Inerrant: Proof per Hebrew Idiom?"

Lord Gelus displayed only mild agitation in response to little man's explanation. He opened his mouth to speak again, apparently having more to say in regard to the Hebrew idiom; but the little man interrupted him.

"Hold off, my dear Lord Gelus, for I can guess what question you would raise next."

"Really," crooned Lord Gelus.

"Correct me if I'm wrong, but I think you would next raise the question of John chapter three, verse sixteen, perhaps the most popular verse in the entire Holy Bible."

"Indeed I would," Lord Gelus conferred. "How could it be that a man should not *only* die, but *also* have eternal life? And I know, for a fact, that this verse contains the Hebrew idiom."

The little man shrugged. "What could make more sense, my dear Lord Gelus? Does not Hebrews chapter nine, verse twenty-seven, plainly state that it is appointed unto man once to die and then the judgment? Has not history made it obvious that Christian men and women who believe in the Son of God still die physical deaths? Clearly Jesus Christ himself pointed out that his followers might still experience physical death by the statement he made in Matthew chapter ten, verse twenty-eight, *And fear not them which kill the body, but are not able to kill the soul*. And this does not conflict with John chapter ten, verse twenty-eight, because the Greek New Testament has words meaning *into the eternal* after the Greek word for *perish* in this verse, so the verse should be translated as saying that Christ's sheep shall never *perish into the eternal*, or shall *never die spiritually*, though I would add that this does not necessarily apply to those sheep who willfully reject Christ's lordship and return to being Satan's goats—nothing can pluck Christ's sheep out of his hand, but this does not mean that Christ will force sheep to remain within his hand who willfully choose to leave. So then, what John chapter three, verse sixteen, reveals, is that those believing in the Son of God should not *only* die physically, but should *also* have eternal life thereafter. You see, Lord Gelus, it makes perfect sense that John chapter three, verse sixteen, is written in the form of the Hebrew idiom.

"And I might add," continued the little man, "that there is no disagreement between John chapter three, verse sixteen, and John chapter eleven, verses twenty-five and twenty-six. A Greek to English translation of the latter part of John chapter eleven, verse twenty-five, is as follows, *anyone believing in me, even if he died, yet shall he live.* And a word for word, direct translation of John chapter eleven, verse twenty-six, is as follows, *and all the having life and believing in me never may have died into the eternal; do you believe this?*' So an accurate translation of that verse is as follows, *and anyone alive who believes in me will never die spiritually; do you believe this?* And in keeping with the context of all New Testament Scripture, it is proper to interpret that Christ is referring to those who not only believe what he says, but who also repent from sin and accept him as Lord and Savior. Jesus Christ taught that he is spiritual bread, and those who partake of that bread will not die spiritually, even though they die physically. In short, Lord Gelus, there is no conflict between the verses in John Chapter three and those in John chapter eleven."

Lord Gelus raised a furry finger and opened his mouth to speak; but again, the little man spoke first.

"And what's more, Lord Gelus, I can now guess your next two rebuttals. First, note that Christ was sent into the world to condemn sin in the flesh, as Romans chapter eight, verse three, so clearly points out, so it is accurate to apply the Hebrew idiom to John chapter three, verse seventeen—Christ came not *only* into the world to condemn the world, but *also* so that the world could be saved. And furthermore, as is made clear in Matthew chapter seven, verse twenty-one, and also in James chapter two, verse nineteen, simply choosing to believe that Christ is the Son of God does not exempt a man from being condemned of sin, rather, it enables such a man to repent of sin and receive deliverance from death through the blood of Christ. In fact, a very strong warning against merely believing the truth, but not repenting from sin, is presented in another verse that contains the Hebrew idiom, namely Second Thessalonians chapter two, verse twelve, ...*that they all might be condemned who were not only believing in the truth but were also taking pleasure in unrighteousness.* Not believing the truth, however, is no better—John chapter three, verses eighteen through twenty-one, points out that men who choose not to believe in Christ do not escape condemnation through such unbelief. Christ is the true light and the only avenue to heaven, and those who reject him are condemned.

"Thus, John chapter three, verse eighteen, makes sense in light of the Hebrew idiom, since those who choose to believe that Jesus is the Son of God are condemned of sin in the flesh, and then may gain forgiveness for their sins through the blood of Christ by repenting of their sins and accepting Christ as Lord and Savior. Those who choose not to believe in Christ have no hope of forgiveness, because they reject belief in Christ. It is by believing that Christ is the Son of God, and by then repenting of sin and accepting his lordship and salvation through his blood, that men are cleansed from sin. This makes it correct to say that not *only* those who believe on the Son of God are condemned of sin in the flesh, but *also* those who do not believe on the Son of God are condemned.

"So then, John chapter three, verse eighteen, points out that those who reject the words of Christ are condemned *already*, meaning that nothing else is required to bring ultimate damnation. In contrast, those who accept the words of Christ are judged by those words, and may experience conviction for their sins, and will hopefully come to repentance and salvation. The first portion of John chapter twelve, verse forty-seven, applies to a man who rejects the gospel as soon as he hears it—*And if any man hear my words, and believe not, I judge him not.* This does not mean that such a man escapes judgment. The latter portion of the next verse states, ...*the word that I have spoken, the same shall judge him in the last day.* So, what this means is that a man who does not believe the words of Christ fails to have his heart opened to Christ's discerning judgment—judgment that can lead to conviction, repentance, and salvation—so in short, that man is destined to damnation. In contrast, those who receive the words of Christ thereby open their hearts to judgment and to the call to salvation. During Christ's ministry on the earth, he did not immediately damn persons to hell who rejected his words—those persons could change their minds and accept the words of Christ if they did so prior to their physical deaths. The same is still true for those who hear the words of Christ today—those persons who reject Christ's words at first, and who are thereby destined to damnation, but who then receive those words later, may still be saved, provided that they accept Christ's words prior to their physical deaths. This clarifies what is written in the Bible in John chapter twelve, verses forty-seven and forty-eight."

Lord Gelus sneered and again opened his mouth to speak...

"Now, now," asserted the little man, "patience, my Lord Gelus. Did I not say that I could guess your next *two* rebuttals? I daresay your second rebuttal would come from the same chapter, namely John chapter three, verse twenty-eight. You would argue, no doubt, that the Hebrew idiom would cause John the Baptist to say that he was not *only* the Christ, but was *also* sent before Him. This seems to present a dilemma in regard to the Hebrew idiom, does it not? Well, one needs only to know that John the Baptist, a man who wore animal hides and ate locusts, did not apply the Hebrew idiom to his speech. Therefore, the Hebrew idiom does not apply to any quotes from John the Baptist, as is made clear in Rule #3 of the list of rules that govern the Hebrew idiom, as found in the book I mentioned previously. Have I not rightly guessed the substance of your rebuttals, Lord Gelus?"

An expression of staid annoyance rested upon Lord Gelus' face. "Perhaps so, a marvel for such a miniature mind. But how would you explain Second Timothy chapter one, verses seven and eight? Has God not *only* given his children the spirit of fear, but *also* of power? And should a man not *only* be ashamed of the testimony of the Lord, but *also* partake of the afflictions of the gospel?"

"Scripture supports Scripture," returned the little man. "Does Proverbs chapter nine, verse ten, not state that the fear of the Lord is the beginning of wisdom? Does Second Corinthians chapter seven, verse one, not speak of perfecting holiness in the fear of God? Does Acts chapter nine, verse thirty-one, not point out that the early churches were edified as the people walked in the fear of the Lord? It is consistent with Scripture, then, that God has not *only* given his children the spirit of fear, but *also* of power, and love, and a sound mind. And a couple more comments on this subject—Romans chapter eight, verse fifteen, another verse containing the Hebrew idiom, reveals that Christians are not *only* bound to God in fear, but are *also* given the wonderful realization of being his children. And First John chapter four, verse eighteen, which also contains the Hebrew idiom, points out that there is not *only* fear in love, but *also* points out that fear is decreased as love is perfected, and in fact, totally perfected love abolishes fear."

The little man paused for a moment and glanced about the room. Andela had become spellbound as she listened to the ongoing debate, and the little man's surveillance of his enemies brought her mind back to the matter of escaping through the ventilation shaft above her. She pretended to scratch an ear as she glanced upward—there was still no rope protruding from the shaft. Then she returned her eyes to the scene before her.

"And next, Lord Gelus," resumed the little man, "let me point out that the Greek word for *ashamed* that appears in Second Timothy chapter one, verse eight, is in the subjunctive mood and passive voice in the Greek text, and let me remind you that the passive voice means that the subject is acted upon by something or someone else, rather than doing the acting himself. And let me also remind you that the subjunctive mood, in the language of the Greek New Testament, is the mood of possibility or probability. Thus, it would be proper to translate First Timothy chapter one, verse eight, as follows, *Do not then only have others probably bestowing shame upon you for the gospel of our lord nor only for me his prisoner, but also be a partaker of the afflictions of the gospel according to the strength of God.* In other words, Lord Gelus, Paul was coaxing Timothy to be bold in his testimony for the Lord, even if it meant he would not *only* suffer social ridicule, but *also* suffer physical persecution. And let me point out that the passive and subjunctive rendition of the word *ashamed* that is found in First Timothy chapter one, verse eight, is in notable contrast to the indicative form of the Greek word for *ashamed* that appears in Romans chapter one, verse sixteen. The first portion of Romans chapter one, verse sixteen, is properly translated, *For I am not ashamed of the gospel of Christ.* And Romans chapter one, verse sixteen, does not contain the Hebrew idiom."

"Perhaps so, perhaps so," Lord Gelus droned. "But what about those verses in the twelfth chapter of Romans? Should God's servants be not *only* conformed to this world, but *also* transformed by the renewing of their minds? And should they be not *only* be overcome of evil, but *also* overcome evil with good?"

The little man did not appear troubled by Lord Gelus' questions. "Rule #5 applies again, Lord Gelus, when it comes to Romans chapter twelve, verse two—this verse does not contain the Hebrew idiom. And in regard to evil overcoming good, the Apostle Paul was well aware that the forces of evil would win a battle now and then. Nonetheless, he encouraged the servants of God to continue fighting and to win a few battles of their own. It makes sense, then, that God's servants should not *only* be overcome of evil, but should *also* overcome evil with good, whether in physical battle, social battle, legislative battle, legal battle, or political battle. And in light of these particulars, Lord Gelus, I think the course of our deliberation has served to validate the conformity and consistency of the Holy Scriptures. And furthermore, it should be evident that the Hebrew idiom serves to establish the remarkable harmony of the infallible New Testament Scriptures as penned in their original Greek language."

"Harmony," Lord Gelus scoffed. "Harmony, you speak of harmony, but what about the obvious discord between First John Chapter five, verse twelve, and John chapter fourteen, verse six? First John Chapter five, verse twelve, indicates that the only way to have life is through the Son of God, but when the Hebrew idiom is applied to the latter portion of John chapter fourteen, verse six, we see that not *only* man cometh to the Father, but *also* by the Son. In other words, John chapter fourteen, verse six, clearly indicates that a man can get to heaven by means other than through the Son of God. Does this not conflict with your idealistic concept of Scriptural harmony?"

The little man shook his head with rebuke. "Now, now, Lord Gelus, you know the Greek New Testament as well as any scholar I've ever met. In the Greek New Testament, there is no Greek word for *but* in John chapter fourteen, verse six. So in the Greek text, this verse is not written in the form of the Hebrew idiom, as is explained in Rule #11 of the rules governing application of the Hebrew idiom. An accurate Greek to English translation of this verse, as I am certain you know, is as follows, *No one comes to the Father if not through me.* So, Lord Gelus, the Holy Scriptures are quite consistent in affirming that the Son of God is the only avenue to heaven. And two other verses that do not contain the Greek word *but* in the Greek New Testament are Revelation chapter twenty-two, verse three, and Revelation chapter twenty-one, verse twenty-seven, so these two verses, likewise, do not contain the Hebrew idiom."

There were several moments of tense silence. When Lord Gelus spoke next, his voice was less calm. "Alright then, you want Greek, I'll give you Greek. Do you think that a bishop should be not *only* given to wine, not *only* a striker, not *only* greedy of filthy lucre, but *also* patient? Is this not absurd? How can you possibly think there is anything to this *Hebrew idiom*?"

Andela clinched her teeth, holding fast to her hope that the little man would successfully rebut Lord Gelus, and the substance beneath her feet remained firm.

"I cannot accuse you of ignorance, Lord Gelus, for you know the words of Holy Scripture incredibly well, and I applaud you for that," returned the little man.

Andela raised her brows.

The little man continued, "However, Lord Gelus, what I do accuse you of is willful deceit. You are fully aware of the seventeen rules that govern application of the Hebrew idiom. Generally speaking, as made clear in Rule #2, a phrase or statement given in the form of the Hebrew idiom only contains the word *not* once, and then contains the word *but* once. If there is more than one item to be included with the term *not* when the Hebrew idiom is used, then the additional items are preceded by words other than *not*, such as the words *neither*, or *nor*, or *and*, or *or*, such as is found in First John chapter three, verse eighteen— *Little children, not only might we love with words nor only with the tongue but also with actions and in sincere truth*, and such as is found in First Timothy chapter two, verse twelve—*...moreover it is not only permitted for a woman to teach, nor only to exercise authority over a man, but also to be quiet*. These two verses are examples of the Hebrew idiom. On the other hand, First Timothy chapter three, verse three, and Titus chapter one, verse seven, are examples of verses where the word *not* appears more than once, so these verses do not contain the Hebrew idiom."

Silence ensued. Andela watched nervously as Lord Gelus sat and stared at the little man with a blank expression. He began tapping on the surface of the stone table with one of his thick, yellow fingernails. Since all other inhabitants of the secluded chamber were frozen in silence, the sound of Lord Gelus' tapping was plainly audible, echoing from wall to wall. At last he stopped tapping and spoke. "Yes, yes, I know all about it," he spoke condescendingly, like a resentful tutor forced to assist a dull student. "In fact, if you look in the original Greek text at Titus chapter one, verse seven, the Greek word for *not* appears five times in succession."

Andela frowned. The words Lord Gelus spoke seemed to support the little man, but his tone of voice was demeaning. She did not trust Lord Gelus in the least.

"So you agree then," the little man returned. There was a note of irony in his voice.

"Perhaps so, though I'm astounded that your limited mental capacity facilitates awareness of such facts. Well then, tell me what works a man must perform in order to obtain salvation, since your Hebrew idiom causes Titus chapter three, verse five, to indicate that man is saved not *only* through his works, but *also* by the mercy of God."

"Easy now, Lord Gelus. First Thessalonians chapter one, verse three, mentions the *work of faith* for which Paul commended the Thessalonians. Although I would agree that the work of faith alone, without any other work in addition to simply believing, is dead, as stated in James chapter two, verse twenty-six—and note that simply believing is even compared to something that devils do, as is written in James chapter two, verse nineteen—and although I would agree that persons will be rewarded according to their works, as stated in Matthew chapter sixteen, verse twenty-seven, I would also point out that men are not saved by the kind of works that are considered great achievements for men to boast about, like giving a lot of money or climbing a high mountain, as stated in Ephesians chapter two, verse nine."

Lord Gelus' eyebrows rose in malignant delight. "Oh really? Just how do you propose to explain that?"

"Quite simply, Lord Gelus. The foundation of salvation is for a man to act upon his faith and repent of dead works and accept the cleansing of his sins through the great work of Jesus Christ on the cross, thereby accepting Jesus Christ as his personal Lord and Savior. This is a work of a man's will, and it is a work that may be accomplished by any person who will repent from dead works and come to salvation through Christ, including those persons deemed the poorest and the weakest and the most undeserving. And do not forget that the greatest work in granting salvation to mankind is done on God's part, including the perfect work accomplished by Jesus Christ through his blood sacrifice on the cross. Thus, a man is not saved by his work of believing, alone, but also by his work of repenting from dead works and accepting Jesus Christ as his personal Lord and Savior, thus receiving salvation through the provision and mercy of God. This is a key point of Scripture. Do you not agree?"

Lord Gelus rose to his full height, scooting the chair backward behind him. "Agree!" he blared. "Sure I agree! I agree that a horde of ancient fools went around jabbering in Hebrew, Greek, or Arabic with the use of a confounded Hebrew idiom!" He picked up the large Bible and slung it across the empty space behind him without even glancing backward. The huge book slammed into the stone wall, crumpling pages and tearing a large section of the manuscript from its binding; and then it slid to the sandy floor where it landed on one end and then plopped backward with a thud.

Lord Gelus continued facing the little man. "What I do not agree with is your oldfangled concept of right and wrong, good and evil, truth and falsehood—that's all rubbish! All that really exists is power and weakness, a truth that all we Resants know fully well."

Threatening murmurs emerged from guttural throats about the chamber. The surface beneath Andela's feet remained solid, but she still felt her pulse quicken and her skin tingle.

"I do not agree with you," stated the little man. "But even if I did agree, the power of good is greater than the power of evil."

Lord Gelus glared at the golden sword that the little man continued to hold aloft. Then he dropped his eyes back down into those of the little man and pointed back toward the crumpled Bible. "You, in your great ignorance, are bound by the words and teachings in that detestable mound of debris, so you cannot use that sword against any creature composed of flesh and blood, such as me and my companions."

"And why not?" challenged the little man, raising his sword higher and causing many of the Resants to take a step backward.

"Have you forgotten Ephesians chapter six, verse twelve—*For we wrestle not against flesh and blood, but against spiritual wickedness*?"

"You've cut the verse a little short," replied the little man. "Nonetheless, you've quoted enough of the passage for me to point out another example of the Hebrew idiom—*...because we fight not only with blood and flesh, but also with the powers, with the authorities, with the rulers of this darkness, with the spirits of evil in the spheres of spiritual activity*. You see, Lord Gelus, true children of God will engage in physical matters and physical battles, as well as engaging in spiritual matters and spiritual battles. And remember Matthew chapter ten, verse thirty-four, a verse that does not contain the Hebrew idiom in light of Rule #2 in the list of rules that govern application of the Hebrew idiom, and a verse teaching that Jesus Christ did not come to bring peace to the earth, but rather, a sword. And note that this verse is not in conflict with Luke 2:14. A direct Greek to English translation of Luke 2:14 is as follows, *Glory within to most high God and upon earth peace within to men of good will*. Thus, Luke 2:14 addresses peace to men of good will, not peace to an evil world where a sword is needed in order to deliver human beings from evil bondage and grant them the freedom to know and worship Jesus Christ. It follows, then, that the term peacemakers in Matthew 5:9 should be interpreted as those who establish freedom to know and worship Jesus Christ and who foster a society where men are encouraged to be of godly disposition."

"Bosh!" swore Lord Gelus. His eyes pored over the little man. "So you claim that a Christian man can engage in physical battle? I ask you, how can he do such a thing without his fleshly body going berserk and committing sinful atrocities? Does the seventh chapter of Romans not make it clear that a man cannot control the actions of his flesh? Does it not say that a man's flesh will commit evil that the man cannot resist? If a man's flesh works evil regardless of the man's will or intentions, then should he not stay far away from any battlefield where his body can become the instrument of evil?"

The little man waited for Lord Gelus to simmer down. "My oh my," he finally remarked, "now you're really reaching for straws. I guess you hoped that I wouldn't know the difference between a man who is *sold under sin*, as stated in Romans chapter seven, verse fourteen, and a man who is *in Christ Jesus*, as stated in Romans chapter eight, verse one. The term *sold under sin* does not refer to a Christian man—a Christian man is redeemed by the blood of the Lamb. A man who is *sold under sin* is the property of the Evil One.

"Therefore, the description of a man who is ruled by the flesh in Romans chapter seven is the description of a man who is the property of the Evil One. This passage describes a man who does not want to be the property of the Evil One, but who cannot redeem himself by his own efforts, and thus he remains subject to the Evil One's control. On the other hand, Romans chapter eight, verse four, features the Hebrew idiom, teaching that those who are in Christ Jesus walk not *only* after the flesh, but *also* after the Spirit. Remember that when the Hebrew idiom applies, the emphasis is on what comes after the word *but*. Christians walk not *only* after the flesh, but *also* after the Spirit, with the emphasis being to walk after the Spirit. It should be obvious that, to some degree, Christians walk after the flesh, feeding and clothing themselves and having sex within godly marriage. However, in the case of true Christians, meaning Christians who go to heaven when they die, the Spirit rules over the flesh. And as verses ten through thirteen of that chapter disclose, the flesh is *quickened* by the Spirit, and the Greek word for *quickened* means to *vitalize* or *give life*. In short, a Christian man does not walk in flesh that is ruled by the flesh, he walks in flesh that is ruled by the Spirit. It would be a shame, don't you think, for fleshly battles to be fought solely by those men who are ruled by the flesh? Would righteous rule and godly kingdoms not be much more likely to arise and flourish if fleshly battles were won by soldiers who were ruled by the Spirit?"

"Bosh again! And double bosh! One of your rules governing the Hebrew idiom, namely Rule #2, keeps the Hebrew idiom from applying to verse one of Romans chapter eight, so this verse is obviously in contradiction to verse four. In other words, *who walk not after the flesh* in verse one is a flagrant contradiction to *who walk not only after the flesh* in verse four."

The little man glanced toward Andela, who was spellbound by the conversation, and winked. He then again faced Lord Gelus. "Would you not agree with me, Lord Gelus, that purposefully speaking lies is evil? You know full well that the phrase *who walk not after the flesh, but after the Spirit* is not found in the Greek text of Romans chapter eight, verse one—a fact that is corrected in the New International Version of the English translation of the New Testament. So, it is Rule #15 that applies to Romans 8:1, not Rule #2."

Despising, yellow eyes turned momentarily upon Andela, and then again addressed the little man. "I admit that I am evil, and I am evil by choice, a choice that I do not regret. So now then, I command you to turn the girl over to me. You cannot resist me, for the Book to which you pledge your allegiance commands that you *resist not evil*. This commandment is stated plainly in Matthew chapter five, verse thirty-nine."

As Lord Gelus mentioned *the girl*, Andela became aware of cruel stares cast in her direction. She darted her eyes about the underground den of voracious cutthroats, and her heart seemed to beat upward into her throat. She looked back toward the little man and his golden sword.

"I have yielded the courtesy of acknowledging your great mental cognizance regarding the words penned in Scripture, Lord Gelus," returned the little man, seemingly ignoring the fact that Lord Gelus gave every indication of an impending assault. "So why must you continue to treat me as one who is completely ignorant of Scriptural content? I am aware that the Greek word for *resist* in Matthew chapter five, verse thirty-nine, derives from the same Greek root word as the word used for *resist* in James chapter four, verse seven—*Resist the devil, and he will flee from you*. I am also aware that a literal Greek to English translation of Hebrews chapter twelve, verse four, reads as follows—*Not yet even to bloodshed have you resisted in striving against sin*. The passage you quote, namely Matthew chapter five, verse thirty-nine, is written in the form of the Hebrew idiom, and it instructs men to not *only* resist evil, but *also* turn the other cheek. And do you know what *turning the other cheek* means, Lord Gelus?"

"Enlighten me," Lord Gelus returned in a voice laden with sarcasm.

"A slap upon the cheek, in the culture of those times, was a means of publicly insulting someone…"

"Any fool knows that," interjected Lord Gelus, sounding impatient.

"Yes, well, and I think that you must agree that you have publicly insulted me by the words you have used to describe me—*trifling, ignorant fool*, and so forth."

"So what?" snapped Lord Gelus. "Given the fact that you are an interfering, mindless half-wit, I do not see how the words I have spoken should be deemed inappropriate."

"No matter," replied the little man, his voice still steady and calm. "This gives me the opportunity to present a good example of *turning the other cheek*. You, Lord Gelus, have publicly insulted me, and you have indicated that you care nothing for me."

"And that is an understatement."

"Okay, so, if I were to simply insult you back, indicating that I care nothing for you either, then I would not be *turning the other cheek*. So then, instead of just snubbing you, even though you are my enemy and I may be forced to overthrow or destroy you, I invite you to repent from your evil ways and become my spiritual brother. I truly hope that you will join the forces of good. Thus, *turning the other cheek* means to continue inviting those who are evil to repent of evil and turn to good, even if they insult you. This is in keeping with the instruction to *love your enemies*. It may leave me vulnerable to further insults, but what is more important, it may result in your salvation."

Andela gazed upon Lord Gelus' burning eyes—they were fixed solely upon the little man, giving the impression of an enraged bull on the verge of charging. But when Lord Gelus spoke again, his voice seemed incongruent with his eyes, much more subdued and sophisticated.

"You speak of loving your enemies," said Lord Gelus. "But if I remember correctly, Luke chapter fourteen, verse twenty-six, teaches that a real disciple should hate his father, hate his mother, hate his wife, hate his children, hate his brethren, hate his sisters, and hate his own life. How can you speak of loving anyone when your Bible so clearly instructs you to hate?"

Again the little man shook his head. "You must be arguing for the sake of arguing, Lord Gelus. Do you not remember the two greatest commandments? The first is to love God, and the second is to love your neighbor as yourself. The Greek word that is translated as *hate* in Luke chapter fourteen, verse twenty-six, can mean to *esteem less* rather than to actually *hate*, and to *esteem less* is certainly what is meant in this verse. Thus, what this verse is teaching is that obedience to God must take precedence over the wishes, desires, or commandments of any other person, agency, or power in the universe. God rightfully reigns supreme, and it would be idolatry to place anyone or anything else above him."

"Perhaps that is so, but then, how can you speak of *loving your enemies* while holding a threatening sword ready for battle?" rebutted Lord Gelus.

Andela was certain that the only thing preventing an immediate attack against her was the raised, golden sword. She surmised that Lord Gelus persisted in conversation solely because he hoped to gain some sort of tactical advantage through dialogue, such as convincing the little man that he should not fight. She shuddered to think what would happen if the little man laid down his sword.

"Loving your enemies means that you want what is best for your enemies, namely that they turn from evil and receive the blessings of life and goodness," explained the little man. "However, Lord Gelus, we are not instructed to *have no enemies*, and thus, we are not instructed to become pacifists who will not battle for any cause. If we are to *love our enemies*, then it should be obvious that we must have enemies. And an enemy, Lord Gelus, is someone you are opposing, perhaps even seeking to overthrow or destroy, as you may confirm by consulting a dictionary. The fact is, Lord Gelus, that my spiritual enemies hold to teachings that result in eternal death, and I will seek to overthrow or destroy those teachings, not only so that my spiritual enemies may themselves be saved, but also so that my spiritual enemies will not lead others down the pathway to eternal death. Meanwhile, I will be kind to my spiritual enemies when I am able to do so, feeding them if they hunger, helping them in need, and lovingly inviting them to turn from false religions to redeeming truth.

"And while we're on the subject of love, let me point out that there are two different Greek words translated as *love* in the New Testament. The first is *agape*, meaning an unconditional desire for someone's ultimate good, a desire that is not dependent on any likeable qualities. The second is *philia*, meaning a strong bond existing between persons who share a common interest or activity, as in a virtuous friendship. Whenever the New Testament instructs persons to love their enemies, the word for love is *agape*, not *philia*. This explains how the New Testament can instruct men and women to love those who they are seeking to overthrow or destroy, because they can hope that their enemies will repent of evil and join them as brothers and sisters in God's eternal family, even when they do not count their enemies as friends.

"And although the Old Testament never plainly declares that we should love or hate our enemies, Ecclesiastes chapter three, verse eight, states that there is a time to love and a time to hate. King David proclaims in chapter one hundred thirty-nine of the Psalms—*Do not I hate them, O Lord, that hate thee? And am not I grieved with those that rise up against thee? I hate them with perfect hatred: I count them mine enemies.* Psalms chapter ninety-seven, verse ten, instructs those that love the Lord to hate evil, and Psalms chapter eight, verse thirteen, states that the fear of the Lord is to hate evil.

"The teachings of the Bible make it clear that while God hates sin, he loves sinners. And since Matthew chapter five, verse forty-eight, teaches children of God to be perfect, even as their Father in heaven is perfect, then Christians should hate the evils that are unacceptable to God, but should love the persons who need saved from such evils. This does not mean, however, that certain individual men and women do not live such lives and make such choices as to achieve the undesirable distinction of procuring God's hatred in addition to God's love—Psalms 5:5 teaches that God hates all of those persons contriving of lawlessness, which may be interpreted as meaning that God hates persons who use cleverness or cunning to foster evil practices or laws, namely practices or laws that are contrary to the laws established by the Word of God. Christians should hate those persons whom God hates, even as David, a man after God's own heart, hated those persons whom God hated. This is true even though Christians, at the same time, should love those persons who rightfully earn their hatred, hoping that those persons whom they both hate and love will repent from evil and receive salvation through the blood of Christ.

"So, Lord Gelus, I deem it appropriate that I both love and dislike you. I have *agape* love for you, but unless you repent of your evil and change your ways, I do not have *philia* love for you—I count you as my enemy, not my friend. It would be a crime if I hated what God my Creator loves, and it would also be a crime if I failed to abhor what God my Creator abhors."

The little man paused; and before speaking again, he made a swipe through the air with his sword.

"I have commented upon my treatment of spiritual enemies, Lord Gelus. So now, let me comment upon my treatment of physical enemies. My physical enemies include those creatures intent upon murdering me

201

or other innocent persons for whom I am physically responsible. And unless those enemies repent of their evil intentions before my sword reaches the napes of their necks, they may find themselves headless."

An uneasy silence followed the little man's words. Lord Gelus peered from side to side across the chamber, seeming to convey some sort of unspoken message to the clan of restless Resants. Andela again glanced behind and upward, and then dropped her face back downward—there was still no sign of a rope. She felt that an attack by the green beasts was imminent; but then the little man spoke again, and his words drew Lord Gelus' attention.

"Do not misinterpret my frank speech, Lord Gelus. I do not desire any sort of bloodshed. Instead, I want you to consider your great potential—just think what an outstanding Cherinede such a refined and educated individual as yourself would make. You must be aware that a Resant may be transformed into a Cherinede by repenting of evil and choosing to join the forces of good. You would be most welcome to join..."

"Silence!" Lord Gelus spewed with ireful vehemence, interrupting the little man and dissipating Andela's mental contemplation as to what a Cherinede might be. "I do not desire to be utterly nauseated." He stared at the little man without blinking. Searing hatred poured from his yellow eyes. "Now let's get to the point—I want you to leave."

"Gladly," responded the little man, "as long as I can take the girl with me."

Once more Lord Gelus raised a great, furry hand and pointed back toward the crumpled Bible. "If that pile of debris is true, as you contest, then she does not need you here. John chapter fourteen, verse fourteen, plainly states—*If ye shall ask any thing in my name, I will do it.* Is the Person who that verse refers to able to rescue the girl? If so, and if that Book is true, then all she has to do is use that Person's name and ask him to rescue her. So, is the Book true, or not?"

The little man shrugged. "The Bible is true, yes, but your misinterpretation of this verse is inexcusable, Lord Gelus. I think you know better."

"Really?" Lord Gelus taunted. "How so?"

The little man took a deep breath. He perceived Lord Gelus' mounting attitude of impatience, and he was glad to see his adversary drawn back into debate. It was his plan to delay any physical battle until Andela was hauled upward through the ventilation shaft.

"To begin with," commenced the little man, "it would be remarkably vain for anyone to think he could get whatever he wanted from God by simply exploiting a particular name. To use God's own name for such a purpose, whether it be the name of God the Father, God the Son, or God the Holy Spirit, would be using the name of God with profound vanity, or in other words, it would be taking name of God in vain. I know you're familiar with the Ten Commandments, as recorded in Exodus chapter twenty. The third Commandment states—*Thou shalt not take the name of the Lord they God in vain.* So, do you really think the verse you quoted from John chapter fourteen means what you have implied?"

Lord Gelus flashed a wicked grin. "I cannot help it if John chapter fourteen, verse fourteen, advises readers to break the Third Commandment," he stated with fiendish delight. "You have previously alluded to the subjunctive mood as it appears in the Greek New Testament, and I can assure you that I am proficient in interpreting all moods in the Greek text, including subjunctive, optative, imperative, and indicative. For example, the Greek word for *give* in John chapter ten, verse twenty-eight, is in the indicative mood, meaning that it presents a definite assertion—*And I give unto them eternal life.* On the other hand, the Greek word for *shall receive* in Mark chapter ten, verse thirty, is in the subjunctive mood, meaning that everything written in that verse about getting houses, and lands, and family, during one's mortal life on earth, is something that may possibly happen—it is not something that will definitely happen. Do you not agree?"

Andela fixed her eyes upon the little man, wondering if he would agree with Lord Gelus. She didn't know what Lord Gelus was up to, but she figured it couldn't be anything good.

"Quite so, I totally agree," the little man said calmly.

Andela was startled by the little man's response. Again she glanced up and behind her—still no rope. Then she again directed her attention toward the debate between the brave little man holding the protective, golden sword; and the gruesome, green monster who sought to gnaw the flesh from her bones. It made her nervous that Lord Gelus seemed to be making gains in the argument, but at least the argument was not making her feel guilty about anything, and the black substance beneath her feet remained solid.

"All right," continued Lord Gelus, "then answer this question. Do you not agree that the Greek word for *do* in John chapter fourteen, verse fourteen, is in the indicative mood?"

"Well...," the little man responded, hesitating while Lord Gelus gazed upon him like a ravished lion expecting to make a kill. "This is a little more challenging than most questions regarding mood forms in the Greek New Testament."

"Bah!" scoffed Lord Gelus. "I'm quite aware that the particular Greek word used for *do* in this verse can be either subjunctive or indicative, depending on the tense. But given the context for that verse, do you not agree that the future tense should be applied?"

"Hmmm, well, I cannot argue against that particular point."

"So you agree then?" Lord Gelus persisted.

"Yes."

"Very well then, do you not agree that the Greek word for *do* should be interpreted in the indicative mood?"

The little man stood and presented a look of contemplation for several seconds, resulting in a low growl of consternation from Lord Gelus' throat. Finally, he shrugged one shoulder and replied. "Yes, I agree."

"Aha!" Lord Gelus proclaimed. "Then you must agree that John chapter fourteen, verse fourteen, overrules the Third Commandment, and means exactly what I pointed out to begin with, so you must either leave the girl, or denounce the Bible."

Initially, there was no response. Andela felt herself beginning to tremble. She couldn't believe the argument had taken such a turn, and she was scared. It would be terrible, of course, if the little man left her alone with the throng of wretched cannibals; but she also felt certain, deep within her heart, that it would be horribly devastating if the little man denounced the Bible. In fact, as she thought about it, she decided that she would prefer being torn to pieces by savage beasts rather than hearing the brave little man denounce the Word of God.

The little man stood in silence for several seconds, but he never lowered the golden sword. When finally he spoke, his voice was surprisingly indifferent. "Not really."

Lord Gelus, despite his menacing visage, appeared utterly dumbfounded. "What? How can it be otherwise?"

Andela felt the trembling dissipate from her body. She smiled in relief.

"Well," began the little man, "for one thing, the word for *give* in John chapter fifteen, verse sixteen, is in the subjunctive mood—*whatsoever ye shall ask of the Father in my name, he may give it you*. This, of course, implies that the Father can decide how to respond to requests. He is not forced to respond exactly as requested simply because a certain name is mentioned."

Lord Gelus stared at the little man with agitated dismay. "So what?" he retorted. "What does it prove if you have found yet another verse that conflicts with John chapter fourteen, verse fourteen? I still say that you must leave the premises or denounce the Bible."

"There is no conflict, Lord Gelus," the little man responded. "You have failed to take into consideration the actual Greek word that is translated as *do* in John chapter fourteen, verse fourteen. It is the same Greek word that is translated as *make* in Matthew chapter twelve, verse thirty-three—*Either 'make' the tree good, and his fruit good; or else 'make' the tree corrupt, and his fruit corrupt*, and it is the same Greek word that is translated as *make* in First John chapter one, verse ten—*If we say that we have not sinned, we 'make' him a liar*. If you were to consult an analytical Greek lexicon, Lord Gelus, I believe you would find that the word translated as *do* in John chapter fourteen, verse fourteen, may also be translated as *consider*.

"Thus, if the Greek word for *do* is translated as *consider* in verses such as John chapter fourteen, verse thirteen, and John chapter fourteen, verse fourteen, then there is no conflict—God gives consideration to all prayers that are issued from his people in the name of his Son, and he responds according to his will. Given this observation, along with the subjunctive mood presented in John chapter fifteen, verse sixteen, it makes sense to interpret any Bible verses stating that those who ask shall receive, as meaning that those who ask in faith shall receive responses from God, according to God's will. And it makes sense to interpret any verses stating that those who *ask* shall be *given*, as meaning that God will respond to such requests according to his will. And likewise, it makes sense to interpret any verses stating that when someone *asks* for something it will be *done*, as meaning that God will respond according to his will. Therefore, John chapter fourteen, verse fourteen, does not conflict with the Third Commandment, and it does not conflict with John chapter fifteen, verse sixteen.

"So then, Lord Gelus, God responds to prayerful requests according to his will and judgment. He does not respond like some fictional genie in a bottle that can be manipulated by the use of some particular name or incantation. And to point out another thing, the last portion of Mark chapter eleven, verse twenty-four, appears in the King James Version of the Bible as—*believe that ye receive them, and ye shall have them.* But this portion of Scripture is properly translated from the Greek as follows—*believe that you have received, and it shall be to you*, meaning that if you believe, in faith, that you have received God's regard and consideration, then God's response to you will come to pass. So again, it is appropriate to interpret this passage of Scripture as meaning that those who pray in faith shall receive a response from God, according to God's will. It also makes sense, then, that if God's children confidently ask for things that are in accordance with his will, then he will hear and grant what is requested, as revealed in First John chapter five, verses fourteen and fifteen."

"That's all quite fine," retorted Lord Gelus, "but what about Matthew chapter seventeen, verse twenty? This verse indicates that the disciples could not cure a lunatic because of their unbelief. Then the verse points out that if they had faith the size of mustard seed, they could tell a mountain to move from one place to another. The verse doesn't say anything about asking God whether it's his will for the mountain to move or not. So then, isn't it clear that God is obliged to do whatever a man requests, as long as that man has faith? And would this not apply to the girl?

"Furthermore," continued Lord Gelus, his foul face indicating the emergence of another thought to use in contention, "verse twenty of that chapter is in disagreement with verse twenty-one. Verse twenty clearly states that the lunatic was not healed because of unbelief on the part of the disciples, and yet verse twenty-one just as clearly states that the lunatic could not be healed without fasting. How could both be true? How could the disciples fail solely because of unbelief, and yet fail because they did not fast? And besides that, if fasting were truly required for success, then how was the lunatic healed? Who fasted?"

Andela was disconcerted by Lord Gelus' passionate rebuttal. His words were confusing, yet it seemed that he might have a point. Nonetheless, she would not let herself doubt the little man's ability to counter Lord Gelus' words. She had no idea what the little man would say, but she trusted it would be something impressive, or at least she hoped so.

A considerable lag of time followed before the little man responded, enough time to cause uneasy shuffling amidst the horde of Resants. The little man was pleased that Lord Gelus had been lured into time-consuming disputation, but he was careful not to disclose this fact. He peered into Lord Gelus' eyes as if he were bewildered. When he finally spoke, he spoke meekly. "Well, it would seem you have asked some good questions, Lord Gelus."

"Then which is it?" Lord Gelus asked in triumph. "Will you leave the room or denounce that heap of rubbish?"

The little man shrugged both shoulders. "Well, I can't really do either, that is, not without a couple of considerations. I may need to address a couple of flaws in your arguments."

Andela exhaled in relief. She had been unconsciously holding her breath.

"Flaws!" snapped Lord Gelus. "What are you gabbing about?"

The little man slightly lowered his sword so that the tip was pointed toward Lord Gelus' forehead. It seemed an invitation for Lord Gelus to contemplate the words that would follow. "First, as you must know, Lord Gelus, there are at least two types of faith presented in the Word of God. There is faith toward God, as disclosed in Acts chapter twenty, verse twenty-one, and also in First Thessalonians chapter one, verse eight, and then there is faith to believe a specific revelation from God, or to carry out a specific instruction from God, as disclosed in Acts chapter twenty-seven, verse twenty-five, and also in Mark chapter nine, verse twenty-three. The discussion we had before, regarding asking God for whatever you want and receiving his response, has to do with faith toward God. In other words, you make a request to God, believing that he will hear and that he will respond according to his will."

The little man paused, but Lord Gelus made no reply. The exuberance in Lord Gelus' horrid green face was fading. He now appeared as a sinister phantom of resentful brooding.

"Let me address the other faith, namely the faith to believe a specific revelation from God," resumed the little man. "Do you remember Peter's reply when Jesus asked his disciples—*But whom say ye that I am*? Peter's reply is recorded in Matthew chapter sixteen, verse sixteen—*Thou art the Christ, the Son of the living God*. And do you remember how Jesus responded to Peter? He told Peter that his reply was a revelation from the Father, and he gave Peter his name, namely Peter, meaning a stone. This response from Jesus acknowledged and honored the solid truth of Peter's reply, or in other words, Peter's reply was solid like a stone. Do you follow me so far?"

Lord Gelus stood like a sullen statue, but the look in his eyes was that of a predator biding his time for the opportune moment to crouch upon hapless prey. He was unresponsive to any of the little man's questions. This, however, did not appear to bother the little man in the least, he simply continued speaking.

"When Christ said *thou art Peter*, the Greek word for *rock*, namely the name given to Peter, is in the masculine form. But when Christ said, *upon this rock I will build my church*, the Greek word for *rock* is in the feminine form, it is not the same word that Christ used to name Peter. And even though the masculine and feminine forms of this Greek word for *rock* have meanings that are considered somewhat interchangeable, the masculine form more generally refers to a small rock or pebble, whereas the feminine form more generally refers to a cliff or boulder. This particular feminine Greek word for *rock* appears in the New Testament sixteen times, and six of those times it is a metaphor referring to Christ, including when it appears in Matthew chapter sixteen. It is never a metaphor referring to Peter or to any other man apart from Jesus Christ. Even Peter used this same Greek word for *rock* to refer to Christ in the second chapter of First Peter. Thus, God's Church is built upon Christ, not upon Peter. Peter is just a stone in the wall that is built upon the foundation, namely Jesus Christ. In fact, all Christians are referred to as stones built upon the foundation of Jesus Christ, as Peter writes in verse five of First Peter, chapter two, where he uses a different Greek word for *rock*. And note that Jesus concluded Matthew chapter sixteen, verse eighteen, by saying that the gates of Hell shall not prevail against the Church, and I would point out that the term *gates of Hell* apparently refers to evil defenses against aggressive activity by the Church, since the gates of a city are erected more for defense than for offense. This indicates that God's Church has the power to overcome evil establishments."

Again the little man paused. There was no change in Lord Gelus' posture. He maintained his looming silence.

"So," recommenced the little man, "now we're getting closer to what I've been leading up to. The next thing I would like to point out is that a literal, word for word translation of Matthew chapter sixteen, verse nineteen, is as follows—*I will give you the keys of the kingdom of the heavens, and that if you may have bound on the earth it shall be having been being bound in the heavens, and that if you may have loosed on the earth it shall be having been being loosed in the heavens.* All things considered, including the fact that keys are associated with power and authority, a good Greek to English transliteration of this verse is as follows—*I will give you authoritative power of heaven, and whatever you may bind on earth shall have been being bound in heaven, and whatever you may loose on earth shall have been being loosed in heaven.* The Greek words in this verse for *bound* and *loosed*, in regard to heaven, are perfect, passive participles following a Greek word for *shall be* that is in the indicative mood. On the other hand, the Greek words in this verse for *bound* and *loosed*, in reference to Peter, are in the subjunctive mood, meaning that Peter may possibly bind or loose, but such binding and loosing is not definite, and this is where Peter's faith plays an important role. And the same subjunctive mood in regard to men, which is in contrast to the indicative mood in regard to heaven, is found in Matthew chapter eighteen, verse eighteen.

"You see, Lord Gelus, when heaven determined that something should be bound or loosed through Peter, such binding or loosing still depended upon Peter's faith. And a word for word, Greek to English translation of John chapter twenty, verse twenty-three would be—*Perhaps any persons you may have forgiven of sins have been forgiven them, perhaps any persons you may hold back have been held back.* So in this verse, we see that being in harmony with the Holy Spirit, and properly understanding communication from the Holy Spirit, may be necessary in order for Christian disciples to make proper judgments as to whether men are forgiven by God or are in need of repentance and salvation.

"God is just, and he respects and honors the free will of mankind. If a man or woman chooses to doubt or disbelieve a message or directive from God, then God respects that doubt, and responds accordingly. We find positive responses to directives from God in Bible verses such as Acts chapter three, verse six, where God heals a lame man through Peter's faith, and in Acts chapter sixteen, verse eighteen, where God frees a damsel from a spirit of divination through Paul's faith, and also in Matthew chapter nine, verse twenty, where God heals a woman through her own faith. In contrast, we find a negative response to a directive from God in Matthew chapter seventeen, verses nineteen and twenty, where the unbelief of the disciples results in God's not curing the lunatic, at least not until later, and not through the disciples."

Lord Gelus perked up at the mention of Matthew chapter seventeen, verse twenty; but he still said nothing. The little man continued.

"When God gives directives through his spirit, then faith comparable to a mustard seed can move a mountain. The last portion of Mark chapter eleven, verse twenty-two, is properly translated from the Greek as—*Have faith of God*, or, *Have faith from God*, and when a man receives such faith, rather than doubting or disbelieving, then his faith can release God's power to accomplish whatever it is that God has directed through him. Thus, the statement about having faith to move mountains in Mark chapter eleven, verse twenty-three, is in regard to having faith in a specific directive from God—it does not mean that an individual can require God to move a mountain by that individual's own volition. In contrast to this, when requests are made to God, then even faith the size of a mountain will not change the fact that God will respond according to his own judgment. Thus, Mark chapter eleven, verse twenty-four, contrasts with Mark chapter eleven, verse twenty-three, in that Mark chapter eleven, verse twenty-four, refers to making requests to God rather than receiving directives from God. And as I pointed out earlier, it is appropriate to interpret Mark chapter eleven, verse twenty-four, as meaning that those who pray in faith shall receive a response from God, according to God's will."

The little man paused. He figured that Lord Gelus was mentally formulating a verbal counterattack. This did not bother him; in fact, it was very much to his liking—such deliberation would be time consuming. Hopefully Andela would be raised through the opening in the stone ceiling before any physical combat erupted. And since Lord Gelus remained calculatingly mute, the little man again resumed speaking, figuring that he could prolong his own dialogue before Lord Gelus responded.

"I trust that I have explained the two different types of faith sufficiently. When a man petitions God through faith, then God will perform anything that he has already promised or directed. On the other hand, when a man petitions God for something that God has not already promised or directed, then the response will be according to God's will and judgment. This clarifies why none of the verses in the Bible pertaining to faith and prayer are in conflict with one another. It also discloses why it would be presumptuous and cowardly for me to depart and leave the girl with her prayers. I may, in fact, be God's response to the girl's prayers."

Lord Gelus cast wicked eyes toward Andela as the little man concluded his statement, causing a shiver of dread to pass upward from the base of Andela's spine. Then the yellow eyes shifted back upon the little man.

"You have extrapolated upon your vagrant viewpoints of faith ad infinitum," grumbled Lord Gelus. "To say that I was bored by your naïve and lengthy dissertation would be like saying that prying one's toenails out by the roots causes a slight annoyance." Lord Gelus flipped his right hand into the empty space above his head and then dropped it back to his side. "All a ploy—all a feeble attempt to misdirect my mind through pitiable and incalculable recitation. Obviously you hoped to make me forget the discrepancy between Matthew chapter seventeen, verse twenty, and Matthew chapter seventeen, verse twenty-one.

"Verse twenty plainly states that the lunatic was not healed because of unbelief on the part of the disciples, and yet verse twenty-one just as plainly states that the lunatic could not be healed without fasting! Again I ask you, how could both be true? If fasting were required to heal the lunatic, then how could the disciples have failed simply due to their unbelief? Would it not also have been a matter of failing to fast? Do you not see how that both of these verses cannot be true? One of them must be thrown out. And if you cannot contest the obvious veracity of my claim, namely that these verses are in conflict with one another, then I categorically proclaim that you are denouncing the Bible."

Andela felt disquieted. Lord Gelus flaunted an intimidating vocabulary, and he was a silver-tongued orator; and he presented his argument plainly enough that she understood his point. If Jesus told the disciples that the only reason the lunatic was not healed was because of their unbelief, then how could the next verse turn around and assert that fasting was required? How could someone defend the validity of both of these Bible verses? She hoped that the little man knew something that she did not know. For a few seconds she fixed her eyes on the raised, golden sword; and then, when the little man began speaking, she dropped her eyes to his face.

"You have asked a worthy question, Lord Gelus. And I must add, you have raised a most delicate and crucial issue."

"Ahaa, haha," cackled Lord Gelus. His evil eyes boasted hellish triumph. "Indeed that is so. I suppose it is a rather delicate matter to denounce the Book that defines all you claim to be, but I presume that you have no other honest choice."

"Not so," returned the little man; and his words bolstered the hope in Andela's heart. "I do not denounce the Bible at all, not in the least. The delicacy I refer to is simply one of defining the Bible."

Lord Gelus raised one brow. His face exuded sinister delight. "So, are you insinuating what I presume? Are you suggesting that Matthew chapter seventeen, verse twenty-one, does not belong in the Bible at all? And in keeping with that, are you suggesting that the words *and fasting* do not belong in Mark chapter nine, verse twenty-nine? That would certainly fix your problem, wouldn't it? After all, there would be no disagreement between verses twenty and twenty-one of Matthew chapter seventeen if verse twenty-one does not belong in the Bible at all. And furthermore, this entire subject of conflict would be dispelled if, in addition to the deletion of Matthew chapter seventeen, verse twenty-one, the words *and fasting* were deleted from Mark chapter nine, verse twenty-nine."

"That would indeed dispel the conflict," the little man responded. "And you are quite right. The words *and fasting* do not belong in Mark chapter nine, verse twenty-nine, and Matthew chapter seventeen, verse twenty-one, should be entirely omitted from the Bible."

Andela's mouth dropped open.

Lord Gelus' eyes narrowed. "Then I must conclude that you do not consider the Textus Receptus, the third edition of the Greek New Testament produced by the Dutch scholar Erasmus in 1522 and slightly modified by Stephanus and Elzevir, to be truth without error? After all, it was this translation of the Greek New Testament that was used in producing the King James Version of the Bible that was published in 1611."

Andela listened intently to every word being spoken. Her mouth still hung open.

"The Bible, as originally penned in its original languages, and comprised of sixty-six books that were canonized in the fourth century A.D., presents wondrously harmonious truth without error," the little man stated. "If Bible verses seem to conflict with one another, Lord Gelus, it indicates that someone has more studying and learning to do. You may refer to the Fifth Revised Edition of the Greek New Testament, and to a book entitled New Testament Supernatural & Inerrant: Proof per Hebrew Idiom, if you desire literary proof of the New Testament's validity."

A spasm of revulsion passed through Lord Gelus' massive body. "So then, the King James Version of the Bible is trash," he jeered.

"Not at all!" retorted the little man. "The King James Version of the Bible is quite wondrously accurate, all things considered. It is certainly useful for leading men to salvation, and for studying the doctrines of Christianity, and for perceiving great truths through the Spirit of God."

Andela sighed, and she was finally able to close her mouth. She had always cherished the King James Version of the Bible.

The little man continued. "The accuracy of the King James Version of the Bible is quite remarkable when one considers that the latest Greek manuscript that Erasmus had in his possession when he put together the Greek New Testament was from about the tenth century."

"Yes, that was too bad," crooned Lord Gelus with feigned sympathy. "And to think, there was an authentic, fourth-century translation of the entire Greek New Testament preserved on animal skins that was discovered in about 1475 and placed in the Vatican. Too bad Christians couldn't get along with each other—Erasmus certainly could have used that fourth century manuscript in producing his version of the Greek New Testament, don't you think?"

"I am aware that additions to the Bible began materializing as early as the fifth century," returned the little man. "Some of this likely resulted from the strong influence of Gnosticism and monasticism. I am also aware that the office of Pontifex Maximus, or Supreme Priest, was shifted from the Roman emperor to the bishop of Rome in 378 A.D., and that additions to the Bible materialized after 378 A.D. from Roman influence. Thankfully, though, the entire New Testament as we know it today was canonized before the year 375 A.D., and notably, the canonized New Testament of that time did not include what is known as the apocrypha, and the Old Testament canon that was recognized during the time of Christ did not include the apocrypha, and the Old Testament canon that was established for Judaism by the time of the second or third century A.D. did not include the apocrypha. Obviously, then, copies of Holy Scripture preserved from periods of time prior to 378 A.D. are critically important, and therefore, I would agree that Erasmus was handicapped by the fact that he did not have access to older translations of the Greek New Testament. So to answer your question, Lord Gelus, if you are implying that there is only one Church, and that all persons born of God through the blood of Christ are members of that Church and should cooperate with each other, then yes, I agree."

"Yes, well, considering that the Vatican sat on their animal skins until after Tischendorf discovered another fourth century Greek New Testament in the middle of the nineteenth century, I would hardly conclude that Christians cooperate," scoffed Lord Gelus.

The little man picked up on the mention of Tishendorf's name. "Tischendorf discovered not only a Greek translation of the entire New Testament, but also a Greek translation of much of the Old Testament," remarked the little man. "He discovered these in the monastery of Saint Catherine on Mount Sinai, and soon after this discovery, he succeeded in getting authorities to make the other fourth century manuscript, the one in the Vatican, available to translators. The fourth century Greek New Testament that was discovered in the monastery of Saint Catherine is known as Codex Sinaiticus, written about 330 to 350 A.D., and the fourth century Greek New Testament that was held in the Vatican is known as Codex Vaticanus, written about 325 to 350 A.D. These two Greek New Testaments, both preserved on animal skins, agree closely with many older Greek manuscripts that contain portions of the Greek New Testament. These older manuscripts were written on papyrus. Papyrus is more fragile than animal skins, but many papyrus manuscripts from the second and third centuries were preserved in the dry sands of southern Egypt.

"Therefore, Lord Gelus, we have amazingly strong evidence for the authenticity and accuracy of the New Testament, especially in regard to the two complete New Testament manuscripts from the fourth century and the many supportive manuscripts from earlier centuries. Also, permit me to mention that the King James Version of the Bible is notably accurate when compared to these early Greek manuscripts. There are some minor differences, but generally these differences are inconsequential."

"Inconsequential!" exclaimed Lord Gelus with an obvious tone of objection. "You may consider the rejection of Matthew chapter seventeen, verse twenty-one, as inconsequential. And you may also consider the rejection of the words *and fasting* from Mark chapter nine, verse twenty-nine, as inconsequential. But I can name twelve other additions to the Greek New Testament that have cropped up over the years. All of these additions were translated into the King James Version of the Bible, and none of them appear in either the Codex Sinaiticus or the Codex Vaticanus, nor are they found in earlier manuscripts. I would challenge you to explain how you think that all twelve of these additions are inconsequential!"

Andela was enthralled. She shifted her eyes back and forth between the little man and Lord Gelus, enticed by the challenges Lord Gelus presented, and awed by the little man's rejoinders.

"Okay, no problem," said the little man. He seemed unruffled. "And to get started, let me name a few of the *additions*, as you call them, and let me point out why each one of them is inconsequential. Are you game?"

"I can't wait," croaked Lord Gelus.

"Well, first of all, the word *God* in First Timothy chapter three, verse sixteen, should actually be translated as the word *which*. I don't see how this would make any great doctrinal difference, and it is more of a minor translational error than an addition. Is this one of your twelve?"

"The most minor one," Lord Gelus acknowledged with a grunt.

"Ah good, so I got one," the little man spoke cheerily. "And speaking of minor ones, please permit me to attempt naming five other *additions*, as you call them, that are all of remarkable insignificance. First, the benediction to the Lord's Prayer, namely the latter portion of Matthew chapter six, verse thirteen—this makes little difference since God's glory, power, and kingdom are well-established without this benediction. Second, Luke chapter twenty-two, verses forty-three through forty-four—this also makes little difference since the sufferings of Christ are well-established, even if he did not sweat blood, and even if an angel did not come down to strengthen him at the Mount of Olives. Third, Acts chapter eight, verse thirty-seven—this also makes little difference since we know that Christ is the Son of God, and since we know that the eunuch was baptized. Fourth, First John chapter five, verse seven—this also makes little difference since the Trinity is well-established without this verse. And fifth, Luke chapter nine, verses fifty-five through fifty-six—this makes little difference since Christ apparently chose not to bring fire down to consume the Samaritans, and notably, verse fifty-six would be rather difficult to explain since it is written in the form of the Hebrew idiom—perhaps whoever added this verse was not well informed in regard to the Hebrew idiom."

"Okay," snapped Lord Gelus. He was obviously annoyed that the little man so handily dispelled the significance of six out of his proposed twelve additions to the original Greek New Testament. He lost no time, however, in downgrading the little man's accomplishment. "You obviously relish the practice of delving into the depths of trivial verbosity, having chosen the six additions that I likely would not have even named. The other six additions are much more consequential."

"Really?" posed the little man. "How is that?"

"Number one," Lord Gelus stated firmly, "is the first portion of Luke chapter twenty-three, verse thirty-four, namely the part about Jesus saying—*Father, forgive them; for they know not what they do*. These words are not in the original Greek texts. So I ask you, is it inconsequential that those who crucified Christ are in hell rather than heaven?"

"Now hold on, Lord Gelus," replied the little man. "You do not know whether the soldiers who crucified Jesus are in heaven or hell. The Bible clearly teaches that any person who believes the Word of God, repents of sin, and chooses Jesus Christ as Lord and Savior, will be saved. There is no sin so great that this truth does not apply."

"No?" rebuffed Lord Gelus. "What about the sin mentioned in Matthew chapter twelve, verse thirty-one? Are you too dim-witted to recall the words—*but the blasphemy against the Holy Ghost shall not be forgiven unto men*?"

"I recall those words quite well, Lord Gelus," the little man replied. "If a man knowingly insults the Holy Spirit of God by professing that the Holy Spirit is Satan, then that man may reach a point of eternal damnation while he yet breathes air upon the earth. You can be certain, however, that such a man will never repent of sin, for without the aid and calling of the Holy Spirit, he will be Satan's prey forever. The same is true for the man described in Hebrews chapter six, verses four through six—these verses describe a man who will never repent of sin. Therefore, Lord Gelus, it still holds true that anyone who will believe the Word of God, repent of sin, and choose Jesus Christ as Lord and Savior, will be saved. There are no exceptions. By repenting of sin, a man proves that he has not committed an unforgivable sin. The Bible does not contradict itself, not when it is translated and interpreted correctly."

"Humph!" snorted Lord Gelus. "You've managed to weasel your way out of that one. But don't get too cocky, I'm only getting started."

"Please proceed," the little man spoke politely.

The little man's civil manner infuriated Lord Gelus. He waited a minute to reply, pretending to contemplate his next verbal challenge as he recollected sufficient emotional composure to converse in a cool, condescending manner. "Alright then, what about my next addition to Scripture, namely Mark chapter sixteen, verses nine through twenty?"

"Totally inconsequential," the little man remarked without hesitation. "The resurrection, appearance, and ascension of the Lord Jesus Christ are all established without these added verses. And even if these verses were authentic, it would be recklessly unwise for any man to purposely drink poison or purposely prod a poisonous snake into biting him. Even Christ, when asked by Satan to cast himself from the pinnacle of a temple in order to prove himself in accordance to Satan's rendition of Scripture, replied by stating—*It is written again, Thou shalt not tempt the Lord thy God.*"

"Maybe so," bleated Lord Gelus, "but what about the addition of the words, *waiting for the moving of the water*, found in John chapter five, verse three? And what about the addition of the entire next verse, namely John chapter five, verse four?"

This time the little man paused and smiled. "And I'll wager that you were next going to mention the addition of the twelve verses beginning with John chapter seven, verse fifty-three. Am I right?"

"You can bet on it," Lord Gelus asserted. He begrudged the fact that the little man identified this passage of Scripture first, rather than affording him the pleasure of bringing it up himself. "Surely you're aware that countless preachers have pored over sermons about the woman caught in adultery, when the entire section of Scripture was merely added to make men and women feel more comfortable about paying off priests for indulgences in sexual sins. What do you have to say about that?"

The little man shook his head and shrugged. "I have already commented upon the fact that some additions to the Bible resulted from Roman and Gnostic influences. In regard to the verses you mentioned from John chapter five—yes, there may have been some intent to attribute magical or miraculous qualities to water or inanimate objects, and to then market such water or objects for monetary gain. However, the Bible makes it clear that forgiveness for sins comes only through repentance and through accepting the blood sacrifice of the Lord Jesus Christ—no amount of money can buy a man's way into heaven. Furthermore, miracles of God are sometimes performed through men, but they are not accomplished by any powers innate to the men themselves. As Christ told His disciples in John chapter fifteen, verse five—*without me ye can do nothing.*

"And when it comes to the woman caught in adultery, of course I object to anyone adding verses to canonized Scripture. Nonetheless, the Bible teaches that God loves sinners and wants them to repent and accept Jesus Christ as Lord and Savior, including adulterers and murderers. The Bible does not teach against the societies of men having civil laws against such sins, nor does the Bible teach against enforcing those laws. But if God loves sinners, then God's children should also love sinners, and the process of loving sinners includes sincerely hoping that sinners will repent of sin and receive eternal life through Christ. I have previously commented upon how Christians may love enemies whom they simultaneously seek to overthrow or destroy, and likewise, Christians may love civil criminals whom they simultaneously punish for committing civil crimes."

For several unsettling seconds, Lord Gelus stood staring at the little man. He now appeared somewhat despondent, but he appeared dangerously despondent rather than passively despondent. He flashed his eyes over the horde of barbarous beasts, and the brutes tensed and crouched in response.

Andela sensed the peril of Lord Gelus' altered mood. It struck her mind that several minutes had passed since she had glanced upward and behind her—she did so, but there was still no rope. She looked back down at the little man.

The little man was also perceptive to Lord Gelus' disposition. He peered back toward Andela to make sure that there was no rope dangling behind her—there was no rope. He again faced Lord Gelus. Somehow he had to delay combat a little longer.

"Well, I guess that about wraps things up," the little man stated. "The King James Version of the Bible is quite sound doctrinally, and your twelve additions make very little difference."

The despondent expression upon Lord Gelus' face gave way to one of suspicion. "You know fully well that you have only addressed ten of my twelve additions," he pointed out with a tone of indignant criticism. "What subject are you attempting to evade?"

The little man feigned an expression of discomfiture. He said nothing.

"Well, I do not think that you are trying to evade discussion of the words, *bless them that curse you, do good to them that hate you,* that were added to Matthew chapter five, verse forty-four," surmised Lord Gelus. "You would simply point out that there have been attempts to turn Christians into pacifists in order to reduce any threat of reformation in regard to evil governments. Besides that, you would also point out that doing good is not always equivalent to being docile, and that doing good might include chopping off the heads of evil enemies during battle."

The little man merely nodded.

"Just as I thought," Lord Gelus proclaimed. "It is the last of my twelve additions that disturbs you, namely, the addition of the words, *without a cause,* appearing in Matthew chapter five, verse twenty-two. In fact, I would expect you to find the entire content of this verse perturbing. To begin with, how can it always be wrong for a man to be angry when even Jesus got angry as shown in Mark chapter three, verse five? And also, how do you explain Ephesians chapter four, verse twenty-six? How can, *Be ye angry, and sin not,* make any sense if it is a sin to be angry in the first place?"

The little man hesitated to answer, partly to expend more time, and partly to sustain Lord Gelus' interest in the debate. When finally he replied, he purposely spoke with a slight quiver to his voice. "Well, I must concede that you have a point. Matthew chapter five, verse twenty-two, is indeed mind-boggling."

Despite her predicament, Andela was interested in hearing how the little man would respond. Matthew chapter five, verse twenty-two, was a verse that had bothered her for years, especially the last portion of the verse; namely, the part that said, *whosoever shall say, Thou fool, shall be in danger of hell fire.* In fact, she had decided to omit the word *fool* from her vocabulary.

"Ah! So then, are you ready to concede that the Bible conflicts with itself and must be denounced?" inquired Lord Gelus. He no longer appeared despondent. In fact, his countenance was one of demonical inspiration.

"Well, um, no, I think I can address the first part of that verse okay," said the little man.

"We shall see," rejoined Lord Gelus.

"Okay," said the little man. "Well, to start out with, the Bible never says that being angry is necessarily a sin. The word for *angry* in Matthew chapter five, verse twenty-two, is in the passive voice in the Greek, so the phrase, *whosoever is angry with his brother shall be in danger of the judgment*, should properly be translated as, *whoever is angering his brother is subject to judgment.* The passive voice in the Greek indicates that the subject is being acted upon, rather than doing the acting himself, so the subject in this verse is receiving anger rather than dishing it out. Thus, the problem is not that the subject is angry, but rather that he is doing something that makes his brother angry.

"Next, permit me to point out that the Greek word for *judgment* in this verse simply means, *to exercise judgment upon.* It does not necessarily mean that the man who is angering his brother will be condemned for doing so, in fact, a judge may determine that he was acting properly, and that his brother got angry for unjust reasons. I certainly do not agree with the addition of the words, *without a cause*, to this verse, because those words are not in the original Greek text. But I also do not agree that being angry is, in and of itself, a sin. So then, it makes sense that if a man causes his brother to be angry, then a judge may end up determining whether that man was in the right or wrong, since the angered brother may take the matter to a judge.

"And before you comment upon my explanation," added the little man, "permit me to expound upon the middle portion of this verse." The little man figured that Lord Gelus would jump ahead to the last portion of the verse if given the opportunity, since the middle portion was not very controversial; so he decided to consume a little more time by discussing the middle portion of the verse before inviting Lord Gelus to respond. "The word *Raca* in this verse derives from an Aramaean term of bitter contempt, and it may be translated as, *worthless fellow*. The word *council* in this verse comes from a Greek word meaning, *judicial council*, and it could apply to the Sanhedrin of that day. So in summary, Jesus is pointing out that a man who contemptuously calls his brother *worthless* may have to face judgment before a judicial council. This makes sense—slander may put an individual in legal jeopardy.

The little man then halted his speech and stood facing Lord Gelus.

"Trite," scorned Lord Gelus, "trite, trite, trite! Shall we discuss the hybridization of oranges in China, or the phenomenal structure of the combustion chamber found within the abdomen of the bombardier beetle? I have more important affairs to occupy my time than chatting all day with some absentminded fool! And speaking of *fool*, permit me to redirect our conversation to the crucial segment of Matthew chapter five, verse twenty-two, namely the last segment. This segment states, *but whosoever shall say, Thou fool, shall be in danger of hell fire.* Unless I'm mistaken, Paul was addressing his brethren in First Corinthians chapter fifteen, verse thirty-six, when he begins the verse by saying, *Thou fool.* So then, did this put Paul in danger of hell fire?"

There was another hesitation, but this time the little man was not just stalling for time, he was thinking. He knew that he could simply reply to Lord Gelus' inquisition, but this did not seem wise. The question posed by Lord Gelus was probably not the last one in the evil savant's academic armamentarium, but it might be the last question that Lord Gelus was capable of recalling in his present state of mind; and the little man didn't want Lord Gelus to run out of subject matter for dispute. After all, if the menacing leader ran short on intellectual ammunition, he would likely resort to physical assault, something that the little man wanted to delay. Then an idea struck the little man's mind—there were certainly a number of controversial topics pertaining to the Bible that he could present in order to spark his cunning adversary's memory. Perhaps there was a subtle way of replying to Lord Gelus' inquiry that would simultaneously supply more fuel for debate.

"Well, that's not really so hard to address. It reminds me of the matter of men reportedly seeing God in the Bible when the Bible also says that no man has seen God," remarked the little man.

Suddenly Lord Gelus' hoary, green head bolted backward; and a dull, sadistic glint that had been smoldering deep within the hollows of his horrible eyes ignited into fires of fiendish festivity. The little man's ploy was successful—Lord Gelus' sinister mind had been stimulated.

"So," continued the little man, now determined to draw out his explanation as long as possible. "Let me point out that the Greek word for *fool* in First Corinthians chapter fifteen, verse thirty-six, is an entirely different Greek word than the Greek word for *fool* in Matthew chapter five, verse twenty-two. In First Corinthians chapter fifteen, verse thirty-six, the Greek word translated as *fool* means, *unwise, simple, religiously unenlightened*, whereas in Matthew chapter five, verse twenty-two, the Greek word translated as *fool* means, *a fool in senseless wickedness*. This explains why Paul was not in danger of hell fire simply from using the term *fool* in regard to his brethren—he was not using the same word as that referred to in Matthew chapter five, verse twenty-two.

"So now then, to help understand why the use of the term meaning, *a fool in senseless wickedness*, could put a man in danger of hell fire, consider the following. First, the Bible teaches that a Christian's body is the temple of the Holy Spirit, as stated in First Corinthians chapter six, verse nineteen. And second, the Bible teaches that blasphemy against the Holy Spirit shall not be forgiven unto men, as disclosed in Matthew chapter twelve, verse thirty-one. Now consider this—if a man accuses a Christian of being *a fool in senseless wickedness*, then such an accusation may be equivalent to accusing the Christian of being a child of Satan. If you will recall, it is blasphemy against the Holy Spirit to accuse the Holy Spirit of being Satan. Therefore, it is logical to conclude that it is blasphemy against the Holy Spirit to accuse a Christian, who is filled with the Holy Spirit, of being a child of Satan. So then, a man should be very, very careful not to accuse a Christian of being a child of Satan. But if a man is worried that he has done that very thing, it is important to remember that any man who will repent of sin and accept salvation through the blood of Christ does not need to worry that he has committed an unforgivable sin.

"And note this, Lord Gelus," the little man continued, "Jesus uses the term *brother* in Matthew chapter five, verse twenty-two, when he warns against causing anger, and he again uses the term *brother* when he warns against saying *Raca*, or *worthless fellow*. But on the other hand, Jesus does not use the term *brother* when he warns against saying, *Thou fool*, or, *fool in senseless wickedness*. Would you like to know why?"

"I can't wait," Lord Gelus muttered with sarcasm. His mind was occupied by issues he planned to address later, but he still listened to every word the little man spoke. This was not because he wanted to learn anything; rather, it was because he hoped to catch the little man saying something that could be used against him. He was like a hunter perched in the branches of a tree, hoping that a deer would wander close enough to shoot a bullet through its heart. In short, Lord Gelus hoped to hear the little man making incongruous statements.

"It's because a true Christian, a brother in Christ, cannot willfully commit dead works," explained the little man, "and blaspheming the Holy Spirit is a dead work. Other dead works are named in First Corinthians chapter six, verses nine and ten, including plunderous robbery. Murder is also a dead work, as noted in First John chapter three, verse fifteen. And bestiality, namely having sex with animals, is also a dead work, as revealed by the Greek word for *unclean person* that appears in Ephesians chapter five, verse five—a word that roughly translates as *sexually licentious person*. A different form of this same basic Greek word is translated as *uncleanness* in Ephesians chapter five, verse three."

"You mentioned thievery," Lord Gelus remarked with a cunning wrinkle in his shaggy brow. "I would wager that almost any human being you refer to as a *true Christian* would stop and pick up a lost dollar on a sidewalk, or perhaps pick up a lost golf ball on a vacant football field, and would then keep such items. How can such thievery be acceptable? Does this not refute your claim that a true Christian cannot commit dead works?"

"Not at all, that is, not if you take the time to interpret the term *thievery* in the context of Scripture," retorted the little man.

"Really? How's that?" challenged Lord Gelus.

"The New Testament is quite free of ridiculous legalism," the little man stated. "Finding items of relatively little value that are lost in the public domain, without knowing who lost those items, and then keeping such items, is not what the Bible means by thievery. Note that Jesus did not instruct his disciples to try and find out who lost the money that they were to find in the mouth of a fish in Matthew chapter seventeen, verse twenty-seven. Rather, they were to use the money for their own need in paying tribute. There is a great difference between absurd legalism and disobeying the Word of God. It is true that facing a firing squad and suffering physical death is preferable to denying the Lord Jesus Christ or willfully committing dead works, but if a Christian finds a dollar bill in a public park, without any way of knowing who the dollar belongs to, then keeping that dollar bill is nothing to feel guilty about—the finder should use the dollar in a good and responsible manner. On the other hand, a lost purse of money containing the owner's address and phone number should be returned to the owner."

"I see," said Lord Gelus. He was engrossed in the exchange of dialogue—he considered the conversation to be an intellectual game of wit that he intended to win in order to procure physical custody of Andela. "So, it sounds like you're saying that a true Christian cannot sin. Is that what you're saying?"

"Hold on now," balked the little man. "To begin with, the Greek word for sin means, *to miss a mark*. There are two distinctly different *marks* presented in the New Testament when it comes to sin, and to fall short of either mark is *sin*, but there is a great difference between falling short of one of the marks as opposed to the other mark."

"Really?" taunted Lord Gelus. "I thought that sin is sin, with no bigger or smaller sins—they're all just sins."

"You know better," reproached the little man. "Don't you recall Jesus mentioning a *greater sin* in John chapter nineteen, verse eleven? Apparently Jesus did not consider all sins to be equal. And in regard to the two *marks* I mentioned before, let me direct your attention to Hebrews chapter six, verse one. The preliminary *mark* presented in this verse is repentance from willfully committing dead works, and faith toward God. And the secondary *mark* is perfection. Falling short of either mark is sin, but falling short of the preliminary mark is impossible for a Christian, as plainly stated in First John chapter three, verse six, and also in First John chapter three, verse nine—*Whosoever is born of God doth not commit sin; for his seed remaineth in him: and he cannot sin, because he is born of God*. The *sin* referred to in these two verses is in regard to missing the preliminary mark, namely repentance from willfully committing dead works and having faith toward God.

"On the other hand, a Christian can fall short of the secondary mark, namely perfection, and such shortcoming is also called sin. Examples of sin short of perfection are found in Titus chapter one, verses five through fourteen, and are given as follows—overly arrogant or self-willed, prone to anger, prone to drinking too much alcohol or being too quarrelsome, prone to fighting or violence, dishonorably greedy for money, and prone to believing false doctrines. Other examples of sin short of perfection are given in Ephesians chapter five, verse four, and are as follows—indecency, dishonorable and foolish talking, and improper jokes or language. Certainly Christians should repent when they find themselves guilty of such sins, and should discipline themselves toward perfection in Christ, but still, such sins can be committed by true Christians that remain Christian, and I would define the term *Christian* as *Begotten of God* and having eternal life."

"Ah!" interjected Lord Gelus. "So then, I guess what you're saying is that if a Christian willfully commits a sin from the *dead works* category, then he is no longer a Christian. Is that right?"

"Hold on again," retorted the little man. "You're getting the cart before the ox. To begin with, a true Christian cannot willfully commit dead works, as I have already established. If a man claims to become a Christian, but he never stops willfully committing dead works, then he never really became a Christian. This is clarified in First John chapter three, verse six—*Whosoever abideth in him sinneth not: whosoever sinneth hath not seen him, neither known him.* The Greek word for the first *sinneth* in this verse is in the present tense, and the Greek word for the second *sinneth* in this verse is a present participle. The tenses of these words, taken in context with the rest of Holy Scripture, make it clear that this verse refers to a man who never departed from willfully committing dead works. So if a man claims to become a Christian, but he continues willfully committing dead works, then his claim to Christianity is false."

"Then there sure are a lot of men making false claims," scoffed Lord Gelus.

"And next," continued the little man, ignoring Lord Gelus' spiteful remark, "let me point out that no external force can remove a Christian from God's family, as revealed in the following verses—Romans chapter eight, verses thirty-eight and thirty-nine, Ephesians chapter one, verse thirteen, Second Corinthians chapter one, verse twenty-two, and Ephesians chapter four, verse thirty. Thus, nothing can force a Christian to willfully commit dead works, and if a Christian discovers that he has unwillingly committed a dead work, such as through ignorance or deception, then he may repent and continue in the lordship of Christ, as shown in First John chapter two, verse one, and in First John chapter one, verse nine. However, a Christian cannot discover that he has unwillingly committed a dead work, and then turn around and willfully commit the same dead work—such willful indulgence in dead works is impossible for a Christian.

"So now then, let me explain how you had the cart before the ox. Certainly God may be displeased when a Christian commits sins short of perfection, and Christians should repent of such sins and seek the empowering of the Holy Spirit to help them do better. On the other hand, a Christian cannot willfully commit dead works, that is, not unless he first willfully chooses to reject the lordship of Jesus Christ. Such rejection of Christ is unspeakably revolting—Peter compares it to a dog returning to its own vomit.

"And before we move on to another subject, let me comment upon the tragic circumstance of an individual who has rejected the lordship of Jesus Christ, thus returning to a state of spiritual death and damnation. One section of Scripture that makes it clear that such an atrocity is possible is Hebrews chapter ten, verses twenty-six through thirty-nine. Verse twenty-six refers to an individual who willfully commits dead works and is no longer covered by the blood of Christ, and the fact that this individual was once a child of God is made evident by the statement in verse twenty-nine, namely that this individual was once sanctified by the blood of Christ. Such tragic rejection of the lordship of Jesus Christ does not mean, however, that there is no hope. James chapter five, verses nineteen and twenty, make it clear that a lost sinner who was previously saved can be saved again, provided that he repents from sin.

"These last two verses in the Book of James clearly show that a man who has departed from God can be saved again. The last words in the second verse, *shall save a soul from death, and shall hide a multitude of sins*, cannot refer to saving a man from physical death, since a man who dies physically is no longer capable of sinning upon the earth. In fact, saving a man from physical death would not be hiding any sins at all—keeping him physically alive would permit him to sin all the more. Rather, these words refer to saving a man from spiritual death, since it is those who are spiritually born of God who cannot sin, meaning that they cannot willfully commit dead works.

"And another verse supporting these truths is Hebrews chapter six, verse three, a verse revealing that when God permits a previously saved sinner to again lay *the foundation of repentance from dead works, and of faith toward God*, then that person is again accepted into God's eternal family through the blood of Christ. Only someone who cannot be persuaded to repent from willfully committing dead works qualifies as someone who may possibly have committed an unforgivable sin."

"And so where does your famous saying fit in?" posed Lord Gelus.

"What famous saying?"

"You know, what all you so-called Christians say—*we're all just sinners saved by grace*."

"That's no saying of mine," retorted the little man. "I realize that it has become a tradition in many churches to refer to those who are born of God as being *sinners saved by grace*, but Jesus warns against putting the traditions of men above the teachings of God. In Mark chapter seven, verses seven and eight, we find the following—*Howbeit in vain do they worship me, teaching for doctrines the commandments of men. For laying aside the commandment of God, ye hold the tradition of men…* In short, Lord Gelus, a Christian should not refer to himself as a *sinner saved by grace*, but rather, as a *saint saved by grace*. Before he entered the family of God through repentance from dead works and acceptance of the blood of Jesus Christ to cleanse him from sin, it was appropriate for him to carry the title of *sinner*. But after being cleansed by the blood of Christ, he should refer to himself as a *saint*."

"A saint? So what makes you think a man has the right to call himself a saint?"

"Do you consider it inappropriate for one who calls himself a Christian to use nomenclature consistent with the Word of God?"

"What do you mean?"

"The words *sinner* and *sinners* appear over forty times in the New Testament, but never once do either of these words refer to an individual who is born of God, unless referring to the previous state of that individual before that person received salvation through Christ. Saint

Paul refers to himself as the chief of those who have been saved from sin, as is found in First Timothy chapter one, verse fifteen, but Paul's claim to having committed horrible sins refers to his former life, prior to his conversion to Christianity, back when he was known as Saul. In verse thirteen of the same chapter, Paul states that he was *before* a blasphemer, and a persecutor, and injurious. The Greek word translated as *before* in this verse is a word meaning *formerly*. Thus, Paul points out that he is chief among those who have been saved from sin because his past sins were so horrendous that they warrant the designation of *chief sinner*. And in verse sixteen of the same chapter, Paul shares how his personal salvation serves as an example of how other persons who have committed horrible sins may also be saved.

"And in addition, the New Testament confers the word *saint* or *saints* upon those individuals who are born of God, and it does so over and over again. I do not mean to imply that the writers of the New Testament were unaware that Christians often commit sins short of perfection, but rather, I would point out that such sins do not warrant the title of *sinner*. In the New Testament, the title of *sinner* is restricted to those who are children of Satan, who are capable of willfully and habitually committing sins designated as *dead works*, and who will receive eternal damnation unless they repent of sin, accept Jesus Christ as Lord, and accept the shed blood of Jesus Christ as the sacrifice and payment for their sins. Christians are referred to as *saints* in fourteen different books of the New Testament, and this use of the term *saints* occurs over fifty times, from the Book of Matthew to the Book of Revelation. Therefore, Lord Gelus, it is in keeping with the Word of God for Christians to refer to themselves as *saints*, and it is in opposition to the Word of God for Christians to refer to themselves as *sinners*."

Lord Gelus stared at the little man as if in a trance, but his brain was busy. "Well," he croaked, "it must be next to impossible for a Christian to decide whether a so-called brother is really a brother or not, if you know what I mean. After all, I believe the New Testament instructs its followers to *judge not* about five times, and then turns around and instructs those same followers to *judge* in several other passages of Scripture. So, which is it? Should a Christian judge others, or not? It seems to me that the Bible is unquestionably at odds with itself."

"Not so!" hailed the little man. "If you look at the Biblical passages teaching Christians to *judge not*, such as those in Matthew chapter seven, verses one through five, and in Luke chapter six, verses thirty-seven through forty-two, you will find that those verses teach Christians not to make judgments about others in regard to things they cannot clearly see. In other words, those verses teach Christians not to jump to conclusions. Those verses also teach Christians not to be overly critical of others.

"In contrast, when the Bible teaches Christians to *judge*, it never instructs them to make unfounded judgments regarding others. Christians are instructed to make *righteous* judgments, as shown in John chapter seven, verse twenty-four, and in Luke chapter twelve, verse fifty-seven. They are also advised to judge matters between themselves, as shown in First Corinthians chapter six, verse five, and they are taught to judge what they hear, as shown in Acts chapter seventeen, verse eleven. Next, in Second Corinthians chapter thirteen, verse five, Christian are instructed to examine themselves, and of course this should be done in light of God's Word and through his Spirit, guided by verses such as Hebrews chapter four, verse twelve, and Romans chapter eight, verse sixteen. And finally, Christians are instructed to judge those persons who claim to be *Christian* and who commit dead works, as revealed in First Corinthians chapter five, verses nine through thirteen. Hypocrites who commit dead works while claiming to be Christian are supposed to receive exceptionally stern judgment—Christians are instructed to not keep company with such frauds, though of course, they should still love them and should still pray for their salvation.

"And by the way, large groups of counterfeit Christians may get together and have church and act spiritual, and yet they may regularly commit dead works such as fornication. Such fake Christians are described in Second Timothy chapter three, verse five—*Having a form of godliness, but denying the power thereof: from such turn away.* The *power* that these fake Christians deny is well-described in First John chapter three, verse nine—*Whosoever is born of God doth not commit sin; for his seed remaineth in him: and he cannot sin, because he is born of God.* Thus, it is the power of the spiritual *seed of God* within true Christians that fake Christians fail to acknowledge, the power that makes it impossible to willfully commit dead works. Such bogus Christians will preach that the blood of Christ saves people from the penalty of sin, but not from the power of sin. But the truth of the matter is that a man who is not saved from the power of sin is not saved from the penalty of sin. And the Bible is consistent in instructing true Christians how to deal with fake Christians—Second Timothy chapter three, verse five, ends with the words, *from such turn away*."

Lord Gelus' face became skewed into an expression of detestation. "So, you managed to weasel your way out again. Well, enough with vague controversies, what about the matter you so foolishly brought up before? There's no way you can tell me that the Bible is consistent when John chapter one, verse eighteen, says that, *no man hath seen God at any time*, when all you have to do is turn to verses such as Genesis chapter seventeen, verse one, and Genesis chapter thirty-two, verse thirty, and Exodus chapter twenty-four, verses nine through eleven, to find that the Bible plainly states that men have seen God. Now then, how do you explain this obvious contradiction?"

The little man smiled. "Dear me, Lord Gelus, you don't think I would have raised an issue that I did not know how to address, do you? The answer to the seeming contradiction you have presented is quite simple. The term *God* in the Bible may refer to the *Being* God, consisting of three Persons in one Being, or it may refer to one specific Person of the *Being* God. Thus, it is appropriate to call Jesus *God*, as Thomas did in John chapter twenty, verse twenty-eight, because Jesus is a Person of the *Being* God. And when Jesus said, *he that hath seen me hath seen the Father*, as recorded in John chapter fourteen, verse nine, he was referring to the fact that there is only one *Being* God—he meant that when you look upon the Son of God, you are also looking upon God the Father, in regard to the *Being* God. On the other hand, it is also appropriate to call God the Father by the title of *God*, as is the case in John chapter one, verse eighteen, the verse indicating that no mortal man has seen God, meaning that no mortal man has seen the face of God the Father.

"When Bible verses indicate that men upon the earth have seen God's face, this is always in regard to men seeing the Person of the Son, or in other words, Jesus. If someone tries to argue that this is not true because Jesus had previously seen the face of his Father, and that he was a man upon the earth, one needs only to point out that Jesus was not just a man, he was, and is, God, so John chapter one, verse eighteen, still holds true—no mere, mortal man has ever seen the face of God the Father. Jesus saw the Person of the Holy Spirit, as recorded in Matthew chapter three, verse sixteen, and Jesus could also claim to have seen the Person of God the Father, even making such claim during the time of his life and ministry upon the earth, as revealed in John chapter six, verse forty-six. No mortal man walking the earth ever saw the Person of God the Father, but Jesus, who is a Person of God, could truthfully make such a claim.

"So, when God tells Moses that no man shall see his face and live, as recorded in Exodus chapter thirty-three, verse twenty, this is referring to the matter of mere, mortal men seeing the face of God the Father. Although men have seen God the Son, and although Stephen beheld the glory of God, as recorded in Acts chapter seven, verse fifty-five, no mere, mortal man upon the earth has seen the face of God the Father, though apparently God the Father once made his back side visible to Moses, as recorded in Exodus chapter thirty-three, verse twenty-three. Furthermore, I think it is noteworthy, Lord Gelus, that the Bible teaches that God is a Spirit, as recorded in John chapter four, verse twenty-four. The Bible also teaches that God is invisible, as recorded in First Timothy chapter one, verse seventeen, and also in Colossians chapter one, verse fifteen. So then, the almighty, immortal, invisible God has chosen to make himself visible to the physical eyes of mortal men from time to time, but not when it comes to the face of God the Father. And note, Lord Gelus, that God the Son can make himself invisible to the eyes of mortal men, as Christ did in Luke chapter twenty-four, verse thirty-one."

Lord Gelus snickered. "I must apologize for referring to you as a weasel," he mocked. "There is no weasel that can compare to you as an escape artist."

The little man nodded politely.

"Nonetheless, the topic you raised regarding men seeing God brought other topics to my mind, and you may not find it so simple to disregard the other contradictions I can name."

"Perhaps not, but I am willing to muster superior effort if such becomes necessary."

Lord Gelus huffed. "Okay then, how can you explain this one? The Bible says not to curse gods or rulers, or to speak wickedly against them, as shown in Acts chapter twenty-three, verse five, and also in Exodus chapter twenty-two, verse twenty-eight. So then, how is it that Nathan cursed Kind David, John the Baptist cursed King Herod, Samuel cursed

King Saul, Elijah cursed King Ahab, Peter cursed the devil, and Jesus cursed King Herod?"

The little man appeared unabashed. "It is true that the Bible teaches men to have respect for the positions of gods and rulers, though both gods and rulers may be evil. Certain levels of reviling and cursing belong to God alone. However, this does not mean that is wrong to point out the wrongdoing of gods or rulers, even face to face. This is what occurred when Nathan pointed out King David's sin in Second Samuel chapter twelve, and when John the Baptist pointed out King Herod's sin in Mark chapter six, verse eighteen, and when Samuel pointed out Saul's folly in First Samuel chapter thirteen, verses thirteen and fourteen, and when Elijah pointed out King Ahab's error in following Baalim in First Kings chapter eighteen, verse eighteen. And if you read these verses carefully, you will also discover that it is not wrong to point out God's judgments against rulers, so long as God directs such discourse.

"Furthermore, it is not unacceptable to describe the nature or disposition of gods and rulers. This occurs when Peter describes the devil as an adversary who is like a roaring lion, a description found in First Peter chapter five, verse eight, and this also occurs when Jesus describes King Herod as a fox, a description found in Luke chapter thirteen, verse thirty-two. So then, none of the examples you gave actually featured men cursing gods or cursing rulers through their own volition, and therefore, none of these men were in breach of Exodus chapter twenty-two, verse twenty-eight, and none of these men were in breach of Acts chapter twenty-three, verse five. And I might also mention that the verses you quoted do not prohibit Christians from viewing gods or rulers as enemies. Jesus certainly identified Satan as an enemy, as seen in Luke chapter ten, verses eighteen and nineteen, and also in Matthew chapter thirteen, verse thirty-nine. And also note that in Second Kings chapter ten, verse thirty, the Lord told Jehu that he had done well in destroying the evil house of King Ahab."

The little man stopped speaking and faced Lord Gelus. It was no secret between the two that they viewed each other as enemies; and although Lord Gelus proclaimed himself as the local ruler, he was aware that the little man was more than willing to use his golden sword against him.

"I take it that the matter of cursing was a familiar subject for you," Lord Gelus remarked. "Well, perhaps the next subject will be more novel. You have spoken high-mindedly regarding this despicable Hebrew idiom of yours, how it brings Biblical Scripture together in congruence and harmony, well, there is one Bible verse where the Hebrew idiom makes complete nonsense, and I have never found anyone who could say otherwise. And before I name the Bible verse, let me point out that the verse was present in Greek manuscripts prior to the fifth century, and let me also point out that the words *not* and *but* are both present in the Greek text, so you will have no grounds for dismissing this verse."

"I'm ready."

"Fine," sneered Lord Gelus. "The verse is Third John eleven, *Beloved, follow not that which is evil, but that which is good. He that doeth good is of God: but he that doeth evil hath not seen God.* So then, when you apply the Hebrew idiom to this verse, you find the verse instructing you to follow not *only* that which is evil, but *also* that which is good. How can that be? Doesn't the rest of the Bible teach men to turn away from evil? How can this verse teach men to follow both that which is evil and that which is good?"

"I'm so glad you asked that," remarked the little man, causing a lugubrious expression to appear upon Lord Gelus' shaggy face. "It is so important to take Bible verses in context, and this verse is a perfect example."

Lord Gelus was dumbstruck, so the little man continued speaking.

"When a statement in the Greek New Testament contains the Hebrew idiom, then the primary emphasis of that statement is focused upon whatever follows the word *but*, which in this case is the phrase, *that which is good.* In the section of Scripture where this verse appears, the author is chastising Diotrephes for self-willed arrogance, and for rejecting persons who should not have been rejected. Diotrephes is identified as a church leader, as seen in verse nine. He is not accused of committing sins named as dead works, nor is he accused of teaching false doctrines, but he is accused of committing sins short of perfection, as revealed in verses nine and ten. To describe Diotrephes' sins succinctly, one might say that he was conceited and cliquish. In contrast to Diotrephes, Gaius and Demetrius are both highly praised.

"In verse eleven, Gaius is advised to follow not *only* that which is evil, but *also* that which is good. The word *evil* appears twice in verse eleven, and both times it is translated from a Greek word that can mean, *of a bad quality or disposition*, and it obviously refers to Diotrephes. Later in verse eleven, the author comments that, *he that doeth evil hath not seen God*. The Greek words translated as *seen God* in verse eleven can mean, *to attain to a true knowledge of God*. Thus, Gaius is being advised to not only listen to a church leader of poorer quality who is conceited and cliquish, such as Diotrephes, but to also listen to a church leader of higher quality, such as Demetrius.

"The author does not recommend kicking Diotrephes out of the church, and he does not recommend rejecting everything Diotrephes has to say, but he does recommend giving more respect to what Demetrius has to say than what Diotrephes has to say. In other words, when there is disagreement between Diotrephes and Demetrius, then Gaius is advised to follow after Demetrius. On the other hand, if both Diotrephes and Demetrius agree on a matter, such as abstaining from fornication, then it is okay to follow after both leaders. Given this context and an understanding of what the author is advising Gaius, it makes perfect sense that this verse is written in the form of the Hebrew idiom—follow not only after the less spiritually enlightened Diotrephes, but follow also, and preferentially, after the more spiritually enlightened Demetrius. If Diotrephes had been guilty of greater sins than arrogance and cliquishness, such as teaching false doctrines and committing dead works, then the author would have surely advised Gaius to reject Diotrephes entirely."

The little man's explanation frustrated Lord Gelus. "Alright then, what about Second Peter chapter three, verse nine? Is it not *only* God's will that any should perish, but *also* that all should come to repentance?"

"Oh, again you have brought up such a good point!" praised the little man.

Lord Gelus scowled.

"This verse makes it clear that individual human beings are not predestined to go to heaven or hell apart from their own freewill choices," stated the little man. "When the Bible speaks of predestination, it is referring to the fact that God has predestined those who exercise their free will to receive Jesus Christ as Lord and Savior to go to heaven, and God has predestined those who exercise their free will to reject Jesus Christ to go to hell. In this particular verse, it is not *only* God's will for those to perish who sin and refuse to repent, but it is *also* God's will for any of those very same persons, if they will repent and accept Jesus Christ as Lord and Savior, to go to heaven. In light of John chapter three, verse sixteen, and in light of Revelation chapter three, verse twenty, it is obviously God's preference that all sinners come to repentance and receive life eternal, but it is still his will for those to perish who will not repent from sin.

"And if there be any man or woman who has committed an *unforgivable sin*, and who can never be brought to repentance, then you can be certain that it was never God's will for that person to commit an unforgivable sin, so Second Peter chapter three, verse nine, still holds true—God was willing for that person to come to repentance prior to committing an *unforgivable sin*, just as he is willing for all sinners who have not committed an *unforgivable sin* to come to repentance prior to experiencing physical death. The person who has committed an unforgivable sin has *perished* already, even before experiencing physical death. Thus, it is the freewill choice of every human being that determines whether or not that individual will end up in heaven or hell. And note that the Greek word for *world* in Ephesians chapter one, verse four, can refer to the human family, or to *the present order of things*, rather than to the physical universe. So, in context with the rest of Scripture, it is appropriate to interpret Ephesians chapter one, verses four and five, as teaching that God foresaw Jesus Christ as the only avenue of salvation for mankind, and that this foresight was present prior to the foundation of human civilization, although not necessarily prior to the creation of Adam and Eve. It is also appropriate to interpret these two verses as teaching that, subsequent to Adam and Eve's sin, God predestined persons to be adopted as his children who would repent from sin and accept Jesus Christ as Lord and Savior. These two verses do not mean that God picked out certain persons to go to heaven, and picked out other persons to go to hell—the choice between heaven and hell rests with the free will of mankind. God prefers that all men repent from sin and be saved, but not all men choose to do what God prefers.

"And let me add, Lord Gelus, that it pains the heart of God for persons to reject his offer of salvation through their refusal to repent from sin. It is his holy nature that cannot permit persons into heaven when those persons stand in need of repentance. God never created himself, as you know, albeit the Son was begotten of the Father, and his holy nature is what it is. And note that the redeeming blood of the Savior cannot cleanse those persons who refuse to lay the foundation of *faith toward God and repentance from dead works*. God honors and respects the free will which he begat within mankind—mankind's free will is an essence of God himself, for it enables the highest form of love—and God will not deny himself."

Lord Gelus scoffed. "And I suppose First John chapter two, verse sixteen, means that the lust of the flesh, and the lust of the eyes, and the pride of life, is not *only* of the Father, but *also* is of the world," sputtered Lord Gelus.

The little man laughed merrily. "You're going backward, Lord Gelus," he said. "This is so simple—one merely needs to be aware of Rule #2 in the rules governing application of the Hebrew idiom. The Greek sentence that begins in the middle of verse fifteen and continues until the end of verse sixteen contains two *Hebrew idiom negatives* prior to the Greek word for *but*, and therefore, the Hebrew idiom does not apply."

There was a pause in the dialogue. The little man's good-natured laughter; and his explanation of First John chapter two, verse sixteen; infuriated Lord Gelus.

"Hang it all," Lord Gelus scoffed. "Why should anyone make any attempt to be righteous? Does it not say in Luke chapter five, verse thirty-two, that Jesus did not come to call the righteous? Does it not say, rather, that he came to call sinners? How can any man make it to heaven if he is not called by Jesus? Shouldn't a man sin, then, so that he can make it to heaven?"

The little man laughed again. Lord Gelus simmered. The room grew quieter than ever.

"You need to control that temper of yours, Lord Gelus—a little self-control may keep you from making the same mistake over and over," remarked the little man. "Luke chapter five, verse thirty-two, obviously contains the Hebrew idiom. Jesus came not *only* to call the righteous, but he *also* came to call sinners to repentance."

Lord Gelus only replied with a snarl.

"This verse emphasizes Jesus' calling sinners to repentance," continued the little man, "but the verse takes for granted that Jesus came to call the righteous."

A look of vindictive cognizance swept Lord Gelus' features. "Oh really!? Well! Just how do you deal with Romans chapter three, verse twenty-three—*For all have sinned, and come short of the glory of God?* How can a man be righteous if he has sinned? So if all have sinned, then how could Jesus have come to call the righteous? And besides that, if men were really righteous, then why would they need called by Jesus at all? Wouldn't they already be on their way to heaven?"

"You know," remarked the little man, "it must bring great joy to the heart of God when a prostitute turns her back on her profession, for Luke chapter fifteen, verse seven, points out there is more rejoicing in heaven over one such sinner who repents than over ninety-nine just persons who need no repentance."

"Do you think that you can evade my question?" roared Lord Gelus. "I've got you, don't I?! You don't have any answer, do you?!"

The little man delayed his response just long enough to let Lord Gelus draw a gloating breath and puff his chest like a toad, and then he produced a smile that incensed Lord Gelus more than any of the laughter that had come before. "You may recall, Lord Gelus, that Isaiah chapter sixty-four, verse six, points out that the righteousness of man is as filthy rags. This verse does not deny that a man can have righteousness, rather, it points out that the best righteousness that a man can achieve through his own efforts falls far short of the righteousness of God. Another verse that sheds light on the Biblical definitions of righteousness is a verse that contains the Hebrew idiom, namely Philippians chapter three, verse nine. In this verse, Paul expresses his goal of not *only* having his own righteousness, which is of the law, but *also* having righteousness that comes from God through faith in Christ, and the emphasis is on the latter righteousness. The righteousness that Paul was able to achieve through his own efforts is well described in Romans chapter seven, where verse fifteen points out that Paul's own righteousness did not even give him the power to keep from doing what he hated, and verse fourteen points out that Paul's own righteousness did not deliver him from being a child of Satan, for he was still *sold under sin*. In contrast, the righteousness of God, which is given to Paul through faith in Christ, gives Paul the power to keep from doing what he hates, and also makes him a child of God. This power is drawn from the redeeming blood of Jesus Christ, and from the indwelling of the Holy Spirit, and this righteousness is described in Romans chapter eight, verses one through four.

"So, Lord Gelus, someone as intellectually blessed as yourself must surely see where my explanation is leading. Remember that the foundation of salvation is presented in Hebrews chapter six, verse one, namely repentance from dead works and faith toward God. There are two levels of righteousness incorporated in this foundation. First, the level of righteousness achieved by the freewill choice to repent from committing dead works…"

"Just a minute!" interrupted Lord Gelus. "I remember that list of *dead works* you blabbed off earlier. What if a man never committed one of those sins? How could a man repent from doing something that he never did? So then, wouldn't a man have to go out and commit a sin that qualifies as a *dead work* before he could obtain salvation, since you say the foundation of salvation starts with repenting from dead works?"

"That's where your verse is so helpful," stated the little man.

"Huh?"

"You know, Romans chapter three, verse twenty-three—*For all have sinned, and come short of the glory of God*. This, of course, refers to all men who reach ages of moral accountability, except for the one man who was also God, namely Jesus Christ. Jesus Christ was the perfect sacrifice, without sin, as pointed out in Hebrews chapter nine, verse fourteen, and also in First Peter chapter one, verse nineteen, and also in Hebrews chapter four, verse fifteen—*but was in all points tempted like as we are, yet without sin*."

"You ramble," rejoined Lord Gelus. "You can't expect me to believe that all men have committed murder, or fornication, or thievery, or…"

"No need to name off the whole list," interjected the little man. "First of all, I daresay a great percentage of men have, in fact, committed a sin off that list, but it really doesn't matter."

"What?"

"Are you totally forgetting James chapter two, verse ten? The verse states—*For whosoever shall keep the whole law, and yet offend in one point, he is guilty of all*. You see, Lord Gelus, the Holy Law of God is like a perfect statue of solid glass that loses its entire essence if marred in any way. And if the statue is marred, it cannot be restored by any human effort. If you damage that statue, whether you scratch the glass, or chip out a chunk of glass, or shatter the entire statue, you are guilty of ruining the whole statue. And the penalty for damaging the statue is death.

"When a man commits any sin at all, no matter how minor, then he has broken the Holy Law of God, and I'm sure you have enough sense to realize that no man of moral capacity lives without sinning at all, that is, no man besides Jesus Christ. And a man who has sinned, even if only guilty of minor sins, cannot withstand the judgment of a perfect and holy God, and the wages of sin is death. That is why the foundation of salvation described in Hebrews chapter six, verse one, applies to all men, for even the smallest of sins leaves one guilty of breaking the whole law, and the law contains commandments against *dead works*. God requires that we exercise the power of free will that he has given us, and that we use that power to turn away from willfully committing dead works. And this is true regardless of how little we have sinned, and regardless of whether or not we have actually committed a sin that meets the definition of a *dead work*. And God also requires that we accept, through faith, the blood sacrifice of Jesus Christ to cleanse us from sin. God may not expect us to live perfect and sinless lives after we obtain salvation, but he puts the power of his Spirit within us, and he points out that this power will keep us from willfully committing those sins defined as *dead works*, so long as we remain *born of God*. This is revealed most emphatically in the second and third chapters of First John.

"And furthermore, as I have pointed out before, the New Testament of our Lord and Savior Jesus Christ directs those who are born of God to refer to themselves as *saints*, for to refer to themselves as *sinners* denies the power of the seed of God within them, and it casts an insult at the Spirit of God who dwells within them, and it is inconsistent with the nomenclature used in regard to sinners and saints in the New Testament, and it also casts insults upon the kings and priests unto God who have been cleansed from sin by the blood of Christ, namely those kings and priests mentioned in Revelation chapter one, verse six.

"So in conclusion, there are two categories of righteousness defined in the New Testament. First, there is the righteousness of repentance from dead works, a righteousness that puts a man in the position to accept the gift of eternal life through the blood of Christ. This was the righteousness obtained by men who accepted the message of repentance preached by John the Baptist, and it is the righteousness referred to by Christ in Luke chapter five, verse thirty-two, when he says that he came to call not *only* the righteous. This righteousness is a good thing, for it is a basic ingredient in the salvation of mankind, and it is a prerequisite to accepting the free gift of eternal life through the blood of Christ. However, this righteousness alone will not get any man into heaven, and it will not deliver the soul of any man from the deplorable condition of being sold under sin—sold to Satan.

"The second category of righteousness is the righteousness of God. Mankind only receives such righteousness through the redeeming blood of Christ, as disclosed in Revelation chapter five, verse nine, a verse that proclaims the worthiness of the risen Lord Jesus. This righteousness is only reached through the second factor named in the foundation of salvation found in Hebrews chapter six, verse one, namely faith toward God. Men believe God, and therefore they believe the Word of God, and they receive the blood sacrifice of Jesus Christ for the forgiveness of their sins, and they are born into the family of God. This is the only righteousness that bears the gift of eternal life."

The look on Lord Gelus' face was a mixture of annoyance, dismay, and fervent animosity. "Your words are nauseating," he spoke with ire. "You leave me no choice but to declare the obvious. One has only to open the very first pages of the Bible to find unsupportable claims."

"I'm sure I do not agree," the little man proclaimed. "But please proceed."

"Very well," Lord Gelus spoke in a tone of discordance. The nature of his voice was drifting farther and farther away from anything suave or refined; he simply sounded angry. "Supposedly God created the earth and all living creatures in six days, and then rested on the seventh day. Well, how could the earth have been created on the first day when the rotation of the earth is used to measure a day? And besides that, how could all the history of creation be referred to as a *day* in Genesis chapter two, verse four, when in Genesis chapter one it took six days? And what's more, did God only work at night? Evening to morning is nighttime, isn't it? Doesn't the first chapter of Genesis state that the evening and the morning comprised the individual days of creation?"

The little man chuckled, which made Lord Gelus all the madder. "What questions!" he declared. "I just love such subject matter."

Lord Gelus frowned.

"To begin with," said the little man, "the evening was the beginning of the Hebrew day, so the term, *the evening and the morning*, can indicate a *beginning and continuing*. And the Hebrew word for *day* can mean an *age*, or an *era*. The exact phrase, *the evening and the morning*, as is found in Genesis chapter one in regard to the days of creation, is also found in Daniel chapter eight, verse twenty-six. In the Book of Daniel, this phrase pertains to the time period encompassed by the vision Daniel describes in chapter eight, a time period great enough to include the conquests of kings, the removal of the daily sacrifice, the transgression of desolation, the cleansing of the sanctuary, and the breaking of the king of fierce countenance that stood up against the Prince of princes. Quite obviously, Lord Gelus, this phrase did not refer to a mere twenty-four hours, but rather, it referred to many years.

"And a similar phrase to, *the evening and the morning*, namely, *evening to morning*, is found in Exodus chapter twenty-seven, verses twenty and twenty-one, and also in Leviticus chapter twenty-four, verses two and three. The meaning of the phrase *evening to morning* in those verses is indicated by other words that appear in those same verses, namely, words such as *always*, *continually*, and *for ever*. Thus, it would be inconsistent with the rest of the Old Testament to interpret the phrase, *the evening and the morning*, that appears in the first chapter of Genesis, as meaning a twenty-four hour day. Therefore, the days of creation should be properly interpreted as eras. Furthermore, the entire period of creation could also be referred to as an era, and any consecutive number of the days of creation could be referred to as an era, so there is no conflict between Genesis chapter two, verse four, and the days of creation in Genesis chapter one. And in addition to that, since the phrase *the evening and the morning* can mean a beginning and continuing, then God may have created new species of plants beyond the third *day* of creation, such as during the creation of insects.

"And for further proof of what I am saying, Leviticus chapter twenty-three, verse thirty-two, defines the Sabbath day that the Jewish people were to observe as being from *even unto even*, and this phrase was referring to a twenty-four hour day. And note how the phrase *even unto even* contrasts with the phrase *the evening and the morning*. And so, Lord Gelus, this means that God did not create everything at night."

"And I suppose that rabbits chewed their cuds back in Old Testament times!" snapped Lord Gelus. He was flustered and irritated.

The little man tightened his grip on the handle of his sword. "Oh," he replied serenely, hoping to have a calming effect upon the adversary facing him. "That's not a bad question. You're referring to the mention of conies and hares chewing the cud in Leviticus chapter eleven, verses five and six."

Lord Gelus glared without replying, but the burning in his eyes eased.

"That could really be a problem, I suppose, if the Old Testament were first written in English. But just as one must realize that the New Testament was originally written in Greek, one must also realize that the Old Testament was originally written in Hebrew. The Hebrew word for *cud* in these verses derives from another Hebrew word meaning, *to drag off roughly*, and by analogy can mean to *saw or chew*. Further, the Hebrew word for *chew* in these verses can mean *to ascend, or cut off*. Thus, the Old Testament phrase, *cheweth the cud*, can mean to *cut, raise, and chew*. This, then, is a description of grazing on vegetation, and it can obviously be applied to creatures such as cattle, goats, sheep, camels, and rabbits."

"And I suppose you think it makes sense that God simply *spoke* the universe into being! As if mere words can create a planet!"

"It makes perfect sense, Lord Gelus, when you consider who the Bible refers to as the *Word*, as found in the first verse of the first chapter of the Book of John. It was the Person of the Son of God who performed material manufacturing—God the Father spoke, and God the Son worked to make the words that were spoken take physical form. Have you never read the first three verses of the gospel of John?"

"Aye, maybe so, but that does not negate another discrepancy. Does Matthew chapter twenty-seven, verse forty-four, not say that both of the thieves who were crucified with Christ reviled him for not supernaturally descending from the cross, whereas the account in Luke chapter twenty-three, verses thirty-nine through forty-three, says that only one of the thieves reviled him while the other supported him? How would you explain that?"

"Quite simple, Lord Gelus. The account in Matthew never says that both thieves reviled Christ, rather, it says that they cast the fact that he remained on the cross in his teeth. One thief reviled Christ, which may have tempted Christ to descend from the cross to prove the thief wrong, and the other thief supported Christ, which may have tempted Christ to descend from the cross to prove the thief right. It is quite reasonable, therefore, to say that the two thieves cast the fact that he remained on the cross in his teeth."

"How clever. So you think you have me stumped, do you? Well then, how do you explain Matthew chapter twenty-seven, verse nine? The prophecy about the thirty pieces of silver was spoken by Zechariah, and yet the verse claims that it was spoken by Jeremiah."

"Not so, Lord Gelus," boomed the little man. "You know good and well that the Book of Matthew was addressed to the Jewish Christians, a group expected to be very knowledgeable in regard to Old Testament Scripture. The word *spoken* in that verse, referring to Jeremiah, is in the passive tense, indicating something *verbally received* through Jeremiah. In contrast to the word *spoken* that refers to Jeremiah, the word *saying* that appears in the same verse, referring to Zechariah, is in the active tense in the Greek, indicating that Zechariah actually spoke the words that follow. Matthew did not need to mention Zechariah by name when he quoted Zechariah, because the Jewish Christians were sufficiently knowledgeable in regard to Old Testament Scripture to know that Zechariah was the one who spoke about the thirty pieces of silver. They were also knowledgeable enough to know that Jeremiah chapter eighteen prophesied about a potter and the remaking of a vessel, an illustration applicable to the ending of an old covenant and the beginning of a new covenant. And Jeremiah chapter thirty-one extensively addressed the establishment of a new covenant. The breaking of a covenant is mentioned in Zechariah, and this precedes the verse prophesying about the thirty pieces of silver and the potter. Thus, the prophesy received through Jeremiah was fulfilled though Christ, and this was made manifest by the fulfillment of prophetic words spoken by Zechariah.

"If the verse had been written to less knowledgeable persons, perhaps it may have said something like the following, *Then the prophecy received through Jeremiah the prophet in regard to the establishment of a new covenant was fulfilled, made evident through the fulfillment of words spoken by Zechariah the prophet pertaining to the breaking of the old covenant. And notably, Zechariah's prophecy regarding the breaking of the old covenant included selling the Lord for thirty pieces of silver that were given to a potter, as fulfilled in the betrayal of Christ. Thus, Christ abolished the old covenant and established a new covenant.* So then, Lord Gelus, does the verse not make perfect sense to one with Biblical knowledge?"

There was a long pause. A hush fell over the chamber. It was obvious that Lord Gelus was losing ground. He looked about at his disheveled mob with embarrassment and ire, then he turned back toward the little man and glared with burning eyes. "You leave me no choice but to dishearten your feeble mind with much more severity than I desired," he fumed, but it was difficult for him to subdue a note of uncertainty. "I hesitate to bestow utter destitution upon your theories of Scriptural integrity, but I am forced to do so. Answer me this question, how do you explain the contradictions in the four gospels, Matthew, Mark, Luke, and John, in regard to the resurrection? How could the women have gone to the sepulcher while it was still dark, and yet have gone at sunrise? How could angels have been sitting, and yet standing? Must I point out more discrepancies?"

The little man shook his head. "Did you never attend kindergarten Sunday school?" he chided. "I'll tell you what, let me explain the story of the resurrection as related by the four gospels, and then you can tell me if I've gotten anything wrong, or if there are any discrepancies. Is that fair enough?"

Lord Gelus puffed out his chest and guffawed. "I look forward to your measly attempt."

"Very well, one needs only to read all four accounts in the four gospels, piece them together, and learn the following…

"There had been an earthquake. The angel of the Lord had descended from heaven and rolled back the stone from the door of the sepulcher where Jesus Christ's body had been placed, and the angel had then sat down on the stone. The Roman guards who were supposed to prevent anyone from stealing the body of Christ were terrified by this happening, but they were not harmed. Those guards were very likely the source of information in regard to this supernatural phenomenon. Notably, the disciples and women who were followers of Christ did not find out about this happening until later.

"Very early that same morning, prior to sunrise, when it was still dark outside, Mary Magdalene, probably in company with one or more other women, went to the sepulcher where Christ's body was placed.

She saw the stone rolled away and assumed that Christ's body had been taken away, so she went and reported this to Peter and John. Peter and John then went to the sepulcher and investigated Mary's claim, and they believed her. Then they went home.

"Remember, Lord Gelus, that Roman guards had been stationed to protect the sepulcher because the Chief priests and Pharisees were afraid that Christian disciples would steal the body of Christ by night and then claim that he rose from the dead. When Mary Magdalene found the tomb empty in the darkness, she may have logically concluded that the Roman guards had moved the body of Christ to a different location to further protect against the body being stolen. She may have also surmised, given that the Chief priests and Pharisees wanted proof that Christ did not rise from the dead, that the body would later be returned for daytime verification of sustained death. It would also have been logical to surmise that when the body was returned, the stone would be rolled back into place.

"Later that same day, still very early in the morning, but now at sunrise when there was more light, Mary Magdalene and other women returned to the sepulcher hoping to find the body of Christ, thinking that his body might have been returned, and thinking they might find that the stone had been rolled back into place. Instead, they found that the sepulcher was open. They entered the sepulcher and did not find the body of Jesus, but then they saw an angel sitting. The angel stood up, and another angel appeared and stood, and the angels proclaimed the resurrection of Christ, with one of the angels serving as primary spokesman. In two of the gospel accounts, only the angel who served as the primary spokesman is mentioned, but notably, neither one of these gospel accounts states that there was only one angel. The women left to tell the disciples, that is, all of the women except for Mary Magdalene.

"Mary Magdalene was not convinced of the resurrection of Christ by the messengers with shining garments, namely the angels. When all the other women left the sepulcher, she remained behind, weeping. She stooped down and looked back into the sepulcher, and saw that the two angels were now sitting. They asked her why she was weeping, and she told them that her Lord had been taken, and that she did not know where he was placed. She then turned away from the angels, and she saw Jesus standing outside, but she did not know that it was Jesus. Jesus asked her why she was weeping, and he also asked her who she was seeking. She thought it was the gardener, and inquired if he knew the whereabouts of Christ's body. Jesus then called her by name, and she turned to him, and recognized him. Then, after conversing with the risen Christ, she went to tell the disciples. Notably, Jesus appeared to the other women who left the sepulcher ahead of Mary Magdalene, and notably, he appeared to them before they reached the disciples.

"When the women, including Mary Magdalene, told the disciples about the angels, and about seeing the risen Lord Jesus, and about the messages that they received from the angels, the disciples did not believe them. Peter, however, returned to the sepulcher to investigate. He did not find any angels, and he did not see Jesus, and he departed wondering what was going on. But later that day Jesus appeared to his disciples, and then they believed, that is, all except for Thomas, who was absent. The other disciples told Thomas that the risen Lord had appeared to them, but he refused to believe their testimony. A few days later Christ appeared to Thomas, and then Thomas believed.

"Thus, it is evident that the disciples did not believe in the resurrection of Christ simply because the tomb was empty. Mary Magdalene did not even believe the testimony of heavenly angels. It was the supernatural risen Christ who convinced the disciples and Mary Magdalene of the truth—he had risen from the dead. And the Word of God gives the most complete description of the events of Christ's resurrection when the accounts of all four gospels, Matthew, Mark, Luke, and John, are pieced together. And notably, the separate accounts of the resurrection presented in the four gospels are not contradictory."

The little man then stopped speaking and nodded toward Lord Gelus, almost winking.

Lord Gelus lost all semblance of his previously debonair carriage. He hunched and stared at the little man like a maddened ape. "It's plain enough that you have an answer for everything," he bellowed. "But you're forgetting one thing, there are a great number of Christians who don't really believe the Bible. It's just a reference book to them, some historical data, a reflection of ancient thinking that is only relevant to particular times and societies."

The little man's face grew stern. "It is only logical and consistent to believe that the same God who inspired and directed the composition of thirty-nine books comprising the canonized Old Testament also inspired and directed the composition of twenty-seven books comprising the canonized New Testament."

"Oh, I'll grant you that," growled Lord Gelus. "But what difference does that make? The Christians who view the Bible as erroneous do not consider the Old Testament to be anything better than the New Testament—if anything, they probably consider the Old Testament to be more nonsensical than the New Testament."

"Then I must point out that your use of the word *Christian* is a misnomer," the little man asserted.

Lord Gelus appeared taken aback. "What do you mean?" he growled.

"Jesus Christ made it clear that those who belong to him hear his voice and heed his words, as shown in John chapter ten, verses three and sixteen, and in John chapter eight, verse forty-seven, and in John chapter eighteen, verse thirty-seven, and in Luke chapter eight, verse twenty-one. Jesus Christ spoke the following words as recorded in John chapter ten, verse thirty-five, *the Scripture cannot be broken*, and he spoke the following words in John chapter seventeen, verse seventeen, *Thy word is truth*. The phrase in the Greek New Testament translated as, *the Scripture cannot be broken*, can also be translated from the Greek text as, *the validity of Scripture cannot be dismissed*. If a man does not agree that the validity of Biblical Scripture cannot be dismissed in regard to the canonized Scripture of the time of Christ, namely most or all of the Old Testament, then he is not hearing and heeding the words of Jesus Christ, so it would be inappropriate to refer to such a man as a *Christian*, and it is reasonable to apply the same standard to a man's view of the twenty-seven canonized books of the New Testament.

"And furthermore, when Christ said, *Thy word is truth*, he granted veracity to Scripture by the mouth of God himself, for Christ is a Person of God. And it is obvious that Christ considered *Scripture* to be the *Word of God*, for when one reads Mark chapter seven, verse thirteen, one finds that Christ refers to Old Testament Scripture as *the word of God*. And Paul supports the New Testament as the Word of God, for he averred that he delivered the *word of God* in First Thessalonians chapter two, verse thirteen—*For this cause also thank we God without ceasing, because, when ye received the word of God which ye heard of us, ye received it not as the word of men, but as it is in truth, the word of God, which effectually worketh also in you that believe*—and this is in addition to the affirmation given in First Timothy, chapter three, verse sixteen. And I would stress, Lord Gelus, that although God may permit or direct the deception of evil men in order to enact his judgments, he never speaks a lie. And by his own mouth, in the Person of Jesus Christ, God has affirmed that the *Word of God* is truth."

Lord Gelus scrunched his shoulders in an odious posture. "Is that so, well, I could really care less," he jeered. "Let's stop this senseless jargon. I know why you're here. You cannot hope to rescue the girl. Does not the Bible that you so gallingly defend make it clear that evil will reign until the *Second Coming of Christ*, at which time God will set up a new kingdom in Israel and the Jews will rule the earth for a thousand years? Christ has not come back yet, so if you fight me now, then I'll win."

The little man laughed. Andela stared upon him in wonder. He leveled his eyes upon Lord Gelus with a look of amusement. "So it comes to this—you resort to fairy tales and rumors."

"Grrrr…," returned Lord Gelus. "So you're calling the canonized Scriptures fairy tales?"

"Not all all, it's your inventful interpretation of Scriptures that I'm calling fairy tales. The present earth will completely pass away at the Second Coming of Christ, as revealed in Second Peter chapter three, verse ten, and in Revelation chapter twenty-one, verse one. Christ's kingdom is spiritual, not physical, as Christ makes clear in John chapter eighteen, verse thirty-six, and in Luke chapter seventeen, verse twenty-one. His powerful kingdom is already established, as shown in Mark chapter one, verse fifteen, and in Colossians chapter one, verse thirteen. And being a racial Jew, or a member of any other group of human beings referred to as a race, makes no difference in regard to being a member of God's kingdom, or in regard to receiving eternal life, as explained in Galatians chapter three, verses twenty-seven through twenty-nine, and in Matthew chapter three, verses eight through ten.

"Furthermore, you should know that the Book of Revelation contains many symbols. The number 1000 is known to represent absolute perfection and completeness. Thus, the *one thousand years* mentioned in Revelation chapter twenty, verse two, represents the perfect completion of Christ's mission through his crucifixion, and through his preaching to the imprisoned dead as disclosed in First Peter chapter three, verse nineteen, and through his resurrection. Don't you think Satan would have attempted to interfere with Christ's preaching to the dead and his redeeming of mankind if Satan were not bound? And note that the period of time from Christ's resurrection to his Second Coming is referred to as *a little season.*

"Verse four of Revelation chapter twenty refers to individuals who were judged worthy of reigning with Christ prior to his resurrection, likely joining ranks with such persons as Moses, Elijah, and Enoch. The period of time these persons reigned with Christ is referred to as *a thousand years.* Verse five reveals that the rest of the dead did not reign with Christ until after the *first resurrection.* There is no second *resurrection* mentioned in the Bible, and this *first resurrection* may also be translated from the Greek as the *chief resurrection,* and notably, this resurrection is ongoing. First Corinthians chapter fifteen, verse sixteen, is properly translated in the present tense—*For if the dead rise not, neither has Christ been raised.* Also, the Greek word for *first* in First Thessalonians chapter four, verse sixteen, may also be translated from the Greek as *formerly,* and it means that Christians who die before the Second Coming of Christ go on to heaven prior to his Second Coming. Those who are included in the *chief resurrection* live and reign with Christ forever, and this *forever* is referred to as *a thousand years* in Revelation chapter twenty, verse six. Thus, the *thousand years* mentioned in verses two, three, and seven of Revelation chapter twenty, is different than the *thousand years* in verse four, and also different than the *thousand years* in verse six. Obviously, then, the *thousand years* in these instances is not a literal thousand years, but rather, it refers to perfect completeness."

Lord Gelus stared upon the little man with hatred. Despite the extensive dialogue that had passed between them, he was not able to invalidate any of the little man's claims. "Well," snarled Lord Gelus, "if you think that all of this makes any difference, then your idiocy is unfathomable. There's no way I'll ever release that gir..."

Lord Gelus ceased speaking. As he began saying the word *girl,* he glanced toward Andela; and then, as he started to look back toward the little man, his face snapped back in her direction and his speech faltered. His great yellow eyes widened in surprise, and then they transformed into smoldering discs of malevolent rage. A bloodcurdling roar burst through his bared fangs. Lord Gelus no longer seemed capable of reason or civilized conversation; instead, he presented an image of rabid hostility.

Andela was entranced by the conversation between the little man and Lord Gelus; and when Lord Gelus unexpectedly transformed into a furious figure of hellish hatred, she found herself petrified in fear. She was unable to think or move.

"The rope! Andela Tidmore! Grab the rope! Now!"

At last the little man's words penetrated Andela's mind, releasing her from paralysis. She saw Resants charging toward her with bestial grimaces and outstretched claws, and she saw a golden sword hacking through shaggy arms, necks and skulls with brilliant furor. The darkness of the shaft engulfed her. Somehow she had turned and grasped the rope, wrapping it around her right forearm and hand and clasping above her right hand with her left hand. Remembering the little man's instruction, she had yanked downward. She wrapped her feet and ankles in the loose end of the rope as she rose upward. At first she ascended smoothly, but then her body was jolted by battling foes on the dangling end of the rope beneath her.

She hung to her lifeline with desperate strength. Her breast pounded. Looking downward past her dangling hair, she glimpsed a glint of gold; and then the rope eased and she continued rising. Apparently the little man had cut the rope. The sounds of battle subsided.

"We'll get you yet!" Andela heard a gruff voice echo through the shaft. She peered downward, but she saw nothing other than a distant circle of dim light.

Chapter 7

Pursuit of Breath

When Bill awoke, he found himself still sprawled out on the plush featherbed in the desert cabin. He surmised that he was not really awake since he was not in his bedroom in Missouri. He also came to another realization, one that distressed him—he was suffocating!

"This room must be airtight," Bill murmured, looking toward the thin line of light showing around the edges of the bedroom door. He slid off the bed and turned on the bedroom light, and then he grabbed the door handle and swung the door wide open. The living room looked the same as before, but the air in the room was every bit as stifling as the air in the bedroom. He crossed the room, flipped up the metal latch to the outside door, and leaned against the door to heave it open, but the door did not budge.

"Not good," Bill muttered. Wearing only socks on his feet, he positioned himself on the wooden floor and lunged against the heavy door with his right shoulder. "Ah!" he grunted, and then he massaged his stunned shoulder as he faced the obstinate door. Breathing harder due to physical exertion, he stepped over to the solitary window. The sounds of tumultuous winds whistled through small cracks in the roof of the cabin, and there were visible whirlwinds skipping across the desert floor. It was dim outside, but Bill could see well enough to determine why the door to the cabin would not open—a sand bank had formed against the side of the cabin, rising to within a foot of the lower edge of the window.

The mental image of a skunk caught in a trap arose within Bill's mind. He drew back from the window and examined the construction of the cabin. The walls were sandstone, and the ceiling was composed of tightly fit logs with reddish clay used to mortar the seams. A good chainsaw might get him out through the ceiling, but he could not remember seeing any tools during his inspection of the cabin. He checked the chimney—the flue was too narrow from front to back to attempt climbing out to the roof. Then his labored breathing brought his thoughts back to the window; he could worry about escaping after he obtained some oxygen. There were several small logs in the fireplace.

Bill selected the largest log and carried it to the window. The glass was brittle and shattered easily; he had no problem knocking all of the glass from within the wooden frame. Sounds of the storm poured into the room. He dropped the log and thrust his face outside, squinting due to blowing sand. After a few seconds of inhaling and exhaling, he deduced that the air outside the window was no better than the air inside; if anything, it was worse.

Dizziness set in as Bill picked up the log and banged the frame of the window loose from the surrounding sandstone structure. Panting for oxygen, he returned to the bedroom and pulled on his boots. Then he staggered into the kitchen and snatched a broom that he remembered seeing in one corner, and he also grabbed one of the kitchen chairs. He returned to the living room and positioned the chair against the wall beneath the square opening. He stood on the chair and thrust the broom through the opening, and then he brushed shattered glass from the sand below. When finished, he tossed the broom aside on the sand.

A feeling of desperation swelled within Bill's chest. The diagonal span of the opening was not quite wide enough for his shoulders. Meanwhile, with his head protruding through the opening, he became convinced that the air outside the cabin was more deficient in oxygen than the air inside the cabin. He climbed down from the chair and rambled to the center of the room. His mind was foggy. He sat down on the thick rug beneath the chandelier. He sat motionless. Taking deep breaths increased his mental coherence.

As Bill's body weakened from lack of oxygen, his mind began racing. He thought about Cowgirl Jane—whatever became of her? Where was she now? Then he mentally chastised himself for thinking about Cowgirl Jane as if she were real. This was all a dream, wasn't it? As unconsciousness approached, he found himself thinking about Andela.

Bill experienced a vague perception of his head thumping against the floor. It seemed that time passed, and it seemed, perhaps, that he dreamed, but how could that be? How could someone have a dream within a dream? By and by he became aware of something extraordinary—he was emerging into the most wonderful corporal sensation he had ever known. A powerful force of affection permeated every cell of his body, and his soul was drawn into an unimaginable dimension of ecstasy. His eyelids parted. Fathomless compassion poured through lovely green eyes.

* * * * * * * * * * * * * * * * * * *

As Andela reached the top of the ventilation shaft, she released her left hand and positioned it against the upper lip of the opening to prevent rough stone from scraping her body. The golden gloves Madam Mercy gave her provided far tougher protection than the sheer golden fabric suggested. She was facing eastward as her body was drawn outside. The Land of the Northern Pool rose in the distance to her left. She was stricken by the dimness of the atmosphere, dusty with whirling winds, and by her labored breathing. The surface air had changed during her ordeal within the horrid underground chamber—the air was suffocating.

Once withdrawn from the shaft, Andela released the rope. Her body was stretched out on a flat stone surface. She peered forward. There was a blurred range of distant mountains, and she could vaguely see the silhouette of something about fifty yards in front of her, something that was moving toward her. She rose to her hands and knees and crawled back to the opening, and then she dropped back down onto her stomach. She dipped her face into the hollow shaft and stared downward. The distant circle of light—the opening into the chamber where she was nearly boiled alive—was small and almost imperceptible. There were no audible sounds coming up through the shaft.

"Thank you," Andela whispered. Then the emotions of her recent experience caught up with her mind and body; she clung to the rocky edges of the hewn hole and let herself cry until she sobbed. Tears dropped downward, liquid pearls of inexpressible gratitude, pearls of heartfelt love for the little man who battled on her behalf. She thought about the sacrifice he made for her, and about his amazing courage, and about the words he spoke—words that enlightened her mind and brought deliverance and healing to her troubled heart—and she remembered that he was invincible. The tears she shed became tears of joy.

Andela felt a hand touch her right shoulder. She knew that it must be the hand of her rescuer. She scooted back from the opening and then rose to her feet and turned around. A petite and beautiful lady with golden hair stood motionless and stared into Andela's eyes. The lady was elvish in appearance, with thick hair flowing downward to her knees. She wore a white silken tunic and a golden satin belt; and there were three small crystal vials hanging between her breasts. The vials were suspended from three golden threads that looped around her neck, with each thread attached to a single vial.

The elvish lady shifted her eyes to Andela's moistened cheeks, and then dropped them to Andela's rising and falling chest, apparently perceptive of Andela's labored breathing. She then lifted her face and addressed Andela with thoughtful eyes—blue eyes that were much like the eyes of the little man who rescued Andela from the savage beasts in the chamber below.

"Your tears are well spent," spoke the elvish lady, stepping closer to Andela so that they stood face to face. She had to raise her face since she was about a foot shorter than Andela. Her voice was clear and sweet. "Whenever he is delayed, there is occasion to mourn, for his presence brings joy and peace while his absence yields frustration and suffering."

Andela gasped for air. It seemed like the atmosphere grew worse with each passing second. "You mean, the little man with the golden sword, the man who rescued me?" asked Andela, panting as she spoke.

"Yes."

Andela squinted as a gust of wind whipped loose sand past her face. "He said that he was invincible. Who is he?"

The little lady's beautiful face displayed momentary surprise. "Truth."

"Truth?"

"Yes, he grew stronger when you came to this land. I am surprised that he did not introduce himself to you."

Andela recalled Madam Mercy mentioning that Hope and Truth would help her. It did not surprise her that the little man who challenged Lord Gelus in debate and delivered her from the fiery trial of false guilt was Truth. The words of John chapter eight, verse thirty-two, came to her mind—*And ye shall know the truth, and the truth shall make you free.*

"We...," began Andela, but then she paused to catch her breath. "We've never really had a good opportunity for introductions. We've always been, well, he's always been busy rescuing me."

The little lady nodded, peering into Andela's eyes. "I am Eovin, a maiden of the oasa trees. I am a Cherinede."

"A Cherinede?" returned Andela. Her mind grew cloudy. Despite deep breathing, her ability to maintain consciousness waned.

Eovin looked downward and reached to her chest with both hands. She unlatched one of the vials from its golden thread, removed a crystal stopper from the top of the vial, and lifted the vial toward Andela's lips. "Here, drink some of this before you pass out. It will help you breathe."

Andela accepted the vial—a translucent crystal tear filled to its brim with a golden liquid. There was a golden band around the neck of the vial, and the band had a small latch, a latch used to fasten the vial to a thread. She brought the vial to her lips with both hands and took a sip. The liquid was aromatic, like dark, wild honey.

"How much do I drink?"

"About half—each half should sustain someone your size for three hours," replied Eovin. She began removing the golden thread that had previously suspended Andela's vial. This required her to lift her hair through the unbroken loop of thread; and as she did so, Andela noted a sleek knife hanging at her right side. Eovin shook her head to drop her hair back into place, and then she handed the golden thread to Andela, along with the crystal stopper that she removed from Andela's vial. She was obviously giving the vial to Andela.

Andela held the thread and stopper in her left hand as she raised the vial in her right hand and sipped some more of the golden fluid, checking the vial to see how much of the fluid remained. When the vial was half empty, she replaced the crystal stopper and latched the vial back onto the golden thread. She passed her head and hair through the thread and suspended the vial between her breasts. There was a warm sensation permeating her abdomen and chest, and she was breathing without difficulty.

"So, Eovin, you say you are a Cherinede. What does that mean?"

Eovin's elvish face grew contemplative. She gazed at Andela. "I will tell you many things with few words, for you must act without delay. The situation is grave."

Andela grew troubled. "Is Bill in danger?"

"Yes. You are aware that Bill is a dead man, right?"

"Yes," returned Andela, choosing not to comment upon the fact that she did not like hearing Bill referred to as a *dead man*.

"Okay then, well, governors that choose death are generally given time to rethink their decisions. They are not immediately damned to hell when they choose death rather than life, because the Creator is mercifully just. Bill is the governor of this land, just like you are the governor of the land that you first entered after your kiss."

Andela was impressed by Eovin's statement. Whatever a Cherinede might be, this one seemed to know what was going on.

"I understand," said Andela.

"Good," said Eovin. "The dead possess a span of time, the time of mortal life, to repent from the sin of choosing a wrongful master, namely any master other than the Creator, though of course, all other masters are simply agents of the Evil One, so there are really only two masters—the Creator, and the Evil One."

"Right," said Andela.

"And when it comes to choosing the wrong master, some of the dead must repent of choosing themselves as their own masters, acting as if they created themselves and can grant themselves meaningful life. Only one Being has the right to ultimate lordship, namely the Creator. Those who choose to be their own masters are easy prey for the Evil One, and he devours them spiritually."

Andela nodded. She had never heard anyone explain what Eovin was saying in quite those words, but she understood; and she realized that Eovin was indicating that Bill had chosen to be his own master.

Eovin resumed speaking. "In order to gain eternal life, the dead must repent from choosing the wrong master and choose the Creator as Master, accepting the perfect sacrifice for forgiveness of sins, the sacrifice provided by the Creator in the Person of his Son. In this land, such a choice by the governor would burst the damn at the edge of the Northern Pool and permit revitalizing water to nourish the land. Meanwhile, the oxygen that temporarily sustains the potential for life in this land is produced by oasa trees. Have you seen the trees with great trunks rising from place to place about the land?"

Again Andela nodded. A couple of questions popped into her mind, but she did not dare delay Eovin with questions that were not direly important. The earnestness in Eovin's eyes convinced her that time was crucial, crucial for Bill.

"These massive trees are oasa trees. They cannot be burned, cut, or otherwise damaged without the governor's permission, and many of these trees contain spacious rooms within their trunks. These rooms within the trunks have natural openings to the outside environment. The air within the magnificent trunks is invigorating to the forces of good, but asphyxiating to evil. Thus, the inner rooms provide a safe haven from Rebelon, Decevon, and other servants of the Evil One."

A nauseous feeling swept through Andela's abdomen as Eovin spoke Decevon's name. The mention of that woman brought back tormenting memories of the whorish spectacle she beheld through the window in the canyon. But her mind regained focus as Eovin continued speaking.

"The atmosphere of lands governed by the dead, such as this land, can only sustain life through oxygen produced by the oasa trees. The trees convert Cherinede hair to oxygen. There are about seventy Cherinedes in this land. Our hair grows fast. We tend to the oasa trees by cutting our hair and burying the trimmings amidst the roots. Without Cherinede hair, the oasa trees cannot produce oxygen, and the land dies, meaning the governor dies. And if the governor dies apart from the True Master, he dies forever."

Andela's eyes widened. Her lips parted; but Eovin began speaking before Andela could utter a sound.

"Bill cannot actually die at this time because he did not come here of his own free will. However, as I believe you know, you may die. Your dying would be of no harm to you, for you would enter the eternal land, but it could be harmful to Bill, and it would be a bad thing for the children. Therefore, we must fight with determination—we must win the present battle and preserve your mortal existence. We must get Bill to reverse his decree."

Andela skewed her brows, but again Eovin resumed speaking before Andela could make any verbal inquiries.

"Bill was deceived by Decevon. He was tricked into commanding Cherinedes to give Rebelon all the hair he requests, and subsequently, Rebelon requested that we Cherinedes give him every single strand of hair removed from our heads. We must do as the governor decrees, and Rebelon uses the hair as he pleases. If Bill had entered this land of his own free will, his decree regarding Cherinede hair would be grievously serious, for it could amount to suicide. However, since he was transported here unknowingly, he will not physically die. But if you die, he will be sent back without you—he will awaken in his own home with only your lifeless corpse lying before him, and that would not be good."

Andela stared into Eovin's eyes. "But I'm not suffocating anymore, so why would I die?"

"Because they'll kill you. Rebelon and his allies are placing just enough Cherinede hair among the roots of the oasa trees to maintain life, but not consciousness. They want to keep Bill alive, because if he dies, or seemingly dies, then both you and Bill will be transported back to Missouri. They plan to keep Bill suspended in unconsciousness until they find you and murder you, whether you are asleep or awake."

"But I'm conscious now, so, how am I receiving oxygen?"

"That is a good question," returned Eovin. She bent over at the waist with the back of her head toward Andela, catching her thick hair with both hands and thrusting it forward so that Andela could see her posterior scalp. Andela winced. There were three raw, sore-looking bald spots on the back of Eovin's head. Eovin straightened back up and dropped her hair back into place. She faced Andela.

"Decevon tricked Bill, but one of our spies, a talking bird named Squarrior, reached an oasa tree before Bill made his decree. I was in the oasa tree with several others. Squarrior overheard Decevon talking to Bill in the canyon, and he reached us just in time. We began ripping the hair from one another's heads, tearing it from the napes of our necks so that our enemies would not be able to detect what we had done, and we tossed the removed hair into a great stone bowl and breathed upon it. The breath of a Cherinede transforms trimmings of Cherinede hair into solista."

"Solista?"

"Yes, the golden liquid within the crystal vials is called solista. And since solista is not hair, Bill's decree does not apply to solista. And furthermore, since the hair that we ripped from our heads was transformed into solista before Bill's decree was made, we are free to use the solista in whatever manner we choose."

"And when you drink solista, it provides you with oxygen?"

"Yes. I am among those of us who were chosen to drink solista in order to maintain consciousness and carry on, hoping to somehow preserve your mortal life. All of the solista has been placed into crystal vials. Our supply of solista is limited because Bill's decree prevents us from making more—any hair removed from our heads must now be given to Rebelon. For that reason, we must use our solista wisely. You were able to breathe while imprisoned by the Resants because oxygen persists longer in the lower chambers. The oasa trees are producing enough oxygen to keep Bill here, but he will be sustained in unconsciousness."

"Unconsciousness?"

"Yes, but if you can find Bill and give him some of the golden fluid from your vial, then he will regain mental alertness and you can plead with him to reverse his decree—he must say that he reverses his decree about Cherinede hair. Some of us have very long hair, and by cutting our hair at shoulder length, we can rapidly bring more oxygen to the atmosphere."

"So the solista helps me breathe?"

"In a manner of speaking, yes. And our enemies can also manufacture solista. They have produced large quantities to use until they can find you and murder you. We must resist them—we must fight them, and we must win. If you die, then the decree regarding our hair will be annulled, but Bill will be worse off than he was before your journey began. There will still be hope for him, but not much hope."

Eovin paused and drew a deep breath. She surmised that Andela comprehended her words. "The solista provides your body with oxygen whether or not you breathe, because it passes oxygen into your bloodstream through your stomach and intestines. You only need to pass air in and out of your lungs to dispel carbon dioxide."

Andela nodded.

"We have to be wary," resumed Eovin. "Our enemies are searching for you. And they suspect something—they are on heightened alert since Truth wagered battle with the Resants, and since Hope snatched Flucheena right out from under Decevon."

"Flucheena?"

Eovin paused and pointed back toward a vaguely visible figure. Andela squinted, peering through the dusty atmosphere. She was able to make out the shadowy outline of a horse.

"Flucheena is one of our land's talking animals. She is on our side. Decevon tricked Flucheena by posing as a heroine cowgirl named Cowgirl Jane, a heroine that Bill has admired since childhood. Hope knows enough Ewanha, the language of the talking beasts, that he was able to reveal Decevon's misdeed to Flucheena, and he was able to send Flucheena to our aid. Unfortunately, Rebelon and a band of his despicable Jealots captured Hope and have detained him, but they cannot kill him, and he drank enough solista before he was captured to keep him awake for many hours."

Andela's brows creased. "What are Jealots?"

"Jealots are much like Resants, but they have green eyes and yellow fur rather than yellow eyes and green fur, and they tend to inhabit the outer regions rather than the hidden caverns. They are the carnal embodiment of ungodly jealousy."

Andela suppressed her curiosity. She straightened to her full height with a look of ready determination. The important thing was to learn how to reach Bill. Her lips remained silent, but her eyes urged Eovin to continue.

"You and Flucheena must go without me. Truth will not be detained for long, and I must wait here and give him some solista. He is invincible, but the lack of oxygen resulting from Bill's decree could weaken his presence within the confines of this land, and our chances of ultimate victory will be much greater if Truth is well and strong."

"Okay," stated Andela. She proffered no further speech, but the tone of her voice evinced firm resolve.

"We know where Bill is—he is caged in a desert cabin. He tried to escape through a window, but he was too large. Flucheena knows the way to the cabin. She is a swift mare, and she is determined to be of service, especially after the misdeed Decevon tricked her into committing—Flucheena would never have aided Decevon knowingly. I gave her two vials of solista, so she should have no problem breathing. I have instructed her to flee to safety after you dismount at the cabin, for I am certain the Jealots would slay her if she remained there. She could not fight them off for long."

Andela nodded. "Are there Jealots at the cabin now?"

"No. Rebelon is keeping the Jealots away from the cabin. If Bill were to see any of them through the cabin window before he succumbs to unconsciousness, he might call for help, and even Jealots would have to respond—they would have to obey the governor of this land. You are almost certain to reach Bill's cabin on the back of Flucheena, even if our enemies spot you on the way. After that, it will be up to you. Any questions?"

Andela's mind was assimilating the information Eovin imparted. She knew that she needed to ride on the back of a horse named Flucheena, and that Flucheena would take her to Bill, and that she needed to revive Bill with some of the solista suspended between her breasts, and she knew that she needed to persuade Bill to reverse his decree about Cherinede hair.

"No questions," stated Andela, but then she realized that there was one thing she wanted to know before she got started—she wanted to know whether or not Bill had sex with Decevon. If that happened, then she and Bill would have to overcome a great emotional hardship in order to continue their relationship, for as Andela knew fully well, this was no mere dream. "Except for, well, I do have one question."

"One question?"

"Yes. Can you tell me what has happened between Bill and Decevon...I mean..."

"I know what you mean," interjected Eovin, "for I am also a woman. There are many men and women who have faced the serious issue of repairing and healing relationships marred by the blight of sexual betrayal. Sometimes, through the power and grace of the Creator, they succeed, if both are willing to grant the Creator supreme lordship in their lives, and if the betrayed partner chooses to make such effort."

Andela felt her heart tighten in pain. "So, they…"

Eovin gazed upon Andela's face with tender eyes. "No, they did not. You reached them in time, and I do not think Bill will be easily tempted to commit fornication after the vivid revelation your earnest cry opened to his mind. And besides that, not all dead men are devoid of moral integrity. I do not think Bill would have fallen to Decevon's temptation anyway, even if your arrival had been delayed."

Andela felt her heart relax. An inner surge of thanksgiving enlivened her. She did not know what kind of vivid revelation her earnest cry opened to Bill's mind, but that hardly mattered—he did not have sex with Decevon, and that was what mattered.

"Okay, I'm ready."

"Fine," said Eovin. "And oh! I almost forgot to tell you. This is very important, so listen closely. If the governor of a land looks into a visitor's eyes while that visitor is within the realm of his land, then that visitor cannot be banished or slain without the governor's permission. You are a visitor here, so if you find Bill, make certain that he looks into your eyes. That way our enemies will need his permission in order to slay you."

"His permission?" returned Andela. She stared at Eovin, and then she shook her head. "Bill would never give permission for anyone to kill me. I just know he wouldn't."

"No," agreed Eovin, "not unless he were manipulated by evil and deceptive forces, but do not underestimate our foes. Now, make sure Bill looks into your eyes, and plead for him to reverse his decree."

Andela nodded. "Okay."

Eovin turned her head and cupped one hand to her mouth. "Flucheena, nasha tum coowaha tean shaha Andela! Nake sherakka tum lauda vern croonfelli—shart!"

The equine figure reared and whinnied, and then her determined hooves pounded against the sand. She bolted to Andela's side and came to an abrupt halt. The rope that was used to hoist Andela from the deep cavern was still secured around her neck. Eovin drew the knife from her right side and cut the trailing rope just below a knot near Flucheena's mane. This left a loop of rope around Flucheena's neck for Andela to grasp. There was no saddle and no reigns, but Andela was an experienced equestrian. She grabbed Flucheena's mane and mounted.

"Flucheena knows that you do not speak the Ewanhan language," said Eovin. "She will take you straight to Bill. Hang on."

"Okay, I'm ready."

"Shart!"

Flucheena was considerate of her rider; beginning with a steady walk, then trotting, and then breaking into a gallop. After galloping for about a minute and sensing that Andela was comfortable and secure upon her back, Flucheena picked up speed and all but flew over the sandy terrain. Andela squinted to keep whipping sand from pelting her eyes, now and then viewing the surrounding landscape through barely parted lashes. At times she just leaned forward and continued holding to Flucheena's mane and the rope, closing her eyes in hopeful prayer. After a couple minutes, Flucheena wheeled to the right. She slowed and dropped downward over the upper edge of a gorge, plodding down a narrow pathway to a riverbed. Then she bolted across the riverbed and up the far bank.

"Carg!" a gruff voice bellowed. "Grab her!"

Andela raised her head and spotted a huge mass of yellow fur charging from her left, but Flucheena was beyond reach of the gruesome attacker before he could lay a finger on horse or rider. Her neck tingled as a cry of rage rose behind her. Flucheena sped forward. Within seconds, the only audible sounds were those of wind, whipping sand, and a mare's hooves pounding the ground.

Andela dropped her head back down toward Flucheena's mane, marveling at the endurance and speed of the steed beneath her. It seemed as though they went on and on for hours, though only a few minutes elapsed. She kept her head near Flucheena's mane to lessen the pain of sand striking her face, and she brooded over the words to say when she found Bill.

"Hatahn!!!"

Andela's eyes snapped open and then narrowed due to flying sand. She peered ahead and to her right, toward the sound of the loud cry. Flucheena ignored Rebelon's command to stop and swerved left without slowing. Andela clung with all her might to keep from sliding off the mare's back. She glimpsed a large man wearing a brilliant red shirt and coal-black trousers. A pang shot through her heart; she knew it was Rebelon, the heartless fiend who nearly crushed Bill in the Land of the Northern Pool. She was still peering back toward Rebelon's fading silhouette when Flucheena's evasive route brought them near the trunk of an oasa tree.

"Aarr! Whack! Thud…"

A nerve-racking roar was followed by a shocking blow; and then Andela's body crashed against the desert floor. For a few moments she lay motionless on the coarse sand, lying flat on her back. Her eyes gazed upward, but her head swam and her vision was blurry. Then just as her head cleared and her eyes regained focus, a burly beast squatted down upon her thighs and grabbed both of her arms. He drew her arms to her sides and pinned them beneath his knees. Then he reached to her neck with a long, green fingernail. She recognized the yellow-furred creature by Eovin's description—a Jealot.

Vile, fetid breath poured downward from the monstrous face above Andela. Leathery yellow skin was contorted in a loathing scowl that featured a pug nose and jutting forehead. The brute snarled as his searing green eyes stared toward her neck, and Andela was certain that her jugular veins would be torn asunder. Her eyes remained open, expecting to see an abhorrent yellow finger rise from her neck with fresh blood dripping downward onto her abdomen. But instead, the merciless fiend ripped the crystal vial from her chest, snapping the golden thread from around her neck. He raised his hand and crushed the vial between the thick pads of his yellow thumb and forefinger, and then he cast shattered glass aside. Andela's mind reeled in agony—the solista meant for Bill's lips was glistening on the monster's hand.

Then the beast fixed his eyes upon Andela's face, growling with hatred. He lifted his right hand high above his head. Andela drew a desperate breath; she thought it would be her last—she had never been so certain that she would die. There was little time to think about death, or Bill, or anything else. Only one quick thought passed through her mind—she was glad that she was one of the living—she was glad that she was ready to meet her Creator.

"Aaaah!!!"

A horrendous roar of pain blasted across the desert. The Jealot's raised hand froze. Flucheena's teeth tore into his scalp as she heaved him upward off Andela and hurled him backward to the ground. The mighty mare's eyes glared like the vindictive orbs of a maddened mother bear battling over her threatened cubs. The Jealot lunged forward and started to rise, but Flucheena was too quick for him—she wheeled around and planted her front hooves, and then kicked both hind legs backward with the force of a battering ram.

"Ka-Bam!!! Splat."

Blood spattered from the face of the Jealot as his head nearly separated from his body, but his neck held securely enough to wrench his body upward off the ground. He was launched into a backward flip, and then his great carcass plopped motionless upon the sand.

Flucheena leaped to Andela's side and dropped her equine head toward Andela's face.

"Nahtush!"

Andela was stunned to hear a horse speak, but that did not keep her from responding. Although she was unfamiliar with the language Flucheena spoke, the nature of the Flucheena's command was obvious. Nodding her head, she sprang to her feet and grabbed Flucheena's mane, and then she vaulted to the mare's back. Her chest, thighs, and left shoulder were sore, but she was able to use her limbs and muscles— she had no serious injuries. She grasped the rope that looped around Flucheena's neck.

"Get them!" roared the voice of Rebelon. He was nearing from behind.

"Ahgrrr, ah!" erupted growls from a group of Jealots closing in on Andela and Flucheena. Flucheena launched forward with such force that the rope bit into Andela's hands and fingers, but Andela held tight. She and Flucheena burst between two of the Jealots, knocking both of them back onto to their rumps; and then Flucheena veered left, circumventing the general area. Andela lowered her face and prayed. A couple of minutes later Flucheena whinnied. Andela lifted her head and peered forward, spotting a cabin.

Flucheena drew to an abrupt halt before the cabin entrance. Andela slid from Flucheena's back and dashed to the door. The mental image of monstrous yellow beasts lumbering across the desert caused adrenalin to pulse through her limbs. She reached down and grabbed the metal handle as she pushed against the door, but then she noted the door's hinges and realized that the door opened to the outside. With sand piled four feet deep against the side of the cabin, it would take forever to dig enough sand away to pry the door open. A panicky sensation rose in her chest—the Jealots could not be far behind. Then she noticed light pouring from a small window to her right.

There were pieces of wood and slivers of glass visible on the ground, but these had been swept from beneath the window, and Andela spotted a broom lying on the sand. Her feet were still shod with the golden slippers given to her by Madam Mercy, and nothing pierced her feet as she approached the window. She dropped to her knees on the sand bank and peered through the window. Her heart quickened—there Bill lay, sprawled out in the middle of the floor.

Andela nudged forward to slide through the window, but then she noticed that Flucheena stood close behind her. "Run!" she said; but Flucheena just stood and stared at her. "They'll kill you, now run!" There was still no response.

Andela stood erect, facing Flucheena. She remembered the word Eovin used to send them on their quest. "Shart!" she commanded, raising a finger toward the western desert, away from approaching enemies.

Flucheena stood her ground and shook her head. "Nay," she whinnied, and this was one word that Andela understood.

"Shart!!!" ordered Andela, stomping a foot on the ground and glaring at Flucheena with a look of resolved determination.

Flucheena stared at Andela with startled respect. Then she spun around and galloped away, disappearing into the hazy atmosphere in the direction that Andela pointed.

It was a bit of a squeeze, but Andela's body slid through the square opening. She braced her hands on the chair that Bill had positioned beneath the window, and then she pulled one leg inside the cabin followed by the other. She stepped down from the chair and lunged to Bill, collapsing at his side. "Bill," she said as she shook his body. There was no response. He was breathing, but he was unconscious. Her stomach sickened as she thought about the crushed vial of solista.

Andela sat up and stared at the small opening in the wall. It was probably too small for a Jealot to enter, or Rebelon either; but she doubted that it would take them long to excavate sand and tear the door from its hinges. Tears swelled in her eyes as she gazed downward between her breasts, downward toward the empty space that should have cradled a golden vial. She paused in mournful silence and sighed, staring at Bill and feeling like her heart would break at any moment; but then, as air passed out from her lungs, an idea entered her mind. She wasn't sure about the scientific and physiological basis of her idea, but it was an idea nonetheless. With kindled hope she surveyed her surroundings, and then she rose and dashed through the doorway to the bedroom. The featherbed was large, but there was enough space on the floor for Bill's body; and with the bedroom door closed, no one would be able to see them through the window.

She returned to Bill, squatting and lifting both of his legs and locking her arms around his ankles. Next she pulled him through the bedroom door and positioned his body beside the bed. Then, after closing the door, she dropped to his side and began mouth-to-mouth resuscitation. She figured that if oxygen was passing into her body from her stomach and digestive tract, somehow produced by the golden liquid manufactured from Eovin's hair, then the oxygen must be entering her bloodstream, and hence the tissue of her lungs, and she figured that oxygen would pass from the capillaries in her lungs to the air in her lungs, or at least she hoped so. Soon air surged into Bill's breast from Andela's lungs, while heartfelt love surged from her heart. She watched his chest rise and fall, hoping for a response, hoping more fervently than she had ever hoped for anything.

Ominous sounds began coming from outside the cabin walls, sounds of scratching and pounding. Andela ignored these sounds. She would continue no matter what—continue until she succeeded, or continue until a ruthless hand tore her body from the side of the man she hoped to marry. Long seconds passed without any sign of consciousness from Bill. A minute seemed an eternity.

Andela lowered her lips to deliver another breath, but then she was startled as Bill's eyes suddenly opened. She held his head and stared into his eyes. "Bill, it's me, Andela."

"Andela," he responded, staring back into her eyes.

"Bill, you were tricked by an evil woman, you must reverse your decree about the Cherinede hair so that we can breathe. Please Bill, please say these words—*I reverse my decree about Cherinede hair.*"

267

Bill continued staring into Andela's eyes. Andela heard the front door to the cabin creak open, but then she blocked all extraneous sounds from her mind. She focused solely upon Bill, pleading with all her heart through beseeching eyes. "I reverse my decree about Cherinede hair," spoke Bill; and then his eyes closed in relapsed unconsciousness. Andela stared upon his face. She felt emotionally drained and she was physically exhausted. He had spoken the required words; he said that he reversed the decree about Cherinede hair. Was that enough?

Andela lowered her lips to breathe more oxygen into Bill's lungs, but the bedroom door burst open just as her lips touched his, and then her body was yanked upward by furry yellow hands. A Jealot, seven feet tall and proportioned like an African ape, held her up by both arms as if she were weightless; and then he carried her from the bedroom with her back and shoulders pressed against his chest. A second Jealot, having broad shoulders and a thick chest but standing no more than four feet in height, shuffled past them toward the bedroom.

The Jealot carrying Andela continued on through the main room and out through the cabin doorway. The sand was cleared from before the door, leaving an open trench about five feet wide and twelve feet long. The door had been torn from its hinges and lay on the ground to the west. The sandstorm had ceased, and the atmosphere was clearing—sand and dust settled to the ground like confetti dropped upon a passing parade.

As the Jealot carried Andela through the open doorway, she noted that the upper edges of the excavated trench were lined with observers, both to the left and to the right. Several hideous Jealots stared downward with smoldering eyes; and though the Jealots appeared very similar to one another, they varied in height from about four feet to eight feet, much like the Resants in the underground chamber. What caught Andela's attention, though, were two figures positioned at the upper edge of the sand bank to her right. Posted with arms crossed upon his chest was Rebelon, and at his right hand stood a wickedly beautiful woman in a black satin gown. The woman's flowing hair was as black as her gown. She wore a black velvet belt tight about her waist; and a curved dagger hung at her right side. Though she appeared much more suave and sophisticated than the temptress that Andela beheld inside the chamber with Bill, Andela knew that the woman was Decevon.

"Up here, Jurf," directed Rebelon, uncrossing his arms and motioning for the large Jealot toting Andela to come up beside him.

Andela noted that Rebelon looked troubled and angry; whereas, the woman beside him presented a cool image of embittered hatred. Rebelon kept his eyes glued to the doorway. The woman, on the other hand, stared brazenly and threateningly at Andela's face. Andela felt her feet drag over the sand as Jurf clambered up the bank and stood behind Rebelon. Decevon turned as the Jealot advanced, repositioning herself so that she never took her eyes off Andela.

No words were spoken. Andela felt vulnerable. The harrowing look in the dark woman's eyes was frightening. She wished the Jealot holding her would turn some other direction, but he stood motionless. Decevon's eyes remained fixed upon her like a ravenous panther eyeing a fawn. Finally a squat figure shuffled out through the cabin entrance; he was the Jealot that passed by Andela as her abductor carried her through the main room of the cabin.

"What news, Quarg?" asked Rebelon.

"Him not waked up, Master," responded Quarg, looking self-important as all eyes focused upon him. He made Andela think of a great yellow toad—a pompous toad. She was thankful that someone drew Decevon's eyes away from her.

"Not awake," reiterated Rebelon. "I guess it's safe to assume, then, that he's unconscious?"

Quarg's repugnant features assumed an uncertain expression. His shoulders drooped for several seconds, but then he puffed his chest outward and replied, chuckling as he spoke. "Aha, yea, that funny, sir, but Master is right, of course—he be very unconkingus—he won't conk no one now, sir."

Andela could not help but pity Quarg for his ludicrous attempt to impress his audience. He was obviously handicapped by a limited vocabulary and had no idea what the word *unconscious* meant. As Quarg finished speaking, haughty jeers erupted from the more intelligent Jealots; but Rebelon gave no verbal response. Instead, he stepped forward and slid down the bank of sand, maintaining his balance well enough to steady himself on Quarg's nearest shoulder. Quarg crumpled to his rump and gazed upward with bewilderment. Rebelon ignored him and strode through the cabin door. Andela's heart quickened as she heard Rebelon's footsteps fade and halt within the cabin—she knew that he was probably kneeling over Bill's body.

Motionless silence beset the gathered horde. Andela could hear air passing in and out of Jurf's lungs as he held her against his chest. The sound of Rebelon's footsteps again became audible. He emerged through the cabin entrance and stopped to address Decevon. "Completely unconscious. Proceed."

Decevon turned and faced Andela, reaching for the dagger that hung at her side. A sadistic smile took shape below gloating eyes. Her intent was obvious. Andela gasped. She jerked and kicked with desperate strength, but she could not break free. Jurf enveloped her upper limbs and body with shaggy arms, and he trapped her legs between his thighs.

Andela's eyes widened as Decevon's hand rose upward—the dagger's steel blade glistened in the clearing atmosphere. The blade plunged downward as a hideous, inhuman snarl poured from Decevon's throat. Andela's body tensed and she closed her eyes.

"Wahaaa!!!" Decevon screamed.

A burst of white light pierced through Andela's closed eyelids. She opened her eyes. Decevon was turning toward Rebelon and clasping her right hand. Andela took a deep breath, a breath that only seconds before seemed unlikely, and then she turned her eyes from side to side, looking for some indication of what happened. There was no one in sight; no one, that is, apart from the group of foul cutthroats who were present when she was carried from the cabin. She wondered how she was saved from the cruel blade. Who saved her?

Rebelon reached downward to the sand at Jurf's feet, down below the level that Andela could see. He lifted what was left of the dagger. The ebony handle was still intact, but only a craggy stub of metal remained where there had been a curved blade. He held the demolished weapon before Decevon's eyes as she opened and closed the fingers of her right hand. "He must have seen her eyes," he said.

Then Andela remembered Eovin's words—*if the governor of a land looks into a visitor's eyes while in the realm of his own land, then that visitor cannot be banished or slain without the governor's permission.* She glanced downward at her breast—there wasn't even a scratch.

"She got to him before he passed out," said Decevon, glaring back at Andela. "Things could be worse, though," she added with a taunting smile; and then she turned her face back toward Rebelon. "We still control the Cherinede…"

"Creech! Creech!" cried a Spite, interrupting Decevon's speech and dropping to Rebelon's shoulder. Andela watched the batlike creature nestle its loathsome snout in Rebelon's ear. It was whispering something. She wondered if it spoke the same language as Flucheena. Rebelon's face blanched, and then grew red with anger. The Spite took flight.

"What is it?" asked Decevon.

Rebelon turned his head and looked at Andela with cold-blooded hatred. His eyes held her in disdain for half a minute before he gained the composure to respond. "The intruder's visit with the governor wreaked havoc. He must have been coherent. The decree has been annulled and our enemies are rejuvenating the atmosphere."

Decevon turned and stood face to face with Andela. Their eyes were not more than a foot apart. "What did you say to him?"

Andela felt pangs of intimidation, but she was no coward. "Why should I tell you?" she inquired coolly.

Decevon cocked her hand backward to slap Andela's cheek; but then she checked her blow, remembering what happened to the dagger. "No matter," she said. A malevolent smile formed upon her lips. "You didn't tell Bill anything, I did."

Andela was troubled by Decevon's remark. She said nothing.

Decevon stretched her hands upward and closed her eyes. She opened her mouth and uttered words that Andela did not understand, but Andela sensed that the words composed a demonic litany. A frigid black cloud formed about Decevon's body, hiding her from sight. Andela shuddered as edges of the icy blackness touched her skin. Then the dark cloud dissipated, and Andela gasped.

It was as if Andela were gazing into a mirror. The height, figure, and attire of the woman standing before her matched her own appearance and clothing perfectly, almost. There was one difference—the eyes—Decevon's eyes were dark brown.

"It won't work," spoke Rebelon, climbing up the sand bank and nudging Jurf backward so that he could stand beside Decevon. "Remember your eyes, they do not change."

Andela stared upon Decevon's eyes as Rebelon and Decevon addressed one another. She was thankful that Decevon's eyes were different from her eyes.

Decevon shrugged as if Rebelon's statement meant nothing. "That doesn't matter. I'm not Andela, I'm Ann, and Andela's not the one who rescued Bill and got him to reverse the awful decree, it was Ann."

Rebelon raised a hand and rubbed his chin in thought.

"Not only did Andela choose not to rescue Bill," resumed Decevon, "she wants to gain control of Bill's land during this *dream* of his, because such control will allow her to manipulate his mind after he awakens back at the farm in Missouri. And the only way Bill can put an end to her selfish conniving, and keep himself free of her egotistic domination, is to permit her termination—just in this dream, of course."

Andela's eyes widened. If Bill granted his approval for her *termination*, then Decevon could wield a dagger that would not rebound from her chest, it would pierce her heart. "Bill!" she yelled. Jurf muffled her mouth with his forearm. For a few tense moments both Rebelon and Decevon turned their faces toward the doorway to the cabin. There was no response.

"It looks like the Jealots can detain her, even if we cannot yet kill her," commented Decevon. "And you know, Rebelon, I think the Arena of Judgment would be a good place to hold trial. After all, she is a criminal, and the governor has every right to serve as judge. What do you think?"

Rebelon stood still and silent, staring at Decevon. Devious contemplations etched a sharply-lined smile across his lips. He turned his face toward the huge Jealot holding Andela. "Jurf, give the prisoner to Kwark and go fetch Lord Gelus. Tell Lord Gelus we need him to serve as a plaintiff attorney in court, and tell him to bring his best jurors, and tell him to make sure they all wear robes large enough to hide their faces."

"Yes master," replied Jurf, transferring Andela into the arms of another large Jealot.

Then Rebelon turned his face back toward Decevon. "All right, I like your idea. But we'd better hurry and get her out of here before he wakes up."

"Bill! Bill! Bi…" cried Andela. Kwark's paw muffled her mouth as he held her in his arms. She stared toward the cabin, contemplating the crucial significance of Rebelon's words. She would be placed on trial, with Bill serving as judge; and with none other than Lord Gelus seeking a sentence of guilt. She felt her emotions laid bare, opened to utter vulnerability. Her relationship with Bill, and her very physical life, would soon be weighed in the balance. But what sort of balance?

"Get her out of here," ordered Rebelon. "We can put her on trial without having her present, so tie her up down in the gorge, down below the Arena, far enough away to keep her voice from being heard, no matter how loud she yells."

Kwark took off toward the east, holding Andela against his chest and continuing to muffle her mouth.

"Cragg, Sturge, go with Kwark and make sure the girl does not escape. I'll have Quarg bring you some stakes and rope," directed Rebelon; and two other Jealots departed, following after Kwark and Andela.

Decevon watched the Jealots tote Andela away. "I guess your plan is best, keeping her away from the trial," she remarked. "It's just that, well...," she paused and turned dark, demonic eyes toward Rebelon, "I'd relish seeing the look on her face when he tells us to go ahead and destroy her."

Chapter 8

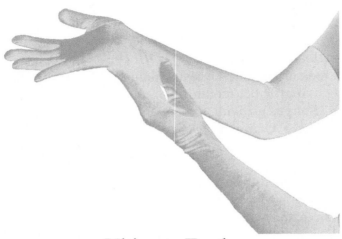

Ultimate Truth

Bill awoke. At first he thought his dream was over, but then he sat straight up on the bedroom floor. He was still in the cabin, but at least now he could breathe. Stretched out on the floor beside him was Andela, or at least he thought it was Andela. She lay with arms and legs extended across the hardwood floor. A beautiful blue gown adorned her lithe body, and her golden hair flowed across the floor. Her face was turned away from him.

"Andela!" said Bill, paying no mind to his belief that he was merely dreaming. He scooted his body across the floor to the woman's side and lifted her head and shoulders. She awoke in his arms and opened her eyes, batting her lashes in feigned timidity. Then she smiled.

Bill knew this woman was not Andela. The eyes looking up at him were chocolate brown, not emerald green; and they conferred nothing similar to the feelings he experienced when Andela peered into his eyes. A confused furrow appeared upon his brow.

"Oh Bill," said the woman, "thank you. You must have succeeded in reversing the decree, otherwise we'd be dead. Thank you so much." Her arms shot upward around Bill's neck and she gave him a hug. Then she released her hold and rose to a semi-reclined position, leaning on her right hand as she folded her legs beneath her. She stared into his eyes. "My name is Ann. Cowgirl Jane told Rebelon that you were here, but she didn't know anything about the evil decree. She just knew that her horse had dropped unconscious and that she was having trouble breathing, so she was worried about you, and it's a good thing that she told Rebelon."

"Rebelon?" returned Bill. He still remembered the name from his encounter with Hope in Andela's land, and from the decree he made regarding Cherinede hair. He also remembered reversing the decree in response to imploring green eyes—unfathomable eyes that hovered above him. Where were those eyes now?

Decevon faced Bill with a look of unbelief. "You don't know who Rebelon is? Oh my, I thought everyone knew Rebelon, especially you." She shook her head playfully and smiled. "He's the lieutenant governor in this land, second in rank to you. He's your right-hand man, and he found out about the decree. If he hadn't gotten me to come and find you and get you to reverse that decree, we'd all be dead. He picked me for the job because I'm a well-conditioned runner, and because I can breathe in low oxygen levels."

Bill was perplexed. His memories of Andela, and the feelings he experienced when he awoke and saw her enchanting eyes, were too potent to dismiss. He did not experience any comparable feelings when this woman hugged his neck or looked into his eyes. And although the presence of this strange woman provided tangible evidence that Andela had not been the one who awakened him, his heart would not accept such evidence. He knew that Andela had been there—he knew that Andela was the one who awakened him—he knew these things more surely than anything else that had taken place during his entire dream.

"So, are you saying that you're the one who got me to reverse my decree about the hair, and that Rebelon sent you?" questioned Bill.

"Of course," replied Decevon. "I could hardly breathe with the air getting so thin, but I managed to get to you in time. But then, I guess I must have been worn out after that long run, and I must have passed out after you reversed the decree. I'm sure you didn't know that the creatures called Cherinedes must never give their hair to anyone, whether friend or foe, or else the oxygen vanishes from the atmosphere. That awful vamp that led you down the canyon fooled you, and she almost ended up killing all of us just to get at you, and she even dragged Rebelon's good name into the whole mess! She's in cahoots with that strange woman, no doubt."

Bill stared at Ann for several moments, and then he dismissed the inconsistencies that arose within his mind by reminding himself that he was dreaming. Anything could happen in a dream. But then something that Decevon spoke struck a troubling chord within his mind.

"Strange woman?"

Again Decevon looked startled, as if surprised that Bill did not know who she referred to. "You know," she stated matter-of-factly, "the strange woman—the woman who followed you into your land—the woman who, for whatever odd reason, looks almost exactly like I do."

Bill figured that Ann was referring to Andela; but then, he was having a bizarre dream, so maybe she was referring to someone else. After all, if he could dream that one woman looked like Andela, then he could dream that several women looked like Andela.

"Do you know the strange woman's name?" he asked.

Decevon wrinkled her nose in spurious contemplation. "You know, Bill, I don't think Rebelon ever mentioned her name to me." For several seconds she tilted her head as if trying to recall something but not quite able to do so; and then she shrugged and rose to her feet. "No matter though, Rebelon can tell you. He said to meet him at the Arena of Judgment."

Bill followed Ann's lead and stood to his feet. "The *Arena of Judgment*?"

"Yep," returned Decevon. She gazed upon Bill's befuddled countenance for a few seconds before resuming speech, as if she were again surprised that he did not know what she was talking about. "Maybe you haven't presided as judge in that court yet. Easy enough to believe, there's hardly any crime in your land, so there's little need for a judge."

"The Arena of Judgment is a court?"

"Sure, the 7th Circuit Court for the grand State of Missouri, whatever that is—I don't think I've ever been to Missouri."

"Missouri!" exclaimed Bill; then he eased his posture, remembering that anything might happen in a dream. "Okay, so it's a State court, and I'm the judge? Is that right?"

"Yep, when you're available."

"Okay, and why does Rebelon want us to meet him there?"

Decevon started to reply, but then paused, appearing somewhat uncertain. "Well, I'm not quite sure why, exactly, but I think it has something to do with your wanting to wake up back at a farm somewhere—something about another life where you're really awake, whatever that means."

Bill's interest peaked. Perhaps Rebelon was a key to waking up—really waking up. "I see. Well, so then, you say that Rebelon will meet us at the court?"

"Yep. Rebelon, and the jury, and the plaintiff attorney, and I think that's all. I don't think there will be any defense attorney. I don't think anyone would stoop that low, or at least that's what Rebelon says."

"What do you mean? Who's the defendant?"

Decevon shook her head as if confused by so many questions. "Well, I'm not entirely sure, I think it may be someone who's keeping you from really waking up, or something like that—someone who's trying to get control over you, trying to manipulate you. Maybe it's that strange woman. I'm not sure."

Bill winced. The thought of Andela on trial disturbed him, and he suspected that the *strange woman* Ann kept mentioning was Andela. Nonetheless, it was all just a dream, and he wanted to wake up—the sooner the better. "Okay," he consented, "let's go meet Rebelon."

Decevon nodded. "We will, but let's eat some grub first. It's about a two mile hike to the Arena, and I'm hungry after all my rescue work. I'll bet you're hungry too."

Bill was more interested in escaping from his consternating dream than in eating, but Ann made him feel indebted to her. It would seem inconsiderate to deny the young woman a simple request for food.

"All right," Bill consented. "There's plenty to eat in the refrigerator, or at least there was the last time I looked."

"Oh, I'm sure there's plenty," said Decevon, smiling slyly after turning her face away from Bill.

* * * * * * * * * * * * * * * * * * *

Bill found himself missing Andela as he walked across the desert with Ann. The food that he and Ann had shared together before beginning their hike was tasty, but the mealtime conversation that passed between them was bland. There was an indefinable aura in Andela's presence, an aura that Ann did not possess; and Bill realized that Andela's aura was something he relished. He was a little annoyed by Ann's comments about the *strange woman*, such as her saying that the *strange woman* wanted to control or manipulate him. Somehow, Ann's words lacked the power that they would have possessed earlier in his dream, before he awoke in the cabin. There was something immeasurably significant about what happened when he awoke and gazed into Andela's eyes. Exactly what that *something* was, Bill did not know; but whatever it was, it was something special.

"There it is," spoke Decevon as she and Bill topped the crest of a dune.

Bill looked ahead. About three hundred yards beyond and below them lay an eye-catching, white marble amphitheater. The landscape sloped downward to the upper edge of the amphitheater where four sections of tiered bleachers stretched farther downward to a stage that lay along the bank of the waterless river gorge. The jurors were already present and seated in white marble chairs on the left side of the stage, to Bill's right; and their royal blue robes contrasted with the white marble of the stage like blueberries on vanilla ice cream. As they drew closer, Bill was impressed by the appearance of two identical statues standing at the left front and right front corners of the stage. Each statue was carved from a solid block of white marble and stood twenty feet high, featuring a draped woman who wore a crown and held a balance in her hands. The statues were magnificent symbols of justice. A man was standing on the sand just outside the rim of the amphitheater. He was poised to greet them.

"That's Rebelon," commented Decevon. They were twenty yards from him. "You've no greater ally in all your land."

The black and red of Rebelon's attire was impressive against the backdrop of the white amphitheater; but as Bill and Decevon continued walking down the sloping dune, Rebelon's figure rose into the reddish-orange background of the terrain beyond the empty gorge. The transformation gave Bill the impression of a human chameleon.

"Governor, welcome!" hailed Rebelon, lifting his right arm in preparation to shake hands with Bill. Though Rebelon's brutal arms had once throttled his throat and chest, Bill had never seen him before, and he did not recognize him.

"Thank you," Bill answered, stepping forward and then stopping and shaking hands. As he looked into Rebelon's dark eyes, he wondered if he were making a mistake to trust this suave gentleman. Rebelon reminded him of a stranger who sold him a three-year subscription to a dairy magazine—it was a magazine he never received; in fact, it was a magazine that never existed.

"I understand you would like to depart from this dream—you're ready to return to your farm," said Rebelon.

"Yes," acknowledged Bill. There were wonderful memories he hoped to carry back to wakeful life, but there were horrors too; and besides, he wanted to see the real Andela. He felt ready to engage her in some serious conversation.

Rebelon turned and gestured downward toward the stage of the amphitheater. "Then my friends and I are ready to help you. Please follow me." He turned his face toward Decevon. "Ann, you may take a seat."

"Thanks," returned Decevon.

Bill followed Rebelon down a marble stairway to the stage. The stairway narrowed as it coursed downward, but it was still wide enough for two persons to walk side by side when it opened onto the floor below the stage. They veered to their left and walked to a flight of steps where they ascended up onto the right side of the stage. Bill was intrigued by the concealing blue robes of the jurors; all twelve jurors sat motionless and silent in marble chairs that were positioned on the left side of the stage, but he could not get a glimpse of their faces. And there was an additional figure cloaked in blue, a tall figure standing before the jurors. The bulky hood of the tall figure's robe was turned toward the center of the amphitheater; and like the seated jurors, Bill could see nothing of his face.

"Have a seat Governor, or perhaps I should say Judge," directed Rebelon, motioning Bill toward an extravagant throne situated in the down-right sector of the stage. Like the female statues, the throne was carved from a solid block of white marble. It faced across the stage toward the jurors.

Bill had to climb up three steps at the base of the throne in order to reach his seat. Once seated, he found that the throne was comfortable— it fit him well. He could not help but reminisce—his parents had wanted him to pursue the study of law, hoping that he would one day be a great attorney, and perhaps a judge.

"I shall serve as the court clerk," stated Rebelon, "and Lord Gelus shall begin conducting proceedings as the plaintiff attorney. Lord Gelus is most experienced and knowledgeable."

Bill nodded as he mused over his parents' dream of his becoming a judge. He had matriculated in law school, and had attempted to find something interesting about the study of law; but there had never been anything that bored him more. He managed to muster a spark of interest in Constitutional law, but when he realized that Federal Courts were massacring the Bill of Rights, he became frustrated and disgusted— dairy farming was much less consternating.

Rebelon took a seat on the front row of the left center section of the amphitheater. Decevon, who had seated herself several rows above, came down and sat beside him. Meanwhile, Lord Gelus sauntered across the stage, waiting until he was in front of the throne before he started speaking.

"Your Honorable Judge, magistrate of this magnificent land, governor of all that transpires within the spacious borders of this vast realm," spoke Lord Gelus. His obsequious voice flowed with polished resonance. "I count it an immense privilege to serve your well-being by fulfilling my role as plaintiff attorney in this unfortunate case of sabotage and insurrection."

Bill stared at the mysterious blue shroud that paced in front of him. After nearing the edge of the stage, it turned without facing him and began pacing back the other direction. The voice emanating from within the shroud carried an air of dignity and authority, giving the unmistakable impression that the speaker was sophisticated, experienced, and confident. Bill was not sure what Lord Gelus meant by *sabotage and insurrection*, but he felt certain that he would find out soon enough; and he had an uneasy feeling that Andela was the unnamed defendant.

"Before I begin my unpalatable albeit necessary task as plaintiff attorney in this 7th Circuit Court for the State of Missouri," resumed Lord Gelus, "permit me to express my sincerest regret that we were unable to secure the services of a defense attorney. The proposition of legal debate inspires me—such debate is my utmost delectation, and we strove with all diligence to find anyone willing to fill such a role, anyone at all, regardless of qualifications, but to no avail."

Bill glanced about at those assembled for the trial. Besides himself, there were twelve jurors who were concealed like hermit crabs in oversized seashells; and there was one plaintiff attorney attired like the jurors; and there were two spectators on the front row of the amphitheater—Rebelon and Ann. Bill looked at Ann, wondering if she had transformed into Andela; but her posture as she sat beside Rebelon convinced him that he was not looking at Andela, her movements were too cocky and too intimate with Rebelon. And besides that, he thought he could discern the dark brown of Ann's eyes. So then, where was the defendant?

"There is no living soul in this mighty kingdom willing to speak on behalf of the malfeasant invader who delays your rightful and customary departure from this dream, a dream already prolonged far beyond any concept of normalcy," continued Lord Gelus. "So I must deploringly…"

"Fear not, my Lord Gelus!" interrupted a vivacious voice from behind the stage. The voice issued upward from the belly of the gorge. "A willing and ready defense attorney has arrived!"

Bill peered back and to his left to espy the new speaker. Appearing over the rear edge of the stage rose a sleek little man wearing silky blue clothing with a golden belt and golden slippers. He bounded over the hind edge of the stage and proceeded to the side of Bill's throne, gazing upward at Bill with sparkling blue eyes that complemented a golden head of hair. Bill was drawn to those eyes—there was something about them that intrigued him, something that reminded him of the look in Andela's eyes.

"How did he escape?" Decevon inquired in a whisper, leaning with her lips near Rebelon's ear.

Rebelon did not reply.

"Well, at least he doesn't have his sword."

"He is a sword," Rebelon replied coldly. There was only one Being he would have abhorred seeing more than Truth, and he wondered if they weren't somehow one in the same—he wondered if Truth weren't simply an extension of his enemy.

"Your Honor," spoke Truth, "allow me to introduce myself…"

"Stop!" shouted Rebelon, rising and stepping forward. He climbed the steps to the stage.

The opening to Lord Gelus' hood shifted from the newcomer to Rebelon.

"This man is a criminal, a liar, and a poison to all that is just or fair," continued Rebelon, speaking with vehemence. "You must order him to maintain silence, Your Honor, immediately!"

"The First Amendment!" retorted Truth. "Freedom of speech!"

"No! Silence him!" roared Rebelon.

Bill was frightened by the spectacle before him. It appeared that Rebelon and the little man might engage in battle, and the little man appeared less than half the size of Rebelon.

"No, leave the little guy alone!" Bill spoke bravely, uncertain as to whether or not he, himself, would be attacked. The response was surprising—Rebelon and the little man both stopped arguing and turned to face him. Bill looked from one to the other, realizing that he was in charge—he was the presiding judge. "I think it is appropriate for both the plaintiff attorney and the defense attorney to be given opportunities to speak," stated Bill.

"Well spoken, Your Honor," interjected the cultured voice of Lord Gelus. He kept the opening of his hood angled away from Bill. "Rebelon means well, I am sure, but members of the audience should not speak unless invited to do so by one of the attorneys or by the judge, so I suggest that Rebelon take his seat and maintain silence in the Court. If he is called upon to bear witness, he may respond at that time."

Rebelon knew that Lord Gelus was more accomplished in the arts of deception and manipulation than he, and it seemed that his flagrant objection to Truth's participation had backfired. Without waiting for Bill to respond, he returned to Decevon's side. Decevon sat speechless and tense as Rebelon rejoined her. She recognized his abbreviated tirade as a tactical blunder.

"What I would suggest, Your Honor," resumed Lord Gelus, "is that you exercise your rightful position in these court proceedings and demand that speakers proceed in turn. In fact, I recommend that you permit only one speaker at a time, and that you disallow any interruption until you decide that it is time for the next speaker to commence. You may then call on the other attorney, or a witness, and so forth."

Decevon relaxed. She appreciated Lord Gelus' subtle manner of assuming control, and she was glad that he was acting as plaintiff attorney rather than Rebelon.

Bill glanced toward the little man, and Truth nodded.

"Very well," conceded Bill. "I so decree."

"And if Shorty does not object to my proceeding first, and I hope the defense attorney recognizes the appropriate nature of assigning him a nickname, one that does not instill prejudice on the part of the judge, then I shall begin," stated Lord Gelus, turning the opening of his hood to face Truth.

Bill was confused by Lord Gelus' concoction of a nickname for the little man. He turned his face toward Truth. "Do you mind being called Shorty?"

"Not at all, Your Honor," responded Truth. "And I do not mind permitting Lord Gelus to speak first, so long as I may speak thereafter."

Bill looked upon the little man in wonder. First the spunky fellow appeared willing to fight a challenger twice his size, and then he expressed willingness to accept a nickname in order to avoid creating prejudice. This made Bill curious about the little man's name, but it did not seem appropriate for a judge to invite prejudice into a court proceeding. Several silent seconds passed, and then Bill realized that everyone was waiting for him to respond. He looked back toward the mysterious plaintiff attorney.

"You may begin, Lord Gelus," proclaimed Bill.

"Thank you, Your Honor," Lord Gelus replied. He began methodical pacing back and forth in front of Bill's throne. "I am delighted, of course, by the arrival of an attorney representing the defendant. It grieves me, therefore, to realize that the court has a serious problem with Shorty's participation. You see, Your Honor, the Supreme Court passed a ruling in 1962 making it clear that the United States Government stands in objection to prayer or religion in any public institution, indicating that there must be a distinct separation between Church and State. That, Your Honor, is where we run into a problem with Shorty."

Lord Gelus paused his pacing long enough to stop and gaze upon Truth, as if ruing the necessity of his own derogatory discourse. Then he continued in the same condescending tone of voice. "The fact is, Your Honor, that Shorty is a religious preacher. If you were to ask him, he would admit to being a preacher of truth, or at least what he considers to be truth. If you ask him if he represents the Church, he would claim to represent the true Church. Thus, he cannot participate as an agent of this Court, since this is an official State Court." Lord Gelus stopped his pacing and again turned toward Truth. "Your Honor, we face the unfortunate but compelling necessity of evicting Shorty from this proceeding."

Bill experienced mixed emotions as Lord Gelus spoke. He realized that Shorty, whatever his real name might be, was probably there to speak on Andela's behalf. Furthermore, the matter Lord Gelus raised, namely the separation of Church and State, was a subject that baffled him when he studied Constitutional law—too many court decisions seemed inconsistent and arbitrary. He wrestled within his mind regarding how he should respond to Lord Gelus' demand to dismiss Shorty. He turned his face toward the little man.

"You have heard the argument of Lord Gelus," spoke Bill, staring straight into Truth's eyes. "Do you wish to respond?"

Truth smiled. "Yes, Your Honor." He stood before Bill. "It is true that I represent the true Church, and it is true that I am a religious preacher, at least in regard to true religion, so I do not wish to proffer any sort of defense to those assertions."

Bill was awed by Shorty's calm demeanor, and by the resolute look in Shorty's eyes.

"However," Truth continued, "let me point out some pertinent facts. Firstly, the 9th Amendment to the Constitution of the United States reads as follows—*The enumeration in the Constitution, of certain rights, shall not be construed to deny or disparage others retained by the people*. Thus, the Supreme Court was unConstitutional in removing the right of prayer in public schools, because this right had been retained for many years by the American people. In other words, the right given to the Supreme Court by the Constitution, namely the right to decide matters questioning the interpretation of the Constitution, cannot be interpreted in such a manner as to remove a right that citizens of the United States have held and exercised for many years. Therefore, this Court, and all courts, should deem the ruling to remove prayer from public schools to be null and void, thereby paying proper respect to the Constitution. And in addition to that, Article III of the Constitution points out that judges of the Supreme Court may be expelled for bad behavior. It is bad behavior for a Supreme Court Judge to make a judgment that disregards the Constitution of the United States—it is judiciary treason against the laws of our land. So then, all Supreme Court judges who vote against the freedom of prayer in public schools should be impeached and removed from office."

Bill's eyes widened. Shorty was a bold speaker; and what was more, he was knowledgeable, able to recite word for word from the Constitution.

"Furthermore," Truth resumed, "the 1962 ruling was a flagrant desecration of the spirit of the Constitution, and an insult to the first and foremost freedom presented in the Bill of Rights. The 1st Amendment to the Constitution of the United States begins as follows—*Congress shall make no law respecting an establishment of religion, or prohibiting the free exercise thereof.* The term *of religion* is an adjective phrase reflecting back upon the word *establishment.* If you look up the word *establishment* in the dictionary, you find that the word can mean, *Permanent place of residence or business; hence, such a place with its grounds, furnishing, staff, etc.,* or, on the other hand, the word *establishment* can mean, *Act of establishing, or state or fact of being established.*

"The phrase *establishment of religion* in the Constitution does not refer to a particular establishment, such as a particular church, or a particular temple, rather, it refers to the *act of establishing religion.* Think about it, if *establishment of religion* referred to a particular establishment, then a neighborhood church could buy and sell human slaves with total immunity from the 13th Amendment, because Congress could not pass any law subsequent to the 1st Amendment that applied to that church, not unless the 1st Amendment were first annulled. This is boloney. The term *establishment of religion* does not refer to a neighborhood church, it refers to the process of officially establishing religion."

Bill's eyes widened further. What Shorty said made sense.

"This first *Right* in the Bill of Rights, ratified on December 15, 1791, gives each State the freedom to establish the religion of its choice. The term *Congress* in the 1st Amendment refers to the Federal Congress, not to individual State Congresses, and the 10th Amendment of the Constitution states the following—*The powers not delegated to the United States by the Constitution, nor prohibited by it to the States, are reserved to the States respectively, or to the people.* So the ruling in 1962 was unConstitutional because the 1st Amendment gives individual States the freedom to establish whatever religion they so choose, and note that the act of establishing religion may include permitting prayer in public State schools. And in addition, it is noteworthy that the 1st Amendment begins by stating—*Congress shall make no law*, it does not state that the Federal Congress cannot practice religion, or pray, or post religious writings on the walls. In short, the Supreme Court ruling of 1962 should be held as errant and intolerable by every court, every school, every local State, and every citizen of the United States of America.

"So then, the 1962 Supreme Court ruling, namely the Engel verses Vitale decision, denied the free right of States to establish the religion of their choice in public schools, and was in breach of the 1st Amendment. It would be un-American, unpatriotic, and unfaithful to the men and women who shed their blood in order to bring freedom to the United States of America, for this Court, or any court, to honor or recognize decisions made in blatant disregard of the very first Right that our forefathers founded when they ratified the Bill of Rights. I contend that religion may be freely practiced at every level of government, including the Federal government, and I further contend that laws establishing religion may be passed by the States, such as the State of Missouri. Therefore, albeit I am a preacher of the Gospel of Truth, I have every right to appear in this Court on behalf of the defendant."

Truth paused. He stepped closer to Bill and raised his face. The look in his eyes was one of utmost sincerity. "Your Honor, I am certain of the validity of my words. The precious freedoms purchased by the blood of your ancestors should never be lost due to indolence or ignorance."

Bill was in awe, not only of Shorty's manner and tone of voice, but also of Shorty's words. The little man's enlightening speech reminded him of the childhood story, *The Emperor's New Clothes*, where a little boy is brave enough to point out that the emperor is naked. What Shorty said was so simple, and made such perfect sense, that it seemed incredible that he had never heard these things before, not even in law school. And furthermore, he had never understood how something openly practiced for decades and accepted by American society in general; namely leading prayers in public schools; could suddenly become unConstitutional in 1962. And in light of what Shorty said, the right of local States to establish prayer in public schools could not become unConstitutional without passing a new Amendment to the Constitution, namely an Amendment to nullify the 1st Amendment, such as the 21st Amendment did to the 18th Amendment.

Bill was leaning so far toward Truth that he nearly toppled out of the throne. He caught himself by clutching the arms of the throne and stomping his left boot against the throne's marble base. Shorty's explanation clarified why religion should be permitted in the 7th Circuit Court for the State of Missouri, and why prayer should be permitted in public schools across the United States of America, and why the essence of the 1st Amendment should have snuffed out the Supreme Court ruling of 1962 before it was ever permitted to set fire to the freedoms that Americans had cherished ever since the inception of their nation.

"Are you okay?" inquired Truth.

"Sure, fine," replied Bill. "Were you finished?"

Truth seated himself on the marble floor beside Bill's throne and motioned toward Lord Gelus, who was again pacing.

"I believe it would be appropriate, Your Honor, to permit rebuttal on the part of the plaintiff attorney," said Truth.

Bill was startled by Shorty's show of sportsmanship; it was not the sort of conduct he expected between opposing attorneys. He found himself liking Shorty more and more. He turned his face toward the robed plaintiff attorney. Lord Gelus stopped pacing and stood expectantly, still keeping the oval opening of his hood turned away from Bill's face.

"Would you like to offer a rebuttal, Lord Gelus?"

"Most certainly, Your Honor," replied Lord Gelus. He deplored the fact that he had convinced Bill to disallow interruptions. He did not expect Truth to be so well versed in matters of Constitutional law and politics. Nonetheless, it was now his turn to engage in verbal warfare, and he esteemed no one more highly than he esteemed himself when it came to a war of words. "I have listened to the comments made by Shorty, and I could make equally compelling arguments to the contrary, but I think I shall proffer information more relevant to the issue."

Truth watched and listened. He was disgusted by Lord Gelus' ability to lie so boldly and eloquently. There was no doubt in his mind that if Lord Gelus could make *equally compelling arguments to the contrary*, then he would do so. But apparently Lord Gelus had some other plan of attack; and the cunning old Resant could be subtle and persuasive. Truth considered it unfortunate that such great talent as that of Lord Gelus was spent in the service of ultimate death.

Following a dramatic pause meant to emphasize the claim that he would present information that was more *relevant*, Lord Gelus resumed pacing back and forth in front of Bill's throne. His posture presented an air of deep contemplation and dignity. As he began speaking, his distinguished voice commanded attention and respect. "We could argue back and forth, Shorty and I, giving our personal opinions of what the Constitution really teaches, and certainly we are all entitled to personal opinions. And we could argue back and forth regarding the character and background of those ladies and gentlemen who are presently assigned to fill seats in the Supreme Court of the United States, but I shall not waste additional time drawing the attention of this Court to the pursuit of such trivialities."

Bill flinched and looked toward Shorty. The words spoken by Shorty hardly seemed trivial—they were the clearest explanation of the first Right mentioned in the 1st Amendment that he ever heard in his entire lifetime, and Lord Gelus' words were obviously meant to downgrade Shorty and discount everything Shorty had said. Surprisingly, Shorty did not appear disturbed.

"What I shall do," continued Lord Gelus, regaining Bill's attention, "is draw this Court's notice to those wise and praiseworthy men who founded this great Nation of ours, and I shall permit the truth and facts regarding the separation of Church and State to be imparted by those voices that indeed deserve our utmost regard. I am sure this Court is familiar with such historical names as those of George Washington, who served as the first President of the United States for eight years, and John Adams, who then served as President for four years, and the noble name of the third President of the United States, serving as President from 1801 to 1809, namely Thomas Jefferson."

Lord Gelus paused again. He had placed special emphasis on his pronunciation of the name *Thomas Jefferson*. Rebelon and Decevon both leaned forward. Truth's words had enraged them, and Rebelon would never have maintained silence if not for Bill's decree. But now they both delighted themselves in Lord Gelus' pompous dismissal of Truth's words, and they hoped his crafty dialogue would succeed in banning Truth from any presence in the Court's ongoing proceedings.

"Thomas Jefferson," Lord Gelus repeated in a tone of reverence. "Now here is a great man, and a great mind. In my opinion, the mind of Thomas Jefferson is the greatest mind in all of American history. It would take hours and days to comment upon all of Thomas Jefferson's magnificent accomplishments, but such commemoration is not necessary. Instead, I will point out the three accomplishments that Thomas Jefferson himself wanted engraved on the tombstone of his grave. First, he wanted it engraved that he was the author of the Declaration of Independence, second, he wanted it engraved that he was the founder of the University of Virginia, and third, he wanted it engraved that he was the author of the Virginia Statute for Religious Freedom. And I would point out that James Madison, the fourth President of the United States, skillfully secured the adoption of the Virginia Statute for Religious Freedom by the Virginia legislature in 1786, thereby establishing this Statute prior to the subsequent ratification of the Constitution of the United States on September 17, 1787."

For the first time since Truth had begun his discourse, Decevon smiled. She did not know what Lord Gelus planned to say, but he possessed an irrefutable charisma. And besides, she knew that Bill was patriotic, and Lord Gelus was appealing to patriotism.

"So, let's consider this Virginia Statute for Religious Freedom, authored by Thomas Jefferson," continued Lord Gelus. "To put this Statute in perspective, remember that the American Revolution disestablished the Anglican Church, a religious organization previously forced upon the American populace by the British Government. Following the Revolution, Jefferson wrote a Statute intended to build a high wall of separation to keep Church and State apart. This Statute not only opposed taxing people to support an established church, it further maintained that religious activity of any sort should be wholly voluntary. Thus, the church should be on one side of the fence, and the government on the other side. The two entities should be totally separate.

"I would further point out that the Virginia Statute for Religious Freedom served as the basis for the *religion clauses* in the Constitution's Bill of Rights. How, then, could the 1st Amendment mean anything other than what I have proffered from the very beginning? There must be a high wall of separation between Church and State. I do not ask, Your Honor, that you take my word for this, and neither do I request that you dismiss Shorty's words based upon my humble albeit well-educated opinions. Rather, I ask that you recognize the fact that we must honor the words and opinions of our founding fathers—we must heed the wisdom and advice of one of the greatest men in all of American history, the honorable Thomas Jefferson. Therefore, Your Honor, we have no choice other than to acknowledge the separation of Church and State, and thus, we must dismiss Shorty from further proceedings in this Court. In fact, Your Honor, I recommend that he be dismissed without encumbering ourselves with further futile dialogue on his part." Lord Gelus stopped his pacing and turned toward Bill, though he kept his visage downcast so that Bill could not see his face. "Your Honor, I recommend that you forbid Shorty from further speech, and that you banish him from the premises."

There was no rustling of robes or sliding of feet—all observers were transfixed, waiting for Bill's response. Bill glanced out toward Rebelon and Decevon, and then surveyed the royal blue garbs encasing the mysterious jurors. Finally, he turned his eyes toward Shorty, who was still seated on the marble floor beside him. The little man's eyes were lifted in earnest plea, and Bill sensed that Shorty was pleading on behalf of someone, and he knew that the *someone* must be Andela, but then, maybe...

Once more Bill crumpled forward, catching himself on the arms of his throne. Shorty's eyes revealed something crucial, something that shocked Bill's cognizance. As he straightened back up, continuing to gaze into the vivid blue eyes, he came to realize that it was actually the judge who was on trial—he, himself, was on trial. Meanwhile, the utter absence of sound persisted within the amphitheater. Bill sensed a battle within his heart and mind, a battle that was externally intangible, yet real.

At last Bill broke his eyes from Shorty and gazed downward. He struggled in deliberation. Lord Gelus had seemingly made a significant point, and Bill was in a position to enact the plaintiff attorney's request to expel Shorty, thus evading whatever issues were stirring within his heart and mind as he peered into Shorty's eyes. But did he desire such evasion? What would he be evading? He raised his eyes and looked upon Lord Gelus, or at least upon the cloak that covered Lord Gelus.

"No, I think I'll let Shorty comment upon your remarks."

For a few moments Lord Gelus did not move or speak. He knew that the tone of his voice, at that moment, might betray him—it might betray the enormity of rage that ignited within his mind and breast. He nodded, and then he turned and resumed his pacing.

Bill turned back toward Shorty. The little man was smiling radiantly, and he had already risen to his feet. "You may speak," said Bill.

Truth bowed, and then turned toward the empty seats of the amphitheater as if addressing the entire world. He spoke with vigorous valor. "I, too, have sincere admiration for the founding fathers of our great and blessed Nation. For this reason, I cringe to hear their gallant ideas and heartfelt passions disparaged. Regarding Lord Gelus' assertion that Thomas Jefferson favored a wall separating Church and State, I will prove that Thomas Jefferson supported each individual State's right to establish the religion of that State's choice, thus supporting the freedom to establish religion in public schools. I will also prove that Thomas Jefferson supported the right of citizens to attend separate, private schools with differing religions, thus giving those citizens the right to avoid public schools altogether. And I will also prove that Thomas Jefferson supported freedom for private schools to establish religions altogether different than the religion established in public schools. But rather than merely commenting upon opinions about what Thomas Jefferson taught, let's examine the exact words spoken and written by Thomas Jefferson himself."

Lord Gelus staggered. A low snarl, not quite loud enough for Bill's ears to perceive, issued through his clenched teeth. The last thing he wanted was for Bill to hear what Thomas Jefferson actually said, or to learn what Thomas Jefferson actually wrote.

"On March fourth, 1805, in his Second Inaugural Address, Thomas Jefferson stated the following—*In matters of religion, I have considered that its free exercise is placed by the Constitution independent of the powers of the General Government. I have therefore undertaken, on no occasion, to prescribe the religious exercises suited to it; but have left them, as the Constitution found them, under the direction and discipline of State or Church authorities acknowledged by the several religious societies.* Thus, Thomas Jefferson made it clear in his inaugural speech that the General Government, meaning the Federal Government, would not prescribe religious exercises, such as praying or not praying in public schools. But rather, the Federal Government would leave such prescription to the local State or Church authorities. Notably, he did not object to States permitting Church authorities to decide what sort of religious practices should be established in public schools, though he also did not object to State governments making such decisions themselves.

"Next, let's take a look at a letter Thomas Jefferson wrote on January 23, 1808—*I consider the government of the United States as interdicted by the Constitution from intermeddling with religious institutions, their doctrines, discipline, or exercises. This results not only from the provisions that no law shall be made respecting the establishment or free exercise of religion, but from that also which reserves to the States the powers not delegated to the United States. Certainly no power to prescribe any religious exercise, or to assume authority in religious discipline, has been delegated to the General Government. It must then rest with the States, as far as it can be in any human authority.* Thus, Thomas Jefferson plainly states his opinion that State governments are free to prescribe religious exercises, and it follows that such prescribed religious exercises can be freely practiced by State courts and by public State schools."

Though the tall blue robe continued pacing before Bill's throne without outward change, the creature within the robe was transforming into an apparition of loathsome ire.

"This, then, reveals a much different perspective regarding the 1st Amendment than Lord Gelus suggested," proclaimed Truth. "And in regard to the 1st Amendment, I would like to point out that the person who introduced the 1st Amendment at the Constitutional Convention, the Convention that created the Constitution of the United States of America, was Fisher Ames, a delegate from Massachusetts. Remarkably, Fisher Ames said that Bible teaching should be in public schools—note this, the very man who introduced the 1st Amendment to the Constitution of the United States of America said that Bible teaching should be in public schools. And until the early 1960s, most States either required Bible teaching in public schools, or left the decision up to the local school boards. Thus, the 1st Amendment was not intended for use in banning prayer from public schools. In fact, the 1st Amendment was created to preserve such freedoms as the freedom to establish prayer in public schools."

Truth's words erased any semblance of a smile from Decevon's lips, and Rebelon clenched his fists so tightly that his nails nearly drew blood from the palms of his hands.

"Finally," continued Truth, "I will show that Thomas Jefferson abhorred the thought of banning or limiting the right of religious men and women to serve in positions of civil authority, such as becoming State and Federal judges, and he would have shunned the idea of prohibiting a preacher from serving as a defense attorney. And furthermore, I will use Thomas Jefferson's own writings to demonstrate that he would have favored the freedom for a man whose religion dogmatically denounces abortion to serve as a member of the Supreme Court. Such freedoms stem from the Holy Bible. The Bible teaches that a man or woman is free to choose between heaven or hell, and thus, a man or woman is free to choose between Christianity and the many other religions, albeit any choice apart from salvation through Jesus Christ leads to damnation. Such damnation applies to those adhering to the religion of Humanism, the belief that human thought, human reason, and human sentiment should take precedence over all else. Humanism may either deny or accept the existence of God. Humanism may make all religions acceptable, or shun religion altogether. Humanism makes mankind the ultimate god."

At this point Shorty paused and looked at Bill. There was no doubt in Bill's mind that Shorty identified him as a Humanist. Shorty's description of Humanism was a description of the religion passed down to him by his parents. His parents taught him that religions were based upon fables, and that God was tolerant of all beliefs, and that the existence of hell was inconceivable. There was one obstacle Bill encountered, however, in accepting what his parents taught him—Jesus Christ. Bill studied the proofs of Jesus' life, his miracles, and his resurrection from death; and these proofs held up to the logical scrutiny of historical records. Furthermore, Bill discovered that Jesus Christ taught that hell was real, and he learned that Jesus Christ claimed to be the only avenue to heaven. Jesus Christ claimed that receiving his blood sacrifice to pay the penalty for sin against God was the only way to escape damnation and receive eternal life; namely, through repenting from sin, accepting his blood sacrifice, and submitting to his lordship. This had impressed Bill deeply; he sensed that a force beyond the material universe endorsed the claims of Jesus Christ, an endorsement he felt within the depths of his heart, mind, soul, and spirit.

"To substantiate my claims," recommenced Truth, again facing out toward the amphitheater as if addressing a large audience, "I will quote from memory the exact wordage that composes the Virginia Statute for Religious Freedom, as penned by Thomas Jefferson. Please excuse some of the Old English grammar. And I quote, *Whereas Almighty God hath created the mind free; that all attempts to influence it by temporal punishments or burthens, or by civil incapacitations, tend only to beget habits of hypocrisy and meanness, and are a departure from the plan of the Holy author of our religion, who being Lord both of body and mind, yet chose not to propagate it by coercions on either, as it was in his Almighty power to do; that the impious presumption of legislators and rulers, civil as well as ecclesiastical, who being themselves but fallible and uninspired men, have assumed dominion over the faith of others, setting up their own opinions and modes of thinking as the only true and infallible, and as such endeavouring to impose them on others, hath established and maintained false religions over the greatest part of the world, and through all time; that to compel a man to furnish contributions of money for the propagation of opinions which he disbelieves, is sinful and tyrannical; that even the forcing him to support this or that teacher of his own religious persuasion, is depriving him of the comfortable liberty of giving his contributions to the particular pastor, whose morals he would make his pattern, and whose powers he feels most persuasive to righteousness, and is withdrawing from the ministry those temporary rewards, which proceeding from an approbation of their personal conduct, are an additional incitement to earnest and unremitting labours for the instruction of mankind; that our civil right have no dependence on our religious opinions, any more than our opinions in physics or geometry; that therefore the proscribing any citizen as unworthy the public confidence by laying upon him an incapacity of being called to offices of trust and emolument, unless he profess or renounce this or that religious opinion, is depriving him injuriously of those privileges and advantages to which in common with his fellow-citizens he has a natural right; that it tends only to corrupt the principles of that religion it is meant to encourage, by bribing with a monopoly of worldly honours and emoluments, those who will externally profess and conform to it; that though indeed these are criminal who do not withstand such temptation, yet neither are those innocent who lay the bait in their way; that to suffer the civil magistrate to intrude his powers into the field of opinion, and to restrain the profession or propagation of principles on supposition of their ill tendency, is a dangerous fallacy, which at once destroys all religious liberty, because he being of course judge of that tendency will make his opinions the rule of judgment, and approve or condemn the sentiments of others only as they shall square with or differ from his own; that it is time enough for the rightful purposes of civil government, for its order; and finally, that truth is great and will prevail if left to herself, that she is the proper and sufficient antagonist to error, and has nothing to fear from the conflict, unless by human interposition disarmed of her natural weapons, free argument and debate, error ceasing to be dangerous when it is permitted freely to contradict them:*

"Be it enacted by the General Assembly, That no man shall be compelled to frequent or support any religious worship, place, or ministry whatsoever, nor shall be enforced, restrained, molested, or burthened in his body or goods, nor shall otherwise suffer on account of his religious opinions or belief; but that all men shall be free to profess, and by argument to maintain, their opinion in matters of religion, and that the same shall in no wise diminish enlarge, or affect their civil capacities.

"And though we well know that this assembly elected by the people for the ordinary purposes of legislation only, have no power to restrain the acts of succeeding assemblies, constituted with powers equal to our own, and that therefore to declare this act to be irrevocable would be of no effect in law; yet we are free to declare, and do declare, that the rights hereby asserted are of the natural rights of mankind, and that if any act shall be hereafter passed to repeal the present, or to narrow its operation, such act shall be an infringement of natural right."

Shorty then paused and turned to face Bill. His words, actually the words and writings of Thomas Jefferson, sounded to Bill like something one might expect to hear from an old-time gospel preacher. Having heard those words, it seemed incredible to Bill that the plaintiff attorney was trying to use the teachings of Thomas Jefferson to eject religion from the courtroom. It seemed more likely that Thomas Jefferson would have favored voluntary prayer and Bible reading at every Federal court session. Shorty had already established Thomas Jefferson's view of the

1st Amendment, namely that individual States are free to establish religion without Federal interference, and the Virginia Statute for Religious Freedom clarified Thomas Jefferson's opinion that religions established by local States should not be forced upon any individual, although such religion may be taught in public schools and practiced in public court rooms.

Bill looked back toward Lord Gelus. "It sounds like Thomas Jefferson did not support your position," he said. He was beginning to suspect that Lord Gelus was capable of dishonest deception.

"So what?" snapped Lord Gelus. The suave tone of his voice began dissipating. "History is history. And what does it matter what our forefathers believed or thought? They were all just a bunch of backward cronies.

"The great government of the United States of America has served the evolutionary function of human endeavor by raising two ruling parties, the Democratic Party and the Republican Party. These parties have served to balance the forward progression of American society, like the right wing and left wing of a majestic eagle. They proffer various experimentations of politics and economics in a manner prone to forward the cause of human existence, and they elevate the condition and enlightenment of the human mind. Through the body of the majestic eagle, these two parties, the two balancing wings, blend the human populace in unity and oneness. It is a system of government worthy of adoration and worship, and it is a system of government that rises far above considerations of petty religion or superstition.

"Do you not see that it would be a great step backward for you to permit this preacher to continue orating in the public domain? I concede that the nation's superstitious forefathers deemed it necessary to safeguard primordial religious inclinations, but have we not evolved beyond all that? Are we not ready to proceed onward to the next level of human evolution? The Constitution of the United States of American is antiquated, and nothing is more antiquated than the First Amendment. Do you not realize that many public leaders, including Supreme Court justices, have long possessed the transcendent realization that the people of the United States need a government that can deliver them from the dark ages and shape their futures in a manner consistent with the Humanistic cause? Don't human beings have the right to decide what is right and best for their own lives?"

Bill gazed at Lord Gelus. He was awed by the persuasive appeal of Lord Gelus' words; but then, he was not so stupid as to realize that Lord Gelus had contradicted himself. Only minutes before, Lord Gelus had praised the nation's founding fathers, such as Thomas Jefferson, as if these men were virtual gods; and now he was casting them aside as ignorant savages. It seemed that Lord Gelus was willing to say whatever served his purpose, and it was obvious that he purposed to curb Shorty's right to speak.

Bill again turned to Shorty. "What do you have to say about that?"

Shorty smiled. "Have you ever seen an eagle try to fly with one good wing and one bad wing? Or what's more, have you ever seen an eagle try to fly with two bad wings?"

Bill creased his forehead in puzzlement, but then he recalled Lord Gelus' remarks about the Republican and Democratic parties. He grinned at Shorty's insinuations. "No, I can't say that I have."

"Well, it's not a pretty sight. And what's more, the Republican and Democratic parties are not the two major parties in the United States of America, they just have people thinking that they are."

"Really?" returned Bill.

Lord Gelus snorted, but Bill ignored the incursion and continued facing Shorty. He couldn't wait to hear what Shorty might say next.

"The two major parties in the United States of America are the Christian Party and the Humanist Party. I've already given the definition of a Humanist. A Christian is someone who is begotten of God and who is subject to the lordship of Jesus Christ. A *party* can simply refer to a group of people who are doing something together, or to a group of people acting together and forming one side in an agreement or dispute. Although the Humanist Party and the Christian Party have not openly professed themselves as political parties, they have functioned as political parties for years, and it would clear the air if they just came forward and identified themselves. The Christian Party should stand on a two-tiered foundation, the primary foundation being the Holy Bible as canonized in the fourth century A.D., and the secondary foundation being the Constitution of the United States of America. Over fifty other countries in the world have Christian political parties, and the correct interpretation of the Constitution of the United States of America certainly does not prohibit the freedom for Christians in the United States to do the same."

"Bash!" interjected Lord Gelus. "What narrow-minded, witless, buffoonery!"

Shorty shook his head. "Your Honor, did you give Lord Gelus leave to speak? I was quite ready to provide evidence to my assertion."

Bill raised one finger. "Shorty has the floor," he stated, without even looking at Lord Gelus. Then he lowered his hand and continued facing Shorty.

Lord Gelus tried to speak, and he tried to take a step forward toward Shorty; but an invisible force restrained him. Bill was indeed governor of the land, and his position was sustained by a power that could not be thwarted.

"Just think back to the last few national presidential elections," resumed Shorty. "I think it was rather obvious that largely Humanist States tended to vote one way while largely Christian States tended to vote another way. Thus, the division of voting that existed between largely Christian States and largely Humanistic States illustrates the existence of the two prevailing political parties in the United States.

"And before we go on," added Shorty, "let me point out that the Christian Party seeks to uphold Constitutional rights and freedoms, whereas the Humanist Party feels free to rewrite and reinterpret the Constitution. And in obtaining the power to reinterpret the Constitution, the Humanist Party cares little about obtaining votes from Christians—they are quite satisfied with obtaining the votes from those Humanists who claim to be Christians, an unfortunately large number of individuals in the United States. These imposters, namely Humanists who claim to be Christians, for whom I have much less respect than I have for admittedly pagan sinners, are easily recognized when they go so far as to condone practices that the Word of God condemns. One must believe the words of Jesus Christ to be Christian, and by his own words, Jesus affirms that the Word of God is true, and that the validity of Scripture cannot be dismissed.

"So, in short, the political arena in the United States has become a moral and intellectual battleground between the two major spiritual forces on planet earth—the Christian children of God, and the Humanist children of Satan."

Bill felt his heart throbbing against his breast. He faced Shorty with resolute courage. "What is your real name?"

"Truth."

Bill felt a shock of enlightenment pierce his soul. "And who do you come to defend?"

"I come to defend the eternal destiny of your soul, and to defend Andela Tidmore, the woman who loves you more than any human being has ever before loved you."

Bill knew that it was true, Andela Tidmore loved him. He also realized, for the first time, exactly what it was about Andela that he desired for himself. He did not even glance toward Lord Gelus, or toward the blue-clad jurors, or toward the two distraught observers seated on a front row of the amphitheater.

"You may speak on behalf of Andela Tidmore."

Truth smiled, but then assumed a very serious expression as he began speaking. "Andela Tidmore came to your home hoping to marry you, but she is of the living—alive through the redemptive blood of Jesus Christ. It would not be proper for her to marry a dead man."

Bill and Truth stood for several long, silent, weighty seconds; peering deeply into one another's eyes. Lord Gelus, Decevon, Rebelon, and each member of the jury stared in baleful trepidation.

"Nor will she!" Bill hailed.

For a moment, misinterpreting Bill's words, Decevon flashed a malicious sneer; but her malevolent celebration was short-lived.

Bill turned toward the golden cliff and the land above, the land he could not see with his physical eyes. It was a land, he knew, that only living, spiritual eyes could behold. "Almighty God," he spoke so loudly that his voice echoed between the canyon walls, "I beg your forgiveness for rejecting you as God, and for choosing Human Reason as my god, and I now repent from sin and choose you as my God—I freely choose the blood of Jesus Christ as my redemption, the immeasurably precious blood of Jesus Christ the Son of God, the blood of Jesus Christ who is God, the blood of Jesus Christ my Lord and Savior."

For a moment all was still; and then the entire land began trembling. Lord Gelus threw off his robe and rushed toward Truth with a bloodcurdling howl and outstretched fingers, but then he vanished. The blue robes of the jurors collapsed into soft, empty shells; and there appeared two disheveled piles of clothing where Decevon and Rebelon were seated moments before. Waves of green grass began sweeping across the desert floor like a verdant tidal wave, and trees shot upward from the ground, sprouting limbs, twigs, leaves, flowers, and fruits. And far to the north, above the head of the empty canyon, burst forth sounds of crumbling stone and gushing water.

Bill wanted to shout, he felt like shouting, and then he did shout. "Whoopee!!!"

Truth laughed, a joyous and uninhibited laugh. Their eyes met in triumphant celebration, and moments later they both heard the galloping sound of horse hooves pounding up the steep, parched side of the canyon wall. Flucheena leaped over the edge of the canyon and landed on the marble surface of the stage, prancing in place. Hope sat upon Flucheena's back with his hands tied behind his back. About his wrists were cords of thin rope secured with convoluted knots. He looked just like Bill remembered him from their previous encounter in Andela's land, tall and muscular with a bright green tunic and matching trousers. He still wore the golden cap and golden belt buckle, and the green plume still rose from his cap, and the brown slippers still matched his leather belt. He also had the same attitude, robust and invigorating. Bill also recognized the horse, but he somehow knew that the horse wasn't Midnight, and that Cowgirl Jane had been an imposter.

Bill stood to his feet and smiled. Hope no longer annoyed him; in fact, Hope's presence inspired him.

"Quick!" remarked Hope, sliding from Flucheena's back and somehow landing upright on his feet. He faced Bill. "Andela's tied to stakes about half-a-mile down the gorge, and the water will be coming like an avalanche. The living can breathe the water as easily as air, but the impact of the torrent could be monstrous. Take the horse and be after her!"

"Ya hasso stuk lard, shart montassa!" Flucheena spoke with excitement.

Bill stared at Flucheena's mouth—he'd never heard a horse speak before. But then he brushed his amazement aside and sprang from the throne as Truth untied Hope's hands. Hope tossed the loosened cords aside and steadied Flucheena as Bill vaulted to her back.

"Sheen shasta, Flucheena shart!" the black mare cried, rearing and turning around on her hind legs.

"What's that mean?" asked Bill.

"We're off, Flucheena away!" hailed both Truth and Hope.

Bill clung to Flucheena's mane and to the solitary loop of rope around her neck. Flucheena bolted southward faster than any horse he'd ever raced or mounted—this was some horse!

"She'll be expecting you!" he heard Hope call.

Air whipped past Bill's ears as the black steed sprinted over parched earth. Greenery swept across the landscape to Bill's right, carpeting the barren ground like green paint splashing over a brown canvas. The sides of the canyon were not as steep as they were farther north, but Bill still had to lean backward and brace his knees as Flucheena swerved to the left and lunged over the edge of the canyon. She cantered down the canyon wall to the riverbed and then swerved back to the right, regaining speed and coursing down the center of the canyon. Seconds later they rounded a wide curve and espied the woman they sought.

Andela was lying on her back, tied with her arms and legs stretched outward between four stakes. A taut rope led from each stake to a wrist or ankle. There was a crude, white cloth fastened around her head and mouth to muffle any attempted cries for help. She was still wearing the blue gown; but now she also wore golden gloves that donned her bound hands, and there were golden slippers on her feet. Her legs were situated toward the north, and her head was lifted with her eyes fixed upon Bill and Flucheena.

The beautiful young women bound to the canyon floor no longer struck Bill as some sort of puzzling mystery; she was a living daughter of God, his sister in Christ, and the woman he wanted to marry.

"Andela," Bill spoke as he slid from Flucheena's back. He dashed to her side, dropping to his knees and reaching to unfasten the gag from her head and face.

"Oh Bill," Andela cried as the detestable gag was withdrawn from her lips. Joyous tears moistened the surface of her eyes. She had guessed what it meant when the Jealots guarding over her disintegrated into nothing, vanishing from sight. She also guessed the cause of the thunderous sound that echoed down the canyon, she knew that the dam above the canyon was rent asunder. Her face grew staid and earnest. "Bill, you've got to get out of the canyon, quick, the water's coming, and you won't have time to untie me. You can come back in for me later."

Bill grinned and lowered himself next to Andela, reaching out and clasping the ropes that bound her wrists. He looked backward toward Flucheena. "Out of the canyon, now! I've got her, we're okay!"

The black mare pawed at the sand and bobbed her head. Roaring sounds of advancing water reverberated down the empty gorge.

"Shart!" hollered Andela.

Flucheena reared and whinnied, and then turned to her right and launched into a gallop, soon scaling the steep wall and disappearing over the edge of the canyon. Bill turned and gazed at Andela in wonder. She was a woman of unceasing amazement, even speaking to a horse in its own language. And what was more, he no longer thought that he was merely dreaming, or if it was a dream, it was altogether more real than anything he had ever experienced while awake.

"Bill," Andela spoke with concern.

"I love you," said Bill.

Andela's concerned expression melted away. She no longer knew where she was or what was happening, other than that a marvelous and living man was staring into her eyes and telling her that he loved her. Bill's lips touched Andela's lips, and there they remained.

Time and space dissolved within ecstasy. Andela and Bill were aware of nothing else, only of one another. As seconds passed, their unspeakable bliss transformed, passing beyond the passionate rejoicing of two separate individuals and entering a foretaste of divine oneness. Neither one of them would ever quantify the time transpiring during this kiss, the first kiss shared between two living persons, and the first kiss shared in the confidence that they would share the remainder of their mortal lives together. They both knew that a power greater than both of them would help sustain their commitment to one another.

When finally their lips parted, they looked into one another's eyes with little regard to their surroundings, though they were vaguely aware that they sat at one end of a familiar sofa. The surroundings in the ranch-house den were unchanged; but the man and woman facing one another were immeasurably and wonderfully transformed, one from death to life, and the other from presumed maidenhood to expectations of joyous matrimony.

"Andela Tidmore, will you marry me?"

"Bill Stroggins, I most assuredly will."

For a few moments they just smiled and gazed into one another's eyes, but then Andela's eyes widened. Her hands were clasped behind Bill's neck.

"What is it?" asked Bill.

She released his neck and held her hands between them, and then they both stared downward upon immaculate, golden gloves.